ARCANE WISDOM

THE GREAT GOD PAN

AND OTHER WEIRD STORIES

By
Arthur Machen

Edited, Introduction and Notes

by

S. T. Joshi

2009

Contents

INTRODUCTION

Arthur Machen (1863–1947) led exactly the kind of life, and wrote exactly the kind of work, that we would expect for an author of tales of horror and the supernatural. Like H. P. Lovecraft, Machen spent the majority of his life in poverty and obscurity; but unlike his great American contemporary and quasi-disciple, Machen was rescued by his receiving a Civil List pension in 1932, which rendered the final years of his long life moderately comfortable, if not luxurious. Whether Machen expected his work to survive after his death is an open question: a good many of his novels, tales, essays, and journalism had already fallen into apparent oblivion by the time he retired to Amersham, Buckinghamshire, in 1929, and he would have been as surprised as anyone to note that his best tales continue to resurface in editions ranging from expensive limited editions to mass-market paperbacks. In the end, Machen may perhaps be chiefly the focus of a devoted band of cognoscenti; but the inherent power of his work, and its significant influence on the horror fiction that followed it, will keep it alive as long as this literature continues to be read.

Born in Caerleon-on-Usk, Wales, on March 3, 1863, and retaining a lifelong love of his native land in spite of the many years he spent away from it, Arthur Llewelyn Jones Machen hoped to become a physician, but in 1880 he failed an examination for the Royal College of Surgeons in London. Returning to Wales briefly, he composed the poem *Eleusinia* and privately published it in an edition of 100 copies. Even though, in later years, Machen found the poem so embarrassingly crude and juvenile that he attempted to buy up all copies of it and destroy them, it is by no means a contemptible piece of work: an evocation of the wonders and terrors of the Eleusinian Mysteries of ancient Greece, the poem in many ways foreshadows much of Machen's work and provides a window to his early philosophical thought. Always of a mystical temperament, Machen came to regard religious ritual as a symbol for the inveterate human yearning for transcendence and connection with God. In later years he would become a vigorous Anglo-Catholic and fervently defend the mysteries of religion against the onslaughts of science and materialism.

Machen decided to go to London in any event, hoping to find work of any kind to support himself. For a time he was a tutor. In 1883 he composed a quaint work of pseudo-scholarship, *The Anatomy of Tobacco*, published the next year. By this time he was working for several publishers, notably George Redway, in various capacities—as editor, translator, cataloguer, and the like. Translating proved to be the most visible—although not by any means the most lucrative—facet of his work. Over the next fifteen years he produced translations of Marguerite de Navarre's *Hemptameron* and, most famously, the entirety of Jacques Casanova's immense *Memoirs*.

But Machen's life took a striking turn upon the death of his father in September 1887, one month after he married Amelia Hogg. From the money he obtained by inheritance, Machen became economically independent for the next decade and a half, and it is this period that saw the production of his greatest work. In 1888 *The Chronicle of Clemendy*, a picaresque novel that displayed Machen's deep-seated interest in the Middle Ages, appeared, although it had been composed in 1884–85. Free to write whatever he wished without thinking of income or markets, he wrote the novella "The Great God Pan" in 1890–91 and the episodic novel *The Three Impostors* in 1890–94. The former was not published until 1894 and the latter until 1895, but both produced a sensation when they appeared.

Machen took a certain masochistic glee in printing in his autobiography *Things Near and Far* (1923) the hostile reviews that greeted *The Great God Pan and The Inmost Light* when that slim booklet appeared. Indeed, the next year later he compiled a piquant volume, *Precious Balms* (1924), that contained nothing but (mostly unfavorable) reviews of his various books. A review of *The Great God Pan*, from the *Westminster Review*, is representative: "It is an incoherent nightmare of sex and the supposed horrible mysteries behind it, such as might conceivably possess a man who was given to a morbid brooding over these matters, but which would soon lead to insanity if unrestrained."[1] In all honesty, there is something to be said for this remark—although the tale is far from "incoherent." For the central theme of "The Great God Pan" really does seem to be a horror of sex—or, perhaps more pertinently, a horror of sexually aggressive women. In this sense, Machen actually shared the pruderies of many of his outraged readers; if he did not, he could not have invested the subject with the shuddering horror that he does. Machen attempts to endow the entire phenomenon with broader philosophical import, suggesting that the scientist Raymond's experiment at the opening of the tale—in which he causes the servant girl Mary to "see" the god Pan—is equivalent to "lifting the veil" that conceals the horrors beyond the bland surface of everyday life; but the working out of the tale very largely focuses on the discomfiture that the sexually adventurous Helen Vaughan (the result of Mary's "seeing" Pan) produces upon the proper Victorian gentlemen who fall under her sway. H. P. Lovecraft, although equally prudish in many ways, recognized this element in the story and in Machen's work generally:

> What Machen probably likes about perverted and forbidden things is their departure from and hostility to the commonplace. . . . People whose minds are—like Machen's—steeped in the orthodox myths of religion, naturally find a poignant fascination in the conception of things which religion brands with outlawry and horror. Such people take the artificial and obsolete concept of "sin" seriously, and find it full of dark allurement. On the other hand, people like myself, with a realistic and scientific point of view, see no charm or mystery whatever in things banned by religious mythology. We recognise the primitiveness and meaninglessness of the religious attitude, and in consequence find no element of attractive defiance or significant escape in those things which happen to contravene it. The whole idea of "sin", with its overtones of unholy fascination, is in 1932 simply a curiosity of intellectual history. The filth and perversion which to Machen's obsoletely orthodox mind meant profound defiances of the universe's foundations, mean to us only a rather prosaic and unfortunate species of organic maladjustment—no more frightful, and no more interesting, than a headache, a fit of colic, or an ulcer on the big toe.[2]

This strikes me as exactly right—although Machen would no doubt have countered that the "scientific point of view" is an illegitimate one that has no validity in the realms of art, morals, or religion. His dim view of science and scientists comes out in several works. In "The Great God Pan," Raymond's callousness and excessive devotion to science is brought forth in his bland utterance that Mary, whom he had rescued from a life of poverty and degradation, was "mine to use as I see fit."

Nevertheless, "The Great God Pan" retains the power to terrify, simply because Machen himself felt the terror behind the figure of

Helen Vaughan and exhibited that terror through a masterful marshalling of prose and incident. It may be, perhaps, that he strains credulity by an excessive use of coincidence—allowing the informal detectives in the case, Clarke and Villiers, to come upon exactly those individuals and those phenomena that allow them to understand that Helen Vaughan is the figure who, under a succession of aliases, has been plaguing a number of men over the years and driving them to suicide. But the spectacular conclusion of the tale, in which Helen is seen to be "changing and melting before your eyes from woman to man, from man to beast, and from beast to worse than beast," still carries a punch and (Lovecraft's comments notwithstanding) injects at least something of a "cosmic" element into the story.

The Three Impostors is also a kind of supernatural detective story, although Machen later came to admit the complaint of many reviewers that he had followed Robert Louis Stevenson a little too closely in both style and structure. The episodic framework of the novel is precisely identical to that found in Stevenson's *New Arabian Nights* (1882) and, in particular, *The Dynamiters* (1885), with its convoluted fabric of narratives within narratives; and the rather jaunty, archly sophisticated style also echoes Stevenson's facile mannerisms a bit too closely. That the "novel" really has no particular unity or integrity is signaled by the fact that one segment, "Novel of the Iron Maid," had already appeared in a magazine as a self-standing story as early as 1890, and the fact that, in subsequent years, Machen had no compunction in allowing other segments—including the two most powerful ones, "Novel of the Black Seal" and "Novel of the White Powder"—to appear as separate tales in anthologies. Indeed, the seriocomic framework of the novel—the attempt by the "three impostors" introduced to us in the prologue to hunt down and capture the "young man with spectacles" in the belief that he has taken a rare coin, the Gold Tiberius, that they are seeking—is merely a flimsy means of stitching together the various "novels" (a term used in the sense of the French *nouvelle*, "tale") into a semblance of a unity.

And yet, there is perhaps more unity in *The Three Impostors* than might be apparent at first glance. The subtitle of the work—"Or The Transmutations," included in the first edition but often omitted in later reprints—is an important clue to the thematic strand that binds the entire work together. The narrator of "Novel of the Black Seal," purporting to be the sister of the protagonist, Francis Leicester, speaks of the "transmutation of my brother's character" upon his taking the baleful white powder of the title. Professor Gregg, at last decoding the hieroglyphics on the black seal, observes portentously: "I read the key to the awful transmutation of the hills." Gregg is not referring merely to landscape, but to the uncovering of monstrous secrets that lurk behind the placid surface of life. And, at the very outset of the novel, we are given what could stand as Machen's manifesto for weird writing, when it is said that the writer's highest skill is in "taking matter apparently commonplace and transmuting it by the high alchemy of style into the pure gold of art."

After the publication of *The Three Impostors*, Machen took the strictures of his critics seriously. Attempting to purge his style of the cheap rhetorical tricks he had picked up from Stevenson, he made the bold utterance, "I will write a 'Robinson Crusoe' of the mind,"[3] and began *The Hill of Dreams*. The two years of agony, from 1895 to 1897, that he spent in painstakingly crafting this work proved well worth the time and effort, even though the novel was not published until 1907. *The Hill of Dreams* remains Machen's signature work in its poignant evocation of the mystical power of Nature (particularly the history and landscape of Wales, especially during its occupation by the Romans in the first several centuries of the Christian era) and its attempt to convey the paradoxical nature of the artist's task—to express the inexpressible. In the literature of horror or fantasy it is only marginally relevant, its only "fantastic" scene being the protagonist Lucian Taylor's vivid dream of being transported to the era of Roman Britain—but all devotees of Machen owe it to themselves to read a work so throbbingly vital in its evocation of the artistic mind.

In some ways, the short novel *A Fragment of Life*—begun in 1899 but not published until 1904—is a pendant to *The Hill of Dreams*. The inclusion of this work in a volume of Machen's "weird tales" would seem problematical, for the weird or fantastic element here seems reduced almost to the vanishing-point, in particular in its opening sections, which seem concerned with nothing but a display, in the manner of such social realists as Jane Austen or George Eliot, of the mundane lives of its protagonists, Edward and Mary Darnell. And yet, Machen is careful to begin the work with the significant sentence, "Edward Darnell awoke from a dream of an ancient wood . . ."—for it is Edward's dreams, and the call of his Welsh ancestry, that is at the heart of this tale. This work must be read in conjunction with Machen's treatise on aesthetics, *Hieroglyphics: A Note upon Ecstasy in Literature* (1902). Here Machen criticized such novelists as Austen, Eliot, and others (excluding his perennial favorite, Charles Dickens) for being too closely devoted to photographic realism, leaving out the "ecstasy" that must be present if a work is to be considered genuine literature. What exactly does Machen mean by "ecstasy"? He is aware that it is a difficult term to define, but he attempts it nonetheless:

> Substitute, if you like, rapture, beauty, adoration, wonder, awe, mystery, sense of the unknown, desire for the unknown. All and each will convey what I mean; for some particular case one term may be more appropriate than another, but in every case there will be that withdrawal from the common life and the common consciousness which justifies my choice of "ecstasy" as the best Symbol of my meaning[4]

Machen does not of course exactly mean that every work must have weirdness or fantasy if it is to qualify as literature instead of what he dismissively refers to as "reading matter"; but he shrewdly points out that, prior to about the eighteenth century, many of the greatest works of literature—Homer's *Odyssey*, Malory's *Morte d'Arthur*, Cervantes' *Don Quixote*, and many others—did indeed include liberal doses of the fantastic. But for Machen, even those works that seem to adhere rigidly to standards of "realism" must be motivated by a broader vision; and it is exactly that vision that we find in *A Fragment of Life*, which resolves in Darnell being led by his dreams and visions to return to his ancestral home in Wales.

But while Machen was writing such delicate works as this, he was not ignoring supernatural horror. Two of his most powerful and ingenious tales, "The Shining Pyramid" (1895) and "The White People" (written in 1899, published in 1904)—were written during this period. "The Shining Pyramid" follows up "Novel of the Black Seal" by treating of the "little people." In adhering to the notion of a primitive, half-human race that was forced to retreat to the secret corners of the earth in the wake of human civilization, Machen felt that he was observing strict scientific fact. In the essay "Folklore and Legends of the North" (1898) he wrote:

> Of recent years abundant proof has been given that a short, non-Aryan race once dwelt beneath ground, in hillocks, throughout Europe, their raths have been explored, and the weird old tales of green hills all lighted up at night have received confirmation. Much in the old legends may be explained by a reference to this primitive race. The stories of changelings, and captive women, become clear on the supposition that the "fairies" occasionally raided the houses of the invaders.[5]

But Machen well knew that the postulation, in a work of fiction, of the continued existence of this race to the present day rendered that work contrary to fact and therefore "supernatural." "The Shining Pyramid" does little more than to accumulate evidence, slowly and systematically, that leads to the inexorable conclusion that such a race does indeed exist. In some ways, this ignorant, violent, aggressive race is a kind of collective version of Helen Vaughan; for her final transformation from female to male to beast signals the primitivism that the prototypically civilized Machen saw as the repository of all horror.

Machen's greatest horror tale, "The White People," in part involves the little people and in part echoes the fear of aberrant sex found in "The Great God Pan." But Machen's genius in this story was in expounding the central narrative entirely in the voice of the nameless child protagonist. Unbenownst to herself, she not only reveals the horrors she has experienced—by way of her nurse's initiation of her into the witch-cult—but shows that she has come to embrace them. As such, Machen's presentation of the girl's diary, in her "green book," aside from containing perhaps the longest single paragraph in literary history, is a masterpiece of artistic restraint. No other means could have been chosen to display the insidiousness of the girl's inculcation into the secret cult that ultimately leads to her self-destruction.

The end of Machen's "great decade" of writing came on a sad note: the death of his wife Amelia in 1899. Even two decades later, the matter was so painful that he could scarcely bring himself to speak of it in his autobiographies. In any case, the depletion of his inheritance in 1901 compelled Machen to go to work, and he did so in an odd way— by becoming a bit player in Frank Benson's Shakespeare Repertory Company, a job he held off and on for eight years. In 1903 he married Purefoy Hudleston, with whom he shared his life for more than forty years. Machen's literary career, however, was not progressing as well as he liked. *The Hill of Dreams*, finally published in 1907, was not well received. In that same year he began work on another novel, *The Secret Glory*, but it did not see print until 1922. This curiously schizophrenic novel, part mysticism and part satire on the British school system, is in some ways a reprise of *A Fragment of Life*, in that its protagonist, Ambrose Meyrick, finally abandons England and returns to his native Wales; but overall it is only sporadically of interest. By this time Machen had turned to journalism to earn his living, and he wrote prolifically for such magazines as the *Academy*, *T.P.'s Weekly*, *the Independent*, and many others. Machen's essays and journalism are occasionally powerful and effective, but collectively they tend to say the same things too many times over and rapidly become tedious and monotonous. But at least they paid the bills, after a fashion.

In 1910 Machen began a career as a reporter for the London *Evening News*, continuing the job until 1921. It was in this capacity that he published a little story, "The Bowmen" (1914), that transformed his life once again. Written at the outbreak of World War I, after the initial battles with their frightfully high casualty counts appalled all Europe, the tale—telling of the ghosts of medieval British archers coming to the rescue of a besieged group of soldiers huddling in trenches—was seized upon by the public and the press as a true account. Several "eye-witnesses" came forth to confirm the story; pamphlets and treatises were written authenticating it; and Machen had a full-time job on his hands in a futile attempt to proclaim that it was all fiction. But in part Machen had himself to blame for the furor the tale caused: his decision to publish it in a newspaper, where it was blandly presented as a news article, naturally caused a traumatized and grieving public to accept it as fact. From a purely aesthetic perspective the tale is indeed a notable success, mingling fantasy and pathos in a distinctive amalgam. Machen's other major weird tale inspired by the war, the short novel *The Terror* (1917), is considerably less successful. In spite of its provocative scenario of animals revolting against the rule of man—later picked up by Daphne du Maurier in "The Birds"—Machen spoils the tale by a lame conclusion in which he once again harps upon the stolid materialism of his age.

Following the war, Machen retreated to a secluded home in St. John's Wood, London, where he completed his autobiographies, *Far Off Things* (1922; begun as early as 1915), *Things Near and Far* (1923), and *The London Adventure* (1924), the last a delightful account of the walks he took all around London. Around this time, a kind of Machen craze took place in America, where the publisher Alfred A. Knopf reissued many of his works in widely distributed editions. Machen also became a collector's item, the first edition of *The Hill of Dreams* selling for the incredible sum of £1500. Vincent Starrett fostered Machen's reputation by publishing two collections of miscellany, *The Shining Pyramid* (1923; not to be confused with a story collection of that title published in England in 1925) and *The Glorious Mystery* (1924). It was then that H. P. Lovecraft discovered Machen, with the result that he promptly wrote several tales—"The Festival" (1923), "Cool Air" (1926), and most notably "The Dunwich Horror" (1928)—that clearly used Machen's tales as a springboard. "The Dunwich Horror" is manifestly an echo of "The Great God Pan" in its basic scenario of a woman impregnated by a "god."

ARTHUR MACHEN

For all his celebrity, however, Machen's own creative work was in decline. *Ornaments in Jade* (1924) is an exquisite collection of prose-poems, but they were largely composed as early as 1897. He wrote only sporadically in the weird vein, and two late collections containing this work—*The Cosy Room* (1936) and *The Children of the Pool* (1936)—are disappointingly uneven. The short novel *The Green Round* (1933) has points of interest but is, on the whole, unfocused and replays many of the themes of his early work. Machen published little in the final decade of his life, and when his beloved wife Purefoy died on March 30, 1947, he seemed to have little to live for. He himself left this earth on December 15, 1947.

Even if the best of Machen's work was written a full half-century prior to his death, that work will survive as both an inextricable component of the "Yellow Nineties" and an imperishable contribution to the literature of supernatural horror. We can trace the Machen influence down through Peter Straub's *Ghost Story* (1979)—yet another variant of the basic plot of "The Great God Pan"—to the recent work of Caitlín R. Kiernan and Laird Barron. At its core, Machen's tales seek to "lift the veil" to reveal both the wonders and the terrors behind the commonplace surface of daily life; and the supernatural elements Machen puts on stage—the little people, the witch-cult, superhuman villains like Helen Vaughan—are symbols for the magic and mystery that Machen fervently hoped had not been banished to the dustbin of history in the wake of scientific progress and modern disillusion.

—S. T. JOSHI

A Note on This Edition

The tales in this volume have been largely taken from the collections in which they originally appeared. "The Great God Pan" is taken from *The House of Souls* (London: Grant Richards, 1906). The text of *Three Impostors* derives from the first edition (London: John Lane; Boston: Roberts Brothers, 1895). "The Shining Pyramid" is taken from *The Three Impostors* (New York: Alfred A. Knopf, 1923). "The White People" and "A Fragment of Life" are taken from *The House of Souls* (1906). "The Bowmen" is taken from *The Angels of Mons: The Bowmen and Other Legends of the War* (London: Simpkin, Marshall, Hamilton, Kent & Co., 1915).

The tales have been annotated to elucidate literary, historical, mythological, and other references that may not be obvious to readers. I have also added a bibliography that lists major editions of Machen's works, both those published in his lifetime and those published after his death, and a selection of the most significant criticism on Machen.

I have benefited from the work of several Machen scholars, notably Roger Dobson, Mark Valentine, Wesley Sweetser, and Andy Sawyer.

Arthur Machen

The Great God Pan

"The Great God Pan" was written in 1890–91. The first chapter of it appeared in the *Whirlwind* (December 13, 1890), but the full text was not published until its appearance in Machen's first story collection, *The Great God Pan and The Inmost Light* (London: John Lane; Boston: Roberts Brothers, 1894). It was subsequently reprinted in Machen's most important story collection, *The House of Souls* (London: Grant Richards, 1906), a large volume that also included *The Three Impostors.* Subsequent editions of *The House of Souls* (e.g., New York: Alfred A. Knopf, 1922), omit *The Three Impostors* and "The Red Hand." The story has proven to be one of Machen's most popular, appearing in many anthologies of horror tales, including Dennis Wheatley's *A Century of Horror Stories* (1935), Herbert A. Wise and Phyllis Fraser's *Great Tales of Horror and the Supernatural* (1944), David G. Hartwell's *Foundations of Fear* (1992), and many others.

I

The Experiment

"I am glad you came, Clarke; very glad indeed. I was not sure you could spare the time."

"I was able to make arrangements for a few days; things are not very lively just now. But have you no misgivings, Raymond? Is it absolutely safe?"

The two men were slowly pacing the terrace in front of Dr. Raymond's house. The sun still hung above the western mountain-line, but it shone with a dull red glow that cast no shadows, and all the air was quiet; a sweet breath came from the great wood on the hillside above, and with it, at intervals, the soft murmuring call of the wild doves. Below, in the long lovely valley, the river wound in and out between the lonely hills, and, as the sun hovered and vanished into the west, a faint mist, pure white, began to rise from the banks. Dr. Raymond turned sharply to his friend.

"Safe? Of course it is. In itself the operation is a perfectly simple one; any surgeon could do it."

"And there is no danger at any other stage?"

"None; absolutely no physical danger whatever, I give you my word. You were always timid, Clarke, always; but you know my history. I have devoted myself to transcendental medicine for the last twenty years. I have heard myself called quack and charlatan and impostor, but all the while I knew I was on the right path. Five years ago I reached the goal, and since then every day has been a preparation for what we shall do to-night."

"I should like to believe it is all true." Clarke knit his brows, and looked doubtfully at Dr. Raymond. "Are you perfectly sure, Raymond, that your theory is not a phantasmagoria—a splendid vision, certainly, but a mere vision after all?"

Dr. Raymond stopped in his walk and turned sharply. He was a middle-aged man, gaunt and thin, of a pale yellow complexion, but as he answered Clarke and faced him, there was a flush on his cheek.

"Look about you, Clarke. You see the mountain, and hill following after hill, as wave on wave, you see the woods and orchards, the fields of ripe corn, and the meadows reaching to the reed-beds by the river. You see me standing here beside you, and hear my voice; but I tell you that all these things—yes, from that star that has just shone out in the sky to the solid ground beneath our feet—I say that all these are but dreams and shadows: the shadows that hide the real world from our eyes. There *is* a real world, but it is beyond this glamour and this vision, beyond these 'chases in Arras, dreams in a career,'[1] beyond them all as beyond a veil. I do not know whether any human being has ever lifted that veil; but I do know, Clarke, that you and I shall see it lifted this very night from before another's eyes. You may think all this strange nonsense; it may be strange, but it is true, and the ancients knew what lifting the veil means. They called it seeing the god Pan."

Clarke shivered; the white mist gathering over the river was chilly.

"It is wonderful indeed," he said. "We are standing on the brink of a strange world, Raymond, if what you say is true. I suppose the knife is absolutely necessary?"

"Yes; a slight lesion in the grey matter, that is all; a trifling rearrangement of certain cells, a microscopical alteration that would escape the attention of ninety-nine brain specialists out of a hundred. I don't want to bother you with 'shop,' Clarke; I might give you a mass of technical detail which would sound very imposing, and would leave you as enlightened as you are now. But I suppose you have read, casually, in out-of-the-way corners of your paper, that immense strides have been made recently in the physiology of the brain. I saw a paragraph the other day about Digby's theory, and Browne Faber's discoveries.[2] Theories and discoveries! Where they are standing now, I stood fifteen years ago, and I need not tell you that I have not been standing still for the last fifteen years. It will be enough if I say that five years ago I made the discovery to which I alluded when I said that then I reached the goal. After years of labour, after years of toiling and groping in the dark, after days and nights of disappointment and sometimes of despair, in which I used now and then to tremble and grow cold with the thought that perhaps there were others seeking for what I sought, at last, after so long, a pang of sudden joy thrilled my soul, and I knew the long journey was at an end. By what seemed then and still seems a chance, the suggestion of a moment's idle thought followed up upon familiar lines and paths that I had tracked a hundred times already, the great truth burst upon me, and I saw, mapped out in lines of light, a whole world, a sphere unknown; continents and islands, and great oceans in which no ship has sailed (to my belief) since a Man first lifted up his eyes and beheld the sun, and the stars of heaven, and the quiet earth beneath. You will think all this high-flown language, Clarke, but it is hard to be literal. And yet; I do not know whether what I am hinting at cannot be set forth in plain and homely terms. For instance, this world of ours is pretty well girdled now with the telegraph wires and cables; thought, with something less than the speed of thought, flashes from sunrise to sunset, from north to south, across the floods and the desert places. Suppose that an electrician of to-day were suddenly to perceive that he and his friends have merely been playing with pebbles and mistaking them for the foundations of the world; suppose that such a man saw uttermost space lie open before the current, and words of men flash forth to the sun and beyond the sun into the systems beyond, and the voices of articulate-speaking men[3] echo in the waste void that bounds our thought. As analogies go, that is a pretty good analogy of what I have done; you can understand now a little of what I felt as I stood here one evening; it was a summer evening, and the valley looked much as it does now; I stood here, and saw before me the unutterable, the unthinkable gulf that yawns profound between two worlds, the world of matter and the world of spirit; I saw the great empty deep stretch dim before me, and in that instant a bridge of light leapt from the earth to the unknown shore, and the abyss was spanned. You may look in Browne Faber's book, if you like, and you will find that to the present day men of science are unable to account for the presence, or to specify the functions of a certain group of nerve-cells in the brain. That group is, as it were, land to let, a mere waste place for fanciful theories. I am not in the position of Browne Faber and the specialists, I am perfectly instructed as to the possible functions of those nerve-centres in the scheme of things. With a touch I can bring them into play, with a touch, I say, I can set free the current, with a touch I can complete the communication between this world of sense and—we shall be able to finish the sentence later on. Yes, the knife is necessary; but think what that knife will effect. It will level utterly the solid wall of sense, and probably for the first time since man was made, a spirit will gaze on a spirit-world. Clarke, Mary will see the god Pan!"

"But you remember what you wrote to me? I thought it would be requisite that she—"

He whispered the rest into the doctor's ear.

"Not at all, not at all. That is nonsense, I assure you. Indeed, it is better as it is; I am quite certain of that."

"Consider the matter well, Raymond. It's a great responsibility. Something might go wrong; you would be a miserable man for the rest of your days."

"No, I think not, even if the worst happened. As you know, I rescued Mary from the gutter, and from almost certain starvation, when she was a child; I think her life is mine to use as I see fit. Come, it is getting late; we had better go in."

Dr. Raymond led the way into the house, through the hall, and down a long dark passage. He took a key from his pocket and opened a heavy door, and motioned Clarke into his laboratory. It had once been a billiard-room, and was lighted by a glass dome in the centre of the ceiling, whence there still shone a sad grey light on the figure of the doctor as he lit a lamp with a heavy shade and placed it on a table in the middle of the room.

Clarke looked about him. Scarcely a foot of wall remained bare; there were shelves all around laden with bottles and phials of all shapes and colours, and at one end stood a little Chippendale book-case. Raymond pointed to this.

"You see that parchment Oswald Crollius?[4] He was one of the first to show me the way, though I don't think he ever found it himself. That is a strange saying of his: 'In every grain of wheat there lies hidden the soul of a star.'"

There was not much of furniture in the laboratory. The table in the centre, a stone slab with a drain in one corner, the two armchairs on which Raymond and Clarke were sitting; that was all, except an odd-looking chair at the furthest end of the room. Clarke looked at it, and raised his eyebrows.

"Yes, that is the chair," said Raymond. "We may as well place it in position." He got up and wheeled the chair to the light, and began raising and lowering it, letting down the seat, setting the back at various angles, and adjusting the foot-rest. It looked comfortable enough, and Clarke passed his hand over the soft green velvet, as the doctor manipulated the levers.

"Now, Clarke, make yourself quite comfortable. I have a couple of hours' work before me; I was obliged to leave certain matters to the last."

Raymond went to the stone slab, and Clarke watched him drearily as he bent over a row of phials and lit the flame under the crucible.

The doctor had a small hand-lamp, shaded as the larger one, on a ledge above his apparatus, and Clarke, who sat in the shadows, looked down the great dreary room, wondering at the bizarre effects of brilliant light and undefined darkness contrasting with one another. Soon he became conscious of an odd odour, at first the merest suggestion of odour, in the room; and as it grew more decided he felt surprised that he was not reminded of the chemist's shop or the surgery. Clarke found himself idly endeavouring to analyse the sensation, and, half conscious, he began to think of a day, fifteen years ago, that he had spent in roaming through the woods and meadows near his old home. It was a burning day at the beginning of August, the heat had dimmed the outlines of all things and all distances with a faint mist, and people who observed the thermometer spoke of an abnormal register, of a temperature that was almost tropical. Strangely that wonderful hot day of the 'fifties rose up in Clarke's imagination; the sense of dazzling all-pervading sunlight seemed to blot out the shadows and the lights of the laboratory, and he felt again the heated air beating in gusts about his face, saw the shimmer rising from the turf, and heard the myriad murmur of the summer.

"I hope the smell doesn't annoy you, Clarke; there's nothing unwholesome about it. It may make you a bit sleepy, that's all."

Clarke heard the words quite distinctly, and knew that Raymond was speaking to him, but for the life of him he could not rouse himself from his lethargy. He could only think of the lonely walk he had taken fifteen years ago; it was his last look at the fields and woods he had known since he was a child, and now it all stood out in brilliant light, as a picture, before him. Above all there came to his nostrils the scent of summer, the smell of flowers mingled, and the odour of the woods, of cool shaded places, deep in the green depths, drawn forth by the sun's heat; and the scent of the good earth, lying as it were with arms stretched forth, and smiling lips, overpowered all. His fancies made him wander, as he had wandered long ago, from the fields into the wood, tracking a little path between the shining undergrowth of beech-trees; and the trickle of water dropping from the limestone rock sounded as a clear melody in the dream. Thoughts began to go astray and to mingle with other recollections; the beech alley was transformed to a path beneath ilex-trees, and here and there a vine climbed from bough to bough, and sent up waving tendrils and drooped with purple grapes, and the sparse grey-green leaves of a wild olive-tree stood out against the dark shadows of the ilex. Clarke, in the deep folds of dream, was conscious that the path from his father's house had led him into an undiscovered country, and he was wondering at the strangeness of it all, when suddenly, in place of the hum and murmur of the summer, an infinite silence seemed to fall on all things, and the wood was hushed, and for a moment of time he stood face to face there with a presence, that was neither man nor beast, neither the living nor the dead, but all things mingled, the form of all things but devoid of all form. And in that moment, the sacrament of body and soul was dissolved, and a voice seemed to cry "Let us go hence," and then the darkness of darkness beyond the stars, the darkness of everlasting.

When Clarke woke up with a start he saw Raymond pouring a few drops of some oily fluid into a green phial, which he stoppered tightly.

"You have been dozing," he said; "the journey must have tired you out. It is done now. I am going to fetch Mary; I shall be back in ten minutes."

Clarke lay back in his chair and wondered. It seemed as if he had but passed from one dream into another. He half expected to see the walls of the laboratory melt and disappear, and to awake in London, shuddering at his own sleeping fancies. But at last the door opened, and the doctor returned and behind him came a girl of about seventeen, dressed all in white. She was so beautiful that Clarke did not wonder at what the doctor had written to him. She was blushing now over face and neck and arms, but Raymond seemed unmoved.

"Mary," he said, "the time has come. You are quite free. Are you willing to trust yourself to me entirely?"

"Yes, dear."

"You hear that, Clarke? You are my witness. Here is the chair, Mary. It is quite easy. Just sit in it and lean back. Are you ready?"

"Yes, dear, quite ready. Give me a kiss before you begin."

The doctor stooped and kissed her mouth, kindly enough. "Now shut your eyes," he said. The girl closed her eyelids, as if she were tired, and longed for sleep, and Raymond held the green phial to her nostrils. Her face grew white, whiter than her dress; she struggled faintly, and then with the feeling of submission strong within her, crossed her arms upon her breast as a little child about to say her prayers. The bright light of the lamp beat full upon her, and Clarke watched changes fleeting over that face as the changes of the hills when the summer clouds float across the sun. And then she lay all white and still, and the doctor turned up one of her eyelids. She was quite unconscious. Raymond pressed hard on one of the levers and the chair instantly sank back. Clarke saw him cutting away a circle, like a tonsure, from her hair, and the lamp was moved nearer. Raymond took a small glittering instrument from a little case, and Clarke turned away shuddering. When he looked again the doctor was binding up the wound he had made.

"She will awake in five minutes." Raymond was still perfectly cool. "There is nothing more to be done; we can only wait."

The minutes passed slowly; they could hear a slow, heavy ticking. There was an old clock in the passage. Clarke felt sick and faint; his knees shook beneath him, he could hardly stand.

Suddenly, as they watched, they heard a long-drawn sigh, and suddenly did the colour that had vanished return to the girl's cheeks, and suddenly her eyes opened. Clarke quailed before them. They shone with an awful light, looking far away, and a great wonder fell upon her face, and her hands stretched out as if to touch what was invisible; but in an instant the wonder faded, and gave place to the most awful terror. The muscles of her face were hideously convulsed, she shook from head to foot; the soul seemed struggling and shuddering within the house of flesh. It was a horrible sight, and Clarke rushed forward, as she fell shrieking to the floor.

Three days later Raymond took Clarke to Mary's bedside. She was lying wide-awake, rolling her head from side to side, and grinning vacantly.

"Yes," said the doctor, still quite cool, "it is a great pity; she is a hopeless idiot. However, it could not be helped; and, after all, she has seen the Great God Pan."

II

MR. CLARKE'S MEMOIRS

Mr. Clarke, the gentleman chosen by Dr. Raymond to witness the strange experiment of the god Pan, was a person in whose character caution and curiosity were oddly mingled; in his sober moments he thought of the unusual and the eccentric with undisguised aversion, and yet, deep in his heart, there was a wide-eyed inquisitiveness with respect to all the more recondite and esoteric elements in the nature of men. The latter tendency had prevailed when he accepted Raymond's invitation, for though his considered judgment had always repudiated the doctor's theories as the wildest nonsense, yet he secretly hugged a belief in fantasy, and would have rejoiced to see that belief confirmed. The horrors that he witnessed in the dreary laboratory were to a certain extent salutary; he was conscious of being involved in an affair not altogether reputable, and for many years afterwards he clung bravely to the commonplace, and rejected all occasions of occult investigation. Indeed, on some homœopathic principle, he for some time attended the séances of distinguished mediums, hoping that the clumsy tricks of these gentlemen would make him altogether disgusted with mysticism of every kind, but the remedy, though caustic, was not efficacious. Clarke knew that he still pined for the unseen, and little by little, the old passion began to reassert itself as the face of Mary shuddering and convulsed with an unknowable terror faded slowly from his memory. Occupied all day in pursuits both serious and lucrative, the temptation to relax in the evening was too great, especially in the winter months, when the fire cast a warm glow over his snug bachelor apartment, and a bottle of some choice claret stood ready by his elbow. His dinner digested, he would make a brief pretence of reading the evening paper, but the mere catalogue of news soon palled upon him, and Clarke would find himself casting glances of warm desire in the direction of an old Japanese bureau, which stood at a pleasant distance from the hearth. Like a boy before a jam-closet, for a few minutes he would hover indecisive, but lust always prevailed, and Clarke ended by drawing up his chair, lighting a candle, and sitting down before the bureau. Its pigeon-holes and drawers teemed with documents on the most morbid subjects, and in the well reposed a large manuscript volume, in which he had painfully entered the gems of his collection. Clarke had a fine contempt for published literature; the most ghostly story ceased to interest him if it happened to be printed; his sole pleasure was in the reading, compiling, arranging, and rearranging what he called his "Memoirs to prove the Existence of the Devil," and engaged in this pursuit the evening seemed to fly and the night appeared too short.

On one particular evening, an ugly December night, black with fog, and raw with frost, Clarke hurried over his dinner, and scarcely deigned to observe his customary ritual of taking up the paper and laying it down again. He paced two or three times up and down the room, and opened the bureau, stood still a moment, and sat down. He leant back, absorbed in one of those dreams to which he was subject, and at length drew out his book and opened it at the last entry. There were three or four pages densely covered with Clarke's round, set penmanship, and at the beginning he had written in a somewhat larger hand:

Singular Narrative told me by my Friend, Dr. Phillips. He assures me that all the Facts related therein are strictly and wholly True, but refuses to give either the Surnames of the Persons concerned, or the Place where these Extraordinary Events occurred.

Mr. Clarke began to read over the account for the tenth time, glancing now and then at the pencil notes he had made when it was told him by his friend. It was one of his humours to pride himself on a certain literary ability; he thought well of his style, and took pains in arranging the circumstances in dramatic order. He read the following story:—

The persons concerned in this statement are Helen V., who, if she is still alive, must now be a woman of twenty-three, Rachel M., since deceased, who was a year younger than the above, and Trevor W.,

26

an imbecile, aged eighteen. These persons were at the period of the story inhabitants of a village on the borders of Wales, a place of some importance in the time of the Roman occupation, but now a scattered hamlet, of not more than five hundred souls. It is situated on rising ground, about six miles from the sea, and is sheltered by a large and picturesque forest.

Some eleven years ago, Helen V. came to the village under rather peculiar circumstances. It is understood that she, being an orphan, was adopted in her infancy by a distant relative, who brought her up in his own house till she was twelve years old. Thinking, however, that it would be better for the child to have playmates of her own age, he advertised in several local papers for a good home in a comfortable farmhouse for a girl of twelve, and this advertisement was answered by Mr. R., a well-to-do farmer in the above-mentioned village. His references proving satisfactory, the gentleman sent his adopted daughter to Mr. R., with a letter, in which he stipulated that the girl should have a room to herself, and stated that her guardians need be at no trouble in the matter of education, as she was already sufficiently educated for the position in life which she would occupy. In fact, Mr. R. was given to understand that the girl was to be allowed to find her own occupations, and to spend her time almost as she liked. Mr. R. duly met her at the nearest station, a town some seven miles away from his house, and seems to have remarked nothing extraordinary about the child, except that she was reticent as to her former life and her adopted father. She was, however, of a very different type from the inhabitants of the village; her skin was a pale, clear olive, and her features were strongly marked, and of a somewhat foreign character. She appears to have settled down easily enough into farmhouse life, and became a favourite with the children, who sometimes went with her on her rambles in the forest, for this was her amusement. Mr. R. states that he has known her to go out by herself directly after their early breakfast, and not return till after dusk, and that, feeling uneasy at a young girl being out alone for so many hours, he communicated with her adopted father, who replied in a brief note that Helen must do as she chose. In the winter, when the forest paths are impassable, she spent most of her time in her bedroom, where she slept alone, according to the instructions of her relative. It was on one of these expeditions to the forest that the first of the singular incidents with which this girl is connected occurred, the date being about a year after her arrival at the village. The preceding winter had been remarkably severe, the snow drifting to a great depth, and the frost continuing for an unexampled period, and the summer following was as noteworthy for its extreme heat. On one of the very hottest days in this summer, Helen V. left the farmhouse for one of her long rambles in the forest, taking with her, as usual, some bread and meat for lunch. She was seen by some men in the fields making for the old Roman Road, a green causeway which traverses the highest part of the wood, and they were astonished to observe that the girl had taken off her hat, though the heat of the sun was already almost tropical. As it happened, a labourer, Joseph W. by name, was working in the forest near the Roman Road, and at twelve o'clock his little son, Trevor, brought the man his dinner of bread and cheese. After the meal, the boy, who was about seven years old at the time, left his father at work, and, as he said, went to look for flowers in the wood, and the man, who could hear him shouting with delight over his discoveries, felt no uneasiness. Suddenly, however, he was horrified at hearing the most dreadful screams, evidently the result of great terror, proceeding from the direction in which his son had gone, and he hastily threw down his tools and ran to see what had happened. Tracing his path by the sound, he met the little boy, who was running headlong, and was evidently terribly frightened, and on questioning him the man at last elicited that after picking a posy of flowers he felt tired, and lay down on the grass and fell asleep. He was suddenly awakened, as he stated, by a peculiar noise, a sort of singing he called it, and on peeping through the branches he saw Helen V. playing on the grass with a "strange naked man," whom he seemed unable to describe more fully. He said he felt dreadfully frightened, and ran away crying for his father. Joseph W. proceeded in the direction indicated by his son, and found Helen V. sitting on the grass in the middle of a glade or open space left by charcoal burners. He angrily charged her with frightening his little boy, but she entirely denied the accusation and laughed at the child's story of a "strange man," to which he himself did not attach much credence. Joseph W. came to the conclusion that the boy had woke up with a sudden fright, as children sometimes do, but Trevor persisted in his story, and continued in such evident distress that at last his father took him home, hoping that his mother would be able to soothe him. For many weeks, however, the boy gave his parents much anxiety; he became nervous and strange in his manner, refusing to leave the cottage by himself, and constantly alarming the household by waking in the night with cries of "The man in the wood! father! father!"

In course of time, however, the impression seemed to have worn off, and about three months later he accompanied his father to the house of a gentleman in the neighbourhood, for whom Joseph W. occasionally did work. The man was shown into the study, and the little boy was left sitting in the hall, and a few minutes later, while the gentleman was giving W. his instructions, they were both horrified by a piercing shriek and the sound of a fall, and rushing out, they found the child lying senseless on the floor, his face contorted with terror. The doctor was immediately summoned, and after some examination he pronounced the child to be suffering from a kind of fit, apparently produced by a sudden shock. The boy was taken to one of the bedrooms, and after some time recovered consciousness, but only to pass into a condition described by the medical man as one of violent hysteria. The doctor administered a strong sedative, and in the course of two hours pronounced him fit to walk home, but in passing through the hall the paroxysms of fright returned and with additional violence. The father perceived that the child was pointing at some object, and heard the old cry, "The man in the wood," and looking in the direction indicated saw a stone head of grotesque appearance, which had been built into the wall above one of the doors. It seems that the owner of the house had recently made alterations in his premises, and on digging the foundations for some offices, the men had found a curious head, evidently of the Roman period, which had been placed in the hall in the manner described. The head is pronounced by the most experienced archæologists of the district to be that of a faun or satyr.[5]

From whatever cause arising, this second shock seemed too severe for the boy Trevor, and at the present date he suffers from a weakness of intellect, which gives but little promise of amending. The matter caused a good deal of sensation at the time, and the girl Helen was closely questioned by Mr. R., but to no purpose, she steadfastly denying that she had frightened or in any way molested Trevor.

The second event with which this girl's name is connected took place about six years ago, and is of a still more extraordinary character.

At the beginning of the summer of 1882 Helen contracted a friendship of a peculiarly intimate character with Rachel M., the daughter of a prosperous farmer in the neighbourhood. This girl, who was a year younger than Helen, was considered by most people to be the prettier of the two, though Helen's features had to a great extent softened as she became older. The two girls, who were together on every available opportunity, presented a singular contrast, the one with her clear olive skin and almost Italian appearance, and the other of the proverbial red and white of our rural districts. It must be stated that the payments made to Mr. R. for the maintenance of Helen were known in the village for their excessive liberality, and the impression was general that she would one day inherit a large sum of money from her relative. The parents of Rachel were therefore not averse from their daughter's friendship with the girl, and even encouraged the intimacy, though they now bitterly regret having done so. Helen still retained her extraordinary fondness for the forest, and on several occasions Rachel accompanied her, the two friends setting out early in the morning, and remaining in the wood till dusk. Once or twice after these excursions Mrs. M. thought her daughter's manner rather peculiar; she seemed languid and dreamy, and as it has been expressed, "different from herself," but these peculiarities seem to have been thought too trifling for remark. One evening, however, after Rachel had come home, her mother heard a noise which sounded like suppressed weeping in the girl's room, and on going in found her lying, half undressed, upon the bed, evidently in the greatest distress. As soon as she saw her mother, she exclaimed, "Ah, mother, mother, why did you let me go to the forest with Helen?" Mrs. M. was astonished at so strange a question, and proceeded to make inquiries. Rachel told her a wild story. She said—

Clarke closed the book with a snap, and turned his chair towards the fire. When his friend sat one evening in that very chair, and told his story, Clarke had interrupted him at a point a little subsequent to this, had cut short his words in a paroxysm of horror. "My God," he exclaimed, "think, think what you are saying! It is too incredible, too monstrous; such things can never be in this quiet world, where men and women live and die, and struggle, and conquer, or maybe fail, and fall down under sorrow, and grieve and suffer strange fortunes for many a year; but not this, Phillips, not such things as this. There must be some explanation, some way out of the terror. Why, man, if such a case were possible, our earth would be a nightmare."

But Phillips had told his story to the end, concluding:

"Her flight remains a mystery to this day; she vanished in broad sunlight; they saw her walking in a meadow, and a few moments later she was not there."

Clarke tried to conceive the thing again, as he sat by the fire, and again his mind shuddered and shrank back, appalled before the sight of such awful, unspeakable elements enthroned as it were, and triumphant in human flesh. Before him stretched the long dim vista of the green causeway in the forest, as his friend had described it: he saw the swaying leaves and the quivering shadows on the grass, he saw the sunlight and the flowers, and far away, far in the long distance, the two figures moved towards him. One was Rachel, but the other?

Clarke had tried his best to disbelieve it all, but at the end of the account, as he had written it in his book, he had placed the inscription:

ET DIABOLUS INCARNATUS EST: ET HOMO FACTUS EST.[6]

III

The City of Resurrections

"Herbert! Good God! Is it possible?"

"Yes, my name's Herbert. I think I know your face, too, but I don't remember your name. My memory is very queer."

"Don't you recollect Villiers of Wadham?"

"So it is, so it is. I beg your pardon, Villiers, I didn't think I was begging of an old college friend. Good-night."

"My dear fellow, this haste is unnecessary. My rooms are close by, but we won't go there just yet. Suppose we walk up Shaftesbury Avenue a little way? But how in heaven's name have you come to this pass, Herbert?"

"It's a long story, Villiers, and a strange one, too, but you can hear it if you like."

"Come on, then. Take my arm, you don't seem very strong."

The ill-assorted pair moved slowly up Rupert Street; the one in dirty, evil-looking rags, and the other attired in the regulation uniform of a man about town, trim, glossy, and eminently well-to-do. Villiers had emerged from his restaurant after an excellent dinner of many courses, assisted by an ingratiating little flask of Chianti, and, in that frame of mind which was with him almost chronic, had delayed a moment by the door, peering round in the dimly-lighted street in search of those mysterious incidents and persons with which the streets of London teem in every quarter and at every hour. Villiers prided himself as a practised explorer of such obscure mazes and byways of London life, and in this unprofitable pursuit he displayed an assiduity which was worthy of more serious employment. Thus he stood beside the lamp-post surveying the passers-by with undisguised curiosity, and with that gravity only known to the systematic diner, had just enunciated in his mind the formula: "London has been called the city of encounters; it is more than that, it is the city of Resurrections," when these reflections were suddenly interrupted by a piteous whine at his elbow, and a deplorable appeal for alms. He looked round in some irritation, and with a sudden shock found himself confronted with the embodied proof of his somewhat stilted fancies. There, close beside him, his face altered and disfigured by poverty and disgrace, his body barely covered by greasy, ill-fitting rags, stood his old friend Charles Herbert, who had matriculated on the same day as himself, with whom he had been merry and wise for twelve revolving terms. Different occupations and varying interests had interrupted the friendship, and it was six years since Villiers had seen Herbert; and now he looked upon this wreck of a man with grief and dismay, mingled with a certain inquisitiveness as to what dreary chain of circumstance had dragged him down to such a doleful pass. Villiers felt together with compassion all the relish of the amateur in mysteries, and congratulated himself on his leisurely speculations outside the restaurant.

They walked on in silence for some time, and more than one passer-by stared in astonishment at the unaccustomed spectacle of a well-dressed man with an unmistakable beggar hanging on to his arm, and, observing this, Villiers led the way to an obscure street in Soho. Here he repeated his question.

"How on earth has it happened, Herbert? I always understood you would succeed to an excellent position in Dorsetshire. Did your father disinherit you? Surely not?"

"No, Villiers; I came into all the property at my poor father's death; he died a year after I left Oxford. He was a very good father to me, and I mourned his death sincerely enough. But you know what young men are; a few months later I came up to town and went a good deal into society. Of course I had excellent introductions, and I managed to enjoy myself very much in a harmless sort of way. I played a little, certainly, but never for heavy stakes, and the few bets I made on races brought me in money—only a few pounds, you know, but enough to pay for cigars and such petty pleasures. It was in my second season that the tide turned. Of course you have heard of my marriage?"

"No, I never heard anything about it."

"Yes, I married, Villiers. I met a girl, a girl of the most wonderful and most strange beauty, at the house of some people whom I knew. I cannot tell you her age; I never knew it, but, so far as I can guess,

I should think she must have been about nineteen when I made her acquaintance. My friends had come to know her at Florence; she told them she was an orphan, the child of an English father and an Italian mother, and she charmed them as she charmed me. The first time I saw her was at an evening party. I was standing by the door talking to a friend, when suddenly above the hum and babble of conversation I heard a voice, which seemed to thrill to my heart. She was singing an Italian song. I was introduced to her that evening, and in three months I married Helen. Villiers, that woman, if I can call her woman, corrupted my soul. The night of the wedding I found myself sitting in her bedroom in the hotel, listening to her talk. She was sitting up in bed, and I listened to her as she spoke in her beautiful voice, spoke of things which even now I would not dare whisper in blackest night, though I stood in the midst of a wilderness. You, Villiers, you may think you know life, and London, and what goes on day and night in this dreadful city; for all I can say you may have heard the talk of the vilest, but I tell you, you can have no conception of what I know, no, not in your most fantastic, hideous dreams can you have imaged forth the faintest shadow of what I have heard—and seen. Yes, seen. I have seen the incredible, such horrors that even I myself sometimes stop in the middle of the street, and ask whether it is possible for a man to behold such things and live. In a year, Villiers, I was a ruined man, in body and soul—in body and soul."

"But your property, Herbert? You had land in Dorset."

"I sold it all; the fields and woods, the dear old house—everything."

"And the money?"

"She took it all from me."

"And then left you?"

"Yes; she disappeared one night. I don't know where she went, but I am sure if I saw her again it would kill me. The rest of my story is of no interest; sordid misery, that is all. You may think, Villiers, that I have exaggerated and talked for effect; but I have not told you half. I could tell you certain things which would convince you, but you would never know a happy day again. You would pass the rest of your life, as I pass mine, a haunted man, a man who has seen hell."

Villiers took the unfortunate man to his rooms, and gave him a meal. Herbert could eat little, and scarcely touched the glass of wine set before him. He sat moody and silent by the fire, and seemed relieved when Villiers sent him away with a small present of money.

"By the way, Herbert," said Villiers as they parted at the door, "what was your wife's name? You said Helen, I think? Helen what?"

"The name she passed under when I met her was Helen Vaughan, but what her real name was I can't say. I don't think she had a name. No, no, not in that sense. Only human beings have names, Villiers; I can't say any more. Good-bye; yes, I will not fail to call if I see any way in which you can help me. Good-night."

The man went out into the bitter night, and Villiers returned to his fireside. There was something about Herbert which shocked him inexpressibly; not his poor rags nor the marks which poverty had set upon his face, but rather an indefinite terror which hung about him like a mist. He had acknowledged that he himself was not devoid of blame; the woman, he had avowed, had corrupted him body and soul, and Villiers felt that this man, once his friend, had been an actor in scenes evil beyond the power of words. His story needed no confirmation: he himself was the embodied proof of it. Villiers mused curiously over the story he had heard, and wondered whether he had heard both the first and the last of it. "No," he thought, "certainly not the last, probably only the beginning. A case like this is like a nest of Chinese boxes; you open one after another and find a quainter workmanship in every box. Most likely poor Herbert is merely one of the outside boxes; there are stranger ones to follow."

Villiers could not take his mind away from Herbert and his story, which seemed to grow wilder as the night wore on. The fire began to burn low, and the chilly air of the morning crept into the room; Villiers got up with a glance over his shoulder, and shivering slightly, went to bed.

A few days later he saw in his club a gentleman of his acquaintance, named Austin, who was famous for his intimate knowledge of London life, both in its tenebrous and luminous phases. Villiers, still full of his encounter in Soho and its consequences, thought Austin might possibly be able to shed some light on Herbert's history, and so after some casual talk he suddenly put the question:

"Do you happen to know anything of a man named Herbert—Charles Herbert?"

Austin turned round sharply and stared at Villiers with some astonishment.

"Charles Herbert? Weren't you in town three years ago? No; then you have not heard of the Paul Street case? It caused a good deal of sensation at the time."

"What was the case?"

"Well, a gentleman, a man of very good position, was found dead, stark dead, in the area of a certain house in Paul Street, off Tottenham Court Road. Of course the police did not make the discovery; if you happen to be sitting up all night and have a light in your window, the constable will ring the bell, but if you happen to be lying dead in somebody's area, you will be left alone. In this instance, as in many others, the alarm was raised by some kind of vagabond; I don't mean a common tramp, or a public-house loafer, but a gentleman, whose business or pleasure, or both, made him a spectator of the London streets at five o'clock in the morning. This individual was, as he said, 'going home,' it did not appear whence or whither, and had occasion to pass through Paul Street between four and five a.m. Something or other caught his eye at Number 20; he said, absurdly enough, that the house had the most unpleasant physiognomy he had ever observed, but, at any rate, he glanced down the area, and was a good deal astonished to see a man lying on the stones, his limbs all huddled together, and his face turned up. Our gentleman thought this face looked peculiarly ghastly, and so set off at a run in search of the nearest policeman. The constable was at first inclined to treat the matter lightly, suspecting common drunkenness; however, he came, and after looking at the man's face, changed his tone, quickly enough. The early bird, who had picked up this fine worm, was sent off for a doctor, and the policeman rang and knocked at the door till a slatternly servant girl came down looking more than half asleep. The constable pointed out the contents of the area to the maid, who screamed loudly enough to wake up the street, but she knew nothing of the man; had never seen him at the house, and so forth. Meanwhile the original discoverer had come back with a medical man, and the next thing was to get into the area. The gate was open, so the whole quartet stumped down the steps. The doctor hardly needed a moment's examination; he said the poor fellow had been dead for several hours, and it was then the case began to get interesting. The dead man had not been robbed, and in one of his pockets were papers identifying him as—well, as a man of good family and means, a favourite in society, and nobody's enemy, so far as could be known. I don't give his name, Villiers, because it has nothing to do with the story, and because it's no good raking up these affairs about the dead when there are relations living. The next curious point was that the medical men couldn't agree as to how he met his death. There were some slight bruises on his shoulders, but they were so slight that it looked as if he had been pushed roughly out of the kitchen door, and not thrown over the railings from the street, or even dragged down the steps. But there were positively no other marks of violence about him, certainly none that would account for his death; and when they came to the autopsy there wasn't a trace of poison of any kind. Of course the police wanted to know all about the people at Number 20, and here again, so

I have heard from private sources, one or two other very curious points came out. It appears that the occupants of the house were a Mr. and Mrs. Charles Herbert; he was said to be a landed proprietor, though it struck most people that Paul Street was not exactly the place to look for county gentry. As for Mrs. Herbert, nobody seemed to know who or what she was, and, between ourselves, I fancy the divers after her history found themselves in rather strange waters. Of course they both denied knowing anything about the deceased, and in default of any evidence against them they were discharged. But some very odd things came out about them. Though it was between five and six in the morning when the dead man was removed, a large crowd had collected, and several of the neighbours ran to see what was going on. They were pretty free with their comments, by all accounts, and from these it appeared that Number 20 was in very bad odour in Paul Street. The detectives tried to trace down these rumours to some solid foundation of fact, but could not get hold of anything. People shook their heads and raised their eyebrows and thought the Herberts rather 'queer,' 'would rather not be seen going into their house,' and so on, but there was nothing tangible. The authorities were morally certain that the man met his death in some way or another in the house and was thrown out by the kitchen door, but they couldn't prove it, and the absence of any indications of violence or poisoning left them helpless. An odd case, wasn't it? But curiously enough, there's something more that I haven't told you. I happened to know one of the doctors who was consulted as to the cause of death, and some time after the inquest I met him, and asked him about it. 'Do you really mean to tell me,' I said, 'that you were baffled by the case, that you actually don't know what the man died of?' 'Pardon me,' he replied, 'I know perfectly well what caused death. Blank died of fright, of sheer, awful terror; I never saw features so hideously contorted in the entire course of my practice, and I have seen the faces of a whole host of dead.' The doctor was usually a cool customer enough, and a certain vehemence in his manner struck me, but I couldn't get anything more out of him. I suppose the Treasury didn't see their way to prosecuting the Herberts for frightening a man to death; at any rate, nothing was done, and the case dropped out of men's minds. Do you happen to know anything of Herbert?"

"Well," replied Villiers, "he was an old college friend of mine."

"You don't say so? Have you ever seen his wife?"

"No, I haven't. I have lost sight of Herbert for many years."

"It's queer, isn't it, parting with a man at the college gate or at Paddington, seeing nothing of him for years, and then finding him pop up his head in such an odd place. But I should like to have seen Mrs.

Herbert; people said extraordinary things about her."

"What sort of things?"

"Well, I hardly know how to tell you. Every one who saw her at the police court said she was at once the most beautiful woman and the most repulsive they had ever set eyes on. I have spoken to a man who saw her, and I assure you he positively shuddered as he tried to describe the woman, but he couldn't tell why. She seems to have been a sort of enigma; and I expect if that one dead man could have told tales, he would have told some uncommonly queer ones. And there you are again in another puzzle; what could a respectable country gentleman like Mr. Blank (we'll call him that if you don't mind) want in such a very queer house as Number 20? It's altogether a very odd case, isn't it?"

"It is indeed, Austin; an extraordinary case. I didn't think, when I asked you about my old friend, I should strike on such strange metal. Well, I must be off; good-day."

Villiers went away, thinking of his own conceit of the Chinese boxes; here was quaint workmanship indeed.

IV

THE DISCOVERY IN PAUL STREET

A few months after Villiers' meeting with Herbert, Mr. Clarke was sitting, as usual, by his after-dinner hearth, resolutely guarding his fancies from wandering in the direction of the bureau. For more than a week he had succeeded in keeping away from the "Memoirs," and he cherished hopes of a complete self-reformation; but, in spite of his endeavours, he could not hush the wonder and the strange curiosity that that last case he had written down had excited within him. He had put the case, or rather the outline of it, conjecturally to a scientific friend, who shook his head, and thought Clarke getting queer, and on this particular evening Clarke was making an effort to rationalize the story, when a sudden knock at his door roused him from his meditations.

"Mr. Villiers to see you, sir."

"Dear me, Villiers, it is very kind of you to look me up; I have not seen you for many months; I should think nearly a year. Come in, come in. And how are you, Villiers? Want any advice about investments?"

"No, thanks, I fancy everything I have in that way is pretty safe. No, Clarke, I have really come to consult you about a rather curious matter that has been brought under my notice of late. I am afraid you will think it all rather absurd when I tell my tale. I sometimes think so myself, and that's just why I made up my mind to come to you, as I know you're a practical man."

Mr. Villiers was ignorant of the "Memoirs to prove the Existence of the Devil."

"Well, Villiers, I shall be happy to give you my advice, to the best of my ability. What is the nature of the case?"

"It's an extraordinary thing altogether. You know my ways; I always keep my eyes open in the streets, and in my time I have chanced upon some queer customers, and queer cases, too, but this, I think, beats all. I was coming out of a restaurant one nasty winter night about three months ago; I had had a capital dinner and a good bottle of Chianti, and I stood for a moment on the pavement, thinking what a mystery there is about London streets and the companies that pass along them. A bottle of red wine encourages these fancies, Clarke, and I dare say I should have thought a page of small type, but I was cut short by a beggar who had come behind me, and was making the usual appeals. Of course I looked round, and this beggar turned out to be what was left of an old friend of mine, a man named Herbert. I asked him how he had come to such a wretched pass, and he told me. We walked up and down one of those long, dark Soho streets, and there I listened to his story. He said he had married a beautiful girl, some years younger than himself, and, as he put it, she had corrupted him body and soul. He wouldn't go into details; he said he dare not, that what he had seen and heard haunted him by night and day, and when I looked in his face I knew he was speaking the truth. There was something about the man that made me shiver. I don't know why, but it was there. I gave him a little money and sent him away, and I assure you that when he was gone I gasped for breath. His presence seemed to chill one's blood."

"Isn't all this just a little fanciful, Villiers? I suppose the poor fellow had made an imprudent marriage, and, in plain English, gone to the bad."

"Well, listen to this." Villiers told Clarke the story he had heard from Austin.

"You see," he concluded, "there can be but little doubt that this Mr. Blank, whoever he was, died of sheer terror; he saw something so awful, so terrible, that it cut short his life. And what he saw, he most certainly saw in that house, which, somehow or other, had got a bad name in the neighbourhood. I had the curiosity to go and look at the place for myself. It's a saddening kind of street; the houses are old enough to be mean and dreary, but not old enough to be quaint. As far as I could see most of them are let in lodgings, furnished and unfurnished, and almost every door has three bells to it. Here and there the ground floors have been made into shops of the commonest kind; it's a dismal street in every way. I found Number 20 was to let, and I went to the agent's and got the key. Of course I should have heard nothing of the Herberts in that quarter, but I asked the man, fair and square, how long they had left the house, and whether there had been other tenants in the meanwhile. He looked at me queerly for a minute, and told me the Herberts had left immediately after the unpleasantness, as he called it, and since then the house had been empty.”

Mr. Villiers paused for a moment.

“I have always been rather fond of going over empty houses; there's a sort of fascination about the desolate empty rooms, with the nails sticking in the walls, and the dust thick upon the window-sills. But I didn't enjoy going over Number 20, Paul Street. I had hardly put my foot inside the passage before I noticed a queer, heavy feeling about the air of the house. Of course all empty houses are stuffy, and so forth, but this was something quite different; I can't describe it to you, but it seemed to stop the breath. I went into the front room and the back room, and the kitchens downstairs; they were all dirty and dusty enough, as you would expect, but there was something strange about them all. I couldn't define it to you, I only know I felt queer. It was one of the rooms on the first floor, though, that was the worst. It was a largish room, and once on a time the paper must have been cheerful enough, but when I saw it, paint, paper, and everything were most doleful. But the room was full of horror; I felt my teeth grinding as I put my hand on the door, and when I went in, I thought I should have fallen fainting to the floor. However, I pulled myself together, and stood against the end wall, wondering what on earth there could be about the room to make my limbs tremble, and my heart beat as if I were at the hour of death. In one corner there was a pile of newspapers littered about on the floor, and I began looking at them; they were papers of three or four years ago, some of them half torn, and some crumpled as if they had been used for packing. I turned the whole pile over, and amongst them I found a curious drawing; I will show it you presently. But I couldn't stay in the room; I felt it was overpowering me. I was thankful to come out, safe and sound, into the open air. People stared at me as I walked along the street, and one man said I was drunk. I was staggering about from one side of the pavement to the other, and it was as much as I could do to take the key back to the agent and get home. I was in bed for a week, suffering from what my doctor called nervous shock and exhaustion. One of those days I was reading the evening paper, and happened to notice a paragraph headed: ‘Starved to Death.’ It was the usual style of thing: a model lodging-house in Marylebone, a door locked for several days, and a dead man in his chair when they broke in. ‘The deceased,’ said the paragraph, ‘was known as Charles Herbert, and is believed to have been once a prosperous country gentleman. His name was familiar to the public three years ago in connection with the mysterious death in

Paul Street, Tottenham Court Road, the deceased being the tenant of the house Number 20 in the area of which a gentleman of good position was found dead under circumstances not devoid of suspicion.' A tragic ending, wasn't it? But, after all, if what he told me were true, which I am sure it was, the man's life was all a tragedy, and a tragedy of a stranger sort than they put on the boards."

"And that is the story, is it?" said Clarke musingly.

"Yes, that is the story."

"Well, really, Villiers, I scarcely know what to say about it. There are, no doubt, circumstances in the case which seem peculiar, the finding of the dead man in the area of Herbert's house, for instance, and the extraordinary opinion of the physician as to the cause of death; but, after all, it is conceivable that the facts may be explained in a straightforward manner. As to your own sensations, when you went to see the house, I would suggest that they were due to a vivid imagination; you must have been brooding, in a semi-conscious way, over what you had heard. I don't exactly see what more can be said or done in the matter; you evidently think there is a mystery of some kind, but Herbert is dead; where then do you propose to look?"

"I propose to look for the woman; the woman whom he married. *She* is the mystery."

The two men sat silent by the fireside; Clarke secretly congratulating himself on having successfully kept up the character of advocate of the commonplace, and Villiers wrapt in his gloomy fancies.

"I think I will have a cigarette," he said at last, and put his hand in his pocket to feel for the cigarette-case.

"Ah!" he said, starting slightly, "I forgot I had something to show you. You remember my saying that I had found a rather curious sketch amongst the pile of old newspapers at the house in Paul Street? Here it is."

Villiers drew out a small thin parcel from his pocket. It was covered with brown paper, and secured with string, and the knots were troublesome. In spite of himself, Clarke felt inquisitive; he bent forward on his chair as Villiers painfully undid the string, and unfolded the outer covering. Inside was a second wrapping of tissue, and Villiers took it off and handed the small piece of paper to Clarke without a word.

There was dead silence in the room for five minutes or more; the two men sat so still that they could hear the ticking of the tall old-fashioned clock that stood outside in the hall, and in the mind of one of them the slow monotony of sound woke up a far, far memory. He was looking intently at the small pen-and-ink sketch of a woman's head; it had evidently been drawn with great care, and by a true artist, for the woman's soul looked out of the eyes, and the lips were parted with a strange smile. Clarke gazed still at the face; it brought to his memory one summer evening long ago; he saw again the long lovely valley, the river winding between the hills, the meadows and the cornfields, the dull red sun, and the cold white mist rising from the water. He heard a voice speaking to him across the waves of many years, and saying, "Clarke, Mary will see the God Pan!" and then he was standing in the grim room beside the doctor, listening to the heavy ticking of the clock, waiting and watching, watching the figure lying on the green chair beneath the lamp-light. Mary rose up, and he looked into her eyes, and his heart grew cold within him.

"Who is this woman?" he said at last. His voice was dry and hoarse.

"That is the woman whom Herbert married."

Clarke looked again at the sketch; it was not Mary after all. There certainly was Mary's face, but there was something else, something he had not seen on Mary's features when the white-clad girl entered the laboratory with the doctor, nor at her terrible awakening, nor when she lay grinning on the bed. Whatever it was, the glance that came from those eyes, the smile on the full lips, or the expression of the whole face, Clarke shuddered before it in his inmost soul, and thought unconsciously of Dr. Phillips's words, "the most vivid presentment of evil I have ever seen." He turned the paper over mechanically in his hand and glanced at the back.

"Good God, Clarke, what is the matter? You are as white as death."

Villiers had started wildly from his chair as Clarke fell back with a groan, and let the paper drop from his hands.

"I don't feel very well, Villiers; I am subject to these attacks. Pour me out a little wine; thanks, that will do. I shall feel better in a few minutes."

Villiers picked up the fallen sketch and turned it over as Clarke had done.

"You saw that?" he said. "That's how I identified it as being a portrait of Herbert's wife, or I should say his widow. How do you feel now?"

"Better, thanks, it was only a passing faintness. I don't think I quite catch your meaning. What did you say enabled you to identify the picture?"

"This word—'Helen'—written on the back. Didn't I tell you her name was Helen? Yes; Helen Vaughan."

Clarke groaned; there could be no shadow of doubt.

"Now don't you agree with me," said Villiers, "that in the story I have told you to-night, and in the part this woman plays in it, there are some very strange points?"

"Yes, Villiers," Clarke muttered, "it is a strange story indeed; a strange story indeed. You must give me time to think it over; I may be able to help you, or I may not. Must you be going now? Well, good-night, Villiers, good-night. Come and see me in the course of a week."

V

THE LETTER OF ADVICE

"Do you know, Austin," said Villiers as the two friends were pacing sedately along Piccadilly one pleasant morning in May, "do you know I am convinced that what you told me about Paul Street and the Herberts is a mere episode in an extraordinary history? I may as well confess to you that when I asked you about Herbert a few months ago I had just seen him."

"You had seen him? Where?"

"He begged of me in the street one night. He was in the most pitiable plight, but I recognized the man, and I got him to tell me his history, or at least the outline of it. In brief, it amounted to this—he had been ruined by his wife."

"In what manner?"

"He would not tell me; he would only say that she had destroyed him, body and soul. The man is dead now."

"And what has become of his wife?"

"Ah, that's what I should like to know, and I mean to find her sooner or later. I know a man named Clarke, a dry fellow, in fact a man of business, but shrewd enough. You understand my meaning; not shrewd in the mere business sense of the word, but a man who really knows something about men and life. Well, I laid the case before him, and he was evidently impressed. He said it needed consideration, and asked me to come again in the course of a week. A few days later I received this extraordinary letter."

Austin took the envelope, drew out the letter, and read it curiously.

It ran as follows:—

"MY DEAR VILLIERS,—I have thought over the matter on which you consulted me the other night, and my advice to you is this. Throw the portrait into the fire, blot out
the story from your mind. Never give it another thought, Villiers, or you will be sorry. You will think, no doubt, that I am
in possession of some secret information, and to a certain extent that is the case. But I only know a little; I am like a traveller who has peered over an abyss, and has drawn back in
terror. What I know is strange enough and horrible enough,
but beyond my knowledge there are depths and horrors more
frightful still, more incredible than any tale told of winter
nights about the fire. I have resolved, and nothing shall shake
that resolve, to explore no whit farther, and if you value your
happiness you will make the same determination.

"Come and see me by all means; but we will talk on more
cheerful topics than this."

Austin folded the letter methodically and returned it to Villiers.

"It is certainly an extraordinary letter," he said; "what does he
mean by the portrait?"

"Ah, I forgot to tell you I have been to Paul Street and have made
a discovery."

Villiers told his story as he had told it to Clarke, and Austin listened in silence. He seemed puzzled.

"How very curious that you should experience such an unpleasant
sensation in that room!" he said at length. "I hardly gather that it was a
mere matter of the imagination; a feeling of repulsion, in short."

"No, it was more physical than mental. It was as if I were inhaling
at every breath some deadly fume, which seemed to penetrate to every
nerve and bone and sinew of my body. I felt racked from head to foot,
my eyes began to grow dim; it was like the entrance of death."

"Yes, yes, very strange, certainly. You see, your friend confesses
that there is some very black story connected with this woman. Did
you notice any particular emotion in him when you were telling your
tale?"

"Yes, I did. He became very faint, but he assured me that it was a
mere passing attack to which he was subject."

"Did you believe him?"

"I did at the time, but I don't now. He heard what I had to say
with a good deal of indifference, till I showed him the portrait. It was

then he was seized with the attack of which I spoke. He looked ghastly, I assure you."

"Then he must have seen the woman before. But there might be another explanation; it might have been the name, and not the face, which was familiar to him. What do you think?"

"I couldn't say. To the best of my belief it was after turning the portrait in his hands that he nearly dropped from his chair. The name, you know, was written on the back."

"Quite so. After all, it is impossible to come to any resolution in a case like this. I hate melodrama, and nothing strikes me as more commonplace and tedious than the ordinary ghost story of commerce; but really, Villiers, it looks as if there were something very queer at the bottom of all this."

The two men had, without noticing it, turned up Ashley Street, leading northward from Piccadilly. It was a long street, and rather a gloomy one, but here and there a brighter taste had illuminated the dark houses with flowers, and gay curtains, and a cheerful paint on the doors. Villiers glanced up as Austin stopped speaking, and looked at one of these houses; geraniums, red and white, drooped from every sill, and daffodil-coloured curtains were draped back from each window.

"It looks cheerful, doesn't it?" he said.

"Yes, and the inside is still more cheery. One of the pleasantest houses of the season, so I have heard. I haven't been there myself, but I've met several men who have, and they tell me it's uncommonly jovial."

"Whose house is it?"

"A Mrs. Beaumont's."

"And who is she?"

"I couldn't tell you. I have heard she comes from South America, but, after all, who she is is of little consequence. She is a very wealthy woman, there's no doubt of that, and some of the best people have taken her up. I hear she has some wonderful claret, really marvellous wine, which must have cost a fabulous sum. Lord Argentine was telling me about it; he was there last Sunday evening. He assures me he has never tasted such a wine, and Argentine, as you know, is an expert. By the way, that reminds me, she must be an oddish sort of woman, this Mrs. Beaumont. Argentine asked her how old the wine was, and what do you think she said? 'About a thousand years, I believe.' Lord Argentine thought she was chaffing him, you know, but when he laughed she said she was speaking quite seriously, and offered to show him the jar. Of course, he couldn't say anything more after that; but it seems rather antiquated for a beverage, doesn't it? Why, here we are at my rooms.

Come in, won't you?"

"Thanks, I think I will. I haven't seen the curiosity-shop for some time."

It was a room furnished richly, yet oddly, where every chair and bookcase and table, and every rug and jar and ornament seemed to be a thing apart, preserving its own individuality.

"Anything fresh lately?" said Villiers after a while.

"No, I think not; you saw those queer jugs, didn't you? I thought so. I don't think I have come across anything for the last few weeks."

Austin glanced round the room from cupboard to cupboard, from shelf to shelf, in search of some new oddity. His eyes fell at last on an old chest, pleasantly and quaintly carved, which stood in a dark corner of the room.

"Ah," he said, "I was forgetting, I have got something to show you." Austin unlocked the chest, drew out a thick quarto volume, laid it on the table, and resumed the cigar he had put down.

"Did you know Arthur Meyrick,[7] the painter, Villiers?"

"A little; I met him two or three times at the house of a friend of mine. What has become of him? I haven't heard his name mentioned for some time."

"He's dead."

"You don't say so! Quite young, wasn't he?"

"Yes; only thirty when he died."

"What did he die of?"

"I don't know. He was an intimate friend of mine, and a thoroughly good fellow. He used to come here and talk to me for hours, and he was one of the best talkers I have met. He could even talk about painting, and that's more than can be said of most painters. About eighteen months ago he was feeling rather overworked, and partly at my suggestion he went off on a sort of roving expedition, with no very definite end or aim about it. I believe New York was to be his first port, but I never heard from him. Three months ago I got this book, with a very civil letter from an English doctor practising at Buenos Ayres, stating that he had attended the late Mr. Meyrick during his illness, and that the deceased had expressed an earnest wish that the enclosed packet should he sent to me after his death. That was all."

"And haven't you written for further particulars?"

"I have been thinking of doing so. You would advise me to write to the doctor?"

"Certainly. And what about the book?"

"It was sealed up when I got it. I don't think the doctor had seen it."

"It is something very rare? Meyrick was a collector, perhaps?"

"No, I think not, hardly a collector. Now, what do you think of those Ainu jugs?"

"They are peculiar, but I like them. But aren't you going to show me poor Meyrick's legacy?"

"Yes, yes, to be sure. The fact is, it's rather a peculiar sort of thing, and I haven't shown it to anyone. I wouldn't say anything about it if I were you. There it is."

Villiers took the book and opened it at haphazard.

"It isn't a printed volume, then?" he said.

"No. It is a collection of drawings in black and white by my poor friend Meyrick."

Villiers turned to the first page, it was blank; the second bore a brief inscription, which he read:

Silet per diem universus, nec sine horrore secretus est; lucet nocturnis ignibus, chorus Ægipanum undique personatur: audiuntur et cantus tibiarum, et tinnitus cymbalorum per oram maritimam.[8]

On the third page was a design which made Villiers start and look up at Austin; he was gazing abstractedly out of the window. Villiers turned page after page, absorbed, in spite of himself, in the frightful Walpurgis Night of evil, strange monstrous evil, that the dead artist had set forth in hard black and white. The figures of Fauns and Satyrs and Ægipans danced before his eyes, the darkness of the thicket, the dance on the mountain-top, the scenes by lonely shores, in green vineyards, by rocks and desert places, passed before him: a world before which the human soul seemed to shrink back and shudder. Villiers whirled over the remaining pages; he had seen enough, but the picture on the last leaf caught his eye, as he almost closed the book.

"Austin!"

"Well, what is it?"

"Do you know who that is?"

It was a woman's face, alone on the white page.

"Know who it is? No, of course not."

"I do."

"Who is it?"

"It is Mrs. Herbert."

"Are you sure?"

"I am perfectly certain of it. Poor Meyrick! He is one more chapter in her history."

"But what do you think of the designs?"

"They are frightful. Lock the book up again, Austin. If I were you

I would burn it; it must be a terrible companion even though it be in a chest."

"Yes, they are singular drawings. But I wonder what connection there could be between Meyrick and Mrs. Herbert, or what link between her and these designs?"

"Ah, who can say? It is possible that the matter may end here, and we shall never know, but in my own opinion this Helen Vaughan, or Mrs. Herbert, is only beginning. She will come back to London, Austin; depend upon it, she will come back and we shall hear more about her then. I don't think it will be very pleasant news."

VI

THE SUICIDES

Lord Argentine was a great favourite in London Society. At twenty he had been a poor man, decked with the surname of an illustrious family, but forced to earn a livelihood as best he could, and the most speculative of money-lenders would not have entrusted him with fifty pounds on the chance of his ever changing his name for a title, and his poverty for a great fortune. His father had been near enough to the fountain of good things to secure one of the family livings, but the son, even if he had taken orders, would scarcely have obtained so much as this, and moreover felt no vocation for the ecclesiastical estate. Thus he fronted the world with no better armour than the bachelor's gown and the wits of a younger son's grandson, with which equipment he contrived in some way to make a very tolerable fight of it. At twenty-five Mr. Charles Aubernoun saw himself still a man of struggles and of warfare with the world, but out of the seven who stood between him and the high places of his family three only remained. These three, however, were "good lives," but yet not proof against the Zulu assegais and typhoid fever, and so one morning Aubernoun woke up and found himself Lord Argentine, a man of thirty who had faced the difficulties of existence, and had conquered. The situation amused him immensely, and he resolved that riches should be as pleasant to him as poverty had always been. Argentine, after some little consideration, came to the conclusion that dining, regarded as a fine art, was perhaps the most amusing pursuit open to fallen humanity, and thus his dinners became famous in London, and an invitation to his table a thing covetously desired. After ten years of lordship and dinners Argentine still declined to be jaded, still persisted in enjoying life, and by a kind of infection had become recognized as the cause of joy in others, in short, as the best of company. His sudden and tragical death, therefore, caused a wide and deep sensation. People could scarce believe it, even though the newspaper was before their eyes, and the cry of "Mysterious Death of a Nobleman" came ringing up from the street. But there stood the brief paragraph: "Lord Argentine was found dead this morning by his valet under distressing circumstances. It is stated that there can be no doubt that his lordship committed suicide, though no motive can be assigned for the act. The deceased nobleman was widely known in society, and much liked for his genial manner and sumptuous hospitality. He is succeeded by," etc., etc.

By slow degrees the details came to light, but the case still remained a mystery. The chief witness at the inquest was the dead nobleman's valet, who said that the night before his death Lord Argentine had dined with a lady of good position, whose name was suppressed in the newspaper reports. At about eleven o'clock Lord Argentine had returned, and informed his man that he should not require his services till the next morning. A little later the valet had occasion to cross the hall and was somewhat astonished to see his master quietly letting himself out at the front door. He had taken off his evening clothes, and was dressed in a Norfolk coat and knickerbockers, and wore a low brown hat. The valet had no reason to suppose that Lord Argentine had seen him, and though his master rarely kept late hours, thought little of the occurrence till the next morning, when he knocked at the bedroom door at a quarter to nine as usual. He received no answer, and, after knocking two or three times, entered the room, and saw Lord Argentine's body leaning forward at an angle from the bottom of the bed. He found that his master had tied a cord securely to one of the short bedposts, and, after making a running noose and slipping it round his neck, the unfortunate man must have resolutely fallen forward to die by slow strangulation. He was dressed in the light suit in which the valet had seen him go out, and the doctor who was summoned pronounced that life had been extinct for more than four hours. All papers, letters, and so forth seemed in perfect order, and nothing was discovered which pointed in the most remote way to any scandal, either great or small. Here the evidence ended; nothing more could be discovered. Several persons had been present at the dinner-party at which Lord Argentine had assisted, and to all these he seemed in his usual genial spirits. The valet, indeed, said he thought his master appeared a little excited when he came home, but he confessed that the alteration in his manner was very slight, hardly noticeable, indeed. It seemed hopeless to seek for any clue, and the suggestion that Lord Argentine had been suddenly attacked by acute suicidal mania was generally accepted.

It was otherwise, however, when within three weeks, three more gentlemen, one of them a nobleman, and the two others men of good position and ample means, perished miserably in almost precisely the same manner. Lord Swanleigh was found one morning in his dressing-room, hanging from a peg affixed to the wall, and Mr. Collier-Stuart and Mr. Herries had chosen to die as Lord Argentine. There was no explanation in either case; a few bald facts; a living man in the evening, and a dead body with a black, swollen face in the morning. The police had been forced to confess themselves powerless to arrest or to explain the sordid murders of Whitechapel;[9] but before the horrible suicides of Piccadilly and Mayfair they were dumbfounded, for not even the mere ferocity which did duty as an explanation of the crimes of the East End, could be of service in the West. Each of these men who had resolved to die a tortured shameful death was rich, prosperous, and to all appearance in love with the world, and not the acutest research could ferret out any shadow of a lurking motive in either case. There was a horror in the air, and men looked at one another's faces when they met, each wondering whether the other was to be the victim of the fifth nameless tragedy. Journalists sought in vain in their scrap-books for materials whereof to concoct reminiscent articles; and the morning paper was unfolded in many a house with a feeling of awe; no man knew when or where the blow would next light.

A short while after the last of these terrible events, Austin came to see Mr. Villiers. He was curious to know whether Villiers had succeeded in discovering any fresh traces of Mrs. Herbert, either through Clarke or by other sources, and he asked the question soon after he had sat down.

"No," said Villiers, "I wrote to Clarke, but he remains obdurate, and I have tried other channels, but without any result. I can't find out what became of Helen Vaughan after she left Paul Street, but I think she must have gone abroad. But to tell the truth, Austin, I haven't paid very much attention to the matter for the last few weeks; I knew poor Herries intimately, and his terrible death has been a great shock to me, a great shock."

"I can well believe it," answered Austin gravely; "you know Argentine was a friend of mine. If I remember rightly, we were speaking of him that day you came to my rooms."

"Yes; it was in connection with that house in Ashley Street, Mrs. Beaumont's house. You said something about Argentine's dining there."

"Quite so. Of course you know it was there Argentine dined the night before—before his death."

"No, I haven't heard that."

"Oh, yes; the name was kept out of the papers to spare Mrs. Beaumont. Argentine was a great favourite of hers, and it is said she was in a terrible state for some time after."

A curious look came over Villiers's face; he seemed undecided whether to speak or not. Austin began again.

"I never experienced such a feeling of horror as when I read the account of Argentine's death. I didn't understand it at the time, and I don't now. I knew him well, and it completely passes my understanding for what possible cause he—or any of the others for the matter of that—could have resolved in cold blood to die in such an awful manner. You know how men babble away each other's characters in London, you may be sure any buried scandal or hidden skeleton would have been brought to light in such a case as this; but nothing of the sort has taken place. As for the theory of mania, that is very well, of course, for the coroner's jury, but everybody knows that it's all nonsense. Suicidal mania is not small-pox."

Austin relapsed into gloomy silence. Villiers sat silent also, watching his friend. The expression of indecision still fleeted across his face; he seemed as if weighing his thoughts in the balance, and the considerations he was revolving left him still silent. Austin tried to shake off the remembrance of tragedies as hopeless and perplexed as the labyrinth of Dædalus, and began to talk in an indifferent voice of the more pleasant incidents and adventures of the season.

"That Mrs. Beaumont," he said, "of whom we were speaking, is a great success; she has taken London almost by storm. I met her the other night at Fulham's; she is really a remarkable woman."

"You have met Mrs. Beaumont?"

"Yes; she had quite a court around her. She would be called very handsome, I suppose, and yet there is something about her face which I didn't like. The features are exquisite, but the expression is strange. And all the time I was looking at her, and afterwards, when I was going home, I had a curious feeling that that very expression was in some way or other familiar to me."

"You must have seen her in the Row."

"No, I am sure I never set eyes on the woman before; it is that which makes it puzzling. And to the best of my belief I have never seen anybody like her; what I felt was a kind of dim far-off memory, vague but persistent. The only sensation I can compare it to, is that odd feeling one sometimes has in a dream, when fantastic cities and wondrous lands and phantom personages appear familiar and accustomed."

Villiers nodded and glanced aimlessly round the room, possibly in search of something on which to turn the conversation. His eyes fell on an old chest somewhat like that in which the artist's strange legacy lay hid beneath a Gothic scutcheon.

"Have you written to the doctor about poor Meyrick?" he asked.

"Yes; I wrote asking for full particulars as to his illness and death. I don't expect to have an answer for another three weeks or a month. I thought I might as well inquire whether Meyrick knew an English-woman named Herbert, and if so, whether the doctor could give me any information about her. But it's very possible that Meyrick fell in with her at New York, or Mexico, or San Francisco; I have no idea as to the extent or direction of his travels."

"Yes, and it's very possible that the woman may have more than one name."

"Exactly. I wish I had thought of asking you to lend me the portrait of her which you possess. I might have enclosed it in my letter to Dr. Matthews."

"So you might; that never occurred to me. We might send it now. Hark! what are those boys calling?"

While the two men had been talking together a confused noise of shouting had been gradually growing louder. The noise rose from the eastward and swelled down Piccadilly, drawing nearer and nearer, a very torrent of sound; surging up streets usually quiet, and making every window a frame for a face, curious or excited. The cries and voices came echoing up the silent street where Villiers lived, growing more distinct as they advanced, and, as Villiers spoke, an answer rang up from the pavement:

"The West End Horrors; Another Awful Suicide; Full Details!"

Austin rushed down the stairs and bought a paper and read out the paragraph to Villiers as the uproar in the street rose and fell. The window was open and the air seemed full of noise and terror.

"Another gentleman has fallen a victim to the terrible epidemic of suicide which for the last month has prevailed in the West End. Mr. Sidney Crashaw, of Stoke House, Fulham, and King's Pomeroy, Devon, was found, after a prolonged search, hanging from the branch of a tree in his garden at one o'clock to-day. The deceased gentleman dined last night at the Carlton Club and seemed in his usual health and spirits. He left the Club at about ten o'clock, and was seen walking leisurely up St. James's Street a little later. Subsequent to this his movements cannot be traced. On the discovery of the body medical aid was at once summoned, but life had evidently been long extinct. So far as is known, Mr. Crashaw had no trouble or anxiety of any kind. This painful suicide, it will be remembered, is the fifth of the kind in the last month. The authorities at Scotland Yard are unable to suggest any explanation of these terrible occurrences."

Austin put down the paper in mute horror.

"I shall leave London to-morrow," he said, "it is a city of nightmares. How awful this is, Villiers!"

Villiers was sitting by the window quietly looking out into the street. He had listened to the newspaper report attentively, and the hint of indecision was no longer on his face.

"Wait a moment, Austin," he replied, "I have made up my mind to mention a little matter that occurred last night. It is stated, I think, that Crashaw was last seen alive in St. James's Street shortly after ten?"

"Yes, I think so. I will look again. Yes, you are quite right."

"Quite so. Well, I am in a position to contradict that statement at all events. Crashaw was seen after that; considerably later indeed."

"How do you know?"

"Because I happened to see Crashaw myself at about two o'clock this morning."

"You saw Crashaw? You, Villiers?"

"Yes, I saw him quite distinctly; indeed, there were but a few feet between us."

"Where, in Heaven's name, did you see him?"

"Not far from here. I saw him in Ashley Street. He was just leaving a house."

"Did you notice what house it was?"

"Yes. It was Mrs. Beaumont's."

"Villiers! Think what you are saying; there must be some mistake. How could Crashaw be in Mrs. Beaumont's house at two o'clock in the morning? Surely, surely, you must have been dreaming, Villiers, you were always rather fanciful."

"No; I was wide awake enough. Even if I had been dreaming as you say, what I saw would have roused me effectually."

"What you saw? What did you see? Was there anything strange about Crashaw? But I can't believe it; it is impossible."

"Well, if you like I will tell you what I saw, or if you please, what I think I saw, and you can judge for yourself."

"Very good, Villiers."

The noise and clamour of the street had died away, though now and then the sound of shouting still came from the distance, and the dull, leaden silence seemed like the quiet after an earthquake or a storm. Villiers turned from the window and began speaking.

"I was at a house near Regent's Park last night, and when I came away the fancy took me to walk home instead of taking a hansom. It was a clear pleasant night enough, and after a few minutes I had the streets pretty much to myself. It's a curious thing, Austin, to be alone in London at night, the gas-lamps stretching away in perspective, and the dead silence, and then perhaps the rush and clatter of a hansom on the stones, and the fire starting up under the horse's hoofs. I walked along pretty briskly, for I was feeling a little tired of being out in the night, and as the clocks were striking two I turned down Ashley Street, which, you know, is on my way. It was quieter than ever there, and the lamps were fewer; altogether, it looked as dark and gloomy as a forest in winter. I had done about half the length of the street when I heard a door closed very softly, and naturally I looked up to see who was abroad like myself at such an hour. As it happens, there is a street lamp close to the house in question, and I saw a man standing on the step. He had just shut the door and his face was towards me, and I recognized Crashaw directly. I never knew him to speak to, but I had often seen him, and I am positive that I was not mistaken in my man. I looked into his face for a moment, and then—I will confess the truth—I set off at a good run, and kept it up till I was within my own door."

"Why?"

"Why? Because it made my blood run cold to see that man's face. I could never have supposed that such an infernal medley of passions could have glared out of any human eyes; I almost fainted as I looked. I knew I had looked into the eyes of a lost soul, Austin, the man's outward form remained, but all hell was within it. Furious lust, and hate that was like fire and the loss of all hope and horror that seemed to shriek aloud to the night, though his teeth were shut; and the utter blackness of despair. I am sure he did not see me; he saw nothing that you or I can see, but he saw what I hope we never shall. I do not know when he died; I suppose in an hour, or perhaps two, but when I passed down Ashley Street and heard the closing door, that man no longer belonged to this world; it was a devil's face that I looked upon."

There was an interval of silence in the room when Villiers ceased speaking. The light was failing, and all the tumult of an hour ago was quite hushed. Austin had bent his head at the close of the story, and his hand covered his eyes.

"What can it mean?" he said at length.

"Who knows, Austin, who knows? It's a black business, but I think we had better keep it to ourselves, for the present at any rate. I will see if I cannot learn anything about that house through private channels of information, and if I do light upon anything I will let you know."

VII

THE ENCOUNTER IN SOHO

Three weeks later Austin received a note from Villiers, asking him to call either that afternoon or the next. He chose the nearer date, and found Villiers sitting as usual by the window, apparently lost in meditation on the drowsy traffic of the street. There was a bamboo table by his side, a fantastic thing, enriched with gilding and queer painted scenes, and on it lay a little pile of papers arranged and docketed as neatly as anything in Mr. Clarke's office.

"Well, Villiers, have you made any discoveries in the last three weeks?"

"I think so; I have here one or two memoranda which struck me as singular, and there is a statement to which I shall call your attention."

"And these documents relate to Mrs. Beaumont? It was really Crashaw whom you saw that night standing on the doorstep of the house in Ashley Street?"

"As to that matter my belief remains unchanged, but neither my inquiries nor their results have any special relation to Crashaw. But my investigations have had a strange issue. I have found out who Mrs. Beaumont is!"

"Who is she? In what way do you mean?"

"I mean that you and I know her better under another name."

"What name is that?"

"Herbert."

"Herbert!" Austin repeated the word dazed with astonishment.

"Yes, Mrs. Herbert of Paul Street, Helen Vaughan of earlier adventures unknown to me. You had reason to recognize the expression of her face; when you go home look at the face in Meyrick's book of horrors, and you will know the sources of your recollection."

"And you have proof of this?"

"Yes, the best of proof; I have seen Mrs. Beaumont, or shall we say Mrs. Herbert?"

"Where did you see her?"

"Hardly in a place where you would expect to see a lady who lives in Ashley Street, Piccadilly. I saw her entering a house in one of the meanest and most disreputable streets in Soho. In fact, I had made an appointment, though not with her, and she was precise both to time and place."

"All this seems very wonderful, but I cannot call it incredible. You must remember, Villiers, that I have seen this woman, in the ordinary adventure of London society, talking and laughing, and sipping her coffee in a commonplace drawing-room with commonplace people. But you know what you are saying."

"I do; I have not allowed myself to be led by surmises or fancies. It was with no thought of finding Helen Vaughan that I searched for Mrs. Beaumont in the dark waters of the life of London, but such has been the issue."

"You must have been in strange places, Villiers."

"Yes, I have been in very strange places. It would have been useless, you know, to go to Ashley Street, and ask Mrs. Beaumont to give me a short sketch of her previous history. No; assuming, as I had to assume, that her record was not of the cleanest, it would be pretty certain that at some previous time she must have moved in circles not quite so refined as her present ones. If you see mud on the top of a stream, you may be sure that it was once at the bottom. I went to the bottom. I have always been fond of diving into Queer Street for my amusement, and I found my knowledge of that locality and its inhabitants very useful. It is, perhaps, needless to say that my friends had never heard the name of Beaumont, and as I had never seen the lady, and was quite unable to describe her, I had to set to work in an indirect way. The people there know me; I have been able to do some of them a service now and again, so they made no difficulty about giving their information; they were aware I had no communication direct or indirect with Scotland Yard. I had to cast out a good many lines, though, before I got what I wanted, and when I landed the fish I did not for a moment suppose it was my fish. But I listened to what I was told out of a constitutional liking for useless information, and I found myself in possession of a very curious story, though, as I imagined, not the story I was looking for. It was to this effect. Some five or six years ago, a woman named Raymond suddenly made her appearance in the neighbourhood to which I am referring. She was described to me as being quite young, probably not more than seventeen or eighteen, very handsome, and looking as if she came from the country. I should be wrong in saying that she found her level in going to this particular quarter, or associating with these people, for from what I was told, I should think the worst den in London far too good for her. The person from whom I got my information, as you may suppose, no great Puritan, shuddered and grew sick in telling me of the nameless infamies which were laid to her charge. After living there for a year, or perhaps a little more, she disappeared as suddenly as she came, and they saw nothing of her till about the time of the Paul Street case. At first she came to her old haunts only occasionally, then more frequently, and finally took up her abode there as before, and remained for six or eight months. It's of no use my going into details as to the life that woman led; if you want particulars you can look at Meyrick's legacy. Those designs were not drawn from his imagination. She again disappeared, and the people of the place saw nothing of her till a few months ago. My informant told me that she had taken some rooms in a house which he pointed out, and these rooms she was in the habit of visiting two or three times a week and always at ten in the morning. I was led to expect that one of these visits would be paid on a certain day about a week ago, and I accordingly managed to be on the look-out in company with my cicerone at a quarter to ten, and the hour and the lady came with equal punctuality. My friend and I were standing under an archway, a little way back from the street, but she saw us, and gave me a glance that I shall be long in forgetting. That look was quite enough for me; I knew Miss Raymond to be Mrs. Herbert; as for Mrs. Beaumont, she had quite gone out of my head. She went into the house, and I watched it till four o'clock, when she came out, and then I followed her. It was a long chase, and I had to be very careful to keep a long way in the background, and yet not to lose sight of the woman. She took me down to the Strand, and then to Westminster, and then up St. James's Street, and along Piccadilly. I felt queerish when I saw her turn up Ashley Street; the thought that Mrs. Herbert was Mrs. Beaumont came into my mind, but it seemed too improbable to be true. I waited at the corner, keeping my eye on her all the time, and I took particular care to note the house at which she stopped. It was the house with the gay curtains, the house of flowers, the house out of which Crashaw came the night he hanged himself in his garden. I was just going away with my discovery, when I saw an empty carriage come round and draw up in front of the house, and I came to the conclusion that Mrs. Herbert was going out for a drive, and I was right. I took a hansom and followed the carriage into the Park. There, as it happened, I met a man I know, and we stood talking together a little distance from the carriage-way, to which I had my back. We had not been there for ten minutes when my friend took off his hat, and I glanced round and saw the lady I had been following all day. 'Who is that?' I said, and his answer was, 'Mrs. Beaumont; lives in Ashley Street.' Of course there could be no doubt after that. I don't know whether she saw me, but I don't think she did. I went home at once, and, on consideration, I thought that I had a sufficiently good case with which to go to Clarke."

"Why to Clarke?"

"Because I am sure that Clarke is in possession of facts about this woman, facts of which I know nothing."

"Well, what then?"

Villiers leaned back in his chair and looked reflectively at Austin for a moment before he answered:

"My idea was that Clarke and I should call on Mrs. Beaumont."

"You would never go into such a house as that? No, no, Villiers, you cannot do it. Besides, consider; what result . . ."

"I will tell you soon. But I was going to say that my information does not end here; it has been completed in an extraordinary manner.

"Look at this neat little packet of manuscript; it is paginated, you see, and I have indulged in the civil coquetry of a ribbon of red tape. It has almost a legal air, hasn't it? Run your eye over it, Austin. It is an account of the entertainment Mrs. Beaumont provided for her choicer guests. The man who wrote this escaped with his life, but I do not think he will live many years. The doctors tell him he must have sustained some severe shock to the nerves."

Austin took the manuscript, but never read it. Opening the neat pages at haphazard his eye was caught by a word and a phrase that followed it; and, sick at heart, with white lips and a cold sweat pouring like water from his temples, he flung the paper down.

"Take it away, Villiers, never speak of this again. Are you made of stone, man? Why, the dread and horror of death itself, the thoughts of the man who stands in the keen morning air on the black platform, bound, the bell tolling in his ears, and waits for the harsh rattle of the bolt, are as nothing compared to this. I will not read it; I should never sleep again."

"Very good. I can fancy what you saw. Yes, it is horrible enough; but after all, it is an old story, an old mystery played in our day, and in dim London streets instead of amidst the vineyards and the olive gardens. We know what happened to those who chanced to meet the Great God Pan, and those who are wise know that all symbols are symbols of something, not of nothing. It was, indeed, an exquisite symbol beneath which men long ago veiled their knowledge of the most awful, most secret forces which lie at the heart of all things; forces before which the souls of men must wither and die and blacken, as their bodies blacken under the electric current. Such forces cannot be named, cannot be spoken, cannot be imagined except under a veil and a symbol, a symbol to the most of us appearing a quaint, poetic fancy, to some a foolish tale. But you and I, at all events, have known something of the terror that may dwell in the secret places of life, manifested under human flesh; that which is without form taking to itself a form. Oh, Austin, how can it be? How is it that the very sunlight does not turn to blackness before this thing, the hard earth melt and boil beneath such a burden?"

Villiers was pacing up and down the room, and the beads of sweat stood out on his forehead. Austin sat silent for a while, but Villiers saw him make a sign upon his breast.

"I say again, Villiers, you will surely never enter such a house as that? You would never pass out alive."

"Yes, Austin, I shall go out alive—I, and Clarke with me."

"What do you mean? You cannot, you would not dare . . ."

"Wait a moment. The air was very pleasant and fresh this morning; there was a breeze blowing, even through this dull street, and I thought I would take a walk. Piccadilly stretched before me a clear, bright vista, and the sun flashed on the carriages and on the quivering leaves in the park. It was a joyous morning, and men and women looked at the sky and smiled as they went about their work or their pleasure, and the wind blew as blithely as upon the meadows and the scented gorse. But somehow or other I got out of the bustle and the gaiety, and found myself walking slowly along a quiet, dull street, where there seemed to be no sunshine and no air, and where the few foot-passengers loitered as they walked, and hung indecisively about corners and archways. I walked along, hardly knowing where I was going or what I did there, but feeling impelled, as one sometimes is, to explore still further, with a vague idea of reaching some unknown goal. Thus I forged up the street, noting the small traffic of the milk-shop, and wondering at the incongruous medley of penny pipes, black tobacco, sweets, newspapers, and comic songs which here and there jostled one another in the short compass of a single window. I think it was a cold shudder that suddenly passed through me that first told me that I had found what I wanted. I looked up from the pavement and stopped before a dusty shop, above which the lettering had faded, where the red bricks of two hundred years ago had grimed to black; where the windows had gathered to themselves the fog and the dirt of winters innumerable. I saw what I required; but I think it was five minutes before I steadied myself and could walk in and ask for it in a cool voice and with a calm face. I think there must even then have been a tremor in my words, for the old man who came out from his back parlour, and fumbled slowly amongst his goods, looked oddly at me as he tied the parcel. I paid what he asked, and stood leaning by the counter, with a strange reluctance to take up my goods and go. I asked about the business, and learnt that trade was bad and the profits cut down sadly; but then the street was not what it was before traffic had been diverted, but that was done forty years ago, 'just before my father died,' he said. I got away at last, and walked along sharply; it was a dismal street indeed, and I was glad to return to the bustle and the noise. Would you like to see my purchase?"

Austin said nothing, but nodded his head slightly; he still looked white and sick. Villiers pulled out a drawer in the bamboo table, and showed Austin a long coil of cord, hard and new; and at one end was a running noose.

"It is the best hempen cord," said Villiers, "just as it used to be made for the old trade, the man told me. Not an inch of jute from end to end."

Austin set his teeth hard, and stared at Villiers, growing whiter as he looked.

"You would not do it," he murmured at last. "You would not have blood on your hands. My God!" he exclaimed, with sudden vehemence, "you cannot mean this, Villiers, that you will make yourself a hangman?"

"No. I shall offer a choice, and leave Helen Vaughan alone with this cord in a locked room for fifteen minutes. If when we go in it is not done, I shall call the nearest policeman. That is all."

"I must go now. I cannot stay here any longer; I cannot bear this. Good-night."

"Good-night, Austin."

The door shut, but in a moment it was opened again and Austin stood, white and ghastly, in the entrance.

"I was forgetting," he said, "that I too have something to tell. I have received a letter from Dr. Harding of Buenos Ayres. He says that he attended Meyrick for three weeks before his death."

"And does he say what carried him off in the prime of life? It was not fever?"

"No, it was not fever. According to the doctor, it was an utter collapse of the whole system, probably caused by some severe shock. But he states that the patient would tell him nothing, and that he was consequently at some disadvantage in treating the case."

"Is there anything more?"

"Yes. Dr. Harding ends his letter by saying: 'I think this is all the information I can give you about your poor friend. He had not been long in Buenos Ayres, and knew scarcely any one, with the exception of a person who did not bear the best of characters, and has since left—a Mrs. Vaughan.'"

VIII

THE FRAGMENTS

Amongst the papers of the well-known physician, Dr. Robert Matheson, of Ashley Street, Piccadilly, who died suddenly, of apoplectic seizure, at the beginning of 1892, a leaf of manuscript paper was found, covered with pencil jottings. These notes were in Latin, much abbreviated, and had evidently been made in great haste. The MS. was only deciphered with great difficulty, and some words have up to the present time evaded all the efforts of the expert employed. The date "xxv Jul. 1888," is written on the right-hand corner of the MS. The following is a translation of Dr. Matheson's manuscript.

"Whether science would benefit by these brief notes if they could be published, I do not know, but rather doubt. But certainly I shall never take the responsibility of publishing or divulging one word of what is here written, not only on account of my oath freely given to those two persons who were present, but also because the details are too abominable. It is probable that, upon mature consideration, and after weighing the good and evil, I shall one day destroy this paper, or at least leave it under seal to my friend D., trusting in his discretion, to use it or to burn it, as he may think fit.

"As was befitting, I did all that my knowledge suggested to make sure that I was suffering under no delusion. At first astounded, I could hardly think, but in a minute's time I was sure that my pulse was steady and regular, and that I was in my real and true senses. I then fixed my eyes quietly on what was before me.

"Though horror and revolting nausea rose up within me, and an odour of corruption choked my breath, I remained firm. I was then privileged or accursed, I dare not say which, to see that which was on the bed, laying there black like ink, transformed before my eyes. The skin, and the flesh, and the muscles, and the bones, and the firm structure of the human body that I had thought to be unchangeable, and permanent as adamant, began to melt and dissolve.

"I knew that the body may be separated into its elements by external agencies, but I should have refused to believe what I saw. For here there was some internal force, of which I knew nothing, that caused dissolution and change.

"Here, too, was all the work by which man has been made repeated before my eyes. I saw the form waver from sex to sex, dividing itself from itself, and then again reunited. Then I saw the body descend to the beasts whence it ascended, and that which was on the heights go down to the depths, even to the abyss of all being. The principle of life, which makes organism, always remained, while the outward form changed.

"The light within the room had turned to blackness, not the darkness of night, in which objects are seen dimly, for I could see clearly and without difficulty. But it was the negation of light; objects were presented to my eyes, if I may say so, without any medium, in such a manner that if there had been a prism in the room I should have seen no colours represented in it.

"I watched, and at last I saw nothing but a substance as jelly. Then the ladder was ascended again . . . [*here the MS. is illegible*] . . . for one instant I saw a Form, shaped in dimness before me, which I will not farther describe. But the symbol of this form may be seen in ancient sculptures, and in paintings which survived beneath the lava, too foul to be spoken of . . . as a horrible and unspeakable shape, neither man nor beast, was changed into human form, there came finally death.

"I who saw all this, not without great horror and loathing of soul, here write my name, declaring all that I have set on this paper to be true.

"ROBERT MATHESON, Med. Dr."

. . . Such, Raymond, is the story of what I know and what I have seen. The burden of it was too heavy for me to bear alone, and yet I could tell it to none but you. Villiers, who was with me at the last, knows nothing of that awful secret of the wood, of how what we both saw die, lay upon the smooth, sweet turf amidst the summer flowers, half in sun and half in shadow, and holding the girl Rachel's hand, called and summoned those companions, and shaped in solid form, upon the earth we tread on, the horror which we can but hint at, which we can only name under a figure. I would not tell Villiers of this, nor of that resemblance, which struck me as with a blow upon my heart, when I saw the portrait, which filled the cup of terror at the end. What this can mean I dare not guess. I know that what I saw perish was not Mary, and yet in the last agony Mary's eyes looked into mine. Whether there by any one who can show the last link in this chain of awful mystery, I do not know, but if there be any one who can do this, you, Raymond, are the man. And if you know the secret, it rests with you to tell it or not, as you please.

I am writing this letter to you immediately on my getting back to town. I have been in the country for the last few days; perhaps you may be able to guess in what part. While the horror and wonder of London was at its height—for "Mrs. Beaumont," as I have told you, was well known in society—I wrote to my friend Dr. Phillips, giving some brief outline, or rather hint, of what had happened, and asking him to tell me the name of the village where the events he had related to me occurred. He gave me the name, as he said with the less hesitation, because Rachel's father and mother were dead, and the rest of the family had gone to a relative in the State of Washington six months before. The parents, he said, had undoubtedly died of grief and horror caused by the terrible death of their daughter, and by what had gone before that death. On the evening of the day on which I received Phillips's letter I was at Caermaen, and standing beneath the moulding Roman walls, white with the winter of seventeen hundred years, I looked over the meadow where once had stood the older temple of the "God of the Deeps," and saw a house gleaming in the sunlight. It was the house where Helen had lived. I stayed at Caermaen for several days. The people of the place, I found, knew little and had guessed less. Those whom I spoke to on the matter seemed surprised that an antiquarian (as I professed myself to be) should trouble about a village tragedy, of which they gave a very commonplace version, and, as you may imagine, I told nothing of what I knew. Most of my time was spent in the great wood that rises just above the village and climbs the hillside, and goes down to the river in the valley; such another long lovely valley, Raymond, as that on which we looked one summer night, walking to and fro before your house. For many an hour I strayed through the maze of the forest, turning now to right and now to left, pacing slowly down the long alleys of undergrowth, shadowy and chill, even under the midday sun, and halting beneath great oaks; lying on the short turf of a clearing where the faint sweet scent of wild roses came to me on the wind and mixed with the heavy perfume of the elder, whose mingled odour is like the odour of the room of the dead, a vapour of incense and corruption. I stood at the edges of the wood, gazing at all the pomp and procession of the foxgloves towering amidst the bracken and shining red in the broad sunshine, and beyond them into deep thickets of close undergrowth where springs boil up from the rock and nourish the water-weeds, dank and evil. But in all my wanderings I avoided one part of the wood; it was not till yesterday that I climbed to the summit of the hill, and stood upon the ancient Roman road that threads the highest ridge of the wood. Here they had walked, Helen and Rachel, along this quiet causeway, upon the pavement of green turf, shut in on either side by high banks of red earth, and tall hedges of shining beech, and here I followed in their steps, looking out, now and again, through partings in the boughs, and seeing on one side the sweep of the wood stretching far to right and left, and sinking into the broad level, and beyond, the yellow sea, and the land over the sea. On the other side was the valley and the river, and hill following hill as wave on wave, and wood and meadow, and cornfield, and white houses gleaming, and a great wall of mountain, and far blue peaks in the north. And so at last I came to the place. The track went up a gentle slope, and widened out into an open space with a wall of thick undergrowth around it, and then, narrowing again, passed on into the distance and the faint blue mist of summer heat. And into this pleasant summer glade Rachel passed a girl, and left it, who shall say what? I did not stay long there.

In a small town near Caermaen there is a museum, containing for the most part Roman remains which have been found in the neighbourhood at various times. On the day after my arrival at Caermaen I walked over to the town in question, and took the opportunity of inspecting this museum. After I had seen most of the sculptured stones, the coffins, rings, coins, and fragments of tessellated pavement which the place contains, I was shown a small square pillar of white stone, which had been recently discovered in the wood of which I have been speaking, and, as I found on inquiry, in that open space where the Roman road broadens out. On one side of the pillar was an inscription, of which I took a note. Some of the letters have been defaced, but I do not think there can be any doubt as to those which I supply. The inscription is as follows:

ARTHUR MACHEN

DEVOMNODENT*i*
FLA*v*IVSSENILISPOSS*Vit*
PROPTERNVP*tias*
*qua*SVIDITSVBVMB*ra*

"To the great god Nodens (the god of the Great Deep or Abyss), Flavius Senilis has erected this pillar on account of the marriage which he saw beneath the shade."[10]

The custodian of the museum informed me that local antiquaries were much puzzled, not by the inscription, or by any difficulty in translating it, but as to the circumstance or rite to which allusion is made.

*   *   *

. . . And now, my dear Clarke, as to what you tell me about Helen Vaughan, whom you say you saw die under circumstances of the utmost and almost incredible horror. I was interested in your account, but a good deal, nay all, of what you told me I knew already. I can understand the strange likeness you remarked both in the portrait and in the actual face; you have seen Helen's mother. You remember that still summer night so many years ago, when I talked to you of the world beyond the shadows, and of the god Pan. You remember Mary. She was the mother of Helen Vaughan, who was born nine months after that night.

Mary never recovered her reason. She lay, as you saw her, all the while upon her bed, and a few days after the child was born she died. I fancy that just at the last she knew me; I was standing by the bed, and the old look came into her eyes for a second, and then she shuddered and groaned and died. It was an ill work I did that night when you were present; I broke open the door of the house of life, without knowing or caring what might pass forth or enter in. I recollect your telling me at the time, sharply enough, and rightly enough too, in one sense, that I had ruined the reason of a human being by a foolish experiment, based on an absurd theory. You did well to blame me, but my theory was not all absurdity. What I said Mary would see, she saw, but I forgot that no human eyes could look on such a vision with impunity. And I forgot, as I have just said, that when the house of life is thus thrown open, there may enter in that for which we have no name, and human flesh may become the veil of a horror one dare not express. I played with energies which I did not understand, and you have seen the ending of it. Helen Vaughan did well to bind the cord about her neck and die, though the death was horrible. The blackened face, the hideous form upon the bed, changing and melting before your eyes from woman to man, from man to beast, and from beast to worse than beast, all the strange horror that you witnessed, surprises me but little. What you say the doctor whom you sent for saw and shuddered at I noticed long ago; I knew what I had done the moment the child was born, and when it was scarcely five years old I surprised it, not once or twice but several times with a playmate, you may guess of what kind. It was for me a constant, an incarnate horror, and after a few years I felt I could bear it no longer, and I sent Helen Vaughan away. You know now what frightened the boy in the wood. The rest of the strange story, and all else that you tell me, as discovered by your friend, I have contrived to learn from time to time, almost to the last chapter. And now Helen is with her companions. . .

Note: *Helan Vaughan was born on August 5th, 1865, at the Red House, Breconshire and died on July 25th, 1888, in her house in a street off Piccadilly, called Ashley Street in the Story.*

The Three Impostors
or
The Transmutations

The Three Impostors (London: John Lane; Boston: Roberts Brothers, 1895) is an episodic novel written over the period 1890–94. "The Novel of the Iron Maid" first appeared in the *St. James's Gazette* (September 13, 1890), and because of copyright restrictions it has been omitted from many reprints of the novel, including the Knopf (1923) and Ballantine (1972) editions. Its two most celebrated segments, "Novel of the Black Seal" and "Novel of the White Powder," appeared separately in Machen's lifetime, the first in Dorothy L. Sayers's *Great Short Stories of Detection, Mystery and Horror* (1928; U.S. edition titled *The Omnibus of Crime*) and the second in T. Everett Harré's *Beware After Dark!* (1929) and other anthologies. Machen discusses the writing and publication of the novel in chapters 7 and 8 of *Things Near and Far* (1923). He also wrote a long introduction to the Knopf edition (see Appendix 1). In addition, an unpublished piece, "On Re-reading *The Three Impostors* and the *Wonder Story*," was written at the behest of August Derleth as a foreword to a planned reprint of the novel by Arkham House. The manuscript of this essay is in the August Derleth Papers at the Wisconsin Historical Society.

PROLOGUE

"And Mr. Joseph Walters is going to stay the night?" said the smooth, clean-shaven man to his companion, an individual not of the most charming appearance, who had chosen to make his ginger-coloured moustache merge into a pair of short chin-whiskers.

The two stood at the hall door, grinning evilly at each other; and presently a girl ran quickly down the stairs and joined them. She was quite young, with a quaint and piquant rather than a beautiful face, and her eyes were of a shining hazel. She held a neat paper parcel in one hand, and laughed with her friends.

"Leave the door open," said the smooth man to the other, as they were going out. "Yes, by ——," he went on with an ugly oath, "we'll leave the front door on the jar. He may like to see company, you know."

The other man looked doubtfully about him.

"Is it quite prudent, do you think, Davies," he said, pausing with his hand on the mouldering knocker. "I don't think Lipsius would like it. What do you say, Helen?"

"I agree with Davies. Davies is an artist, and you are commonplace, Richmond, and a bit of a coward. Let the door stand open, of course. But what a pity Lipsius had to go away! He would have enjoyed himself."

"Yes," replied the smooth Mr. Davies, "that summons to the west was very hard on the doctor."

The three passed out, leaving the hall door, cracked and riven with frost and wet, half open, and they stood silent for a moment under the ruinous shelter of the porch.

"Well," said the girl, "it is done at last. We shall hurry no more on the track of the young man with spectacles."

"We owe a great deal to you," said Mr. Davies politely; "the doctor said so before he left. But have we not all three some farewells to make? I, for my part, propose to say good-bye here, before this picturesque but mouldy residence, to my friend, Mr. Burton, dealer in the antique and curious," and the man lifted his hat with an exaggerated bow.

"And I," said Richmond, "bid adieu to Mr. Wilkins, the private secretary, whose company has, I confess, become a little tedious."

"Farewell to Miss Lally, and to Miss Leicester also," said the girl, making as she spoke a delicious curtsy. "Farewell to all occult adventure; the farce is played."

Mr. Davies and the lady seemed full of grim enjoyment, but Richmond tugged at his whiskers nervously.

"I feel a bit shaken up," he said. "I've seen rougher things in the States, but that crying noise he made gave me a sickish feeling."

The three friends moved away from the door, and began to walk slowly up and down what had been a gravel path, but now lay green and pulpy with damp mosses. It was a fine autumn evening, and a faint sunlight shone on the yellow walls of the old deserted house, and showed the patches of gangrenous decay, the black drift of rain from the broken pipes, the scabrous blots where the bare bricks were exposed, the green weeping of a gaunt laburnum that stood beside the porch, and ragged marks near the ground where the reeking clay was gaining on the worn foundations. It was a queer, rambling old place, the centre perhaps two hundred years old, with dormer-windows sloping from the tiled roof, and on each side there were Georgian wings; bow windows had been carried up to the first floor, and two dome-like cupolas that had once been painted a bright green were now grey and neutral. Broken urns lay upon the path, and a heavy mist seemed to rise from the unctuous clay; the neglected shrubberies, grown all tangled and unshapen, smelt dank and evil, and there was an atmosphere all about the deserted mansion that proposed thoughts of an open grave. The three friends looked dismally at the rough grasses and the nettles that grew thick over lawn and flower-beds; and at the sad water-pool in the midst of the weeds. There, above green and oily scum instead of lilies, stood a rusting Triton on the rocks, sounding a dirge through a shattered horn;[1] and beyond, beyond the sunk fence and the far meadows, the sun slid down and shone red through the bars of the elm trees.

Richmond shivered and stamped his foot.

"We had better be going soon," he said; "there is nothing else to be done here."

"No," said Davies; "it is finished at last. I thought for some time we should never get hold of the gentleman with the spectacles. He was a clever fellow, but, Lord! he broke up badly at last. I can tell you, he looked white at me when I touched him on the arm in the bar. But where could he have hidden the thing? We can all swear it was not on him."

The girl laughed, and they turned away, when Richmond gave a violent start.

"Ah!" he cried, turning to the girl, "what have you got there? Look, Davies, look; it's all oozing and dripping."

The young woman glanced down at the little parcel she was carrying, and partially unfolded the paper.

"Yes, look, both of you," she said; "it's my own idea. Don't you think it will do nicely for the doctor's museum? It comes from the right hand, the hand that took the Gold Tiberius."

Mr. Davies nodded with a good deal of approbation, and Richmond lifted his ugly highcrowned bowler, and wiped his forehead with a dingy handkerchief.

"I'm going," he said, "you two can stay if you like."

The three went round by the stable-path, past the withered wilderness of the old kitchen-garden, and struck off by a hedge at the back, making for a particular point in the road. About five minutes later two gentlemen, whom idleness had led to explore these forgotten outskirts of London, came sauntering up the shadowy carriage-drive. They had spied the deserted house from the road, and as they observed all the heavy desolation of the place, they began to moralize in the great style, with considerable debts to Jeremy Taylor.[2]

"Look, Dyson," said the one, as they drew nearer; "look at those upper windows; the sun is setting, and, though the panes are dusty, yet—

'The grimy sash an oriel burns.'"[3]

"Phillipps," replied the elder and (it must be said) the more pompous of the two, "I yield to fantasy; I cannot withstand the influence of the grotesque. Here, where all is falling into dimness and dissolution, and we walk in cedarn gloom, and the very air of heaven goes mouldering to the lungs, I cannot remain commonplace. I look at that deep glow on the panes, and the house lies all enchanted; that very room, I tell you, is within all blood and fire."

Adventure of the Gold Tiberius

The acquaintance between Mr. Dyson and Mr. Charles Phillipps arose from one of those myriad chances which are every day doing their work in the streets of London. Mr. Dyson was a man of letters, and an unhappy instance of talents misapplied. With gifts that might have placed him in the flower of his youth among the most favoured of Bentley's favourite novelists,[4] he had chosen to be perverse; he was, it is true, familiar with scholastic logic, but he knew nothing of the logic of life, and he flattered himself with the title of artist, when he was in fact but an idle and curious spectator of other men's endeavours. Amongst many delusions, he cherished one most fondly, that he was a strenuous worker; and it was with a gesture of supreme weariness that he would enter his favourite resort, a small tobacco-shop in Great Queen Street, and proclaim to any one who cared to listen that he had seen the rising and setting of two successive suns. The proprietor of the shop, a middle-aged man of singular civility, tolerated Dyson partly out of good nature, and partly because he was a regular customer. He was allowed to sit on an empty cask, and to express his sentiments on literary and artistic matters till he was tired, or the time for closing came; and if no fresh customers were attracted, it is believed that none were turned away by his eloquence. Dyson was addicted to wild experiments in tobacco; he never wearied of trying new combinations; and one evening he had just entered the shop, and given utterance to his last preposterous formula, when a young fellow of about his own age, who had come in a moment later, asked the shopman to duplicate the order on his account, smiling politely, as he spoke, to Mr. Dyson's address. Dyson felt profoundly flattered, and after a few phrases the two entered into conversation, and in an hour's time the tobacconist saw the new friends sitting side by side on a couple of casks, deep in talk.

"My dear sir," said Dyson, "I will give you the task of the literary man in a phrase. He has got to do simply this—to invent a wonderful story, and to tell it in a wonderful manner."

"I will grant you that," said Mr. Phillipps, "but you will allow me to insist that in the hands of the true artist in words all stories are marvellous and every circumstance has its peculiar wonder. The matter is of little consequence; the manner is everything. Indeed, the highest skill is shown in taking matter apparently commonplace and transmuting it by the high alchemy of style into the pure gold of art."

"That is indeed a proof of great skill, but it is great skill exerted foolishly, or at least unadvisedly. It is as if a great violinist were to show us what marvellous harmonies he could draw from a child's banjo."

"No, no, you are really wrong. I see you take a radically mistaken view of life. But we must thresh this out. Come to my rooms; I live not far from here."

It was thus that Mr. Dyson became the associate of Mr. Charles Phillipps, who lived in a quiet square not far from Holborn. Thenceforth they haunted each other's rooms at intervals, sometimes regular, and occasionally the reverse, and made appointments to meet at the shop in Queen Street, where their talk robbed the tobacconist's profit of half its charm. There was a constant jarring of literary formulas, Dyson exalting the claims of the pure imagination; while Phillipps, who was a student of physical science and something of an ethnologist, insisted that all literature ought to have a scientific basis. By the mistaken benevolence of deceased relatives both young men were placed out of reach of hunger, and so, meditating high achievements, idled their time pleasantly away, and revelled in the careless joys of a Bohemianism devoid of the sharp seasoning of adversity.

One night in June Mr. Phillipps was sitting in his room in the calm retirement of Red Lion Square. He had opened the window, and was smoking placidly, while he watched the movement of life below. The sky was clear, and the afterglow of sunset had lingered long about it. The flushing twilight of a summer evening vied with the gas-lamps in the square, and fashioned a chiaroscuro that had in it something unearthly; and the children, racing to and fro upon the pavement, the lounging idlers by the public-house, and the casual passers-by rather flickered and hovered in the play of lights than stood out substantial things. By degrees in the houses opposite one window after another leapt out a square of light; now and again a figure would shape itself against a blind and vanish, and to all this semi-theatrical magic the runs and flourishes of brave Italian opera played a little distance off on a piano-organ seemed an appropriate accompaniment, while the deep-muttered bass of the traffic of Holborn never ceased. Phillipps enjoyed the scene and its effects; the light in the sky faded and turned to darkness, and the square gradually grew silent, and still he sat dreaming at the window, till the sharp peal of the house-bell roused him, and looking at his watch, he found that it was past ten o'clock. There was a knock at the door, and his friend Mr. Dyson entered, and, according to his custom, sat down in an arm-chair and began to smoke in silence.

"You know, Phillipps," he said at length, "that I have always battled for the marvellous. I remember your maintaining in that chair that one has no business to make use of the wonderful, the improbable, the odd coincidence in literature, and you took the ground that it was wrong to do so, because as a matter of fact the wonderful and the improbable don't happen, and men's lives are not really shaped by odd coincidence. Now, mind you, if that were so, I would not grant your conclusion, because I think the 'criticism-of-life' theory is all nonsense;[5] but I deny your premise. A most singular thing has happened to me tonight."

"Really, Dyson, I am very glad to hear it. Of course, I oppose your argument, whatever it may be; but if you would be good enough to tell me of your adventure, I should be delighted."

"Well, it came about like this. I have had a very hard day's work; indeed I have scarcely moved from my old bureau since seven o'clock last night. I wanted to work out that idea we discussed last Tuesday, you know, the notion of the fetish-worshipper?"

"Yes, I remember. Have you been able to do anything with it?"

"Yes; it came out better than I expected; but there were great difficulties, the usual agonies between the conception and the execution. Anyhow, I got it done about seven o'clock to-night, and I thought I should like a little of the fresh air. I went out and wandered rather aimlessly about the streets; my head was full of my tale, and I didn't much notice where I was going. I got into those quiet places to the north of Oxford Street as you go west, the genteel residential neighbourhood of stucco and prosperity. I turned east again without knowing it, and it was quite dark when I passed along a sombre little by-street, ill-lighted and empty. I did not know at the time in the least where I was, but I found out afterwards that it was not very far from Tottenham Court Road. I strolled idly along, enjoying the stillness; on one side there seemed to be the back premises of some great shop; tier after tier of dusty windows lifted up into the night, with gibbet-like contrivances for raising heavy goods, and below large doors, fast closed and bolted, all dark and desolate. Then there came a huge pantechnicon[6] ware-house; and over the way a grim blank wall, as forbidding as the wall of a gaol, and then the headquarters of some volunteer regiment, and afterwards a passage leading to a court where waggons were standing to be hired; it was, one might almost say, a street devoid of inhabitants, and scarce a window showed the glimmer of a light. I was wonder-ing at the strange peace and dimness there, where it must be close to some roaring main artery of London life, when suddenly I heard the noise of dashing feet tearing along the pavement at full speed, and from a narrow passage, a mews or something of that kind, a man was discharged as from a catapult under my very nose, and rushed past me, flinging something from him as he ran. He was gone, and down another street in an instant, almost before I knew what had happened; but I didn't much bother about him, I was watching something else. I told you he had thrown something away; well, I watched what seemed a line of flame flash through the air and fly quivering over the pave-ment, and in spite of myself I could not help tearing after it. The im-petus lessened, and I saw something like a bright halfpenny roll slower and slower, and then deflect towards the gutter, hover for a moment on the edge, and dance down into a drain. I believe I cried out in positive despair, though I hadn't the least notion what I was hunting; and then, to my joy, I saw that, instead of dropping into a sewer, it had fallen flat across two bars. I stooped down and picked it up and whipped it into my pocket, and I was just about to walk on when I heard again that sound of dashing footsteps. I don't know why I did it, but as a matter of fact I dived down into the mews, or whatever it was, and stood as much in the shadow as possible. A man went by with a rush a few paces from where I was standing, and I felt uncommonly pleased that I was hiding. I couldn't make out much feature, but I saw his eyes gleaming and his teeth showing, and he had an ugly-looking knife in one hand, and I thought things would be very unpleasant for gentleman number one if the second robber, or robbed, or what you like, caught him up. I can tell you, Phillipps, a fox-hunt is exciting enough, when the horn blows clear on a winter morning, and the hounds give tongue, and the red-coats charge away, but it's nothing to a man-hunt, and that's what I had a slight glimpse of to-night. There was murder in the fellow's eyes as he went by, and I don't think there was much more than fifty seconds between the two. I only hope it was enough."

Dyson leant back in his arm-chair, relit his pipe, and puffed thoughtfully. Phillipps began to walk up and down the room, musing over the story of violent death fleeting in chase along the pavement, the knife shining in the lamplight, the fury of the pursuer, and the terror of the pursued.

"Well," he said at last, "and what was it, after all, that you rescued from the gutter?"

Dyson jumped up, evidently quite startled. "I really haven't a notion. I didn't think of looking. But we shall see."

He fumbled in his waistcoat pocket, drew out a small and shining object, and laid it on the table. It glowed there beneath the lamp with the radiant glory of rare old gold; and the image and the letters stood out in high relief, clear and sharp, as if it had but left the mint a month before. The two men bent over it, and Phillipps took it up and examined it closely.

"Imp. Tiberius Cæsar Augustus,"[7] he read the legend, and then looking at the reverse of the coin, he stared in amazement, and at last turned to Dyson with a look of exultation.

"Do you know what you have found?" he said.

"Apparently a gold coin of some antiquity," said Dyson coolly.

"Quite so, a gold Tiberius. No, that is wrong. You have found *the* gold Tiberius. Look at the reverse."

Dyson looked and saw the coin was stamped with the figure of a faun standing amidst reeds and flowing water. The features, minute as they were, stood out in delicate outline; it was a face lovely and yet terrible, and Dyson thought of the well-known passage of the lad's playmate, gradually growing with his growth and increasing with his stature till the air was filled with the rank fume of the goat.

"Yes," he said; "it is a curious coin. Do you know it?"

"I know about it. It is one of the comparatively few historical objects in existence; it is all storied like those jewels we have read of. A whole cycle of legend has gathered round the thing; the tale goes that it formed part of an issue struck by Tiberius to commemorate an infamous excess. You see the legend on the reverse: 'Victoria.' It is said that by an extraordinary accident the whole issue was thrown into the melting-pot, and that only this one coin escaped. It glints through history and legend, appearing and disappearing, with intervals of a hundred years in time, and continents in place. It was 'discovered' by an Italian humanist, and lost and rediscovered. It has not been heard of since 1727, when Sir Joshua Byrde, a Turkey merchant, brought it home from Aleppo, and vanished with it a month after he had shown it to the virtuosi, no man knew or knows where. And here it is!"

"Put it in your pocket, Dyson," he said, after a pause. "I would not let any one have a glimpse of the thing if I were you. I would not talk about it. Did either of the men you saw see you?"

"Well, I think not. I don't think the first man, the man who was vomited out of the dark passage, saw anything at all; and I am sure that he could not have seen me."

"And you didn't really see them. You couldn't recognize either the one or the other if you met him in the street to-morrow?"

"No, I don't think I could. The street, as I said, was dimly lighted, and they ran like madmen."

The two men sat silent for some time, each weaving his own fancies of the story; but the lust of the marvellous was slowly overpowering Dyson's more sober thoughts.

"It is all more strange than I fancied," he said at last. "It is queer enough what I saw; a man is sauntering along a quiet, sober, everyday London street, a street of grey houses and blank walls, and there, for a moment, a veil seems drawn aside, and the very fume of the pit steams up through the flagstones, the ground glows, red-hot, beneath his feet, and he seems to hear the hiss of the infernal caldron. A man flying in mad terror for his life, and furious hate pressing hot on his steps with knife drawn ready; here, indeed, is horror; but what is all that to what you have told me? I tell you, Phillipps, I see the plot thicken; our steps will henceforth be dogged with mystery, and the most ordinary incidents will teem with significance. You may stand out against it, and shut your eyes, but they will be forced open; mark my words, you will have to yield to the inevitable. A clue, tangled if you like, has been placed by chance in our hands; it will be our business to follow it up. As for the guilty person or persons in this strange case, they will be unable to escape us, our nets will be spread far and wide over this great city, and suddenly, in the streets and places of public resort, we shall in some way or other be made aware that we are in touch with the unknown criminal. Indeed I almost fancy I see him slowly approaching this quiet square of yours; he is loitering at street corners, wandering, apparently without aim, down far-reaching thoroughfares, but all the while coming nearer and nearer, drawn by an irresistible magnetism, as ships were drawn to the Loadstone Rock in the Eastern tale."[8]

"I certainly think," replied Phillipps, "that if you pull out that coin and flourish it under people's noses as you are doing at the present moment, you will very probably find yourself in touch with the criminal, or a criminal. You will undoubtedly be robbed with violence. Otherwise, I see no reason why either of us should be troubled. No one saw you secure the coin, and no one knows you have it. I, for my part, shall sleep peacefully, and go about my business with a sense of security and a firm dependence on the natural order of things. The events of the evening, the adventure in the street, have been odd, I grant you, but I resolutely decline to have any more to do with the matter, and, if necessary, I shall consult the police. I will not be enslaved by a gold Tiberius, even though it swims into my ken in a manner which is somewhat melodramatic."

"And I, for my part," said Dyson, "go forth like a knight-errant in search of adventure. Not that I shall need to seek; rather adventure will seek me; I shall be like a spider in the midst of his web, responsive to every movement, and ever on the alert."

Shortly afterwards Dyson took his leave, and Mr. Phillipps spent the rest of the night in examining some flint arrow-heads which he had purchased. He had every reason to believe that they were the work of a modern and not a palæolithic man; still he was far from gratified when a close scrutiny showed him that his suspicions were well founded. In his anger at the turpitude which would impose on an ethnologist, he completely forgot Dyson and the gold Tiberius; and when he went to bed at first sunlight, the whole tale had faded utterly from his thoughts.

THE ENCOUNTER OF THE PAVEMENT

Mr. Dyson, walking leisurely along Oxford Street, and staring with bland inquiry at whatever caught his attention, enjoyed in all its rare flavours the sensation that he was really very hard at work. His observation of mankind, the traffic, and the shop windows tickled his faculties with an exquisite bouquet; he looked serious, as one looks on whom charges of weight and moment are laid; and he was attentive in his glances to right and left, for fear lest he should miss some circumstance of more acute significance. He had narrowly escaped being run over at a crossing by a charging van, for he hated to hurry his steps, and indeed the afternoon was warm; and he had just halted by a place of popular refreshment, when the astounding gestures of a well-dressed individual on the opposite pavement held him enchanted and gasping like a fish. A treble line of hansoms, carriages, vans, cabs, and omnibuses was tearing east and west, and not the most daring adventurer of the crossings would have cared to try his fortune; but the person who had attracted Dyson's attention seemed to rage on the very edge of the pavement, now and then darting forward at the hazard of instant death, and at each repulse absolutely dancing with excitement, to the rich amusement of the passers-by. At last a gap that would have tried the courage of a street-boy appeared between the serried lines of vehicles, and the man rushed across in a frenzy, and escaping by a hair's-breadth, pounced upon Dyson as a tiger pounces on her prey. "I saw you looking about you," he said, sputtering out his words in his intense eagerness; "would you mind telling me this? Was the man who came out of the Aerated Bread Shop and jumped into the hansom three minutes ago a youngish-looking man with dark whiskers and spectacles? Can't you speak, man? For heaven's sake, can't you speak? Answer me; it's a matter of life and death."

The words bubbled and boiled out of the man's mouth in the fury of his emotion, his face went from red to white, and the beads of sweat stood out on his forehead; he stamped his feet as he spoke, and tore with his hand at his coat, as if something swelled and choked him, stopping the passage of his breath.

"My dear sir," said Dyson, "I always like to be accurate. Your observation was perfectly correct. As you say, a youngish man—a man, I should say, of somewhat timid bearing—ran rapidly out of the shop here, and bounced into a hansom that must have been waiting for him, as it went eastwards at once. Your friend also wore spectacles, as you say. Perhaps you would like me to call a hansom for you to follow the gentleman?"

"No, thank you; it would be a waste of time." The man gulped down something which appeared to rise in his throat, and Dyson was alarmed to see him shaking with hysterical laughter; he clung hard to a lamp-post, and swayed and staggered like a ship in a heavy gale.

"How shall I face the doctor?" he murmured to himself. "It is too hard to fail at the last moment." Then he seemed to recollect himself; he stood straight again, and looked quietly at Dyson.

"I owe you an apology for my violence," he said at last. "Many men would not be so patient as you have been. Would you mind adding to your kindness by walking with me a little way? I feel a little sick; I think it's the sun."

Dyson nodded assent, and devoted himself to a quiet scrutiny of this strange personage as they moved on together. The man was dressed in quiet taste, and the most scrupulous observer could find nothing amiss with the fashion or make of his clothes; yet, from his hat to his boots, everything seemed inappropriate. His silk hat, Dyson thought, should have been a high bowler of odious pattern, worn with a baggy morning-coat, and an instinct told him that the fellow did not commonly carry a clean pocket-handkerchief. The face was not of the most agreeable pattern, and was in no way improved by a pair of bulbous chin-whiskers of a ginger hue, into which moustaches of like colour merged imperceptibly. Yet, in spite of these signals hung out by nature, Dyson felt that the individual beside him was something more than compact of vulgarity. He was struggling with himself, holding his feelings in check; but now and again passion would mount black to his face, and it was evidently by a supreme effort that he kept himself from raging like a madman. Dyson found something curious, and a little terrible, in the spectacle of an occult emotion thus striving for the mastery, and threatening to break out at every instant with violence; and they had gone some distance before the person whom he had met by so odd a hazard was able to speak quietly.

"You are really very good," he said. "I apologize again; my rudeness was really most unjustifiable. I feel my conduct demands an explanation, and I shall be happy to give it to you. Do you happen to know of any place near here where one could sit down? I should really be very glad."

"My dear sir," said Dyson solemnly, "the only café in London is close by. Pray do not consider yourself as bound to offer me any explanation, but at the same time I should be most happy to listen to you. Let us turn down here."

They walked down a sober street and turned into what seemed a narrow passage past an iron-barred gate thrown back. The passage was paved with flagstones, and decorated with handsome shrubs in pots on either side, and the shadow of the high walls made a coolness which was very agreeable after the hot breath of the sunny street. Presently the passage opened out into a tiny square, a charming place, a morsel of France transplanted into the heart of London. High walls rose on either side, covered with glossy creepers, flower-beds beneath were gay with nasturtiums, and marigolds, and odorous mignonette, and in the centre of the square a fountain, hidden by greenery, sent a cool shower continually plashing into the basin beneath. Chairs and tables were disposed at convenient intervals, and at the other end of the court broad doors had been thrown back; beyond was a long, dark room, and the turmoil of traffic had become a distant murmur. Within the room one or two men were sitting at the tables, writing and sipping, but the courtyard was empty.

"You see, we shall be quiet," said Dyson. "Pray sit down here, Mr.—?"

"Wilkins. My name is Henry Wilkins."

"Sit here, Mr. Wilkins. I think you will find that a comfortable seat. I suppose you have not been here before? This is the quiet time; the place will be like a hive at six o'clock, and the chairs and tables will overflow into that little alley there."

A waiter came in response to the bell; and after Dyson had politely inquired after the health of M. Annibault, the proprietor, he ordered a bottle of the wine of Champigny.

"The wine of Champigny," he observed to Mr. Wilkins, who was evidently a good deal composed by the influence of the place, "is a

Tourainian wine of great merit.[9] Ah, here it is; let me fill your glass. How do you find it?"

"Indeed," said Mr. Wilkins, "I should have pronounced it fine Burgundy. The bouquet is very exquisite. I am fortunate in lighting upon such a good Samaritan as yourself: I wonder you did not think me mad. But if you knew the terrors that assailed me, I am sure you would no longer be surprised at conduct which was certainly most unjustifiable."

He sipped his wine, and leant back in his chair, relishing the drip and trickle of the fountain, and the cool greenness that hedged in this little port of refuge.

"Yes," he said at last, "that is indeed an admirable wine. Thank you; you will allow me to offer you another bottle?"

The waiter was summoned, and descended through a trap-door in the floor of the dark apartment and brought up the wine. Mr. Wilkins lit a cigarette, and Dyson pulled out his pipe.

"Now," said Mr. Wilkins, "I promised to give you an explanation of my strange behaviour. It is rather a long story, but I see, sir, that you are no mere cold observer of the ebb and flow of life. You take, I think, a warm and an intelligent interest in the chances of your fellow-creatures, and I believe you will find what I have to tell not devoid of interest."

Mr. Dyson signified his assent to these propositions; and though he thought Mr. Wilkins's diction a little pompous, prepared to interest himself in his tale. The other, who had so raged with passion half an hour before, was now perfectly cool, and when he had smoked out his cigarette, he began in an even voice to relate the

NOVEL OF THE DARK VALLEY

I am the son of a poor but learned clergyman in the west of England—but I am forgetting, these details are not of special interest. I will briefly state, then, that my father, who was, as I have said, a learned man, had never learnt the specious arts by which the great are flattered, and would never condescend to the despicable pursuit of self-advertisement. Though his fondness for ancient ceremonies and quaint customs, combined with a kindness of heart that was unequalled and a primitive and fervent piety, endeared him to his moorland parishioners, such were not the steps by which clergy then rose in the Church, and at sixty my father was still incumbent of the little benefice he had accepted in his thirtieth year. The income of the living was barely sufficient to support life in the decencies which are expected of the Angli-can parson; and when my father died a few years ago, I, his only child, found myself thrown upon the world with a slender capital of less than a hundred pounds, and all the problem of existence before me. I felt that there was nothing for me to do in the country, and as usually happens in such cases, London drew me like a magnet. One day in August, in the early morning, while the dew still glittered on the turf, and on the high green banks of the lane, a neighbour drove me to the railway station, and I bade good-bye to the land of the broad moors and unearthly battlements of the wild tors. It was six o'clock as we neared London; the faint, sickly fume of the brickfields about Acton came in puffs through the open window, and a mist was rising from the ground. Presently the brief view of successive streets, prim and uni-form, struck me with a sense of monotony; the hot air seemed to grow hotter; and when we had rolled beneath the dismal and squalid houses, whose dirty and neglected backyards border the line near Paddington, I felt as if I should be stifled in this fainting breath of London. I got a hansom and drove off, and every street increased my gloom; grey houses with blinds drawn down, whole thoroughfares almost desolate, and the foot-passengers who seemed to stagger wearily along rather than walk, all made me feel a sinking at heart. I put up for the night at a small hotel in a street leading from the Strand, where my father had stayed on his few brief visits to the town; and when I went out after dinner, the real gaiety and bustle of the Strand and Fleet Street could cheer me but little, for in all this great city there was no single human being whom I could claim even as an acquaintance. I will not weary you with the history of the next year, for the adventures of a man who sinks are too trite to be worth recalling. My money did not last me long; I found that I must be neatly dressed, or no one to whom I applied would so much as listen to me; and I must live in a street of decent reputation if I wished to be treated with common civility. I applied for various posts, for which, as I now see, I was completely devoid of quali-fication; I tried to become a clerk without having the smallest notion of business habits; and I found, to my cost, that a general knowledge of literature and an execrable style of penmanship are far from being looked upon with favour in commercial circles. I had read one of the most charming of the works of a famous novelist of the present day, and I frequented the Fleet Street taverns in the hope of making literary friends, and so getting the introductions which I understood were in-dispensable in the career of letters. I was disappointed; I once or twice ventured to address gentlemen who were sitting in adjoining boxes, and I was answered, politely indeed, but in a manner that told me my advances were unusual. Pound by pound, my small resources melted; I could no longer think of appearances; I migrated to a shy quarter, and my meals became mere observances. I went out at one and returned to my room at two, but nothing but a mere milk-cake had occurred in the interval. In short, I became acquainted with misfortune; and as I sat amidst slush and ice on a seat in Hyde Park, munching a piece of bread, I realized the bitterness of poverty, and the feelings of a gentleman reduced to something far below the condition of a vagrant. In spite of all discouragement I did not desist in my efforts to earn a living. I consulted advertisement columns, I kept my eyes open for a chance, I looked in at the windows of stationers' shops, but all in vain. One evening I was sitting in a Free Library, and I saw an advertisement in one of the papers. It was something like this: "Wanted by a gentleman a person of literary tastes and abilities as secretary and amanuensis. Must not object to travel." Of course I knew that such an advertisement would have answers by the hundred, and I thought my own chances of securing the post extremely small; however I applied at the address given, and wrote to Mr. Smith, who was staying at the West End. I must confess that my heart gave a jump when I received a note a couple of days later, asking me to call at the Cosmopole at my earliest convenience. I do not know, sir, what your experiences of life may have been, and so I cannot tell you whether you have known such moments. A slight sickness, my heart beating rather more rapidly than usual, a choking in the throat, and a difficulty of utterance; such were my sensations as I walked to the Cosmopole; I had to mention the name twice before the hall porter could understand me, and as I went upstairs my hands were wet. I was a good deal struck by Mr. Smith's appearance; he looked younger than I did, and there was something mild and hesitating about his expression. He was reading when I came in, and he looked up when I gave my name. "My dear sir," he said, "I am really delighted to see you. I have read very carefully the letter you were good enough to send me. Am I to understand that this document is in your own handwriting?" He showed me the letter I had written, and I told him I was not so fortunate as to be able to keep a secretary myself. "Then, sir," he went on, "the post I advertised is at your service. You have no objection to travel, I presume?" As you may imagine, I closed pretty eagerly with the offer he made, and thus I entered the service of Mr. Smith. For the first few weeks I had no special duties; I had received a quarter's salary, and a handsome allowance was made me in lieu of board and lodging. One morning, however, when I called at the hotel according to instructions, my master informed me that I must hold myself in readiness for a sea-voyage, and, to spare unnecessary detail, in the course of a fortnight we had landed at New York. Mr. Smith told me that he was engaged on a work of a special nature, in the compilation of which some peculiar researches had to be made; in short, I was given to understand that we were to travel to the far West.

After about a week had been spent in New York we took our seats in the cars, and began a journey tedious beyond all conception. Day after day, and night after night, the great train rolled on, threading its way through cities the very names of which were strange to me, passing at slow speed over perilous viaducts, skirting mountain ranges and pine forests, and plunging into dense tracts of wood, where mile after mile and hour after hour the same monotonous growth of brushwood met the eye, and all along the continual clatter and rattle of the wheels upon the ill-laid lines made it difficult to hear the voices of our fellow-passengers. We were a heterogeneous and ever-changing company; often I woke up in the dead of night with a sudden grinding jar of the breaks, and looking out found that we had stopped in the shabby street of some frame-built town, lighted chiefly by the flaring windows of the saloon. A few rough-looking fellows would often come out to stare at the cars, and sometimes passengers got down, and sometimes there was a party of two or three waiting on the wooden sidewalk to get on board. Many of the passengers were English; humble households torn up from the moorings of a thousand years, and bound for some problematical paradise in the alkali desert or the Rockies. I heard the men talking to one another of the great profits to be made on the virgin soil of America, and two or three, who were mechanics, expatiated on the wonderful wages given to skilled labour on the railways and in the factories of the States. This talk usually fell dead after a few minutes, and I could see a sickness and dismay in the faces of these men as they looked at the ugly brush or at the desolate expanse of the prairie, dotted here and there with frame houses, devoid of garden or flowers or trees, standing all alone in what might have been a great sea frozen into stillness. Day after day the waving sky-line, and the desolation of a land without form or colour or variety, appalled the hearts of such of us as were Englishmen, and once in the night as I lay awake I heard a woman sobbing and asking what she had done to come to such a place. Her husband tried to comfort her in the broad speech of Gloucestershire, telling her the ground was so rich that one had only to plough it up and it would grow sunflowers of itself, but she cried for her mother and their old cottage and the beehives like a little child. The sadness of it all overwhelmed me, and I had no heart to think of other matters; the question of what Mr. Smith could have to do in such a country, and of what manner of literary research could be carried on in the wilderness, hardly troubled me. Now and again my situation struck me as peculiar; I had been engaged as a literary assistant at a handsome salary, and yet my master was still almost a stranger to me; sometimes he would come to where I was sitting in the cars and make a few banal remarks about the country, but for the most part of the journey he sat by himself, not speaking to any one, and so far as I could judge, deep in his thoughts. It was, I think, on the fifth day from New York when I received the intimation that we should shortly leave the cars; I had been watching some distant mountains which rose wild and savage be-fore us, and I was wondering if there were human beings so unhappy as to speak of home in connection with those piles of lumbered rock, when Mr. Smith touched me lightly on the shoulder. "You will be glad to be done with the cars, I have no doubt, Mr. Wilkins," he said. "You were looking at the mountains, I think? Well, I hope we shall be there to-night. The train stops at Reading, and I dare say we shall manage to find our way."

A few hours later the breaksman brought the train to a standstill at the Reading depôt, and we got out. I noticed that the town, though of course built almost entirely of frame-houses, was larger and busier than any we had passed for the last two days. The depôt was crowded; and as the bell and whistle sounded, I saw that a number of persons were preparing to leave the cars, while an even greater number were waiting to get on board. Besides the passengers, there was a pretty dense crowd of people, some of whom had come to meet or to see off their friends and relatives, while others were merely loafers. Several of our English fellow-passengers got down at Reading, but the confu-sion was so great that they were lost to my sight almost immediately. Mr. Smith beckoned me to follow him, and we were soon in the thick of the mass; and the continual ringing of bells, the hubbub of voices, the shrieking of whistles, and the hiss of escaping steam, confused my senses, and I wondered dimly, as I struggled after my employer, where we were going, and how we should be able to find our way through an unknown country. Mr. Smith had put on a wide-brimmed hat, which he had sloped over his eyes, and as all the men wore hats of the same pattern, it was with some difficulty that I distinguished him in the crowd. We got free at last, and he struck down a side street, and made one or two sharp turns to right and left. It was getting dusk, and we seemed to be passing through a shy portion of the town; there were few people about in the ill-lighted streets, and these few were men of the unprepossessing pattern. Suddenly we stopped before a corner house. A man was standing at the door, apparently on the look-out for some one, and I noticed that he and Smith gave sharp glances one to the other.

"From New York City, I expect, mister?"

"From New York."

"All right; they're ready, and you can have 'em when you choose. I know my orders, you see, and I mean to run this business through."

"Very well, Mr. Evans, that is what we want. Our money is good, you know. Bring them round."

I had stood silent, listening to this dialogue and wondering what it meant. Smith began to walk impatiently up and down the street, and the man Evans was still standing at his door. He had given a sharp whistle, and I saw him looking me over in a quiet, leisurely way, as if to make sure of my face for another time. I was thinking what all this could mean, when an ugly slouching lad came up a side passage, leading two raw-boned horses.

"Get up, Mr. Wilkins, and be quick about it," said Smith; "we ought to be on our way."

We rode off together into the gathering darkness, and before long I looked back and saw the far plain behind us, with the lights of the town glimmering faintly; and in front rose the mountains. Smith guided his horse on the rough track as surely as if he had been riding along Piccadilly, and I followed as well as I could. I was weary and exhausted, and scarcely took note of anything; I felt that the track was a gradual ascent, and here and there I saw great boulders by the road. The ride made but little impression on me. I have a faint recollection of passing through a dense black pine forest, where our horses had to pick their way among the rocks, and I remember the peculiar effect of the rarefied air as we kept still mounting higher and higher. I think I must have been half asleep for the latter half of the ride, and it was with a shock that I heard Smith saying—

"Here we are, Wilkins. This is Blue Rock Park. You will enjoy the view to-morrow. Tonight we will have something to eat, and then go to bed."

A man came out of a rough-looking house and took the horses, and we found some fried steak and coarse whiskey awaiting us inside. I had come to a strange place. There were three rooms—the room in which we had supper, Smith's room, and my own. The deaf old man who did the work slept in a sort of shed, and when I woke up the next morning and walked out I found that the house stood in a sort of hollow amongst the mountains; the clumps of pines and some enormous bluish-grey rocks that stood here and there between the trees had given the place the name of Blue Rock Park. On every side the snow-covered mountains, surrounded us, the breath of the air was as wine, and when

I climbed the slope and looked down, I could see that, so far as any human fellowship was concerned, I might as well have been wrecked on some small island in mid-Pacific. The only trace of man I could see was the rough log-house where I had slept, and in my ignorance I did not know that there were similar houses within comparatively easy distance, as distance is reckoned in the Rockies. But at the moment, the utter, dreadful loneliness rushed upon me, and the thought of the great plain and the great sea that parted me from the world I knew caught me by the throat, and I wondered if I should die there in that mountain hollow. It was a terrible instant, and I have not yet forgotten it. Of course, I managed to conquer my horror; I said I should be all the stronger for the experience, and I made up my mind to make the best of everything. It was a rough life enough, and rough enough board and lodging. I was left entirely to myself. Smith I scarcely ever saw, nor did I know when he was in the house. I have often thought he was far away, and have been surprised to see him walking out of his room, locking the door behind him, and putting the key in his pocket; and on several occasions, when I fancied he was busy in his room, I have seen him come in with his boots covered with dust and dirt. So far as work went I enjoyed a complete sinecure; I had nothing to do but to walk about the valley, to eat and to sleep. With one thing and another I grew accustomed to the life, and managed to make myself pretty comfortable, and by degrees I began to venture farther away from the house, and to explore the country. One day I had contrived to get into the neighbouring valley, and suddenly I came upon a group of men sawing timber. I went up to them, hoping that perhaps some of them might be Englishmen; at all events, they were human beings, and I should hear articulate speech; for the old man I have mentioned, besides being half blind and stone deaf, was wholly dumb so far as I was concerned. I was prepared to be welcomed in rough and ready fashion, without much of the forms of politeness, but the grim glances and the short, gruff answers I received astonished me. I saw the men glance oddly at each other; and one of them, who had stopped work, began fingering a gun, and I was obliged to return on my path uttering curses on the fate which had brought me into a land where men were more brutish than the very brutes. The solitude of the life began to oppress me as with a nightmare, and a few days later I determined to walk to a kind of station some miles distant, where a rough inn was kept for the accommodation of hunters and tourists. English gentlemen occasionally stopped there for the night, and I thought I might perhaps fall in with some one of better manners than the inhabitants of the country. I found, as I had expected, a group of men lounging about the door of the log-house that served as a hotel, and as I came nearer I could see that heads were put together and looks interchanged, and when I walked up the six or seven trappers stared at me in stony ferocity, and with something of the disgust that one eyes a loathsome and venomous snake. I felt that I could bear it no longer, and I called out—

"Is there such a thing as an Englishman here, or any one with a little civilization?"

One of the men put his hand to his belt, but his neighbour checked him, and answered me—

"You'll find we've got some of the resources of civilization before very long, mister, and I expect you'll not fancy them extremely. But, anyway, there's an Englishman tarrying here, and I've no doubt he'll be glad to see you. There you are; that's Mr. D'Aubernoun."

A young man, dressed like an English country squire, came and stood at the door, and looked at me. One of the men pointed to me and said—

"That's the individual we were talking about last night. Thought you might like to have a look at him, squire, and here he is."

The young fellow's good-natured English face clouded over, and he glanced sternly at me, and turned away with a gesture of contempt and aversion.

"Sir," I cried, "I do not know what I have done to be treated in this manner. You are my fellow-countryman, and I expected some courtesy."

He gave me a black look and made as if he would go in, but he changed his mind and faced me.

"You are rather imprudent, I think, to behave in this manner. You must be counting on a forbearance which cannot last very long, which may last a very short time indeed. And let me tell you this, sir, you may call yourself an Englishman, and drag the name of England through the dirt, but you need not count on any English influence to help you. If I were you, I would not stay here much longer."

He went into the inn, and the men quietly watched my face as I stood there, wondering whether I was going mad. The woman of the house came out and stared at me as if I were a wild beast or a savage, and I turned to her, and spoke quietly—

"I am very hungry and thirsty. I have walked a long way. I have plenty of money. Will you give me something to eat and drink?"

"No, I won't," she said. "You had better quit this."

I crawled home like a wounded beast, and lay down on my bed. It was all a hopeless puzzle to me; I knew nothing but rage, and shame, and terror, and I suffered little more when I passed by a house in an adjacent valley, and some children who were playing outside ran from me shrieking. I was forced to walk to find some occupation; I should have died if I had sat down quietly in Blue Rock Park and looked all day at the mountains; but wherever I saw a human being I saw the same glance of hatred and aversion, and once as I was crossing a thick brake I heard a shot and the venomous hiss of a bullet close to my ear.

One day I heard a conversation which astounded me; I was sitting behind a rock resting, and two men came along the track and halted. One of them had got his feet entangled in some wild vines, and swore fiercely, but the other laughed, and said they were useful things sometimes.

"What the hell do you mean?"

"Oh, nothing much. But they're uncommon tough, these here vines, and sometimes rope is skerse and dear."

The man who had sworn chuckled at this, and I heard them sit down and light their pipes.

"Have you seen him lately?" asked the humorist.

"I sighted him the other day, but the darned bullet went high. He's got his master's luck, I expect, sir, but it can't last much longer. You heard about him going to Jinks's and trying his brass, but the young Britisher downed him pretty considerable, I can tell you."

"What the devil is the meaning of it?"

"I don't know, but I believe it'll have to be finished, and done in the old style too. You know how they fix the niggers?"

"Yes, sir, I've seen a little of that. A couple of gallons of kerosene 'll cost a dollar at Brown's store, but I should say it's cheap anyway."

They moved off after this, and I lay still behind the rock, the sweat pouring down my face. I was so sick that I could barely stand, and I walked home as slowly as an old man, leaning on my stick. I knew that the two men had been talking about me, and I knew that some terrible death was in store for me. That night I could not sleep; I tossed on the rough bed and tortured myself to find out the meaning of it all. At last, in the very dead of night, I rose from the bed and put on my clothes, and went out. I did not care where I went, but I felt that I must walk till I had tired myself out. It was a clear moonlight night, and in a couple of hours I found I was approaching a place of dismal reputation in the mountains, a deep cleft in the rocks, known as Black Gulf Cañon. Many years before an unfortunate party of Englishmen and English women had camped here and had been surrounded by Indians. They were captured, outraged, and put to death with almost inconceivable tortures, and the roughest of the trappers or woodsmen gave the cañon a wide berth even in the daytime. As I crushed through the dense brushwood which grew above the cañon I heard voices; and wondering who could be in such a place at such a time, I went on, walking more carefully, and making as little noise as possible. There was a great tree growing on the very edge of the rocks, and I lay down and looked out from behind the trunk. Black Gulf Cañon was below me, the moonlight shining bright into its very depths from midheaven, and casting shadows as black as death from the pointed rock, and all the sheer rock on the other side, overhanging the cañon, was in darkness. At intervals a light veil obscured the moonlight, as a filmy cloud fleeted across the moon, and a bitter wind blew shrill across the gulf. I looked down, as I have said, and saw twenty men standing in a semicircle round a rock; I counted them one by one, and knew most of them. They were the vilest of the vile, more vile than any den in London could show, and there was murder, worse than murder, on the heads of not a few. Facing them and me stood Mr. Smith, with the rock before him, and on the rock was a great pair of scales, such as are used in the stores. I heard his voice ringing down the cañon as I lay beside the tree, and my heart turned cold as I heard it.

"Life for gold," he cried, "a life for gold. The blood and the life of an enemy for every pound of gold."

A man stepped and raised one hand, and with the other flung a bright lump of something into the pan of the scales, which clanged down, and Smith muttered something in his ear. Then he cried again—

"Blood for gold, for a pound of gold, the life of an enemy. For every pound of gold upon the scales, a life."

One by one the men came forward, each lifting up his right hand; and the gold was weighed in the scales, and each time Smith leant forward and spoke to each man in his ear. Then he cried again—

"Desire and lust for gold on the scales. For every pound of gold enjoyment of desire."

I saw the same thing happen as before; the uplifted hand and the metal weighed, and the mouth whispering, and black passion on every face.

Then, one by one, I saw the men again step up to Smith. A muttered conversation seemed to take place. I could see that Smith was explaining and directing, and I noticed that he gesticulated a little as one who points out the way, and once or twice he moved his hands quickly as if he would show that the path was clear and could not be missed. I kept my eyes so intently on his figure that I noted little else, and at last it was with a start that I realized the cañon was empty. A moment before I thought I had seen the group of villainous faces, and the two standing, a little apart, by the rock; I had looked down a moment, and when

I glanced again into the cañon there was no one there. In dumb terror I made my way home, and I fell asleep in an instant from exhaustion. No doubt I should have slept on for many hours, but when I woke up the sun was only rising, and the light shone in on my bed. I had started up from sleep with the sensation of having received a violent shock; and as I looked in confusion about me, I saw, to my amazement, that there were three men in the room. One of them had his hand on my shoulder and spoke to me—

"Come, mister, wake up. Your time's up now, I reckon, and the boys are waiting for you outside, and they're in a big hurry. Come on; you can put on your clothes; it's kind of chilly this morning."

I saw the other two men smiling sourly at each other, but I understood nothing. I simply pulled on my clothes and said I was ready.

"All right; come on, then. You go first, Nichols, and Jim and I will give the gentleman an arm."

They took me out into the sunlight, and then I understood the meaning of the dull murmur that had vaguely perplexed me while I was dressing. There were about two hundred men waiting outside, and some women too, and when they saw me there was a low muttering growl. I did not know what I had done, but that noise made my heart beat and the sweat come out on my face. I saw confusedly, as through a veil, the tumult and tossing of the crowd, discordant voices were speaking, and amongst all those faces there was not one glance of mercy, but a fury of lust that I did not understand. I found myself presently walking in a sort of procession up the slope of the valley, and on every side of me there were men with revolvers in their hands. Now and then a voice struck me, and I heard words as sentences of which I could form no connected story. But I understood that there was one sentence of execration; I heard scraps of stories that seemed strange and improbable. Some one was talking of men, lured by cunning devices from their homes and murdered with hideous tortures, found writhing like wounded snakes in dark and lonely places, only crying for some one to stab them to the heart, and so end their anguish; and I heard another voice speaking of innocent girls who had vanished for a day or two, and then come back and died, blushing red with shame even in the agonies of death. I wondered what it all meant, and what was to happen; but I was so weary that I walked on in a dream, scarcely longing for anything but sleep. At last we stopped. We had reached the summit of the hill overlooking Blue Rock Valley, and I saw that I was standing beneath a clump of trees where I had often sat. I was in the midst of a ring of armed men, and I saw that two or three men were very busy with piles of wood, while others were fingering a rope. Then there was a stir in the crowd, and a man was pushed forward. His hands and feet were tightly bound with cord; and though his face was unutterably villainous, I pitied him for the agony that worked his features and twisted his lips. I knew him; he was amongst those that had gathered round Smith in Black Gulf Cañon. In an instant he was unbound and stripped naked, borne beneath one of the trees, and his neck encircled by a noose that went around the trunk. A hoarse voice gave some kind of order; there was a rush of feet, and the rope tightened; and there before me I saw the blackened face and the writhing limbs and the shameful agony of death. One after another half a dozen men, all of whom I had seen in the cañon the night before, were strangled before me, and their bodies were flung forth on the ground. Then there was a pause, and the man who had roused me a short while before came up to me, and said—

"Now, mister, it's your turn. We give you five minutes to cast up your accounts, and when that's clocked, by the living God, we will burn you alive at that tree."

It was then I awoke and understood. I cried out—

"Why, what have I done? Why should you hurt me? I am a harmless man; I never did you any wrong." I covered my face with my hands; it seemed so pitiful, and it was such a terrible death.

"What have I done?" I cried again. "You must take me for some other man. You cannot know me."

"You black-hearted devil," said the man at my side, "we know you well enough. There's not a man within thirty miles of this that won't curse Jack Smith when you are burning in hell."

"My name is not Smith," I said, with some hope left in me. "My name is Wilkins. I was Mr. Smith's secretary, but I knew nothing of him."

"Hark at the black liar," said the man. "Secretary be damned! You were clever enough, I dare say, to slink out at night and keep your face in the dark, but we've tracked you out at last. But your time's up. Come along."

I was dragged to the tree and bound to it with chains; I saw the piles of wood heaped all about me, and shut my eyes. Then I felt myself drenched all over with some liquid, and looked again, and a woman grinned at me. She had just emptied a great can of petroleum over me and over the wood. A voice shouted, "Fire away!" and I fainted, and knew nothing more.

When I opened my eyes I was lying on a bed in a bare, comfortless room. A doctor was holding some strong salts to my nostrils, and a gentleman standing by the bed, whom I afterwards found to be the sheriff, addressed me.

"Say, mister," he began, "you've had an uncommon narrow squeak for it. The boys were just about lighting up when I came along with the posse, and I had as much as I could do to bring you off, I can tell you. And, mind you, I don't blame them; they had made up their minds, you see, that you were the head of the Black Gulf gang, and at first nothing I could say would persuade them you weren't Jack Smith. Luckily, a man from here named Evans, that came along with us, allowed he had seen you with Jack Smith, and that you were yourself. So we brought you along and gaoled you, but you can go if you like when you're through with this faint turn."

I got on the cars next day, and in three weeks I was in London; again almost penniless. But from that time my fortune seemed to change; I made influential friends in all directions; bank directors courted my company, and editors positively flung themselves into my arms. I had only to choose my career, and after a while I determined that I was meant by nature for a life of comparative leisure. With an ease that seemed almost ridiculous, I obtained a well-paid position in connection with a prosperous political club. I have charming chambers in a central neighbourhood, close to the parks, the club chef exerts himself when I lunch or dine, and the rarest vintages in the cellar are always at my disposal. Yet, since my return to London, I have never known a day's security or peace; I tremble when I awake lest Smith should be standing at my bed, and every step I take seems to bring me nearer to the edge of the precipice. Smith, I knew, had escaped free from the raid of the Vigilantes, and I grew faint at the thought that he would in all probability return to London, and that suddenly and unprepared I should meet him face to face. Every morning as I left my house I would peer up and down the street, expecting to see that dreaded figure awaiting me; I have delayed at street-corners, my heart in my mouth, sickening at the thought that a few quick steps might bring us together; I could not bear to frequent the theatres or music-halls, lest by some bizarre chance he should prove to be my neighbour. Sometimes I have been forced, against my will, to walk out at night, and then in silent squares the shadows have made me shudder, and in the medley of meetings in the crowded thoroughfares I have said to myself, "It must come sooner or later; he will surely return to London, and I shall see him when I feel most secure." I scanned the newspapers for hint or intimation of approaching danger, and no small type nor report of trivial interest was allowed to pass unread. Especially I read and re-read the advertisement columns, but without result; months passed by, and I was undisturbed till, though I felt far from safe, I no longer suffered from the intolerable oppression of instant and ever-present terror. This afternoon, as I was walking quietly along Oxford Street, I raised my eyes and looked across the road, and then at last I saw the man who had so long haunted my thoughts."

Mr. Wilkins finished his wine, and leant back in his chair, looking sadly at Dyson; and then, as if a thought struck him, fished out of an inner pocket a leather letter-case, and handed a newspaper cutting across the table.

Dyson glanced closely at the slip, and saw that it had been extracted from the columns of an evening paper. It ran as follows:—

WHOLESALE LYNCHING

SHOCKING STORY

"A Dalziel telegram[10] from Reading (Colorado)[11] states that advices received there from Blue Rock Park report a frightful instance of popular vengeance. For some time the neighbourhood has been terrorized by the crimes of a gang of desperadoes, who, under the cover of a carefully planned organization, have perpetrated the most infamous cruelties on men and women. A Vigilance Committee was formed, and it was found that the leader of the gang was a person named Smith, living in Blue Rock Park. Action was taken, and six of the worst in the band were summarily strangled in the presence of two or three hundred men and women. Smith is said to have escaped."

"This is a terrible story," said Dyson; "I can well believe that your days and nights are haunted by such fearful scenes, as you have described. But surely you have no need to fear Smith? He has much more cause to fear you. Consider: you have only to lay your information before the police, and a warrant would be immediately issued for his arrest. Besides, you will, I am sure, excuse me for what I am going to say."

"My dear sir," said Mr. Wilkins, "I hope you will speak to me with perfect freedom."

"Well, then, I must confess that my impression was that you were rather disappointed at not being able to stop the man before he drove off. I thought you seemed annoyed that you could not get across the street."

"Sir, I did not know what I was about. I caught sight of the man, but it was only for a moment, and the agony you witnessed was the agony of suspense. I was not perfectly certain of the face, and the horrible thought that Smith was again in London overwhelmed me. I shuddered at the idea of this incarnate fiend, whose soul is black with shocking crimes, mingling free and unobserved amongst the harmless crowds, meditating perhaps a new and more fearful cycle of infamies. I tell you, sir, that an awful being stalks through the streets, a being before whom the sunlight itself should blacken, and the summer air grow chill and dank. Such thoughts as these rushed upon me with the force of a whirlwind; I lost my senses."

"I see. I partly understand your feelings, but I would impress on you that you have nothing really to fear. Depend upon it, Smith will not molest you in any way. You must remember he himself has had a warning; and indeed, from the brief glance I had of him, he seemed to me to be a frightened-looking man. However, I see it is getting late, and if you will excuse me, Mr. Wilkins, I think I will be going. I dare say we shall often meet here."

Dyson walked off smartly, pondering the strange story chance had brought him, and finding on cool reflection that there was something a little strange in Mr. Wilkins's manner, for which not even so weird a catalogue of experiences could altogether account.

Adventure of the Missing Brother

Mr. Charles Phillipps was, as has been hinted, a gentleman of pronounced scientific tastes. In his early days he had devoted himself with fond enthusiasm to the agreeable study of biology, and a brief monograph on the Embryology of the Microscopic Holothuria[12] had formed his first contribution to the *belles lettres*. Later he had somewhat relaxed the severity of his pursuits, and had dabbled in the more frivolous subjects of palæontology and ethnology; he had a cabinet in his sitting-room whose drawers were stuffed with rude flint implements, and a charming fetish from the South Seas was the dominant note in the decorative scheme of the apartment. Flattering himself with the title of materialist, he was in truth one of the most credulous of men, but he required a marvel to be neatly draped in the robes of Science before he would give it any credit, and the wildest dreams took solid shape to him if only the nomenclature were severe and irreproachable. He laughed at the witch, but quailed before the powers of the hypnotist, lifting his eyebrows when Christianity was mentioned, but adoring protyle and the ether. For the rest, he prided himself on a boundless scepticism; the average tale of wonder he heard with nothing but contempt, and he would certainly not have credited a word or syllable of Dyson's story of the pursuer and pursued, unless the gold coin had been produced as visible and tangible evidence. As it was, he half suspected that Dyson had imposed upon him; he knew his friend's disordered fancies, and his habit of conjuring up the marvellous to account for the entirely commonplace; and, on the whole, he was inclined to think that the so-called facts in the odd adventure had been gravely distorted in the telling. Since the evening on which he had listened to the tale he paid Dyson a visit, and had delivered himself of some serious talk on the necessity of accurate observation, and the folly, as he put it, of using a kaleidoscope instead of a telescope in the view of things, to which remarks his friend had listened with a smile that was extremely sardonic. "My dear fellow," Dyson had remarked at last, "you will allow me to tell you that I see your drift perfectly. However, you will be astonished to hear that I consider you to be the visionary, while I am the sober and serious spectator of human life. You have gone round the circle; and while you fancy yourself far in the golden land of new philosophies, you are in reality a dweller in a metaphorical Clapham; your scepticism has defeated itself and become a monstrous credulity; you are, in fact, in the position of the bat or owl, I forget which it was, who denied the existence of the sun at noonday, and I shall be astonished if you do not one day come to me full of contrition for your manifold intellectual errors, with a humble resolution to see things in their true light for the future." This tirade had left Mr. Phillipps unimpressed; he considered Dyson as hopeless, and he went home to gloat over some primitive stone implements that a friend had sent him from India. He found that his landlady, seeing them displayed in all their rude formlessness upon the table, had removed the collection to the dustbin, and had replaced it by lunch; and the afternoon was spent in malodorous research. Mrs. Brown, hearing these stones spoken of as very valuable knives, had called him in his hearing "poor Mr. Phillipps," and between rage and evil odours he spent a sorry afternoon. It was four o'clock before he had completed his work of rescue; and overpowered with the flavours of decaying cabbage leaves, Phillipps felt that he must have a walk to gain an appetite for the evening meal. Unlike Dyson he walked fast, with his eyes on the pavement, absorbed in his thoughts, and oblivious of the life around him; and he could not have told by what streets he had passed, when he suddenly lifted up his eyes and found himself in Leicester Square. The grass and flowers pleased him, and he welcomed the opportunity of resting for a few minutes, and glancing round, he saw a bench which had only one occupant, a lady, and as she was seated at one end, Phillipps took up a position at the other extremity, and began to pass in angry review the events of the afternoon. He had noticed as he came up to the bench that the person already there was neatly dressed, and to all appearance young; her face he could not see, as it was turned away in apparent contemplation of the shrubs, and, moreover, shielded with her hand; but it would be doing wrong to Mr. Phillipps to imagine that his choice of seat was dictated by any hopes of an affair of the heart, he had simply preferred the company of one lady to that of five dirty children, and having seated himself, was immersed directly in thoughts of his misfortunes. He had meditated changing his lodgings; but now, on a judicial review of the case in all its bearings, his calmer judgment told him that the race of landladies is like to the race of the leaves, and that there was but little to choose between them. He resolved, however, to talk to Mrs. Brown, the offender, very coolly and yet severely, to point out the extreme indiscretion of her conduct, and to express a hope for better things in the future. With this decision registered in his mind, Phillipps was about to get up from the seat and move off, when he was intensely annoyed to hear a stifled sob, evidently from the lady, who still continued her contemplation of the shrubs and flower-beds. He clutched his stick desperately, and in a moment would have been in full retreat, when the lady turned her face towards him, and with mute entreaty bespoke his attention. She was a young girl with a quaint and piquant rather than a beautiful face, and she was evidently in the bitterest distress. Mr. Phillipps sat down again, and cursed his chances heartily. The young lady looked at him with a pair of charming eyes of a shining hazel, which showed no trace of tears, though a handkerchief was in her hand; she bit her lip, and seemed to struggle with some overpowering grief, and her whole attitude was all-beseeching and imploring. Phillipps sat on the edge of the bench gazing awkwardly at her, and wondering what was to come next, and she looked at him still without speaking.

"Well, madam," he said at last, "I understood from your gesture that you wished to speak to me. Is there anything I can do for you? Though, if you will pardon me, I cannot help saying that that seems highly improbable."

"Ah, sir," she said in a low, murmuring voice, "do not speak harshly to me. I am in sore straits, and I thought from your face that I could safely ask your sympathy, if not your help."

"Would you kindly tell me what is the matter?" said Phillipps. "Perhaps you would like some tea?"

"I knew I could not be mistaken," the lady replied. "That offer of refreshment bespeaks a generous mind. But tea, alas! is powerless to console me. If you will let me, I shall endeavour to explain my trouble."

"I should be glad if you would."

"I shall do so, and I shall try to be brief, in spite of the numerous complications which have made me, young as I am, tremble before what seems the profound and terrible mystery of existence. Yet the grief which now racks my very soul is but too simple; I have lost my brother."

"Lost your brother! How on earth can that be?"

Arthur Machen

"I see I must trouble you with a few particulars. My brother, then, who is by some years my elder, is a tutor in a private school in the extreme north of London. The want of means deprived him of the advantages of a University education; and lacking the stamp of a degree, he could not hope for that position which his scholarship and his talents entitled him to claim. He was thus forced to accept the post of classical master at Dr. Saunderson's Highgate Academy for the Sons of Gentlemen, and he has performed his duties with perfect satisfaction to his principal for some years. My personal history need not trouble you; it will be enough if I tell you that for the last month I have been governess in a family residing at Tooting. My brother and I have always cherished the warmest mutual affection; and though circumstances into which I need not enter have kept us apart for some time, yet we have never lost sight of one another. We made up our minds that unless one of us was absolutely unable to rise from a bed of sickness, we should never let a week pass by without meeting, and some time ago we chose this square as our rendezvous on account of its central position and its convenience of access. And indeed, after a week of distasteful toil, my brother felt little inclination for much walking, and we have often spent two or three hours on this bench, speaking of our prospects and of happier days, when we were children. In the early spring it was cold and chilly; still we enjoyed the short respite, and I think that we were often taken for a pair of lovers as we sat close together, eagerly talking. Saturday after Saturday we have met each other here; and though the doctor told him it was madness, my brother would not allow the influenza to break the appointment. That was some time ago; last Saturday we had a long and happy afternoon, and separated more cheerfully than usual, feeling that the coming week would be bearable, and resolving that our next meeting should be if possible still more pleasant. I arrived here at the time agreed upon, four o'clock, and sat down and watched for my brother, expecting every moment to see him advancing towards me from the gate at the north side of the square. Five minutes passed by, and he had not arrived; I thought he must have missed his train, and the idea that our interview would be cut short by twenty minutes, or perhaps half an hour, saddened me; I had hoped we should be so happy together to-day. Suddenly, moved by I know not what impulse, I turned abruptly round, and how can I describe to you my astonishment when I saw my brother advancing slowly towards me from the southern side of the square, accompanied by another person? My first thought, I remember, had in it something of resentment that this man, whoever he was, should intrude himself into our meeting; I wondered who it could possibly be, for my brother had, I may say, no intimate friends. Then as I looked still at the advancing figures, another feeling took possession of me; it was a sensation of bristling fear, the fear of the child in the dark, unreasonable and unreasoning, but terrible, clutching at my heart as with the cold grip of a dead man's hands. Yet I overcame the feeling, and looked steadily at my brother, waiting for him to speak, and more closely at his companion. Then I noticed that this man was leading my brother rather than walking arm-in-arm with him; he was a tall man, dressed in quite ordinary fashion. He wore a high bowler hat, and, in spite of the warmth of the day, a plain black overcoat, tightly buttoned, and I noticed his trousers, of a quiet black and grey stripe. The face was commonplace too, and indeed I cannot recall any special features, or any trick of expression; for though I looked at him as he came near, curiously enough his face made no impression on me—it was as though I had seen a well-made mask. They passed in front of me, and to my unutterable astonishment, I heard my brother's voice speaking to me, though his lips did not move, nor his eyes look into mine. It was a voice I cannot describe, though I knew it, but the words came to my ears as if mingled with splashing water and the sound of a shallow brook flowing amidst stones. I heard, then, the words, 'I cannot stay,' and for a moment the heavens and the earth seemed to rush together with the sound of thunder, and I was thrust forth from the world into a black void without beginning and without end. For, as my brother passed me, I saw the hand that held him by the arm, and seemed to guide him, and in one moment of horror I realized that it was a formless thing that has mouldered for many years in the grave. The flesh was peeled in strips from the bones, and hung apart dry and granulated, and the fingers that encircled my brother's arm were all unshapen, claw-like things, and one was but a stump from which the end had rotted off. When I recovered my senses I saw the two passing out by the gate. I paused for a moment, and then with a rush of fire to my heart I knew that no horror could stay me, but that I must follow my brother and save him, even though all hell rose up against me. I ran out, and looked up the pavement, and saw the two figures walking amidst the crowd. I ran across the road, and saw them turn up that side street, and I reached the corner a moment later. In vain I looked to right and left, for neither my brother nor his strange guardian was in sight; two elderly men were coming down arm-in-arm, and a telegraph boy was walking lustily along whistling. I remained there a moment horrorstruck, and then I bowed my head and returned to this seat, where you found me. Now, sir, do you wonder at my grief? Oh, tell me what has happened to my brother, or I feel I shall go mad!"

Mr. Phillipps, who had listened with exemplary, patience to this tale, hesitated a moment before he spoke.

"My dear madam," he said at length, "you have known how to engage me in your service, not only as a man, but as a student of science. As a fellow-creature I pity you most profoundly; you must have suffered extremely from what you saw, or rather from what you fancied you saw. For, as a scientific observer, it is my duty to tell you the plain truth, which, indeed, besides being true, must also console you. Allow me to ask you then to describe your brother."

"Certainly," said the lady eagerly; "I can describe him accurately. My brother is a somewhat young-looking man; he is pale, has small black whiskers, and wears spectacles. He has rather a timid, almost a frightened expression, and looks about him nervously from side to side. Think, think! Surely you must have seen him. Perhaps you are an *habitué* of this engaging quarter; you may have met him on some previous Saturday. I may have been mistaken in supposing that he turned up that side street; he may have gone on, and you may have passed each other. Oh, tell me, sir, whether you have not seen him!"

"I am afraid I do not keep a very sharp lookout when I am walking," said Phillipps, who would have passed his mother unnoticed; "but I am sure your description is admirable. And now will you describe the person who, you say, held your brother by the arm?"

"I cannot do so. I told you his face seemed devoid of expression or salient feature. It was like a mask."

"Exactly; you cannot describe what you have never seen. I need hardly point out to you the conclusion to be drawn; you have been the victim of an hallucination. You expected to see your brother, you were alarmed because you did not see him, and unconsciously, no doubt, your brain went to work, and finally you saw a mere projection of your own morbid thoughts—a vision of your absent brother, and a mere confusion of terrors incorporated in a figure which you can't describe. Of course your brother has been in some way prevented from coming to meet you as usual. I expect you will hear from him in a day or two."

The lady looked seriously at Mr. Phillipps, and then for a second there seemed almost a twinkling as of mirth about her eyes, but her face clouded sadly at the dogmatic conclusions to which the scientist was led so irresistibly.

"Ah!" she said, "you do not know. I cannot doubt the evidence of my waking senses. Besides, perhaps I have had experiences even more terrible. I acknowledge the force of your arguments, but a woman has intuitions which never deceive her. Believe me, I am not hysterical; feel my pulse, it is quite regular."

She stretched out her hand with a dainty gesture, and a glance that enraptured Phillipps in spite of himself. The hand held out to him was soft and white and warm, and as, in some confusion, he placed his fingers on the purple vein, he felt profoundly touched by the spectacle of love and grief before him.

"No," he said, as he released her wrist, "as you say, you are evidently quite yourself. Still, you must be aware that living men do not possess dead hands. That sort of thing doesn't happen. It is, of course, barely possible that you did see your brother with another gentleman, and that important business prevented him from stopping. As for the wonderful hand, there may have been some deformity, a finger shot off by accident, or something of that sort."

The lady shook her head mournfully.

"I see you are a determined rationalist," she said. "Did you not hear me say that I have had experiences even more terrible? I too was once a sceptic, but after what I have known I can no longer doubt."

"Madam," replied Mr. Phillipps, "no one shall make me deny my faith. I will never believe, nor will pretend to believe that two and two make five, nor will I on any pretences admit the existence of two-sided triangles."

"You are a little hasty," rejoined the lady. "But may I ask you if you ever heard the name of Professor Gregg, the authority on ethnology and kindred subjects?"

"I have done much more than merely hear of Professor Gregg," said Phillipps. "I always regarded him as one of our most acute and clearheaded observers; and his last publication, the '*Textbook of Ethnology*,' struck me as being admirable in its kind. Indeed, the book had but come into my hands when I heard of the terrible accident which cut short Gregg's career. He had, I think, taken a country house in the West of England for the summer, and is supposed to have fallen into a river. So far as I remember, his body was never recovered."

"Sir, I am sure that you are discreet. Your conversation seems to declare as much, and the very title of that little work of yours which you mentioned assures me that you are no empty trifler. In a word, I feel that I may depend on you. You appear to be under the impression that Professor Gregg is dead; I have no reason to believe that that is the case."

"What?" cried Phillipps, astonished and perturbed. "You do not hint that there was anything disgraceful? I cannot believe it. Gregg was a man of the clearest character; his private life was one of great benevolence; and though I myself am free from delusions, I believe him to have been a sincere and devout Christian. Surely you cannot mean to insinuate that some disreputable history forced him to flee the country?"

"Again you are in a hurry," replied the lady. "I said nothing of all this. Briefly, then, I must tell you that Professor Gregg left his house one morning in full health both of mind and body. He never returned, but his watch and chain, a purse containing three sovereigns in gold, and some loose silver, with a ring that he wore habitually, were found three days later on a wild and savage hillside, many miles from the river. These articles were placed beside a limestone rock of fantastic form; they had been wrapped into a parcel with a kind of rough parchment which was secured with gut. The parcel was opened, and the inner side of the parchment bore an inscription done with some red substance; the characters were undecipherable, but seemed to be a corrupt cuneiform."

"You interest me intensely," said Phillipps. "Would you mind continuing your story? The circumstance you have mentioned seems to me of the most inexplicable character, and I thirst for elucidation."

The young lady seemed to meditate for a moment, and she then proceeded to relate the

NOVEL OF THE BLACK SEAL

I must now give you some fuller particulars of my history. I am the daughter of a civil engineer, Steven Lally by name, who was so unfortunate as to die suddenly at the outset of his career, and before he had accumulated sufficient means to support his wife and her two children.

My mother contrived to keep the small household going on resources which must have been incredibly small; we lived in a remote country village, because most of the necessaries of life were cheaper than in a town, but even so we were brought up with the severest economy. My father was a clever and well-read man, and left behind him a small but select collection of books, containing the best Greek, Latin, and English classics, and these books were the only amusement we possessed. My brother, I remember, learnt Latin out of Descartes' "*Meditationes*,"[13] and I, in place of the little tales which children are usually told to read, had nothing more charming than a translation of the "*Gesta Romanorum*."[14] We grew up thus, quiet, and studious children, and in course of time my brother provided for himself in the manner I have mentioned. I continued to live at home; my poor mother had become an invalid, and demanded my continual care, and about two years ago she died after many months of painful illness. My situation was a terrible one; the shabby furniture barely sufficed to pay the debts I had been forced to contract, and the books I dispatched to my brother, knowing how he would value them. I was absolutely alone; I was aware how poorly my brother was paid; and though I came up to London in the hope of finding employment, with the understanding that he would defray my expenses, I swore it should only be for a month, and that if I could not in that time find some work, I would starve rather than deprive him of the few miserable pounds he had laid by for his day of trouble. I took a little room in a distant suburb, the cheapest that I could find; I lived on bread and tea, and I spent my time in vain answering of advertisements, and vainer walks to addresses I had noted.[15] Day followed on day, and week on week, and still I was unsuccessful, till at last the term I had appointed drew to a close, and I saw before me the grim prospect of slowly dying of starvation. My landlady was good-natured in her way; she knew the slenderness of my means, and I am sure that she would not have turned me out of doors; it remained for me then to go away, and to try to die in some quiet place. It was winter then and a thick white fog gathered in the early part of the afternoon, becoming more dense as the day wore on; it was a Sunday, I remember, and the people of the house were at chapel. At about three o'clock I crept out and walked away as quickly as I could, for I was weak from abstinence. The white mist wrapped all the streets in silence, a hard frost had gathered thick upon the bare branches of the trees, and frost crystals glittered on the wooden fences, and on the cold, cruel ground beneath my feet. I walked on, turning to right and left in utter haphazard, without caring to look up at the names of the streets, and all that I remember of my walk on that Sunday afternoon seems but the broken fragments of an evil dream. In a confused vision I stumbled on, through roads half town and half country, grey fields melting into the cloudy world of mist on one side of me, and on the other comfortable villas with a glow of firelight flickering on the walls, but all unreal; red brick walls and lighted windows, vague trees, and glimmering country, gas-lamps beginning to star the white shadows, the vanishing perspectives of the railway line beneath high embankments, the green and red of the signal lamps,—all these were but momentary pictures flashed on my tired brain and senses numbed by hunger. Now and then I would hear a quick step ringing on the iron road, and men would pass me well wrapped up, walking fast for the sake of warmth, and no doubt eagerly foretasting the pleasures of a glowing hearth, with curtains tightly drawn about the frosted panes, and the welcomes of their friends; but as the early evening darkened and night approached, foot-passengers got fewer and fewer, and I passed through street after street alone. In the white silence I stumbled on, as desolate as if I trod the streets of a buried city; and as I grew more weak and exhausted, something of the horror of death was folding thickly round my heart. Suddenly, as I turned a corner, some one accosted me courteously beneath the lamp-post, and I heard a voice asking if I could kindly point the way to Avon Road. At the sudden shock of human accents I was prostrated, and my strength gave way; I fell all huddled on the sidewalk, and wept and sobbed and laughed in violent hysteria. I had gone out prepared to die, and as I stepped across the threshold that had sheltered me, I consciously bade adieu to all hopes and all remembrances; the door clanged behind me with the noise of thunder, and I felt that an iron curtain had fallen on the brief passages of my life, that henceforth I was to walk a little way in a world of gloom and shadow; I entered on the stage of the first act of death. Then came my wandering in the mist, the whiteness wrapping all things, the void streets, and muffled silence, till when that voice spoke to me it was as if I had died and life returned to me. In a few minutes I was able to compose my feelings, and as I rose I saw that I was confronted by a middle-aged gentleman of pleasing appearance, neatly and correctly dressed. He looked at me with an expression of great pity, but before I could stammer out my ignorance of the neighbourhood, for indeed I had not the slightest notion of where I had wandered, he spoke.

"My dear madam," he said, "you seem in some terrible distress. You cannot think how you alarmed me. But may I inquire the nature of your trouble? I assure you that you can safely confide in me."

"You are very kind," I replied, "but I fear there is nothing to be done. My condition seems a hopeless one."

"Oh, nonsense, nonsense! You are too young to talk like that. Come, let us walk down here, and you must tell me your difficulty. Perhaps I may be able to help you."

There was something very soothing and persuasive in his manner, and as we walked together I gave him an outline of my story, and told of the despair that had oppressed me almost to death.

"You were wrong to give in so completely," he said, when I was silent. "A month is too short a time in which to feel one's way in London. London, let me tell you, Miss Lally, does not lie open and undefended; it is a fortified place, fossed and double-moated with curious intricacies. As must always happen in large towns, the conditions of life have become hugely artificial; no mere simple palisade is run up to oppose the man or woman who would take the place by storm, but serried lines of subtle contrivances, mines, and pitfalls which it needs a strange skill to overcome. You, in your simplicity, fancied you had only to shout for these walls to sink into nothingness, but the time is gone for such startling victories as these. Take courage; you will learn the secret of success before long."

"Alas! sir," I replied, "I have no doubt your conclusions are correct, but at the present moment I seem to be in a fair way to die of starvation. You spoke of a secret; for heaven's sake tell it me, if you have any pity for my distress."

He laughed genially. "There lies the strangeness of it all. Those who know the secret cannot tell it if they would; it is positively as ineffable as the central doctrine of Freemasonry. But I may say this, that you yourself have penetrated at least the outer husk of the mystery," and he laughed again.

"Pray do not jest with me," I said. "What have I done, *que sçais-je*.[216] I am so far ignorant that I have not the slightest idea of how my next meal is to be provided."

"Excuse me. You ask what you have done. You have met me. Come, we will fence no longer. I see you have self-education, the only education which is not infinitely pernicious, and I am in want of a governess for my two children. I have been a widower for some years; my name is Gregg. I offer you the post I have named, and shall we say a salary of a hundred a year?"

I could only stutter out my thanks, and slipping a card with his address, and a banknote by way of earnest into my hand, Mr Gregg bade me good-bye, asking me to call in a day or two.

Such was my introduction to Professor Gregg, and can you wonder that the remembrance of despair and the cold blast that had blown from the gates of death upon me made me regard him as a second father? Before the close of the week I was installed in my new duties. The professor had leased an old brick manor-house in a western suburb of London, and here, surrounded by pleasant lawns and orchards, and soothed with the murmur of ancient elms that rocked their boughs above the roof, the new chapter of my life began. Knowing as you do the nature of the professor's occupations, you will not be surprised to hear that the house teemed with books, and cabinets full of strange, and even hideous, objects filled every available nook in the vast low rooms. Gregg was a man whose one thought was for knowledge, and I too before long caught something of his enthusiasm,, and strove to enter into his passion for research. In a few months I was perhaps more his secretary than the governess of the two children, and many a night I have sat at the desk in the glow of the shaded lamp while he, pacing up and down in the rich gloom of the firelight, dictated to me the substance of his "*Textbook of Ethnology.*" But amidst these more sober and accurate studies I always detected a something hidden, a longing and desire for some object to which he did not allude; and now and then he would break short in what he was saying and lapse into reverie, entranced, as it seemed to me, by some distant prospect of adventurous discovery. The textbook was at last finished, and we began to receive proofs from the printers, which were entrusted to me for a first reading, and then underwent the final revision of the professor. All the while his weariness of the actual business he was engaged on increased, and it was with the joyous laugh of a schoolboy when term is over that he one day handed me a copy of the book. "There," he said, "I have kept my word; I promised to write it, and it is done with. Now I shall be free to live for stranger things; I confess it, Miss Lally, I covet the renown of Columbus; you will, I hope, see me play the part of an explorer."

"Surely," I said, "there is little left to explore. You have been born a few hundred years too late for that."

"I think you are wrong," he replied; "there are still, depend upon it, quaint, undiscovered countries and continents of strange extent. Ah, Miss Lally! believe me, we stand amidst sacraments and mysteries full of awe, and it doth not yet appear what we shall be. Life, believe me, is no simple thing, no mass of grey matter and congeries of veins and muscles to be laid naked by the surgeon's knife; man is the secret which I am about to explore, and before I can discover him I must cross over weltering seas indeed, and oceans and the mists of many thousand years. You know the myth of the lost Atlantis; what if it be true, and I am destined to be called the discoverer of that wonderful land?"

I could see the excitement boiling beneath his words, and in his face was the heat of the hunter; before me stood a man who believed himself summoned to tourney with the unknown. A pang of joy possessed me when I reflected that I was to be in a way associated with him in the adventure, and I too burned with the lust of the chase, not pausing to consider that I knew not what we were to unshadow.

The next morning Professor Gregg took me into his inner study, where, ranged against the wall, stood a nest of pigeon-holes, every drawer neatly labelled, and the results of years of toil classified in a few feet of space.

"Here," he said, "is my life; here are all the facts which I have gathered together with so much pains, and yet it is all nothing. No, nothing to what I am about to attempt. Look at this"; and he took me to an old bureau, a piece fantastic and faded, which stood in a corner of the room. He unlocked the front and opened one of the drawers.

"A few scraps of paper," he went on, pointing to the drawer, "and a lump of black stone, rudely annotated with queer marks and scratch-es—that is all that drawer holds. Here you see is an old envelope with the dark red stamp of twenty years ago, but I have pencilled a few lines at the back; here is a sheet of manuscript, and here some cuttings from obscure local journals. And if you ask me the subject-matter of the col-lection, it will not seem extraordinary—a servant-girl at a farmhouse, who disappeared from her place and has never been heard of, a child supposed to have slipped down some old working on the mountains, some queer scribbling on a limestone rock, a man murdered with a blow from a strange weapon; such is the scent I have to go upon. Yes, as you say, there is a ready explanation for all this; the girl may have run away to London, or Liverpool, or New York; the child may be at the bottom of the disused shaft; and the letters on the rock may be the idle whims of some vagrant. Yes, yes, I admit all that; but I know I hold the true key. Look!" and he held out a slip of yellow paper.

Characters found inscribed on a limestone rock on the Grey Hills, I read, and then there was a word erased, presumably the name of a county, and a date some fifteen years back. Beneath was traced a number of uncouth characters, shaped somewhat like wedges or daggers, as strange and outlandish as the Hebrew alphabet.

"Now the seal," said Professor Gregg, and he handed me the black stone, a thing about two inches long, and something like an old-fashioned tobacco-stopper, much enlarged.

I held it up to the light, and saw to my surprise the characters on the paper repeated on the seal.

"Yes," said the professor, "they are the same. And the marks on the limestone rock were made fifteen years ago, with some red sub-stance. And the characters on the seal are four thousand years old at least. Perhaps much more."

"Is it a hoax?" I said.

"No, I anticipated that. I was not to be led to give my life to a practical joke. I have tested the matter very carefully. Only one person besides myself knows of the mere existence of that black seal. Besides, there are other reasons which I cannot enter into now."

"But what does it all mean?" I said. "I cannot understand to what conclusion all this leads."

"My dear Miss Lally, that is a question I would rather leave un-answered for some little time. Perhaps I shall never be able to say what secrets are held here in solution; a few vague hints, the outlines of vil-lage tragedies, a few marks done with red earth upon a rock, and an ancient seal. A queer set of data to go upon? Half a dozen pieces of evidence, and twenty years before even so much could be got together;

and who knows what mirage or *terra incognita*[17] may be beyond all this? I look across deep waters, Miss Lally, and the land beyond may be but a haze after all. But still I believe it is not so, and a few months will show whether I am right or wrong."

He left me, and alone I endeavoured to fathom the mystery, wondering to what goal such eccentric odds and ends of evidence could lead. I myself am not wholly devoid of imagination, and I had reason to respect the professor's solidity of intellect; yet I saw in the contents of the drawer but the materials of fantasy, and vainly tried to conceive what theory could be founded on the fragments that had been placed before me. Indeed, I could discover in what I had heard and seen but the first chapter of an extravagant romance; and yet deep in my heart I burned with curiosity, and day after day I looked eagerly in Professor Gregg's face for some hint of what was to happen.

It was one evening after dinner that the word came.

"I hope you can make your preparations without much trouble," he said suddenly to me. "We shall be leaving here in a week's time."

"Really!" I said in astonishment. "Where are we going?"

"I have taken a country house in the west of England, not far from Caermaen, a quiet little town, once a city, and the headquarters of a Roman legion. It is very dull there, but the country is pretty, and the air is wholesome."

I detected a glint in his eyes, and guessed that this sudden move had some relation to our conversation of a few days before.

"I shall just take a few books with me," said Professor Gregg, "that is all. Everything else will remain here for our return. I have got a holiday," he went on, smiling at me, "and I shan't be sorry to be quit for a time of my old bones and stones and rubbish. Do you know," he went on, "I have been grinding away at facts for thirty years; it is time for fancies."

The days passed quickly; I could see that the professor was all quivering with suppressed excitement, and I could scarce credit the eager appetence of his glance as we left the old manorhouse behind us and began our journey. We set out at midday, and it was in the dusk of the evening that we arrived at a little county station. I was tired and excited, and the drive through the lanes seems all a dream. First the deserted streets of a forgotten village, while I heard Professor Gregg's voice talking of the Augustan Legion and the clash of arms, and all the tremendous pomp that followed the eagles; then the broad river swimming to full tide with the last afterglow glimmering duskily in the yellow water, the wide meadows, the cornfields whitening, and the deep lane winding on the slope between the hills and the water. At last we began to ascend, and the air grew rarer. I looked down and saw the pure white mist tracking the outline of the river like a shroud, and a vague and shadowy country; imaginations and fantasy of swelling hills and hanging woods, and half-shaped outlines of hills beyond, and in the distance the glare of the furnace fire on the mountain, growing by turns a pillar of shining flame and fading to a dull point of red. We were slowly mounting a carriage drive, and then there came to me the cool breath and the secret of the great wood that was above us; I seemed to wander in its deepest depths, and there was the sound of trickling water, the scent of the green leaves, and the breath of the summer night. The carriage stopped at last, and I could scarcely distinguish the form of the house as I waited a moment at the pillared porch. The rest of the evening seemed a dream of strange things bounded by the great silence of the wood and the valley and the river.

The next morning, when I awoke and looked out of the bow window of the big, old-fashioned bedroom, I saw under a grey sky a country that was still all mystery. The long, lovely valley, with the river winding in and out below, crossed in mid-vision by a mediæval bridge of vaulted and buttressed stone, the clear presence of the rising ground beyond, and the woods that I had only seen in shadow the night before, seemed tinged with enchantment, and the soft breath of air that sighed in at the opened pane was like no other wind. I looked across the valley, and beyond, hill followed on hill as wave on wave, and here a faint blue pillar of smoke rose still in the morning air from the chimney of an ancient grey farmhouse, there was a rugged height crowned with dark firs, and in the distance I saw the white streak of a road that climbed and vanished into some unimagined country. But the boundary of all was a great wall of mountain, vast in the west, and ending like a fortress with a steep ascent and a domed tumulus clear against the sky.

I saw Professor Gregg walking up and down the terrace path below the windows, and it was evident that he was revelling in the sense of liberty, and the thought that he had for a while bidden good-bye to task-work. When I joined him there was exultation in his voice as he pointed out the sweep of valley and the river that wound beneath the lovely hills.

"Yes," he said, "it is a strangely beautiful country; and to me, at least, it seems full of mystery. You have not forgotten the drawer I showed you, Miss Lally? No; and you guessed that I have come here not merely for the sake of the children and the fresh air?"

"I think I have guessed as much as that," I replied; "but you must remember I do not know the mere nature of your investigations; and as for the connection between the search and this wonderful valley, it is past my guessing."

He smiled queerly at me. "You must not think I am making a mystery for the sake of a mystery," he said. "I do not speak out because, so far, there is nothing to be spoken, nothing definite, I mean, nothing that can be set down in hard black and white, as dull and sure and irreproachable as any blue-book. And then I have another reason: Many years ago a chance paragraph in a newspaper caught my attention, and focussed in an instant the vagrant thoughts and half-formed fancies of many idle and speculative hours into a certain hypothesis. I saw at once that I was treading on a thin crust; my theory was wild and fantastic in the extreme, and I would not for any consideration have written a hint of it for publication. But I thought that in the company of scientific men like myself, men who knew the course of discovery, and were aware that the gas that blazes and flares in the gin-palace was once a wild hypothesis—I thought that with such men as these I might hazard my dream—let us say Atlantis, or the philosopher's stone, or what you like—without danger of ridicule. I found I was grossly mistaken; my friends looked blankly at me and at one another, and I could see something of pity, and something also of insolent contempt, in the glances they exchanged. One of them called on me next day, and hinted that I must be suffering from overwork and brain exhaustion. 'In plain terms,' I said, 'you think I am going mad. I think not'; and I showed him out with some little appearance of heat. Since that day I vowed that I would never whisper the nature of my theory to any living soul; to no one but yourself have I ever shown the contents of that drawer. After all, I may be following a rainbow; I may have been misled by the play of coincidence; but as I stand here in this mystic hush and silence amidst the woods and the wild hills, I am more than ever sure that I am hot on the scent. Come, it is time we went in."

To me in all this there was something both of wonder and excitement; I knew how in his ordinary work Professor Gregg moved step by step, testing every inch of the way, and never venturing on assertion without proof that was impregnable. Yet I divined more from his glance and the vehemence of his tone than from the spoken word, that he had in his every thought the vision of the almost incredible continually with him; and I, who was with some share of imagination no little of a sceptic, offended at a hint of the marvellous, could not help asking myself whether he were cherishing a monomania, and barring out from this one subject all the scientific method of his other life.

Yet, with this image of mystery haunting my thoughts, I surrendered wholly to the charm of the country. Above the faded house on the hillside began the great forest—a long, dark line seen from the opposing hills, stretching above the river for many a mile from north to south, and yielding in the north to even wilder country, barren and savage hills, and ragged common-land, a territory all strange and un-visited, and more unknown to Englishmen than the very heart of Africa. The space of a couple of steep fields alone separated the house from the wood, and the children were delighted to follow me up the long alleys of undergrowth, between smooth pleached walls of shining beech, to the highest point in the wood, whence one looked on one side across the river and the rise and fall of the country to the great western mountain wall, and on the other over the surge and dip of the myriad trees of the forest, over level meadows and the shining yellow sea to the faint coast beyond. I used to sit at this point on the warm sunlit turf which marked the track of the Roman Road, while the two children raced about hunting for the whinberries that grew here and there on the banks. Here beneath the deep blue sky and the great clouds rolling, like olden galleons with sails full-bellied, from the sea to the hills, as I listened to the whispered charm of the great and ancient wood, I lived solely for delight, and only remembered strange things when we would return to the house and find Professor Gregg either shut up in the little room he had made his study, or else pacing the terrace with the look, patient and enthusiastic, of the determined seeker.

One morning, some eight or nine days after our arrival, I looked out of my window and saw the whole landscape transmuted before me. The clouds had dipped low and hidden the mountain in the west; a southern wind was driving the rain in shifting pillars up the valley, and the little brooklet that burst the hill below the house now raged, a red torrent, down to the river. We were perforce obliged to keep snug within-doors; and when I had attended to my pupils, I sat down in the morning-room where the ruins of a library still encumbered an old-fashioned bookcase. I had inspected the shelves once or twice, but their contents had failed to attract me; volumes of eighteenth-century sermons, an old book on farriery,[18] a collection of *Poems* by "persons of quality," Prideaux's *Connection*,[19] and an odd volume of Pope, were the boundaries of the library, and there seemed little doubt that every-thing of interest or value had been removed. Now however, in despera-tion, I began to re-examine the musty sheepskin and calf bindings, and found, much to my delight, a fine old quarto printed by the Stephani,[20] containing the three books of Pomponius Mela, *De Situ Orbis*,[21] and other of the ancient geographers. I knew enough of Latin to steer my way through an ordinary sentence, and I soon became absorbed in the odd mixture of fact and fancy—light shining on a little space of the world, and beyond, mist and shadow and awful forms. Glancing over the clear-printed pages, my attention was caught by the heading of a chapter in Solinus,[22] and I read the words:—

"MIRA DE INTIMIS GENTIBUS LIBYAE, DE LAPIDE HEXECONTALITHO,"

—"The wonders of the people that inhabit the inner parts of Libya, and of the stone called Sixtystone."

The odd title attracted me, and I read on: "Gens ista avia et secreta habitat, in montibus horrendis foeda mysteria celebrat. De hominibus nihil aliud illi praeferunt quam figuram, ab humano ritu prorsus exulant, oderunt deum lucis. Stridunt potius quam loquuntur; vox absona nee sine horrore auditur. Lapide quodam gloriantur, quem Hexecontalithon vocant; dicunt enim hunc lapidem sexaginta notas ostendere. Cujus lapidis nomen secretum ineffabile colunt: quod Ixaxar."

"This folk," I translated to myself, "dwells in remote and secret places, and celebrates foul mysteries on savage hills. Nothing have they in common with men save the face, and the customs of humanity are wholly strange to them; and they hate the sun. They hiss rather than speak; their voices are harsh, and not to be heard without fear. They boast of a certain stone, which they call Sixtystone; for they say that it displays sixty characters. And this stone has a secret unspeakable name; which is Ixaxar."

I laughed at the queer inconsequence of all this, and thought it fit for "Sinbad the Sailor," or other of the supplementary Nights.[23] When I saw Professor Gregg in the course of the day, I told him of my find in the bookcase, and the fantastic rubbish I had been reading. To my surprise he looked up at me with an expression of great interest.

"That is really very curious," he said. "I have never thought it worth while to look into the old geographers, and I dare say I have missed a good deal. Ah, that is the passage, is it? It seems a shame to rob you of your entertainment, but I really think I must carry off the book."

The next day the professor called me to come to the study. I found him sitting at a table in the full light of the window, scrutinizing something very attentively with a magnifying glass.

"Ah, Miss Lally," he began, "I want to use your eyes. This glass is pretty good, but not like my old one that I left in town. Would you mind examining the thing yourself, and telling me how many characters are cut on it?"

He handed me the object in his hand. I saw that it was the black seal he had shown me in London, and my heart began to beat with the thought that I was presently to know something. I took the seal, and, holding it up to the light, checked off the grotesque dagger-shaped characters one by one.

"I make sixty-two," I said at last.

"Sixty-two? Nonsense; it's impossible. Ah, I see what you have done, you have counted that and that," and he pointed to two marks which I had certainly taken as letters with the rest.

"Yes, yes," Professor Gregg went on, "but those are obvious scratches, done accidentally; I saw that at once. Yes, then that's quite right. Thank you very much, Miss Lally."

I was going away, rather disappointed at my having been called in merely to count the number of marks on the black seal, when suddenly there flashed into my mind what I had read in the morning.

"But, Professor Gregg," I cried, breathless, "the seal, the seal. Why, it is the stone Hexecontalithos that Solinus writes of; it is Ixaxar."

"Yes," he said, "I suppose it is. Or it may be a mere coincidence. It never does to be too sure, you know, in these matters. Coincidence killed the professor."

I went away puzzled at what I had heard, and as much as ever at a loss to find the ruling clue in this maze of strange evidence. For three days the bad weather lasted, changing from driving rain to a dense mist, fine and dripping, and we seemed to be shut up in a white cloud that veiled all the world away from us. All the while Professor Gregg was darkling in his room, unwilling, it appeared, to dispense confidences or talk of any kind, and I heard him walking to and fro with a quick, impatient step, as if he were in some way wearied of inaction. The fourth morning was fine, and at breakfast the professor said briskly—

"We want some extra help around the house; a boy of fifteen or sixteen, you know. There are a lot of little odd jobs that take up the maids' time which a boy could do much better."

"The girls have not complained to me in any way," I replied. "Indeed, Anne said there was much less work than in London, owing to there being so little dust."

"Ah, yes, they are very good girls. But I think we shall do much better with a boy. In fact, that is what has been bothering me for the last two days."

"Bothering you?" I said in astonishment, for as a matter of fact the professor never took the slightest interest in the affairs of the house.

"Yes," he said, "the weather, you know. I really couldn't go out in that Scotch mist; I don't know the country very well, and I should have lost my way. But I am going to get the boy this morning."

"But how do you know there is such a boy as you want anywhere about?"

"Oh, I have no doubt as to that. I may have to walk a mile or two at the most, but I am sure to find just the boy I require."

I thought the professor was joking, but though his tone was airy enough there was something grim and set about his features that puzzled me. He got his stick, and stood at the door looking meditatively before him, and as I passed through the hall he called to me.

"By the way, Miss Lally, there was one thing I wanted to say to you. I dare say you may have heard that some of these country lads are not over bright; idiotic would be a harsh word to use, and they are usually called 'naturals,' or something of the kind. I hope you won't mind if the boy I am after should turn out not too keen-witted; he will be perfectly harmless, of course, and blacking boots doesn't need much mental effort."

With that he was gone, striding up the road that led to the wood, and I remained stupefied; and then for the first time my astonishment was mingled with a sudden note of terror, arising I knew not whence, and all unexplained even to myself, and yet I felt about my heart for an instant something of the chill of death, and that shapeless, formless dread of the unknown that is worse than death itself. I tried to find courage in the sweet air that blew up from the sea, and in the sunlight after rain, but the mystic woods seemed to darken around me; and the vision of the river coiling between the reeds, and the silver grey of the ancient bridge, fashioned in my mind symbols of vague dread, as the mind of a child fashions terror from things harmless and familiar.

Two hours later Professor Gregg returned. I met him as he came down the road, and asked quietly if he had been able to find a boy.

"Oh, yes," he answered; "I found one easily enough. His name is Jervase Cradock, and I expect he will make himself very useful. His father has been dead for many years, and the mother, whom I saw, seemed very glad at the prospect of a few shillings extra coming in on Saturday nights. As I expected, he is not too sharp, has fits at times, the mother said; but as he will not be trusted with the china, that doesn't much matter, does it? And he is not in any way dangerous, you know, merely a little weak."

"When is he coming?"

"To-morrow morning at eight o'clock. Anne will show him what he has to do, and how to do it. At first he will go home every night, but perhaps it may ultimately turn out more convenient for him to sleep here, and only go home for Sundays."

I found nothing to say to all this; Professor Gregg spoke in a quiet tone of matter-of-fact, as, indeed was warranted by the circumstance;

and yet I could not quell my sensation of astonishment at the whole affair. I knew that in reality no assistance was wanted in the housework, and the professor's prediction that the boy he was to engage might prove a little "simple," followed by so exact a fulfilment, struck me as bizarre in the extreme. The next morning I heard from the housemaid that the boy Cradock had come at eight, and that she had been trying to make him useful. "He doesn't seem quite all there, I don't think, miss," was her comment, and later in the day I saw him helping the old man who worked in the garden. He was a youth of about fourteen, with black hair and black eyes and an olive skin, and I saw at once from the curious vacancy of his expression that he was mentally weak. He touched his forehead awkwardly as I went by, and I heard him answering the gardener in a queer, harsh voice that caught my attention; it gave me the impression of some one speaking deep below under the earth, and there was a strange sibilance, like the hissing of the phonograph as the pointer travels over the cylinder. I heard that he seemed anxious to do what he could, and was quite docile and obedient, and Morgan the gardener, who knew his mother, assured me he was perfectly harmless. "He's always been a bit queer," he said, "and no wonder, after what his mother went through before he was born. I did know his father, Thomas Cradock, well, and a very fine workman he was too, indeed. He got something wrong with his lungs owing to working in the wet woods, and never got over it, and went off quite sudden like. And they do say as how Mrs. Cradock was quite off her head; anyhow, she was found by Mr. Hillyer, Ty Coch, all crouched up on the Grey Hills, over there, crying and weeping like a lost soul. And Jervase, he was born about eight months afterwards, and as I was saying, he was a bit queer always; and they do say when he could scarcely walk he would frighten the other children into fits with the noises he would make."

A word in the story had stirred up some remembrance within me, and, vaguely curious, I asked the old man where the Grey Hills were.

"Up there," he said, with the same gesture he had used before; "you go past the 'Fox and Hounds,' and through the forest, by the old ruins. It's a good five mile from here, and a strange sort of a place. The poorest soil between this and Monmouth, they do say, though it's good feed for sheep. Yes, it was a sad thing for poor Mrs. Cradock."

The old man turned to his work, and I strolled on down the path between the espaliers, gnarled and gouty with age, thinking of the story I had heard, and groping for the point in it that had some key to my memory. In an instant it came before me; I had seen the phrase "Grey Hills" on the slip of yellowed paper that Professor Gregg had taken from the drawer in his cabinet. Again I was seized with pangs of mingled curiosity and fear; I remembered the strange characters copied from the limestone rock, and then again their identity with the inscription on the age-old seal, and the fantastic fables of the Latin geographer. I saw beyond doubt that, unless coincidence had set all the scene and disposed all these bizarre events with curious art, I was to be a spectator of things far removed from the usual and customary traffic and jostle of life. Professor Gregg I noted day by day; he was hot on his trail, growing lean with eagerness; and in the evenings, when the sun was swimming on the verge of the mountain, he would pace the terrace to and fro with his eyes on the ground, while the mist grew white in the valley, and the stillness of the evening brought far voices near, and the blue smoke rose a straight column from the diamond-shaped chimney of the grey farm-house, just as I had seen it on the first morning. I have told you I was of sceptical habit; but though I understood little or nothing, I began to dread, vainly proposing to myself the iterated dogmas of science that all life is material, and that in the system of things there is, no undiscovered land, even beyond the remotest stars, where the supernatural can find a footing. Yet there struck in on this the thought that matter is as really awful and unknown as spirit, that science itself but dallies on the threshold, scarcely gaining more than a glimpse of the wonders of the inner place.

There is one day that stands up from amidst the others as a grim red beacon, betokening evil to come. I was sitting on a bench in the garden, watching the boy Cradock weeding, when I was suddenly alarmed by a harsh and choking sound, like the cry of a wild beast in anguish, and I was unspeakably shocked to see the unfortunate lad standing in full view before me, his whole body quivering and shaking at short intervals as though shocks of electricity were passing through him, his teeth grinding, foam gathering on his lips, and his face all swollen and blackened to a hideous mask of humanity. I shrieked with terror, and Professor Gregg came running; and as I pointed to Cradock, the boy with one convulsive shudder fell face forward, and lay on the wet earth, his body writhing like a wounded blind worm, and an inconceivable babble of sounds bursting and rattling and hissing from his lips. He seemed to pour forth an infamous jargon, with words, or what seemed words, that might have belonged to a tongue dead since untold ages, and buried deep beneath Nilotic mud, or in the inmost recesses of the Mexican forest. For a moment the thought passed through my mind, as my ears were still revolted with that infernal clamour, "Surely this is the very speech of hell," and then I cried out again and again, and ran away shuddering to my inmost soul. I had seen Professor Gregg's face as he stooped over the wretched boy and raised him, and I was appalled by the glow of exultation that shone on every lineament and feature. As I sat in my room with drawn blinds, and my eyes hidden in my hands, I heard heavy steps beneath, and I was told afterwards that Professor Gregg had carried Cradock to his study, and had locked the door. I heard voices murmur indistinctly, and I trembled to think of what might be passing within a few feet of where I sat; I longed to escape to the woods and sunshine, and yet I dreaded the sights that might confront me on the way; and at last, as I held the handle of the door nervously, I heard Professor Gregg's voice calling to me with a cheerful ring. "It's all right now, Miss Lally," he said. "The poor fellow has got over it, and I have been arranging for him to sleep here after to-morrow. Perhaps I may be able to do something for him."

"Yes," he said later, "it was a very painful sight, and I don't wonder you were alarmed. We may hope that good food will build him up a little, but I am afraid he will never be really cured," and he affected the dismal and conventional air with which one speaks of hopeless illness; and yet beneath it I detected the delight that leapt up rampant within him, and fought and struggled to find utterance. It was as if one glanced down on the even surface of the sea, clear and immobile, and saw beneath raging depths and a storm of contending billows. It was indeed to me a torturing and offensive problem that this man, who had so bounteously rescued me from the sharpness of death, and showed himself in all the relations of life full of benevolence, and pity, and kindly forethought, should so manifestly be for once on the side of the demons, and take a ghastly pleasure in the torments of an afflicted fellow-creature. Apart, I struggled with the horned difficulty, and strove to find the solution; but without the hint of a clue, beset by mystery and contradiction. I saw nothing that might help me, and began to wonder whether, after all, I had not escaped from the white mist of the suburb at too dear a rate. I hinted something of my thought to the professor; I said enough to let him know that I was in the most acute perplexity, but the moment after regretted what I had done when I saw his face contort with a spasm of pain.

"My dear Miss Lally," he said, "you surely do not wish to leave us? No, no, you would not do it. You do not know how I rely on you; how confidently I go forward, assured that you are here to watch over my children. You, Miss Lally, are my rearguard; for let me tell you the business in which I am engaged is not wholly devoid of peril. You have not forgotten what I said the first morning here; my lips are shut by an old and firm resolve till they can open to utter no ingenious hypothesis or vague surmise but irrefragable fact, as certain as a demonstration in mathematics. Think over it, Miss Lally: not for a moment would I endeavour to keep you here against your own instincts, and yet I tell you frankly that I am persuaded it is here, here amidst the woods, that your duty lies."

I was touched by the eloquence of his tone, and by the remembrance that the man, after all, had been my salvation, and I gave him my hand on a promise to serve him loyally and without question. A few days later the rector of our church—a little church, grey and severe and quaint, that hovered on the very banks of the river and watched the tides swim and return—came to see us, and Professor Gregg easily persuaded him to stay and share our dinner. Mr. Meyrick was a member of an antique family of squires, whose old manor-house stood amongst the hills some seven miles away, and thus, rooted in the soil, the rector was a living store of all the old fading customs and lore of the country. His manner, genial, with a deal of retired oddity, won on Professor Gregg; and towards the cheese, when a curious Burgundy had begun its incantations, the two men glowed like the wine, and talked of philology with the enthusiasm of a burgess over the peerage. The parson was expounding the pronunciation of the Welsh *ll*, and producing sounds like the gurgle of his native brooks, when Professor Gregg struck in.

"By the way," he said, "that was a very odd word I met the other day. You know my boy, poor Jervase Cradock? Well, he has got the bad habit of talking to himself, and the day before yesterday I was walking in the garden here and heard him; he was evidently quite unconscious of my presence. A lot of what he said I couldn't make out, but one word struck me distinctly. It was such an odd sound, half sibilant, half guttural, and as quaint as those double *ls* you have been demonstrating. I do not know whether I can give you an idea of the sound; 'Ishakshar' is perhaps as near as I can get. But the *k* ought to be a Greek *chi* or a Spanish *j*. Now what does it mean in Welsh?"

"In Welsh?" said the parson. "There is no such word in Welsh, nor any word remotely resembling it. I know the book-Welsh, as they call it, and the colloquial dialects as well as any man, but there's no word like that from Anglesea to Usk. Besides, none of the Cradocks speaks a word of Welsh; it's dying out about here."

"Really. You interest me extremely, Mr. Meyrick. I confess the word didn't strike me as having the Welsh ring. But I thought it might be some local corruption."

"No, I never heard such a word, or anything like it. Indeed," he added, smiling whimsically, "if it belongs to any language, I should say it must be that of the fairies—the Tylwydd Têg, as we call them."

The talk went on to the discovery of a Roman villa in the neighbourhood; and soon after I left the room, and sat down apart to wonder at the drawing together of such strange clues of evidence. As the professor had spoken of the curious word, I had caught the glint of his eye upon me; and though the pronunciation he gave was grotesque in the extreme, I recognized the name of the stone of sixty characters mentioned by Solinus, the black seal shut up in some secret drawer of the study, stamped for ever by a vanished race with signs that no man could read, signs that might, for all I knew, be the veils of awful things done long ago, and forgotten before the hills were moulded into form.

When the next morning I came down, I found Professor Gregg pacing the terrace in his eternal walk.

"Look at that bridge," he said, when he saw me; "observe the quaint and Gothic design, the angles between the arches, and the silvery grey of the stone in the awe of the morning light. I confess it seems to me symbolic; it should illustrate a mystical allegory of the passage from one world to another."

"Professor Gregg," I said quietly, "it is time that I knew something of what has happened, and of what is to happen."

For the moment he put me off, but I returned again with the same question in the evening, and then Professor Gregg flamed with excitement. "Don't you understand yet?" he cried. "But I have told you a good deal; yes, and shown you a good deal; you have heard pretty nearly all that I have heard, and seen what I have seen; or at least," and his voice chilled as he spoke, "enough to make a good deal clear as noonday. The servants told you, I have no doubt, that the wretched boy Cradock had another seizure the night before last; he awoke me with cries in that voice you heard in the garden, and I went to him, and God forbid you should see what I saw that night. But all this is useless; my time here is drawing to a close; I must be back in town in three weeks, as I have a course of lectures to prepare, and need all my books about me. In a very few days it will all be over, and I shall no longer hint, and no longer be liable to ridicule as a madman and a quack. No, I shall speak plainly, and I shall be heard with such emotions as perhaps no other man has ever drawn from the breasts of his fellows."

He paused, and seemed to grow radiant with the joy of great and wonderful discovery.

"But all that is for the future, the near future certainly, but still the future," he went on at length. "There is something to be done yet; you will remember my telling you that my researches were not altogether devoid of peril? Yes, there is a certain amount of danger to be faced; I did not know how much when I spoke on the subject before, and to a certain extent I am still in the dark. But it will be a strange adventure, the last of all, the last demonstration in the chain."

He was walking up and down the room as he spoke, and I could hear in his voice the contending tones, of exultation and despondence, or perhaps I should say awe, the awe of a man who goes forth on unknown waters, and I thought of his allusion to Columbus on the night he had laid his book before me. The evening was a little chilly, and a fire of logs had been lighted in the study where we were; the remittent flame and the glow on the walls reminded me of the old days. I was sitting silent in an arm-chair by the fire, wondering over all I had heard, and still vainly speculating as to the secret springs concealed from me under all the phantasmagoria I had witnessed, when I became suddenly aware of a sensation that change of some sort had been at work in the room, and that there was something unfamiliar in its aspect. For some time I looked about me, trying in vain to localize the alteration that I knew had been made; the table by the window, the chairs, the faded settee were all as I had known them. Suddenly, as a sought-for recollection flashes into mind, I knew what was amiss. I was facing the professor's desk, which stood on the other side of the fire, and above the desk was a grimy-looking bust of Pitt,[24] that I had never seen there before. And then I remembered the true position of this work of art; in the furthest corner by the door was an old cupboard, projecting into the room, and on the top of the cupboard, fifteen feet from the floor, the bust had been, and there, no doubt, it had delayed, accumulating dirt, since the early years of the century.

I was utterly amazed, and sat silent still, in a confusion of thought. There was, so far as I knew, no such thing as a step-ladder in the house, for I had asked for one to make some alterations in the curtains of my room, and a tall man standing on a chair would have found it impossible to take down the bust. It had been placed, not on the edge of the cupboard, but far back against the wall; and Professor Gregg was, if anything, under the average height.

"How on earth did you manage to get down Pitt?" I said at last.

The professor looked curiously at me, and seemed to hesitate a little.

"They must have found you a step-ladder, or perhaps the gardener brought in a short ladder from outside?"

"No, I have had no ladder of any kind. Now, Miss Lally," he went on with an awkward simulation of jest, "there is a little puzzle for you; a problem in the manner of the inimitable Holmes; there are the facts, plain and patent; summon your acuteness to the solution of the puzzle. For Heaven's sake," he cried with a breaking voice, "say no more about it! I tell you, I never touched the thing," and he went out of the room with horror manifest on his face, and his hand shook and jarred the door behind him.

I looked round the room in vague surprise, not at all realizing what had happened, making vain and idle surmises by way of explanation, and wondering at the stirring of black waters by an idle word and the trivial change of an ornament. "This is some petty business, some whim on which I have jarred," I reflected; "the professor is perhaps scrupulous and superstitious over trifles, and my question may have outraged unacknowledged fears, as though one killed a spider or spilled the salt before the very eyes of a practical Scotchwoman." I was immersed in these fond suspicions, and began to plume myself a little on my immunity from such empty fears, when the truth fell heavily as lead upon my heart, and I recognized with cold terror that some awful influence had been at work. The bust was simply inaccessible; without a ladder no one could have touched it.

I went out to the kitchen and spoke as quietly as I could to the housemaid.

"Who moved that bust from the top of the cupboard, Anne?" I said to her. "Professor Gregg says he has not touched it. Did you find an old step-ladder in one of the outhouses?"

The girl looked at me blankly.

"I never touched it," she said. "I found it where it is now the other morning when I dusted the room. I remember now, it was Wednesday morning, because it was the morning after Cradock was taken bad in the night. My room is next to his, you know, miss," the girl went on piteously, "and it was awful to hear how he cried and called out names that I couldn't understand. It made me feel all afraid; and then master came, and I heard him speak, and he took down Cradock to the study and gave him something."

"And you found that bust moved the next morning?"

"Yes, miss. There was a queer sort of smell in the study when I came down and opened the windows; a bad smell it was, and I wondered what it could be. Do you know, miss, I went a long time ago to the Zoo in London with my cousin Thomas Barker, one afternoon that I had off, when I was at Mrs. Prince's in Stanhope Gate, and we went into the snake-house to see the snakes, and it was just the same sort of smell; very sick it made me feel, I remember, and I got Barker to take me out. And it was just the same kind of a smell in the study, as I was saying, and I was wondering what it could be from, when I see that bust with Pitt cut in it, standing on the master's desk, and I thought to myself, Now who has done that, and how have they done it? And when I came to dust the things, I looked at the bust, and I saw a great mark on it where the dust was gone, for I don't think it can have been touched with a duster for years and years, and it wasn't like finger-marks, but a large patch like, broad and spread out. So I passed my hand over it, without thinking what I was doing, and where that patch was it was all sticky and slimy, as if a snail had crawled over it. Very strange, isn't it, miss? and I wonder who can have done it, and how that mess was made."

The well-meant gabble of the servant touched me to the quick; I lay down upon my bed, and bit my lip that I should not cry out loud in the sharp anguish of my terror and bewilderment. Indeed, I was almost mad with dread; I believe that if it had been daylight I should have fled hot foot, forgetting all courage and all the debt of gratitude that was due to Professor Gregg, not caring whether my fate were that I must starve slowly, so long as I might escape from the net of blind and panic fear that every day seemed to draw a little closer round me. If I knew, I thought, if I knew what there were to dread, I could guard against it; but here, in this lonely house, shut in on all sides by the olden woods and the vaulted hills, terror seems to spring inconsequent from every covert, and the flesh is aghast at the half-heard murmurs of hor-rible things. All in vain I strove to summon scepticism to my aid, and endeavoured by cool common sense to buttress my belief in a world of natural order, for the air that blew in at the open window was a mystic breath, and in the darkness I felt the silence go heavy and sorrowful as a mass of requiem, and I conjured images of strange shapes gathering fast amidst the reeds, beside the wash of the river.

In the morning from the moment that I set foot in the breakfast-room, I felt that the unknown plot was drawing to a crisis; the profes-sor's face was firm and set, and he seemed hardly to hear our voices when we spoke.

"I am going out for a rather long walk," he said when the meal was over. "You mustn't be expecting me, now, or thinking anything has happened if I don't turn up to dinner. I have been getting stupid, lately, and I dare say a miniature walking tour will do me good. Perhaps I may even spend the night in some little inn, if I find any place that looks clean and comfortable."

I heard this and knew by my experience of Professor Gregg's manner that it was no ordinary business or pleasure that impelled him. I knew not, nor even remotely guessed, where he was bound, nor had I the vaguest notion of his errand, but all the fear of the night before returned; and as he stood, smiling, on the terrace, ready to set out, I implored him to stay, and to forget all his dreams of the undiscovered continent.

"No, no, Miss Lally," he replied still smiling, "it's too late now. *Vestigia nulla retrorsum*,[25] you know, is the device of all true explorers, though I hope it won't be literally true in my case. But, indeed, you are wrong to alarm yourself so; I look upon my little expedition as quite commonplace; no more exciting than a day with the geological hammers. There is a risk, of course, but so there is on the commonest excursion. I can afford to be jaunty; I am doing nothing so hazardous as 'Arry does a hundred times over in the course of every Bank Holiday. Well, then, you must look more cheerfully; and so good-bye till to-morrow at latest."

He walked briskly up the road, and I saw him open the gate that marks the entrance of the wood, and then he vanished in the gloom of the trees.

All the day passed heavily with a strange darkness in the air, and again I felt as if imprisoned amidst the ancient woods, shut in an olden land of mystery and dread, and as if all was long ago and forgotten by the living outside. I hoped and dreaded; and when the dinner-hour came waited, I expecting to hear the professor's step in the hall, and his voice exulting at I knew not what triumph. I composed my face to welcome him gladly, but the night descended dark, and he did not come.

In the morning, when the maid knocked at my door, I called out to her, and asked if her master had returned; and when she replied that his bedroom stood open and empty, I felt the cold clasp of despair. Still, I fancied he might have discovered genial company, and would return for luncheon, or perhaps in the afternoon, and I took the children for a walk in the forest, and tried my best to play and laugh with them, and to shut out the thoughts of mystery and veiled terror. Hour after hour I waited, and my thoughts grew darker; again the night came and found me watching, and at last, as I was making much ado to finish my dinner, I heard steps outside and the sound of a man's voice.

The maid came in and looked oddly at me. "Please, miss," she began, "Mr. Morgan the gardener wants to speak to you for a minute, if you didn't mind."

"Show him in, please," I answered, and set my lips tight.

The old man came slowly into the room, and the servant shut the door behind him.

"Sit down, Mr. Morgan," I said; "what is it that you want to say to me?"

"Well, miss, Mr. Gregg he gave me something for you yesterday morning, just before he went off; and he told me particular not to hand it up before eight o'clock this evening exactly, if so be as he wasn't back home again before, and if he should come home before I was just to return it to him in his own hands. So, you see, as Mr. Gregg isn't here yet, I suppose I'd better give you the parcel directly."

He pulled out something from his pocket, and gave it to me, half rising. I took it silently, and seeing that Morgan seemed doubtful as to what he was to do next, I thanked him and bade him good-night, and he went out. I was left alone in the room with the parcel in my hand— a paper parcel neatly sealed and directed to me, with the instructions Morgan had quoted, all written in the professor's large loose hand. I broke the seals with a choking at my heart, and found an envelope inside, addressed also, but open, and I took the letter out.

"My Dear Miss Lally," it began,—"To quote the old logic manual, the case of your reading this note is a case of my having made a blunder of some sort, and, I am afraid, a blunder that turns these lines into a farewell. It is practically certain that neither you nor any one else will ever see me again. I have made my will with provision for this eventuality, and I hope you will consent to accept the small remembrance addressed to you, and my sincere thanks for the way in which you joined your fortunes to mine. The fate which has come upon me is desperate and terrible beyond the remotest dreams of man; but this fate you have a right to know—if you please. If you look in the left-hand drawer of my dressing-table, you will find the key of the escritoire, properly labelled. In the well of the escritoire is a large envelope sealed and addressed to your name. I advise you to throw it forthwith into the fire; you will sleep better of nights if you do so. But if you must know the history of what has happened, it is all written down for you to read."

The signature was firmly written below, and again I turned the page and read out the words one by one, aghast and white to the lips, my hands cold as ice, and sickness choking me. The dead silence of the room, and the thought of the dark woods and hills closing me in on every side, oppressed me, helpless and without capacity, and not knowing where to turn for counsel. At last I resolved that though knowledge should haunt my whole life and all the days to come, I must know the meaning of the strange terrors that had so long tormented me, rising grey, dim, and awful, like the shadows in the wood at dusk. I carefully carried out Professor Gregg's directions, and not without reluctance broke the seal of the envelope, and spread out his manuscript before me. That manuscript I always carry with me, and I see that I cannot deny your unspoken request to read it. This, then, was what I read that night, sitting at the desk, with a shaded lamp beside me.

The young lady who called herself Miss Lally then proceeded to recite

THE THREE IMPOSTORS

The Statement of William Gregg, F. R. S., etc.

It is many years since the first glimmer of the theory which is now almost, if not quite, reduced to fact dawned on my mind. A somewhat extensive course of miscellaneous and obsolete reading had done a good deal to prepare the way, and, later, when I became somewhat of a specialist, and immersed myself in the studies known as ethnological, I was now and then startled by facts that would not square with orthodox scientific opinion, and by discoveries that seemed to hint at something still hidden for all our research. More particularly I became convinced that much of the folk-lore of the world is but an exaggerated account of events that really happened, and I was especially drawn to consider the stories of the fairies, the good folk of the Celtic races. Here I thought I could detect the fringe of embroidery and exaggeration, the fantastic guise, the little people dressed in green and gold sporting in the flowers, and I thought I saw a distinct analogy between the name given to this race (supposed to be imaginary) and the description of their appearance and manners. Just as our remote ancestors called the dreadful beings "fair" and "good" precisely because they dreaded them, so they had dressed them up in charming forms, knowing the truth to be the very reverse. Literature, too, had gone early to work, and had lent a powerful hand in the transformation, so that the playful elves of Shakespeare are already far removed from the true original, and the real horror is disguised in a form of prankish mischief. But in the older tales, the stories that used to make men cross themselves as they sat round the burning logs, we tread a different stage; I saw a widely opposed spirit in certain histories of children and of men and women who vanished strangely from the earth. They would be seen by a peasant in the fields walking towards some green and rounded hillock, and seen no more on earth; and there are stories of mothers who have left a child quietly sleeping, with the cottage door rudely barred with a piece of wood, and have returned, not to find the plump and rosy little Saxon, but a thin and wizened creature, with sallow skin and black, piercing eyes, the child of another race. Then, again, there were myths darker still; the dread of witch and wizard, the lurid evil of the Sabbath, and the hint of demons who mingled with the daughters of men. And just as we have turned the terrible "fair folk" into a company of benignant, if freakish, elves, so we have hidden from us the black foulness of the witch and her companions under a popular *diablerie* of old women and broomsticks and a comic cat with tail on end. So the Greeks called the hideous furies benevolent ladies,[26] and thus the northern nations have followed their example. I pursued my investigations, stealing odd hours from other and more imperative labours, and I asked myself the question: Supposing these traditions to be true, who were the demons who are reported to have attended the Sabbaths? I need not say that I laid aside what I may call the supernatural hypothesis of the Middle Ages, and came to the conclusion that fairies and devils were of one and the same race and origin; invention, no doubt, and the Gothic fancy of old days, had done much in the way of exaggeration and distortion; yet I firmly believe that beneath all this imagery there was a black background of truth. As for some of the alleged wonders, I hesitated. While I should be very loath to receive any one specific instance of modern spiritualism as containing even a grain of the genuine, yet I was not wholly prepared to deny that human flesh may now and then, once perhaps in ten million cases, be the veil of powers which seem magical to us—powers which, so far from proceeding from the heights and leading men thither, are in reality survivals from the depth of being. The amœba and the snail have powers which we do not possess; and I thought it possible that the theory of reversion might explain many things which seem wholly inexplicable. Thus stood my position; I saw good reason to believe that much of the tradition, a vast deal of the earliest and uncorrupted tradition of the so-called fairies, represented solid fact, and I thought that the purely supernatural element in these traditions was to be accounted for on the hypothesis that a race which had fallen out of the grand march of evolution might have retained, as a survival, certain powers which would be to us wholly miraculous. Such was my theory as it stood conceived in my mind; and working with this in view, I seemed to gather confirmation from every side, from the spoils of a tumulus or a barrow, from a local paper reporting an antiquarian meeting in the country, and from general literature of all kinds. Amongst other instances, I remember being struck by the phrase "articulate-speaking men" in Homer,[27] as if the writer knew or had heard of men whose speech was so rude that it could hardly be termed articulate; and on my hypothesis of a race who had lagged far behind the rest, I could easily conceive that such a folk would speak a jargon but little removed from the inarticulate noises of brute beasts.

Thus I stood, satisfied that my conjecture was at all events not far removed from fact, when a chance paragraph in a small country print one day arrested my attention. It was a short account of what was to all appearance the usual sordid tragedy of the village—a young girl unaccountably missing, and evil rumour blatant and busy with her reputation. Yet, I could read between the lines that all this scandal was purely hypocritical, and in all probability invented to account for what was in any other manner unaccountable. A flight to London or Liverpool, or an undiscovered body lying with a weight about its neck in the foul depths of a woodland pool, or perhaps murder—such were the theories of the wretched girl's neighbours. But as I idly scanned the paragraph, a flash of thought passed through me with the violence of an electric shock: what if the obscure and horrible race of the hills still survived, still remained haunting the wild places and barren hills, and now and then repeating the evil of Gothic legend, unchanged and unchangeable as the Turanian Shelta,[28] or the Basques of Spain? I have said that the thought came with violence; and indeed I drew in my breath sharply, and clung with both hands to my elbow-chair, in a strange confusion of horror and elation. It was as if one of my *confrères* of physical science, roaming in a quiet English wood, had been suddenly stricken aghast by the presence of the slimy and loathsome terror of the ichthyosaurus, the original of the stories of the awful worms killed by valorous knights, or had seen the sun darkened by the pterodactyl, the dragon of tradition. Yet as a resolute explorer of knowledge, the thought of such a discovery threw me into a passion of joy, and I cut out the slip from the paper and put it in a drawer in my old bureau, resolved that it should be but the first piece in a collection of the strangest significance. I sat long that evening dreaming of the conclusions I should establish, nor did cooler reflection at first dash my confidence. Yet as I began to put the case fairly, I saw that I might be building on an unstable foundation; the facts might possibly be in accordance with local opinion, and I regarded the affair with a mood of some reserve. Yet I resolved to remain perched on the look-out, and I hugged to myself the thought that I alone was watching and wakeful, while the great crowd of thinkers and searchers stood heedless and indifferent, perhaps letting the most prerogative facts pass by unnoticed.

Several years elapsed before I was enabled to add to the contents of the drawer; and the second find was in reality not a valuable one, for it was a mere repetition of the first, with only the variation of another and distant locality. Yet I gained something; for in the second case, as in the first, the tragedy took place in a desolate and lonely country, and so far my theory seemed justified. But the third piece was to me far more decisive. Again, amongst outland hills, far even from a main road of traffic, an old man was found done to death, and the instrument of execution was left beside him. Here, indeed, there was rumour and conjecture, for the deadly tool was a primitive stone axe, bound by gut to the wooden handle, and surmises the most extravagant and improbable were indulged in. Yet, as I thought with a kind of glee, the wildest conjectures went far astray; and I took the pains to enter into correspondence with the local doctor, who was called at the inquest. He, a man of some acuteness, was dumbfoundered. "It will not do to speak of these things in country places," he wrote to me; "but frankly, there is some hideous mystery here. I have obtained possession of the stone axe, and have been so curious as to test its powers. I took it into the back-garden of my house one Sunday afternoon when my family and the servants were all out, and there, sheltered by the poplar hedges, I made my experiments. I found the thing utterly unmanageable; whether there is some peculiar balance, some nice adjustment of weights, which require incessant practice, or whether an effectual blow can be struck only by a certain trick of the muscles, I do not know; but I can assure you that I went into the house with but a sorry opinion of my athletic capacities. It was like an inexperienced man trying 'putting the hammer'; the force exerted seemed to return on oneself, and I found myself hurled backwards with violence, while the axe fell harmless to the ground. On another occasion I tried the experiment with a clever woodman of the place; but this man, who had handled his axe for forty years, could do nothing with the stone implement, and missed every stroke most ludicrously. In short, if it were not so supremely absurd, I should say that for four thousand years no one on earth could have struck an effective blow with the tool that undoubtedly was used to murder the old man." This, as may be imagined, was to me rare news; and afterwards, when I heard the whole story, and learned that the unfortunate old man had babbled tales of what might be seen at night on a certain wild hillside, hinting at unheard-of wonders, and that he had been found cold one morning on the very hill in question, my exultation was extreme, for I felt I was leaving conjecture far behind me. But the next step was of still greater importance. I had possessed for many years an extraordinary stone seal—a piece of dull black stone, two inches long from the handle to the stamp, and the stamping end a rough hexagon an inch and a quarter in diameter. Altogether, it presented the appearance of an enlarged tobacco stopper of an old-fashioned make. It had been sent to me by an agent in the East, who informed me that it had been found near the site of the ancient Babylon. But the characters engraved on the seal were to me an intolerable puzzle. Somewhat of the cuneiform pattern, there were yet striking differences, which I detected at the first glance, and all efforts to read the inscription on the hypothesis that the rules for deciphering the arrow-headed writing would apply proved futile. A riddle such as this stung my pride, and at odd moments I would take the Black Seal out of the cabinet, and scrutinize it with so much idle perseverance that every letter was familiar to my mind, and I could have drawn the inscription from memory without the slightest error. Judge, then, of my surprise when I one day received from a correspondent in the west of England a letter and an enclosure that positively left me thunderstruck. I saw carefully traced on a large piece of paper the very characters of the Black Seal, without alteration of any kind, and above the inscription my friend had written: *Inscription found on a limestone rock on the Grey Hills, Monmouthshire. Done in some red earth, and quite recent.* I turned to the letter. My friend wrote: "I sent you the enclosed inscription with all due reserve. A shepherd who passed by the stone a week ago swears that there was then no mark of any kind. The characters, as I have noted, are formed by drawing some red earth over the stone, and are of an average height of one inch. They look to me like a kind of cuneiform character, a good deal altered, but this, of course,

134

is impossible. It may be either a hoax, or more probably some scribble of the gypsies, who are plentiful enough in this wild country. They have, as you are aware, many hieroglyphics which they use in communicating with one another. I happened to visit the stone in question two days ago in connection with a rather painful incident which has occurred here."

As may be supposed, I wrote immediately to my friend, thanking him for the copy of the inscription, and asking him in a casual manner the history of the incident he mentioned. To be brief, I heard that a woman named Cradock, who had lost her husband a day before, had set out to communicate the sad news to a cousin who lived some five miles away. She took a short cut which led by the Grey Hills. Mrs. Cradock, who was then quite a young woman, never arrived at her relative's house. Late that night a farmer who had lost a couple of sheep, supposed to have wandered from the flock, was walking over the Grey Hills, with a lantern and his dog. His attention was attracted by a noise, which he described as a kind of wailing, mournful and pitiable to hear; and, guided by the sound, he found the unfortunate Mrs. Cradock crouched on the ground by the limestone rock, swaying her body to and fro, and lamenting and crying in so heartrending a manner that the farmer was, as he says, at first obliged to stop his ears, or he would have run away. The woman allowed herself to be taken home, and a neighbour came to see to her necessities. All the night she never ceased her crying, mixing her lament with words of some unintelligible jargon, and when the doctor arrived he pronounced her insane. She lay on her bed for a week, now wailing, as people said, like one lost and damned for eternity, and now sunk in a heavy coma; it was thought that grief at the loss of her husband had unsettled her mind, and the medical man did not at one time expect her to live. I need not say that I was deeply interested in this story, and I made my friend write to me at intervals with all the particulars of the case. I heard then that in the course of six weeks the woman gradually recovered the use of her faculties, and some months later she gave birth to a son, christened Jervase, who unhappily proved to be of weak intellect. Such were the facts known to the village; but to me, while I whitened at the suggested thought of the hideous enormities that had doubtless been committed, all this was nothing short of conviction, and I incautiously hazarded a hint of something like the truth to some scientific friends. The moment the words had left my lips I bitterly regretted having spoken, and thus given way the great secret of my life, but with a good deal of relief mixed with indignation I found my fears altogether misplaced, for my friends ridiculed me to my face, and I was regarded as a madman; and beneath a natural anger I chuckled to myself, feeling as secure amidst these blockheads as if I had confided what I knew to the desert sands.

But now, knowing so much, I resolved I would know all, and I concentrated my efforts on the task of deciphering the inscription on the Black Seal. For many years I made this puzzle the sole object of my leisure moments; for the greater portion of my time was, of course, devoted to other duties, and it was only now and then that I could snatch a week of clear research. If I were to tell the full history of this curi-ous investigation, this statement would be wearisome in the extreme, for it would contain simply the account of long and tedious failure. By what I knew already of ancient scripts I was well equipped for the chase, as I always termed it to my-self. I had correspondents amongst all the scientific men in Europe, and indeed, in the world, and I could not believe that in these days any character, however ancient and however perplexed, could long resist the search-light I should bring to bear upon it. Yet, in point of fact, it was fully fourteen years before I succeeded. With every year my professional duties increased, and my leisure became smaller. This no doubt re-tarded me a good deal; and yet, when I look back on those years, I am astonished at the vast scope of my investigation of the Black Seal. I made my bureau a centre, and from all the world and from all the ages I gathered transcripts of ancient writing. Nothing, I resolved, should pass me unawares, and the faintest hint should be welcomed and followed up. But as one covert after another was tried and proved empty of result, I began in the course of years to despair, and to won-der whether the Black Seal were the sole relic of some race that had vanished from the world and left no other trace of its existence—had perished, in fine, as Atlantis is said to have done, in some great cataclysm, its secrets perhaps drowned beneath the ocean or moulded into the heart of the hills. The thought chilled my warmth a little, and though I still persevered, it was no longer with the same certainty of faith. A chance came to the rescue. I was staying in a considerable town in the north of England, and took the opportunity of going over the very creditable museum that had for some time been established in the place. The curator was one of my correspondents; and, as we were looking through one of the mineral cases, my attention was struck by a specimen, a piece of black stone some four inches square, the appearance of which reminded me in a measure of the Black Seal. I took it up carelessly, and was turning it over in my hand, when I saw, to my astonishment, that the under side was inscribed. I said, quietly enough, to my friend the curator that the specimen interested me, and that I should be much obliged if he would allow me to take it with me to my hotel for a couple of days. He, of course, made no objection, and I hurried to my rooms and found that my first glance had not deceived me. There were two inscriptions; one in the regular cuneiform character, another, in the character of the Black Seal, and I realized that my task was accomplished. I made an exact copy of the two inscriptions; and when I got to my London study, and had the Seal before me, I was able seriously to grapple with the great problem. The interpreting inscription on the museum specimen, though in itself curious enough, did not bear on my quest, but the transliteration made me master of the secret of the Black Seal. Conjecture, of course, had to enter into my calculations; there was here and there uncertainty about a particular ideograph, and one sign recurring again and again on the seal baffled me for many successive nights. But at last the secret stood open before me in plain English, and I read the key of the awful transmutation of the hills. The last word was hardly written, when with fingers all trembling and unsteady I tore the scrap of paper into the minutest fragments, and saw them flame and blacken in the red hollow of the fire, and then I crushed the grey films that remained into finest powder. Never since then have I written those words; never will I write the phrases which tell how man can be reduced to the slime from which he came, and be forced to put on the flesh of the reptile and the snake. There was now but one thing remaining. I knew, but I desired to see, and I was after some time able to take a house in the neighbourhood of the Grey Hills, and not far from the cottage where Mrs. Cradock and her son Jervase resided. I need not go into a full and detailed account of the apparently inexplicable events which have occurred here, where I am writing this. I knew that I should find in Jervase Cradock something of the blood of the "Little People," and I found later that he had more than once encountered his kinsmen in lonely places in that lonely land. When I was summoned one day to the garden, and found him in a seizure speaking or hissing the ghastly jargon of the Black Seal, I am afraid that exultation prevailed over pity, I heard bursting from his lips the secrets of the underworld, and the word of dread, "Ishakshar," signification of which I must be excused from giving.

But there is one incident I cannot pass over unnoticed. In the waste hollow of the night I awoke at the sound of those hissing syllables I knew so well; and on going to the wretched boy's room, I found him convulsed and foaming at the mouth, struggling on the bed as if he strove to escape the grasp of writhing demons. I took him down to my room and lit the lamp, while he lay twisting on the floor, calling on the power within his flesh to leave him. I saw his body swell and become distended as a bladder, while the face blackened before my eyes; and then at the crisis I did what was necessary according to the directions on the Seal, and putting all scruple on one side, I became a man of science, observant of what was passing. Yet the sight I had to witness was horrible, almost beyond the power of human conception and the most fearful fantasy. Something pushed out from the body there on the floor, and stretched forth, a slimy, wavering tentacle, across the room, grasped the bust upon the cupboard, and laid it down on my desk.

When it was over, and I was left to walk up and down all the rest of the night, white and shuddering, with sweat pouring from my flesh, I vainly tried to reason with myself: I said, truly enough, that I had seen nothing really supernatural, that a snail pushing out his horns and drawing them in was but an instance on a smaller scale of what I had witnessed; and yet horror broke through all such reasonings and left me shattered and loathing myself for the share I had taken in the night's work.

There is little more to be said. I am going now to the final trial and encounter; for I have determined that there shall be nothing wanting, and I shall meet the "Little People" face to face. I shall have the Black Seal and the knowledge of its secrets to help me, and if I unhappily do not return from my journey, there is no need to conjure up here a picture of the awfulness of my fate.

Pausing a little at the end of Professor Gregg's statement, Miss Lally continued her tale in the following words:—

Such was the almost incredible story that the professor had left behind him. When I had finished reading it, it was late at night, but the next morning I took Morgan with me, and we proceeded to search the Grey Hills for some trace of the lost professor. I will not weary you with a description of the savage desolation of that tract of country, a tract of utterest loneliness, of bare green hills, dotted over with grey limestone boulders, worn by the ravages of time into fantastic semblances of men and beasts. Finally, after many hours of weary searching, we found what I told you—the watch and chain, the purse, and the ring—wrapped in a piece of coarse parchment. When Morgan cut the gut that bound the parcel together, and I saw the professor's property, I burst into tears, but the sight of the dreaded characters of the Black Seal repeated on the parchment froze me to silent horror, and I think I understood for the first time the awful fate that had come upon my late employer.

I have only to add that Professor Gregg's lawyer treated my account of what had happened as a fairy tale, and refused even to glance at the documents I laid before him. It was he who was responsible for the statement that appeared in the public press, to the effect that Professor Gregg had been drowned, and that his body must have been swept into the open sea.

Miss Lally stopped speaking, and looked at Mr. Phillipps, with a glance of some inquiry. He, for his part, was sunken in a deep reverie of thought; and when he looked up and saw the bustle of the evening gathering in the square, men and women hurrying to partake of dinner, and crowds already besetting the music-halls, all the hum and press of actual life seemed unreal and visionary, a dream in the morning after an awakening.

"I thank you," he said at last, "for your most interesting story; interesting to me, because I feel fully convinced of its exact truth."

"Sir," said the lady, with some energy of indignation, "you grieve and offend me. Do you think I should waste my time and yours by concocting fictions on a bench in Leicester Square?"

"Pardon me, Miss Lally, you have a little misunderstood me. Before you began I knew that whatever you told would be told in good faith, but your experiences have a far higher value than that of *bona fides*. The most extraordinary circumstances in your account are in perfect harmony with the very latest scientific theories. Professor Lodge[29] would, I am sure, value a communication from you extremely; I was charmed from the first by his daring hypothesis in explanation of the wonders of spiritualism (so called), but your narrative puts the whole matter out of the range of mere hypothesis."

"Alas! sir, all this will not help me. You forget, I have lost my brother under the most startling and dreadful circumstances. Again, I ask you, did you not see him as you came here? His black whiskers, his spectacles, his timid glance to right and left; think, do not these particulars recall his face to your memory?"

"I am sorry to say I have never seen any one of the kind," said Phillipps, who had forgotten all about the missing brother. "But let me ask you a few questions. Did you notice whether Professor Gregg—"

"Pardon me, Sir, I have stayed too long. My employers will be expecting me. I thank you for your sympathy. Good-bye."

Before Mr. Phillipps had recovered from his amazement at this abrupt departure Miss Lally had disappeared from his gaze, passing into the crowd that now thronged the approaches to the Empire. He walked home in a pensive frame of mind, and drank too much tea. At ten o'clock he had made his third brew, and had sketched out the outlines of a little work to be called *Protoplasmic Reversion.*

Incident of the Private Bar

Mr. Dyson often meditated at odd moments over the singular tale he had listened to at the café de la Touraine. In the first place, he cherished a profound conviction that the words of truth were scattered with a too niggardly and sparing hand over the agreeable history of Mr. Smith and the Black Gulf Cañon; and secondly, there was the undeniable fact of the profound agitation of the narrator, and his gestures on the pavement, too violent to be simulated. The idea of a man going about London haunted by the fear of meeting a young man with spectacles struck Dyson as supremely ridiculous; he searched his memory for some precedent in romance, but without success; he paid visits at odd times to the little café, hoping to find Mr. Wilkins there; and he kept a sharp watch on the great generation of the spectacled men, without much doubt that he would remember the face of the individual whom he had seen dart out of the aerated bread shop. All his peregrinations and researches, however, seemed to lead to nothing of value, and Dyson needed all his warm conviction of his innate detective powers and his strong scent for mystery to sustain him in his endeavours. In fact, he had two affairs on hand; and every day, as he passed through streets crowded or deserted, lurked in the obscure districts and watched at corners, he was more than surprised to find that the affair of the gold coin persistently avoided him, while the ingenious Wilkins, and the young man with spectacles, whom he dreaded, seemed to have vanished from the pavements.

He was pondering these problems one evening in a house of call in the Strand, and the obstinacy with which the persons he so ardently desired to meet hung back gave the modest tankard before him an additional touch of bitter. As it happened, he was alone in his compartment, and, without thinking, he uttered aloud the burden of his meditations. "How bizarre it all is!" he said, "a man walking the pavement with the dread of a timid-looking young man with spectacles continually hovering before his eyes. And there was some tremendous feeling at work, I could swear to that." Quick as thought, before he had finished the sentence, a head popped round the barrier, and was withdrawn again; and while Dyson was wondering what this could mean, the door of the compartment was swung open, and a smooth, clean-shaven, and smiling gentleman entered.

"You will excuse me, sir," he said politely, "for intruding on your thoughts, but you made a remark a minute ago."

"I did," said Dyson; "I have been puzzling over a foolish matter, and I thought aloud. As you heard what I said, and seem interested, perhaps you may be able to relieve my perplexity?"

"Indeed, I scarcely know; it is an odd coincidence. One has to be cautious. I suppose, sir, that you would be glad to assist the ends of justice."

"Justice," replied Dyson, "is a term of such wide meaning, that I too feel doubtful about giving an answer. But this place is not altogether fit for such a discussion; perhaps you would come to my rooms?"

"You are very kind; my name is Burton, but I am sorry to say I have not a card with me. Do you live near here?"

"Within ten minutes' walk."

Mr. Burton took out his watch, and seemed to be making a rapid calculation.

"I have a train to catch," he said; "but after all, it is a late one. So if you don't mind, I think I will come with you. I am sure we should have a little talk together. We turn up here?"

The theatres were filling as they crossed the Strand; the street seemed alive, and Dyson looked fondly about him. The glittering lines of gas-lamps, with here and there the blinding radiance of an electric light, the hansoms that flashed to and fro with ringing bells, the laden 'buses, and the eager hurrying east and west of the foot passengers, made his most enchanting picture; and the graceful spire of St. Mary le Strand on the one hand, and the last flush of sunset on the other, were to him a cause of thanksgiving, as the gorse blossom to Linnæus. Mr. Burton caught his look of fondness as they crossed the street.

"I see you can find the picturesque in London," he said. "To me this great town is as I see it is to you—the study and the love of life.

Yet how few there are that can pierce the veils of apparent monotony and meanness! I have read in a paper, which is said to have the largest circulation in the world, a comparison between the aspects of London and Paris, a comparison which should be positively laureate as the great masterpiece of fatuous stupidity. Conceive if you can a human being of ordinary intelligence preferring the Boulevards to our London streets; imagine a man calling for the wholesale destruction of our most charming city, in order that the dull uniformity of that whited sepulchre called Paris should be reproduced here in London. Is it not positively incredible?"

"My dear sir," said Dyson, regarding Burton with a good deal of interest, "I agree most heartily with your opinions, but I really can't share your wonder. Have you heard how much George Eliot received for 'Romola'?[30] Do you know what the circulation of 'Robert Elsmere' was?[31] Do you read 'Tit-Bits' regularly?[32] To me, on the contrary, it is constant matter for wonder and thanksgiving that London was not boulevardized twenty years ago. I praise that exquisite jagged skyline that stands up against the pale greens and fading blues and flushing clouds of sunset, but I wonder even more than I praise. As for St. Mary le Strand, its preservation is a miracle, nothing more or less. A thing of exquisite beauty *versus* four 'buses abreast! Really, the conclusion is too obvious. Didn't you read the letter of the man who proposed that the whole mysterious system, the immemorial plan of computing Easter, should be abolished off-hand, because he doesn't like his son having his holidays as early as March 25th? But shall we be going on?"

They had lingered at the corner of a street on the north side of the Strand, enjoying the contrasts and the glamour of the scene. Dyson pointed the way with a gesture, and they strolled up the comparatively deserted streets, slanting a little to the right, and thus arriving at Dyson's lodging on the verge of Bloomsbury. Mr. Burton took a comfortable arm-chair by the open window, while Dyson lit the candles and produced the whisky and soda and cigarettes.

"They tell me these cigarettes are very good," he said; "but I know nothing about it myself. I hold at last that there is only one tobacco, and that is shag. I suppose I could not tempt you to try a pipeful?"

Mr. Burton smilingly refused the offer, and picked out a cigarette from the box. When he had smoked it half through, he said with some hesitation—

"It is really kind of you to have me here, Mr. Dyson; the fact is that the interests at issue are far too serious to be discussed in a bar, where, as you found for yourself, there may be listeners, voluntary or involuntary, on each side. I think the remark I heard you make was something about the oddity of an individual going about London in deadly fear of a young man with spectacles?"

"Yes; that was it."

"Well, would you mind confiding to me the circumstances that gave rise to the reflection?"

"Not in the least. It was like this." And he ran over in brief outline the adventure in Oxford Street, dwelling on the violence of Mr. Wilkins's gestures, but wholly suppressing the tale told in the café. "He told me he lived in constant terror of meeting this man; and I left him when I thought he was cool enough to look after himself," said Dyson, ending his narrative.

"Really," said Mr. Burton. "And you actually saw this mysterious person?"

"Yes."

"And could you describe him?"

"Well, he looked to me a youngish man, pale and nervous. He had small black side-whiskers, and wore rather large spectacles."

"But this is simply marvellous! You astonish me. For I must tell you that my interest in the matter is this. I'm not in the least in terror of meeting a dark young man with spectacles, but I shrewdly suspect a person of that description would much rather not meet me. And yet the account you give of the man tallies exactly. A nervous glance to right and left—is it not so? And, as you observed, he wears prominent spectacles, and has small black whiskers. There cannot be, surely, two people exactly identical—one a cause of terror, and the other, I should imagine, extremely anxious to get out of the way. But have you seen this man since?"

"No, I have not; and I have been looking out for him pretty keenly. But of course he may have left London, and England too, for the matter of that."

"Hardly, I think. Well, Mr. Dyson, it is only fair that I should explain my story, now that I have listened to yours. I must tell you, then, that I am an agent for curiosities and precious things of all kinds. An odd employment, isn't it? Of course, I wasn't brought up to the business; I gradually fell into it. I have always been fond of things queer and rare, and by the time I was twenty I had made half a dozen collections. It is not generally known how often farm-labourers come upon rarities; you would be astonished if I told you what I have seen turned up by the plough. I lived in the country in those days, and I used to buy anything the men on the farms brought me; and I had the queerest set of rubbish, as my friends called my collection. But that's how I got the scent of the business, which means everything; and, later on,

144

it struck me that I might very well turn my knowledge to account and add to my income. Since those early days I have been in most quarters of the world, and some very valuable things have passed through my hands, and I have had to engage in difficult and delicate negotiations. You have possibly heard of the Khan opal—called in the East 'The Stone of a Thousand and One Colours'? Well, perhaps the conquest of that stone was my greatest achievement. I call it myself the stone of the thousand and one lies, for I assure you that I had to invent a cycle of folk-lore before the Rajah who owned it would consent to sell the thing. I subsidized wandering story-tellers, who told tales in which the opal played a frightful part; I hired a holy man—a great ascetic—to prophesy against the thing in the language of Eastern symbolism; in short, I frightened the Rajah out of his wits. So, you see, there is room for diplomacy in the traffic I am engaged in. I have to be ever on my guard, and I have often been sensible that unless I watched every step and weighed every word, my life would not last me much longer. Last April I became aware of the existence of a highly valuable antique gem; it was in southern Italy, and in the possession of persons who were ignorant of its real value. It has always been my experience that it is precisely the ignorant who are most difficult to deal with. I have met farmers who were under the impression that a shilling of George the First was a find of almost incalculable value; and all the defeats I have sustained have been at the hands of people of this description. Reflecting on these facts, I saw that the acquisition of the gem would be an affair demanding the nicest diplomacy; I might possibly have got it by offering a sum approaching its real value, but I need not point out to you that such a proceeding would be most unbusinesslike. Indeed, I doubt whether it would have been successful; for the cupidity of such persons is aroused by a sum which seems enormous, and the low cunning which serves them in place of intelligence immediately suggests that the object for which such an amount is offered must be worth at least double. Of course, when it is a matter of an ordinary curiosity—an old jug, a carved chest, or a queer brass lantern—one does not much care; the cupidity of the owner defeats its object; the collector laughs and goes away, for he is aware that such things are by no means unique. But this gem I fervently desired to possess; and as I did not see my way to giving more than a hundredth part of its value, I was conscious that all my, let us say, imaginative and diplomatic powers would have to be exerted. I am sorry to say that I came to the conclusion that I could not undertake to carry the matter through single-handed, and I determined to confide in my assistant, a young man named William Robbins, whom I judged to be by no means devoid of capacity. My idea was that Robbins should get himself up as a low-class dealer in precious stones; he could patter a little Italian, and would go to the town in question and manage to see the gem we were after, possibly by offering some trifling articles of jewellery for sale, but that I left to be decided. Then my work was to begin, but I will not trouble you with a tale told twice over. In due course, then, Robbins went off to Italy with an assortment of uncut stones and a few rings, and some jewellery I bought in Birmingham on purpose for his expedition. A week later I followed him, travelling leisurely, so that I was a fortnight later in arriving at our common destination. There was a decent hotel in the town, and on my inquiring of the landlord whether there were many strangers in the place, he told me very few; he had heard there was an Englishman staying in a small tavern, a pedlar, he said, who sold beautiful trinkets very cheaply, and wanted to buy old rubbish. For five or six days I took life leisurely, and I must say I enjoyed myself. It was part of my plan to make the people think I was an enormously rich man; and I knew that such items as the extravagance of my meals, and the price of every bottle of wine I drank, would not be suffered, as Sancho Panza puts it, to rot in the landlord's breast. At the end of the week I was fortunate enough to make the acquaintance of Signor Melini, the owner of the gem I coveted, at the café, and with his ready hospitality, and my geniality, I was soon established as a friend of the house. On my third or fourth visit I managed to make the Italians talk about the English pedlar, who, they said, spoke a most detestable Italian. 'But that does not matter,' said the Signora Melini, 'for he has beautiful things, which he sells very, very cheap.' 'I hope you may not find he has cheated you,' I said, 'for I must tell you that English people give these fellows a very wide berth. They usually make a great parade of the cheapness of their goods, which often turn out to be double the price of better articles in the shops.' They would not hear of this, and Signora Melini insisted on showing me the three rings and the bracelet she had bought of the pedlar. She told me the price she had paid; and after scrutinizing the articles carefully, I had to confess that she had made a bargain, and indeed Robbins had sold her the things at about fifty per cent below market value. I admired the trinkets as I gave them back to the lady, and I hinted that the pedlar must be a somewhat foolish specimen of his class. Two days later, as I was taking my vermouth at the café with Signor Melini, he led the conversation back to the pedlar, and mentioned casually that he had shown the man a little curiosity, for which he had made rather a handsome offer. 'My dear sir,' I said, 'I hope you will be careful. I told you that the travelling tradesman does not bear a very high reputation in England; and notwithstanding his apparent simplicity, this fellow may turn out to be an arrant cheat. May I ask you what is the nature of the curiosity you have shown him?' He told me it was a little thing, a pretty little stone with some figures cut on it: people said it was old. 'I should like to examine it;' I replied, 'as it happens I have seen a good deal of these gems. We have a fine collection of them in our Museum at London.' In due course I was shown the article, and I held the gem I so coveted between my fingers. I looked at it coolly, and put it down carelessly on the table. 'Would you mind telling me, Signor,' I said, 'how much my fellow-countryman offered you for this?' 'Well,' he said, 'my wife says the man must be mad; he said he would give me twenty lire for it.'

"I looked at him quietly, and took up the gem and pretended to examine it in the light more carefully; I turned it over and over, and finally pulled out a magnifying glass from my pocket, and seemed to search every line in the cutting with minutest scrutiny. 'My dear sir,' I said at last, 'I am inclined to agree with Signora Melini. If this gem were genuine, it would be worth some money; but as it happens to be a rather bad forgery, it is not worth twenty centesimi. It was sophisticated, I should imagine, some time in the last century, and by a very unskilful hand.' 'Then we had better get rid of it,' said Melini. 'I never thought it was worth anything myself. Of course, I am sorry for the pedlar, but one must let a man know his own trade. I shall tell him we will take the twenty lire.' 'Excuse me,' I said, 'the man wants a lesson. It would be a charity to give him one. Tell him that you will not take anything under eighty lire, and I shall be much surprised if he does not close with you at once.'

"A day or two later I heard that the English pedlar had gone away, after debasing the minds of the country people with Birmingham art jewellery; for I admit that the gold sleeve-links like kidney beans, the silver chains made apparently after the pattern of a dog-chain, and the initial brooches, have always been heavy on my conscience. I cannot acquit myself of having indirectly contributed to debauch the taste of a simple folk; but I hope that the end I had in view may finally outbalance this heavy charge. Soon afterwards I paid a farewell visit at the Melinis', and the signor informed me with an oily chuckle that the plan I had suggested had been completely successful. I congratulated him on his bargain, and went away after expressing a wish that Heaven might send many such pedlars in his path.

"Nothing of interest occurred on my return journey. I had arranged that Robbins was to meet me at a certain place on a certain day, and I went to the appointment full of the coolest confidence; the gem had been conquered, and I had only to reap the fruits of victory. I am sorry to shake that trust in our common human nature which I am sure you possess, but I am compelled to tell you that up to the present date I have never set eyes on my man Robbins, or on the antique gem in his custody. I have found out that he actually arrived in London, for he was seen three days before my arrival in England by a pawnbroker of my acquaintance, consuming his favourite beverage—four ale—in the tavern where we met tonight. Since then he has not been heard of. I hope you will now pardon my curiosity as to the history and adventures of dark young men with spectacles. You will, I am sure, feel for me in my position; the savour of life has disappeared for me; it is a bitter thought that I have rescued one of the most perfect and exquisite specimens of antique art from the hands of ignorant, and indeed unscrupulous persons, only to deliver it into the keeping of a man who is evidently utterly devoid of the very elements of commercial morality."

"My dear sir," said Dyson, "you will allow me to compliment you on your style; your adventures have interested me exceedingly. But, forgive me, you just now used the word morality; would not some persons take exception to your own methods of business? I can conceive, myself, flaws of a moral kind being found in the very original conception you have just described to me; I can imagine the Puritan shrinking in dismay from your scheme, pronouncing it unscrupulous—nay, dishonest."

Mr. Burton helped himself very frankly to some more whisky.

"Your scruples entertain me," he said. "Perhaps you have not gone very deeply into these questions of ethics. I have been compelled to do so myself, just as I was forced to master a system of book-keeping. Without book-keeping, and still more without a system of ethics, it is impossible to conduct a business such as mine. But I assure you that I am often profoundly saddened, as I pass through the crowded streets and watch the world at work, by the thought of how few amongst all these hurrying individuals, black-hatted, well-dressed, educated we may presume sufficiently,—how few amongst them have any reasoned system of morality. Even you have not weighed the question; although you study life and affairs, and to a certain extent penetrate the veils and masks of the comedy of man, even you judge by empty conventions, and the false money which is allowed to pass current as sterling coin. Allow me to play the part of Socrates; I shall teach you nothing that you do not know. I shall merely lay aside the wrappings of prejudice and bad logic, and show you the real image which you possess in your soul. Come, then. Do you allow that happiness is anything?"

"Certainly," said Dyson.

"And happiness is desirable or undesirable?"

"Desirable, of course."

"And what shall we call the man who gives happiness? Is he not a philanthropist?"

"I think so."

"And such a person is praiseworthy, and the more praiseworthy in the proportion of the persons whom he makes happy?"

"By all means."

"So that he who makes a whole nation happy is praiseworthy in the extreme, and the action by which he gives happiness is the highest virtue?"

"It appears so, O Burton," said Dyson, who found something very exquisite in the character of his visitor.

"Quite so; you find the several conclusions inevitable. Well, apply them to the story I have told you. I conferred happiness on myself by obtaining (as I thought) possession of the gem; I conferred happiness on the Melinis by getting them eighty lire instead of an object for which they had not the slightest value, and I intended to confer happiness on the whole British nation by selling the thing to the British Museum, to say nothing of the happiness a profit of about nine thousand per cent would have conferred on me. I assure you, I regard Robbins as an interferer with the cosmos and fair order of things. But that is nothing; you perceive that I am an apostle of the very highest morality; you have been forced to yield to argument."

"There certainly seems a great deal in what you advance," said Dyson. "I admit that I am a mere amateur of ethics, while you, as you say, have brought the most acute scrutiny to bear on these perplexed and doubtful questions. I can well understand your anxiety to meet the fallacious Robbins, and I congratulate myself on the chance which has made us acquainted. But you will pardon my seeming inhospitality; I see it is half-past eleven, and I think you mentioned a train."

"A thousand thanks, Mr. Dyson. I have just time, I see. I will look you up some evening, if I may. Good-night."

THE DECORATIVE
IMAGINATION

In the course of a few weeks Dyson became accustomed to the constant incursions of the ingenious Mr. Burton, who showed himself ready to drop in at all hours, not averse to refreshment, and a profound guide in the complicated questions of life. His visits at once terrified and delighted Dyson, who could no longer seat himself at his bureau secure from interruption while he embarked on literary undertakings, each one of which was to be a masterpiece. On the other hand, it was a vivid pleasure to be confronted with views so highly original; and if here and there Mr. Burton's reasonings seemed tinged with fallacy, yet Dyson freely yielded to the joy of strangeness, and never failed to give his visitor a frank and hearty welcome. Mr. Burton's first inquiry was always after the unprincipled Robbins, and he seemed to feel the stings of disappointment when Dyson told him that he had failed to meet this outrage on all morality, as Burton styled him, vowing that sooner or later he would take vengeance on such a shameless betrayal of trust.

One evening they had sat together for some time discussing the possibility of laying down for this present generation and our modern and intensely complicated order of society some rules of social diplomacy, such as Lord Bacon gave to the courtiers of King James I. "It is a book to make," said Mr. Burton, "but who is there capable of making it? I tell you, people are longing for such a book; it would bring fortune to its publisher. Bacon's Essays[33] are exquisite, but they have now no practical application; the modern strategist can find but little use in a treatise *De Re Militari*, written by a Florentine in the fifteenth century.[34]

Scarcely more dissimilar are the social conditions of Bacon's time and our own; the rules that he lays down so exquisitely for the courtier and diplomatist of James the First's age will avail us little in the rough-and-tumble struggle of to-day. Life, I am afraid, has deteriorated; it gives little play for fine strokes such as formerly advanced men in the state. Except in such businesses as mine, where a chance does occur now and then, it has all become, as I said, an affair of rough and tumble; men still desire to attain, it is true, but what is their *moyen de parvenir.*[285] A mere imitation—and not a gracious one—of the arts of the soap vendor and the proprietor of baking-powder. When I think of these things, my dear Dyson, I confess that I am tempted to despair of my century."

"You are too pessimistic, my dear fellow; you set up too high a standard. Certainly, I agree with you, that the times are decadent in many ways. I admit a general appearance of squalor; it needs much philosophy to extract the wonderful and the beautiful from the Cromwell Road or the Nonconformist conscience. Australian wines of fine Burgundy character, the novels alike of the old women and the new women, popular journalism,—these things, indeed, make for depression. Yet we have our advantages: before us is unfolded the greatest spectacle the world has ever seen—the mystery of the innumerable, unending streets, the strange adventures that must infallibly arise from so complicated a press of interests. Nay, I will say that he who has stood in the ways of a suburb, and has seen them stretch before him all shining, void, and desolate at noonday, has not lived in vain. Such a sight is in reality more wonderful than any perspective of Bagdad or Grand Cairo. And, to set on one side the entertaining history of the gem which you told me, surely you must have had many singular adventures in your own career?"

"Perhaps not so many as you would think; a good deal—the larger part of my business—has been as commonplace as linen-drapery. But, of course, things happen now and then. It is ten years since I established my agency, and I suppose that a house- and estate-agent who had been in trade for an equal time could tell you some queer stories. But I must give you a sample of my experiences some night."

"Why not to-night?" said Dyson. "This evening seems to me admirably adapted for an odd chapter. Look out into the street; you can catch a view of it if you crane your neck from that chair of yours. Is it not charming? The double row of lamps growing closer in the distance, the hazy outline of the plane-tree in the square, and the lights of the hansoms swimming to and fro, gliding and vanishing; and above, the sky all clear and blue and shining. Come, let us have one of your *cent nouvelles nouvelles*."[36]

"My dear Dyson, I am delighted to amuse you." With these words Mr. Burton prefaced the

NOVEL OF THE IRON MAID

I think the most extraordinary event which I can recall took place about five years ago. I was then still feeling my way; I had declared for business, and attended regularly at my office; but I had not succeeded in establishing a really profitable connection, and consequently I had a good deal of leisure time on my hands. I have never thought fit to trouble you with the details of my private life; they would be entirely devoid of interest. I must briefly say, however, that I had a numerous circle of acquaintance, and was never at a loss as to how to spend my evenings. I was so fortunate as to have friends in most of the ranks of the social order; there is nothing so unfortunate, to my mind, as a specialised circle, wherein a certain round of ideas is continually traversed and retraversed. I have always tried to find out new types and persons whose brains contained something fresh to me; one may chance to gain information even from the conversation of city men on an omnibus. Amongst my acquaintance I knew a young doctor, who lived in a far outlying suburb, and I used often to brave the intolerably slow railway journey to have the pleasure of listening to his talk. One night we conversed so eagerly together over our pipes and whisky that the clock passed unnoticed; and when I glanced up, I realised with a shock that I had just five minutes in which to catch the last train. I made a dash for my hat and stick, jumped out of the house and down the steps, and tore at full speed up the street. It was no good, however; there was a shriek of the engine-whistle, and I stood there at the station door and saw far on the long, dark line of the embankment a red light shine and vanish, and a porter came down and shut the door with a bang.

"How far to London?" I asked him.

"A good nine miles to Waterloo Bridge." And with that he went off.

Before me was the long suburban street, its dreary distance marked by rows of twinkling lamps, and the air was poisoned by the faint, sickly smell of burning bricks; it was not a cheerful prospect by any means, and I had to walk through nine miles of such streets, deserted as those of Pompeii. I knew pretty well what direction to take, so I set out wearily, looking at the stretch of lamps vanishing in perspective; and as I walked, street after street branched off to right and left, some far-reaching, to distances that seemed endless, communicating with other systems of thoroughfare, and some mere protoplasmic streets, beginning in orderly fashion with serried two-storied houses, and ending suddenly in waste, and pits, and rubbish-heaps, and fields whence the magic had departed. I have spoken of systems of thoroughfare, and I assure you that walking alone through these silent places I felt fantasy growing on me, and some glamour of the infinite. There was here, I felt, an immensity as in the outer void of the universe; I passed from unknown to unknown, my way marked by lamps like stars, and on either hand was an unknown world where myriads of men dwelt and slept, street leading into street, as it seemed to world's end. At first the road by which I was travelling was lined with houses of unutterable monotony, a wall of grey brick pierced by two stories of windows, drawn close to the very pavement; but by degrees I noticed an improvement, there were gardens, and these grew larger; the suburban builder began to allow himself a wider scope; and for a certain distance each flight of steps was guarded by twin lions of plaster, and scents of flowers prevailed over the fume of heated bricks. The road began to climb a hill, and looking up a side street I saw the half moon rise over plane-trees, and there on the other side was as if a white cloud had fallen, and the air around it was sweetened as with incense; it was a may-tree in full bloom. I pressed on stubbornly, listening for the wheels and the clatter of some belated hansom; but into that land of men who go to the city in the morning and return in the evening the hansom rarely enters, and I had resigned myself once more to the walk, when I sudclenly became aware that some one was advancing to meet me along the sidewalk. The man was strolling rather aimlessly; and though the time and the place would have allowed an unconventional style of dress, he was vested in the ordinary frockcoat, black tie, and silk hat of civilisation. We met each other under the lamp, and, as often happens in this great town, two casual passengers brought face to face found each in the other an acquaintance.

"Mr. Mathias, I think?" I said.

"Quite so. And you are Frank Burton. You know you are a man with a Christian name, so I won't apologise for my familiarity. But may I ask where you are going?"

I explained the situation to him, saying I had traversed a region as unknown to me as the darkest recesses of Africa. "I think I have only about five miles further," I concluded.

"Nonsense! you must come home with me. My house is close by; in fact, I was just taking my evening walk when we met. Come along; I dare say you will find a makeshift bed easier than a five-mile walk."

I let him take my arm and lead me along, though I was a good deal surprised at so much geniality from a man who was, after all, a mere casual club acquaintance. I suppose I had not spoken to Mr. Mathias half a dozen times; he was a man who would sit silent in an arm-chair for hours, neither reading nor smoking, but now and again moistening his lips with his tongue and smiling queerly to himself. I confess he had never attracted me, and on the whole I should have preferred to continue my walk. But he took my arm and led me up a side street, and stopped at a door in a high wall. We passed through the still, moonlit garden, beneath the black shadow of an old cedar, and into an old red-brick house with many gables. I was tired enough, and I sighed with relief as I let myself fall into a great leather arm-chair. You know the infernal grit with which they strew the sidewalk in those suburban districts; it makes walking a penance, and I felt my four-mile tramp had made me more weary than ten miles on an honest country road. I looked about the room with some curiosity; there was a shaded lamp, which threw a circle of brilliant light on a heap of papers lying on an old brass-bound secretaire of the last century, but the room was all vague and shadowy, and I could only see that it was long and low, and that it was filled with indistinct objects which might be furniture. Mr. Mathias sat down in a second arm-chair, and looked about him with that odd smile of his. He was a queer-looking man, clean shaven, and white to the lips. I should think his age was something between fifty and sixty.

"Now I have got you here," he began, "I must inflict my hobby on you. You knew I was a collector? Oh yes, I have devoted many years to collecting curiosities, which I think are really curious. But we must have a better light."

He advanced into the middle of the room, and lit a lamp which hung from the ceiling; and as the bright light flashed round the wick, from every corner and space there seemed to start a horror. Great wooden frames, with complicated apparatus of ropes and pulleys, stood against the wall; a wheel of strange shape had a place beside a thing that looked like a gigantic gridiron; little tables glittered with bright steel instruments carelessly put down as if ready for use; a screw and vice loomed out, casting ugly shadows, and in another nook was a saw with cruel jagged teeth.

"Yes," said Mr. Mathias, "they are, as you suggest, instruments of torture—of torture and death. Some—many, I may say—have been used; a few are reproductions after ancient examples. Those knives were used for flaying; that frame is a rack, and a very fine specimen. Look at this; it comes from Venice. You see that sort of collar, some-

154

thing like a big horse-shoe? Well, the patient, let us call him, sat down quite comfortably, and the horse-shoe was neatly fitted round his neck. Then the two ends were joined with a silken band, and the executioner began to turn a handle connected with the band. The horse-shoe contracted very gradually as the band tightened, and the turning continued till the man was strangled. It all took place quietly, in one of those queer garters under the leads. But these things are all European; the Orientals are, of course, much more ingenious. These are the Chinese contrivances; you have heard of the 'Heavy Death'? It is my hobby, this sort of thing. Do you know, I often sit here, hour after hour, and meditate over the collection. I fancy I see the faces of the men who have suffered, faces lean with agony, and wet with sweats of death growing distinct out of the gloom, and I hear the echoes of their cries for mercy. But I must show you my latest acquisition. Come into the next room."

I followed Mr. Mathias out. The weariness of the walk, the late hour, and the strangeness of it all made me feel like a man in a dream; nothing would have surprised me very much. The second room was as the first, crowded with ghastly instruments; but beneath the lamp was a wooden platform, and a figure stood on it. It was a large statue of a naked woman, fashioned in green bronze, the arms were stretched out, and there was a smile on the lips; it might well have been intended for a Venus, and yet there was about the thing an evil and a deadly look.

Mr. Mathias looked at it complacently. "Quite a work of art, isn't it?" he said. "It's made of bronze, as you see, but it has long had the name of the Iron Maid. I got it from Germany, and it was only unpacked this afternoon; indeed, I have not yet had time to open the letter of advice. You see that very small knob between the breasts? Well, the victim was bound to the Maid, the knob was pressed, and the arms slowly tightened round the neck. You can imagine the result."

As Mr. Mathias talked, he patted the figure affectionately. I had turned away, for I sickened at the sight of the man and his loathsome treasure. There was a slight click, of which I took no notice; it was not much louder than the tick of a clock; and then I heard a sudden whirr, the noise of machinery in motion, and I faced round. I have never forgotten the hideous agony on Mathias's face as those relentless arms tightened about his neck; there was a wild struggle as of a beast in the toils, and then a shriek that ended in a choking groan. The whirring noise had suddenly changed into a heavy droning. I tore with all my might at the bronze arms, and strove to wrench them apart, but I could do nothing. The head had slowly bent down, and the green tips were on the lips of Mathias.

Of course, I had to attend at the inquest. The letter which had accompanied the figure was found unopened on the study table. The German firm of dealers cautioned their client to be most careful in touching the Iron Maid, as the machinery had been put in thorough working order.

*   *   *

For many revolving weeks Mr. Burton delighted Dyson by his agreeable conversation, diversified by anecdote, and interspersed with the narration of singular adventures. Finally, however, he vanished as suddenly as he had appeared, and on the occasion of his last visit he contrived to loot a copy of his namesake's *Anatomy*.[37] Dyson, considering this violent attack on the rights of property, and certain glaring inconsistencies in the talk of his late friend, arrived at the conclusion that his stories were fabulous, and that the Iron Maid only existed in the sphere of a decorative imagination.

THE RECLUSE OF
BAYSWATER

Amongst the many friends who were favoured with the occasional pleasure of Mr. Dyson's society was Mr. Edgar Russell, realist and obscure struggler, who occupied a small back room on the second floor of a house in Abingdon Grove, Notting Hill. Turning off from the main street, and walking a few paces onward, one was conscious of a certain calm, a drowsy peace, which made the feet inclined to loiter, and this was ever the atmosphere of Abingdon Grove. The houses stood a little back, with gardens where the lilac, and laburnum, and blood-red may blossomed gaily in their seasons, and there was a corner where an older house in another street had managed to keep a back garden of real extent, a walled-in garden, whence there came a pleasant scent of greenness after the rains of early summer, where old elms held memories of the open fields, where there was yet sweet grass to walk on. The houses in Abingdon Grove belonged chiefly to the nondescript stucco period of thirty-five years ago, tolerably built, with passable accommodation for moderate incomes; they had largely passed into the state of lodgings, and cards bearing the inscription "Furnished Apartments" were not infrequent over the doors. Here, then, in a house of sufficiently good appearance, Mr. Russell had established himself; for he looked upon the traditional dirt and squalor of Grub Street as a false and obsolete convention, and preferred, as he said, to live within sight of green leaves. Indeed, from his room one had a magnificent view of a long line of gardens, and a screen of poplars shut out the melancholy back premises of Wilton Street during the summer months. Mr. Russell lived chiefly on bread and tea, for his means were of the smallest; but when Dyson came to see him, he would send out the slavey for six ale, and Dyson was always at liberty to smoke as much of his tobacco as he pleased. The landlady had been so unfortunate as to have her drawing-room floor vacant for many months; a card had long proclaimed the void within; and Dyson, when he walked up the steps one evening in early autumn, had a sense that something was missing, and, looking at the fanlight, saw the appealing card had disappeared.

"You have let your first floor, have you?" he said, as he greeted Mr. Russell.

"Yes; it was taken about a fortnight ago by a lady."

"Indeed," said Dyson, always curious; "a young lady?"

"Yes; I believe so. She is a widow, and wears a thick crape veil. I have met her once or twice on the stairs and in the street; but I should not know her face."

"Well," said Dyson, when the beer had arrived, and the pipes were in full blast, "and what have you been doing? Do you find the work getting any easier?"

"Alas!" said the young man, with an expression of great gloom, "the life is a purgatory, and all but a hell. I write, picking out my words, weighing and balancing the force of every syllable, calculating the minutest effects that language can produce, erasing and rewriting, and spending a whole evening over a page of manuscript. And then, in the morning, when I read what I have written— Well, there is nothing to be done but to throw it in the waste-paper basket, if the verso has been already written on, or to put it in the drawer if the other side happens to be clean. When I have written a phrase which undoubtedly embodies a happy turn of thought, I find it dressed up in feeble commonplace; and when the style is good, it serves only to conceal the baldness of superannuated fancies. I sweat over my work, Dyson—every finished line means so much agony. I envy the lot of the carpenter in the side street who has a craft which he understands. When he gets an order for a table he does not writhe with anguish; but if I were so unlucky as to get an order for a book, I think I should go mad."

"My dear fellow, you take it all too seriously. You should let the ink flow more readily. Above all, firmly believe, when you sit down to write, that you are an artist, and that whatever you are about is a masterpiece. Suppose ideas fail you, say, as I heard one of our most exquisite artists say, 'It's of no consequence; the ideas are all there, at the bottom of that box of cigarettes!' You, indeed, smoke a pipe, but the application is the same. Besides, you must have some happy moments; and these should be ample consolation."

"Perhaps you are right. But such moments are so few; and then there is the torture of a glorious conception matched with execution beneath the standard of the 'Family Story Paper.' For instance, I was happy for two hours a night or two ago; I lay awake and saw visions. But then the morning!"

"What was your idea?"

"It seemed to me a splendid one: I thought of Balzac and the 'Comédie Humaine,' of Zola and the Rougon-Macquart family.[38] It dawned on me that I would write the history of a street. Every house should form a volume. I fixed upon the street, I saw each house, and read as clearly as in letters the physiology and psychology of each; the little byway stretched before me in its actual shape—a street that I know and have passed down a hundred times, with some twenty houses, prosperous and mean, and lilac bushes in purple blossom. And yet it was, at the same time, a symbol, a *via dolorosa*[39] of hopes cherished and disappointed, of years of monotonous existence without content or discontent, of tragedies and obscure sorrows; and on the door of one of those houses I saw the red stain of blood, and behind a window two shadows, blackened and faded on the blind, as they swayed on tightened cords—the shadows of a man and a woman hanging in a vulgar gaslit parlour. These were my fancies; but when pen touched paper they shrivelled and vanished away."

"Yes," said Dyson, "there is a lot in that. I envy you the pains of transmuting vision into reality, and, still more, I envy you the day when you will look at your bookshelf and see twenty goodly books upon the shelves—the series complete and done for ever. Let me entreat you to have them bound in solid parchment, with gold lettering. It is the only real cover for a valiant book. When I look in at the windows of some choice shop, and see the bindings of Levant morocco, with pretty tools and panellings, and your sweet contrasts of red and green, I say to myself, 'These are not books, but *bibelots*.'[40] A book bound so—a true book, mind you—is like a Gothic statue draped in brocade of Lyons."

"Alas!" said Russell, "we need not discuss the binding—the books are not begun."

The talk went on as usual till eleven o'clock, when Dyson bade his friend good-night. He knew the way downstairs, and walked down by himself; but, greatly to his surprise, as he crossed the first-floor landing the door opened slightly, and a hand was stretched out, beckoning.

Dyson was not the man to hesitate under such circumstances. In a moment he saw himself involved in adventure; and, as he told himself, the Dysons had never disobeyed a lady's summons. Softly, then, with due regard for the lady's honour, he would have entered the room, when a low but clear voice spoke to him—

"Go downstairs and open the door and shut it again rather loudly. Then come up to me; and for Heaven's sake, walk softly."

Dyson obeyed her commands, not without some hesitation, for he was afraid of meeting the landlady or the maid on his return journey. But, walking like a cat, and making each step he trod on crack loudly, he flattered himself that he had escaped observation; and as he gained the top of the stairs the door opened wide before him, and he found himself in the lady's drawing-room, bowing awkwardly.

"Pray be seated, sir. Perhaps this chair will be the best; it was the favoured chair of my landlady's deceased husband. I would ask you to smoke, but the odour would betray me. I know my proceedings must seem to you unconventional; but I saw you arrive this evening, and I do not think you would refuse to help a woman who is so unfortunate as I am."

Mr. Dyson looked shyly at the young lady before him. She was dressed in deep mourning, but the piquant smiling face and charming hazel eyes ill accorded with the heavy garments and the mouldering surface of the crape.

"Madam," he said gallantly, "your instinct has served you well. We will not trouble, if you please, about the question of social conventions; the chivalrous gentleman knows nothing of such matters. I hope I may be privileged to serve you."

"You are very kind to me, but I knew it would be so. Alas! sir, I have had experience of life, and I am rarely mistaken. Yet man is too often so vile and so misjudging that I trembled even as I resolved to take this step, which, for all I knew, might prove to be both desperate and ruinous."

"With me you have nothing to fear," said Dyson. "I was nurtured in the faith of chivalry, and I have always endeavoured to remember the proud traditions of my race. Confide in me, then, and count upon my secrecy, and if it prove possible, you may rely on my help."

"Sir, I will not waste your time, which I am sure is valuable, by idle parleyings. Learn, then, that I am a fugitive, and in hiding here; I place myself in your power; you have but to describe my features, and I fall into the hands of my relentless enemy."

Mr. Dyson wondered for a passing instant how this could be, but he only renewed his promise of silence, repeating that he would be the embodied spirit of dark concealment.

"Good," said the lady, "the Oriental fervour of your style is delightful. In the first place, I must disabuse your mind of the conviction that I am a widow. These gloomy vestments have been forced on me by strange circumstance; in plain language, I have deemed it expedient to go disguised. You have a friend, I think, in the house, Mr. Russell? He seems of a coy and retiring nature."

"Excuse me, madam," said Dyson, "he is not coy, but he is a realist; and perhaps you are aware that no Carthusian monk can emulate the cloistral seclusion in which a realistic novelist loves to shroud himself. It is his way of observing human nature."

"Well, well," said the lady; "all this, though deeply interesting, is not germane to our affair. I must tell you my history."

With these words the young lady proceeded to relate the

NOVEL OF THE WHITE POWDER

My name is Leicester; my father, Major-General Wyn Leicester, a distinguished officer of artillery, succumbed five years ago to a complicated liver complaint acquired in the deadly climate of India. A year later my only brother, Francis, came home after an exceptionally brilliant career at the University, and settled down with the resolution of a hermit to master what has been well called the great legend of the law. He was a man who seemed to live in utter indifference to everything that is called pleasure; and though he was handsomer than most men, and could talk as merrily and wittily as if he were a mere vagabond, he avoided society, and shut himself up in a large room at the top of the house to make himself a lawyer. Ten hours a day of hard reading was at first his allotted portion; from the first light in the east to the late afternoon he remained shut up with his books, taking a hasty half-hour's lunch with me as if he grudged the wasting of the moments, and going out for a short walk when it began to grow dusk. I thought that such relentless application must be injurious, and tried to cajole him from the crabbed textbooks, but his ardour seemed to grow rather than diminish, and his daily tale of hours increased. I spoke to him seriously, suggesting some occasional relaxation, if it were but an idle afternoon with a harmless novel; but he laughed, and said that he read about feudal tenures when he felt in need of amusement, and scoffed at the notions of theatres, or a month's fresh air. I confessed that he looked well, and seemed not to suffer from his labours, but I knew that such unnatural toil would take revenge at last, and I was not mistaken. A look of anxiety began to lurk about his eyes, and he seemed languid, and at last he avowed that he was no longer in perfect health; he was troubled, he said, with a sensation of dizziness, and awoke now and then of nights from fearful dreams, terrified and cold with icy sweats. "I am taking care of myself," he said, "so you must not trouble; I passed the whole of yesterday afternoon in idleness, leaning back in that comfortable chair you gave me, and scribbling nonsense on a sheet of paper. No, no; I will not overdo my work; I shall be well enough in a week or two depend upon it."

Yet in spite of his assurances I could see that he grew no better, but rather worse; he would enter the drawing-room with a face all miserably wrinkled and despondent, and endeavour to look gaily when my eyes fell on him, and I thought such symptoms of evil omen, and was frightened sometimes at the nervous irritation of his movements, and at glances which I could not decipher. Much against his will, I prevailed on him to have medical advice, and with an ill grace he called in our old doctor.

Dr. Haberden cheered me after examination of his patient.

"There is nothing really much amiss," he said to me. "No doubt he reads too hard and eats hastily, and then goes back again to his books in too great a hurry, and the natural sequence is some digestive trouble and a little mischief in the nervous system. But I think—I do indeed, Miss Leicester—that we shall be able to set this all right. I have written him a prescription which ought to do great things. So you have no cause for anxiety."

My brother insisted on having the prescription made up by a chemist in the neighbourhood. It was an odd, old-fashioned shop, devoid of the studied coquetry and calculated glitter that make so gay a show on the counters and shelves of the modern apothecary; but Francis liked the old chemist, and believed in the scrupulous purity of his drugs. The medicine was sent in due course, and I saw that my brother took it regularly after lunch and dinner. It was an innocent-looking white powder, of which a little was dissolved in a glass of cold water; I stirred it in, and it seemed to disappear, leaving the water clear and colorless. At first Francis seemed to benefit greatly; the weariness vanished from his face, and he became more cheerful than he had ever been since the time when he left school; he talked gaily of reforming himself, and avowed to me that he had wasted his time.

"I have given too many hours to law," he said, laughing; "I think you have saved me in the nick of time. Come, I shall be Lord Chancellor yet, but I must not forget life. You and I will have a holiday together before long; we will go to Paris and enjoy ourselves, and keep away from the Bibliothèque Nationale."

I confessed myself delighted with the prospect.

"When shall we go?" I said. "I can start the day after to-morrow if you like."

"Ah! that is perhaps a little too soon; after all, I do not know London yet, and I suppose a man ought to give the pleasures of his own country the first choice. But we will go off together in a week or two, so try and furbish up your French. I only know law French myself, and I am afraid that wouldn't do."

We were just finishing dinner, and he quaffed off his medicine with a parade of carousal as if it had been wine from some choicest bin.

"Has it any particular taste?" I said.

"No; I should not know I was not drinking water," and he got up from his chair and began to pace up and down the room as if he were undecided as to what he should do next.

"Shall we have coffee in the drawing-room?" I said; "or would you like to smoke?"

"No, I think I will take a turn; it seems a pleasant evening. Look at the afterglow; why, it is as if a great city were burning in flames, and down there between the dark houses it is raining blood fast. Yes, I will go out; I may be in soon, but I shall take my key; so good-night, dear, if I don't see you again."

The door slammed behind him, and I saw him walk lightly down the street, swinging his malacca cane, and I felt grateful to Dr. Haberden for such an improvement.

I believe my brother came home very late that night, but he was in a merry mood the next morning.

"I walked on without thinking where I was going," he said, "enjoying the freshness of the air, and livened by the crowds as I reached more frequented quarters. And then I met an old college friend, Orford, in the press of the pavement, and then—well, we enjoyed ourselves. I have felt what it is to be young and a man; I find I have blood in my veins, as other men have. I made an appointment with Orford for to-night; there will be a little party of us at the restaurant. Yes; I shall enjoy myself for a week or two, and hear the chimes at midnight, and then we will go for our little trip together."

Such was the transmutation of my brother's character that in a few days he became a lover of pleasure, a careless and merry idler of western pavements, a hunter out of snug restaurants, and a fine critic of fantastic dancing; he grew fat before my eyes, and said no more of Paris, for he had clearly found his paradise in London. I rejoiced, and yet wondered a little; for there was, I thought, something in his gaiety that indefinitely displeased me, though I could not have defined my feeling. But by degrees there came a change; he returned still in the cold hours of the morning, but I heard no more about his pleasures, and one morning as we sat at breakfast together I looked suddenly into his eyes and saw a stranger before me.

"Oh, Francis!" I cried. "Oh, Francis, Francis, what have you done?" and rending sobs cut the words short. I went weeping out of the room; for though I knew nothing, yet I knew all, and by some odd play of thought I remembered the evening when he first went abroad, and the picture of the sunset sky glowed before me; the clouds like a city in burning flames, and the rain of blood. Yet I did battle with such thoughts, resolving that perhaps, after all, no great harm had been done, and in the evening at dinner I resolved to press him to fix a day for our holiday in Paris. We had talked easily enough, and my brother had just taken his medicine, which he continued all the while. I was about to begin my topic when the words forming in my mind vanished, and I wondered for a second what icy and intolerable weight oppressed my heart and suffocated me as with the unutterable horror of the coffin-lid nailed down on the living.

We had dined without candles; the room had slowly grown from twilight to gloom, and the walls and corners were indistinct in the shadow. But from where I sat I looked out into the street; and as I thought of what I would say to Francis, the sky began to flush and shine, as it had done on a well-remembered evening, and in the gap between two dark masses that were houses an awful pageantry of flame appeared—lurid whorls of writhed cloud, and utter depths burning, grey masses like the fume blown from a smoking city, and an evil glory blazing far above shot with tongues of more ardent fire, and below as if there were a deep pool of blood. I looked down to where my brother sat facing me, and the words were shaped on my lips, when I saw his hand resting on the table. Between the thumb and forefinger of the closed hand there was a mark, a small patch about the size of a sixpence, and somewhat of the colour of a bad bruise. Yet, by some sense I cannot define, I knew that what I saw was no bruise at all; oh! if human flesh could burn with flame, and if flame could be black as pitch, such was that before me. Without thought or fashioning of words grey horror shaped within me at the sight, and in an inner cell it was known to be a brand. For the moment the stained sky became dark as midnight, and when the light returned to me I was alone in the silent room, and soon after I heard my brother go out.

Late as it was, I put on my hat and went to Dr. Haberden, and in his great consulting room, ill lighted by a candle which the doctor brought in with him, with stammering lips, and a voice that would break in spite of my resolve, I told him all, from the day on which my brother began to take the medicine down to the dreadful thing I had seen scarcely half an hour before.

When I had done, the doctor looked at me for a minute with an expression of great pity on his face.

"My dear Miss Leicester," he said, "you have evidently been anxious about your brother; you have been worrying over him, I am sure. Come, now, is it not so?"

"I have certainly been anxious," I said. "For the last week or two I have not felt at ease."

"Quite so; you know, of course, what a queer thing the brain is?"

"I understand what you mean; but I was not deceived. I saw what I have told you with my own eyes."

"Yes, yes, of course. But your eyes had been staring at that very curious sunset we had tonight. That is the only explanation. You will see it in the proper light to-morrow, I am sure. But, remember, I am always ready to give any help that is in my power; do not scruple to come to me, or to send for me if you are in any distress."

I went away but little comforted, all confusion and terror and sorrow, not knowing where to turn. When my brother and I met the next day, I looked quickly at him, and noticed, with a sickening at heart, that the right hand, the hand on which I had clearly seen the patch as of a black fire, was wrapped up with a handkerchief.

"What is the matter with your hand, Francis?" I said in a steady voice.

"Nothing of consequence. I cut a finger last night, and it bled rather awkwardly. So I did it up roughly to the best of my ability."

"I will do it neatly for you, if you like."

"No, thank you, dear; this will answer very well. Suppose we have breakfast; I am quite hungry."

We sat down and I watched him. He scarcely ate or drank at all, but tossed his meat to the dog when he thought my eyes were turned away; there was a look in his eyes that I had never yet seen, and the thought flashed across my mind that it was a look that was scarcely human. I was firmly convinced that awful and incredible as was the thing I had seen the night before, yet it was no illusion, no glamour of bewildered sense, and in the course of the evening I went again to the doctor's house.

He shook his head with an air puzzled and incredulous, and seemed to reflect for a few minutes.

"And you say he still keeps up the medicine? But why? As I understand, all the symptoms he complained of have disappeared long ago; why should he go on taking the stuff when he is quite well? And by the by, where did he get it made up? At Sayce's? I never send any one there; the old man is getting careless. Suppose you come with me to the chemist's; I should like to have some talk with him."

We walked together to the shop; old Sayce knew Dr. Haberden, and was quite ready to give any information.

"You have been sending that in to Mr. Leicester for some weeks, I think, on my prescription," said the doctor, giving the old man a pencilled scrap of paper.

The chemist put on his great spectacles with trembling uncertainty, and held up the paper with a shaking hand.

"Oh, yes," he said, "I have very little of it left; it is rather an uncommon drug, and I have had it in stock some time. I must get in some more, if Mr. Leicester goes on with it."

"Kindly let me have a look at the stuff," said Haberden, and the chemist gave him a glass bottle. He took out the stopper and smelt the contents, and looked strangely at the old man.

"Where did you get this?" he said, "and what is it? For one thing, Mr. Sayce, it is not what I prescribed. Yes, yes, I see the label is right enough, but I tell you this is not the drug."

"I have had it a long time," said the old man in feeble terror; "I got it from Burbage's in the usual way. It is not prescribed often, and I have had it on the shelf for some years. You see there is very little left."

"You had better give it to me," said Haberden. "I am afraid something wrong has happened."

We went out of the shop in silence, the doctor carrying the bottle neatly wrapped in paper under his arm.

"Dr. Haberden," I said, when we had walked a little way—"Dr. Haberden."

"Yes," he said, looking at me gloomily enough.

"I should like you to tell me what my brother has been taking twice a day for the last month or so."

"Frankly, Miss Leicester, I don't know. We will speak of this when we get to my house."

We walked on quickly without another word till we reached Dr. Haberden's. He asked me to sit down, and began pacing up and down the room, his face clouded over, as I could see, with no common fears.

"Well," he said at length, "this is all very strange; it is only natural that you should feel alarmed, and I must confess that my mind is far from easy. We will put aside, if you please, what you told me last night and this morning, but the fact remains that for the last few weeks Mr. Leicester has been impregnating his system with a drug which is completely unknown to me. I tell you, it is not what I ordered; and what the stuff in the bottle really is remains to be seen."

He undid the wrapper, and cautiously tilted a few grains of the white powder on to a piece of paper, and peered curiously at it.

"Yes," he said, "it is like the sulphate of quinine, as you say; it is flaky. But smell it."

He held the bottle to me, and I bent over it. It was a strange, sickly smell, vaporous and overpowering, like some strong anæsthetic.

"I shall have it analyzed," said Haberden; "I have a friend who has devoted his whole life to chemistry as a science. Then we shall have something to go upon. No, no; say no more about that other matter; I cannot listen to that; and take my advice and think no more about it yourself."

That evening my brother did not go out as usual after dinner.

"I have had my fling," he said with a queer laugh, "and I must go back to my old ways. A little law will be quite a relaxation after so sharp a dose of pleasure," and he grinned to himself, and soon after went up to his room. His hand was still all bandaged.

Dr. Haberden called a few days later.

"I have no special news to give you," he said. "Chambers is out of town, so I know no more about that stuff than you do. But I should like to see Mr. Leicester, if he is in."

"He is in his room," I said; "I will tell him you are here."

"No, no, I will go up to him; we will have a little quiet talk together. I dare say that we have made a good deal of fuss about very little; for, after all, whatever the powder may be, it seems to have done him good."

The doctor went upstairs, and standing in the hall I heard his knock, and the opening and shutting of the door; and then I waited in the silent house for an hour, and the stillness grew more and more intense as the hands of the clock crept round. Then there sounded from above the noise of a door shut sharply, and the doctor was coming down the stairs. His footsteps crossed the hall, and there was a pause at the door; I drew a long, sick breath with difficulty, and saw my face white in a little mirror, and he came in and stood at the door. There was an unutterable horror shining in his eyes; he steadied himself by holding the back of a chair with one hand, his lower lip trembled like a horse's, and he gulped and stammered unintelligible sounds before he spoke.

"I have seen that man," he began in a dry whisper. "I have been sitting in his presence for the last hour. My God! And I am alive and in my senses! I, who have dealt with death all my life, and have dabbled with the melting ruins of the earthly tabernacle. But not this, oh! not this," and he covered his face with his hands as if to shut out the sight of something before him.

"Do not send for me again, Miss Leicester," he said with more composure. "I can do nothing in this house. Good-bye."

As I watched him totter down the steps, and along the pavement towards his house, it seemed to me that he had aged by ten years since the morning.

My brother remained in his room. He called out to me in a voice I hardly recognized that he was very busy, and would like his meals brought to his door and left there, and I gave the order to the servants. From that day it seemed as if the arbitrary conception we call time had been annihilated for me; I lived in an ever-present sense of horror, going through the routine of the house mechanically, and only speaking a few necessary words to the servants. Now and then I went out and paced the streets for an hour or two and came home again; but whether I were without or within, my spirit delayed before the closed door of the upper room, and, shuddering, waited for it to open. I have said that I scarcely reckoned time; but I suppose it must have been a fortnight after Dr. Haberden's visit that I came home from my stroll a little refreshed and lightened. The air was sweet and pleasant, and the hazy form of green leaves, floating cloud-like in the square, and the smell of blossoms, had charmed my senses, and I felt happier and walked more briskly. As I delayed a moment at the verge of the pavement, waiting for a van to pass by before crossing over to the house, I happened to look up at the windows, and instantly there was the rush and swirl of deep cold waters in my ears, my heart leapt up and fell down, down as into a deep hollow, and I was amazed with a dread and terror without form or shape. I stretched out a hand blindly through the folds of thick darkness, from the black and shadowy valley, and held myself from falling, while the stones beneath my feet rocked and swayed and tilted, and the sense of solid things seemed to sink away from under me. I had glanced up at the window of my brother's study, and at that moment the blind was drawn aside, and something that had life stared out into the world. Nay, I cannot say I saw a face or any human likeness; a living thing, two eyes of burning flame glared at me, and they were in the midst of something as formless as my fear, the symbol and presence of all evil and all hideous corruption. I stood shuddering and quaking as with the grip of ague, sick with unspeakable agonies of fear and loathing, and for five minutes I could not summon force or motion to my limbs. When I was within the door, I ran up the stairs to my brother's room and knocked.

"Francis, Francis," I cried, "for Heaven's sake, answer me. What is the horrible thing in your room? Cast it out, Francis; cast it from you."

I heard a noise as of feet shuffling slowly and awkwardly, and a choking, gurgling sound, as if some one was struggling to find utterance, and then the noise of a voice, broken and stifled, and words that I could scarcely understand.

"There is nothing here," the voice said. "Pray do not disturb me. I am not very well to-day."

I turned away, horrified, and yet helpless. I could do nothing, and I wondered why Francis had lied to me, for I had I seen the appearance beyond the glass too plainly to be deceived, though it was but the sight of a moment. And I sat still, conscious that there had been something else, something I had seen in the first flash of terror, before those burning eyes had looked at me. Suddenly I remembered; as I lifted my face the blind was being drawn back, and I had had an instant's glance of the thing that was moving it, and in my recollection I knew that a hideous image was engraved forever on my brain. It was not a hand; there were no fingers that held the blind, but a black stump pushed it aside, the mouldering outline and the clumsy movement as of a beast's paw had glowed into my senses before the darkling waves of terror had overwhelmed me as I went down quick into the pit. My mind was aghast at the thought of this, and of the awful presence that dwelt with my brother in his room; I went to his door and cried to him again, but no answer came. That night one of the servants came up to me and told me in a whisper that for three days food had been regularly placed at the door and left untouched; the maid had knocked but had received no answer; she had heard the noise of shuffling feet that I had noticed. Day after day went by, and still my brother's meals were brought to his door and left untouched; and though I knocked and called again and again, I could get no answer. The servants began to talk to me; it appeared they were as alarmed as I; the cook said that when my brother first shut himself up in his room she used to hear him come out at night and go about the house; and once, she said, the hall door had opened and closed again, but for several nights she had heard no sound. The climax came at last; it was in the dusk of the evening, and I was sitting in the darkening dreary room when a terrible shriek jarred and rang harshly out of the silence, and I heard a frightened scurry of feet dashing down the stairs. I waited, and the servant-maid staggered into the room and faced me, white and trembling.

"Oh, Miss Helen!" she whispered; "oh! for the Lord's sake, Miss Helen, what has happened? Look at my hand, miss; look at that hand!"

I drew her to the window, and saw there was a black wet stain upon her hand.

"I do not understand you," I said. "Will you explain to me?"

"I was doing your room just now," she began. "I was turning down the bed-clothes, and all of a sudden there was something fell upon my hand, wet, and I looked up, and the ceiling was black and dripping on me."

I looked hard at her and bit my lip.

"Come with me," I said. "Bring your candle with you."

The room I slept in was beneath my brother's, and as I went in I felt I was trembling. I looked up at the ceiling, and saw a patch, all black and wet, and a dew of black drops upon it, and a pool of horrible liquor soaking into the white bedclothes.

I ran upstairs and knocked loudly.

"Oh, Francis, Francis, my dear brother," I cried, "what has happened to you."

And I listened. There was a sound of choking, and a noise like water bubbling and regurgitating, but nothing else, and I called louder, but no answer came.

In spite of what Dr. Haberden had said, I went to him; with tears streaming down my cheeks I told him all that had happened, and he listened to me with a face set hard and grim.

"For your father's sake," he said at last, "I will go with you, though I can do nothing."

We went out together; the streets were dark and silent, and heavy with heat and a drought of many weeks. I saw the doctor's face white under the gas-lamps, and when we reached the house his hand was shaking.

We did not hesitate, but went upstairs directly. I held the lamp, and he called out in a loud, determined voice—

"Mr. Leicester, do you hear me? I insist on seeing you. Answer me at once."

There was no answer, but we both heard that choking noise I have mentioned.

"Mr. Leicester, I am waiting for you. Open the door this instant, or I shall break it down." And he called a third time in a voice that rang and echoed from the walls—

"Mr. Leicester! For the last time I order you to open the door."

"Ah!" he said, after a pause of heavy silence, "we are wasting time here. Will you be so kind as to get me a poker, or something of the kind?"

I ran into a little room at the back where odd articles were kept, and found a heavy adze-like tool that I thought might serve the doctor's purpose.

"Very good," he said, "that will do, I dare say. I give you notice,

Mr. Leicester," he cried loudly at the keyhole, "that I am now about to break into your room."

Then I heard the wrench of the adze, and the wood-work split and cracked under it; with a loud crash the door suddenly burst open, and for a moment we started back aghast at a fearful screaming cry, no human voice, but as the roar of a monster, that burst forth inarticulate and struck at us out of the darkness.

"Hold the lamp," said the doctor, and we went in and glanced quickly round the room.

"There it is," said Dr. Haberden, drawing a quick breath; "look, in that corner."

I looked, and a pang of horror seized my heart as with a white-hot iron. There upon the floor was a dark and putrid mass, seething with corruption and hideous rottenness, neither liquid nor solid, but melting and changing before our eyes, and bubbling with unctuous oily bubbles like boiling pitch. And out of the midst of it shone two burning points like eyes, and I saw a writhing and stirring as of limbs, and something moved and lifted up what might have been an arm. The doctor took a step forward, raised the iron bar and struck at the burning points; he drove in the weapon, and struck again and again in the fury of loathing.

*　　*　　*

A week or two later, when I had recovered to some extent from the terrible shock, Dr. Haberden came to see me.

"I have sold my practice," he began, "and to-morrow I am sailing on a long voyage. I do not know whether I shall ever return to England; in all probability I shall buy a little land in California, and settle there for the remainder of my life. I have brought you this packet, which you may open and read when you feel able to do so. It contains the report of Dr. Chambers on what I submitted to him. Good-bye, Miss Leicester, good-bye."

When he was gone I opened the envelope; I could not wait, and proceeded to read the papers within. Here is the manuscript, and if you will allow me, I will read you the astounding story it contains.

"My dear Haberden," the letter began, "I have delayed inexcusably in answering your questions as to the white substance you sent me. To tell you the truth, I have hesitated for some time as to what course I should adopt, for there is a bigotry and orthodox standard in physical science as in theology, and I knew that if I told you the truth I should offend rooted prejudices which I once held dear myself. However, I have determined to be plain with you, and first I must enter into a short personal explanation.

"You have known me, Haberden, for many years as a scientific man; you and I have often talked of our profession together, and discussed the hopeless gulf that opens before the feet of those who think to attain to truth by any means whatsoever except the beaten way of experiment and observation in the sphere of material things. I remember the scorn with which you have spoken to me of men of science who have dabbled a little in the unseen, and have timidly hinted that perhaps the senses are not, after all, the eternal, impenetrable bounds of all knowledge, the everlasting walls beyond which no human being has ever passed. We have laughed together heartily, and I think justly, at the 'occult' follies of the day, disguised under various names—the mesmerisms, spiritualisms, materializations, theosophies, all the rabble rout of imposture, with their machinery of poor tricks and feeble conjuring, the true back-parlour of shabby London streets. Yet, in spite of what I have said, I must confess to you that I am no materialist, taking the word of course in its usual signification. It is now many years since I have convinced myself—convinced myself, a sceptic, remember— that the old ironbound theory is utterly and entirely false. Perhaps this confession will not wound you so sharply as it would have done twenty years ago; for I think you cannot have failed to notice that for some time hypotheses have been advanced by men of pure science which are nothing less than transcendental, and I suspect that most modern chemists and biologists of repute would not hesitate to subscribe the *dictum* of the old Schoolman, *Omnia exeunt in mysterium*,[41] which means, I take it, that every branch of human knowledge if traced up to its source and final principles vanishes into mystery. I need not trouble you now with a detailed account of the painful steps which led me to my conclusions; a few simple experiments suggested a doubt as to my then standpoint, and a train of thought that rose from circumstances comparatively trifling brought me far; my old conception of the universe has been swept away, and I stand in a world that seems as strange and awful to me as the endless waves of the ocean seen for the first time, shining, from a peak in Darien.[42] Now I know that the walls of sense that seemed so impenetrable, that seemed to loom up above the heavens and to be founded below the depths, and to shut us in for evermore, are no such everlasting impassable barriers as we fancied, but thinnest and most airy veils that melt away before the seeker, and dissolve as the early mist of the morning about the brooks. I know that you never adopted the extreme materialistic position; you did not go about trying to prove a universal negative, for your logical sense withheld you from that crowning absurdity; but I am sure that you will find all that I am saying strange and repellent to your habits of thought. Yet, Haberden, what I tell you is the truth, nay, to adopt our common language, the sole and scientific truth, verified by experience; and the universe is verily more splendid and more awful than we used to dream. The whole universe, my friend, is a tremendous sacrament; a mystic, ineffable force and energy, veiled by an outward form of matter; and man, and the sun and the other stars, and the flower of the grass, and the crystal in the test-tube, are each and every one as spiritual, as material, and subject to an inner working.

"You will perhaps wonder, Haberden, whence all this tends; but I think a little thought will make it clear. You will understand that from such a standpoint the whole view of things is changed, and what we thought incredible and absurd may be possible enough. In short, we must look at legend and belief with other eyes, and be prepared to accept tales that had become mere fables. Indeed this is no such great demand. After all, modern science will concede as much, in a hypocritical manner; you must not, it is true, believe in witchcraft, but you may credit hypnotism; ghosts are out of date, but there is a good deal to be said for the theory of telepathy. Give superstition a Greek name, and believe in it, should almost be a proverb.

"So much for my personal explanation. You sent me, Haberden, a phial, stoppered and sealed, containing a small quantity of flaky white powder, obtained from a chemist who has been dispensing it to one of your patients. I am not surprised to hear that this powder refused to yield any results to your analysis. It is a substance which was known to a few many hundred years ago, but which I never expected to have submitted to me from the shop of a modern apothecary. There seems no reason to doubt the truth of the man's tale; he no doubt got, as he says, the rather uncommon salt you prescribed from the wholesale chemist's; and it has probably remained on his shelf for twenty years, or perhaps longer. Here what we call chance and coincidence begin to work; during all these years the salt in the bottle was exposed to certain recurring variations of temperature, variations probably ranging from 40° to 80°. And, as it happens, such changes, recurring year after year at irregular intervals, and with varying degrees of intensity and duration, have constituted a process, and a process so complicated and so delicate, that I question whether modern scientific apparatus directed with the utmost precision could produce the same result. The white powder you sent me is something very different from the drug you prescribed; it is the powder from which the wine of the Sabbath, the *Vinum Sabbati*, was prepared. No doubt you have read of the Witches'

Sabbath, and have laughed at the tales which terrified our ancestors; the black cats, and the broomsticks, and dooms pronounced against some old woman's cow. Since I have known the truth I have often reflected that it is on the whole a happy thing that such burlesque as this is believed, for it serves to conceal much that it is better should not be known generally. However, if you care to read the appendix to Payne Knight's monograph,[43] you will find that the true Sabbath was something very different, though the writer has very nicely refrained from printing all he knew. The secrets of the true Sabbath were the secrets of remote times surviving into the Middle Ages, secrets of an evil science which existed long before Aryan man entered Europe. Men and women, seduced from their homes on specious pretences, were met by beings well qualified to assume, as they did assume, the part of devils, and taken by their guides to some desolate and lonely place, known to the initiate by long tradition, and unknown to all else. Perhaps it was a cave in some bare and windswept hill, perhaps some inmost recess of a great forest, and there the Sabbath was held. There, in the blackest hour of night, the *Vinum Sabbati* was prepared, and this evil graal was poured forth and offered to the neophytes, and they partook of an infernal sacrament; *sumentes calicem principis inferorum,*[44] as an old author well expresses it. And suddenly, each one that had drunk found himself attended by a companion, a shape of glamour and unearthly allurement, beckoning him apart, to share in joys more exquisite, more piercing than the thrill of any dream, to the consummation of the marriage of the Sabbath. It is hard to write of such things as these, and chiefly because that shape that allured with loveliness was no hallucination, but, awful as it is to express, the man himself. By the power of that Sabbath wine, a few grains of white powder thrown into a glass of water, the house of life was riven asunder and the human trinity dissolved, and the worm which never dies, that which lies sleeping within us all, was made tangible and an external thing, and clothed with a garment of flesh. And then, in the hour of midnight, the primal fall was repeated and re-presented, and the awful thing veiled in the mythos of the Tree in the Garden was done anew. Such was the *nuptiæ Sabbati.*

"I prefer to say no more; you, Haberden, know as well as I do that the most trivial laws of life are not to be broken with impunity; and for so terrible an act as this, in which the very inmost place of the temple was broken open and defiled, a terrible vengeance followed. What began with corruption ended also with corruption."

Underneath is the following in Dr. Haberden's writing:—

"The whole of the above is unfortunately strictly and entirely true. Your brother confessed all to me on that morning when I saw him in his room. My attention was first attracted to the bandaged hand, and I forced him to show it me. What I saw made me, a medical man of many years' standing, grow sick with loathing, and the story I was forced to listen to was infinitely more frightful than I could have believed possible. It has tempted me to doubt the Eternal Goodness which can permit nature to offer such hideous possibilities; and if you had not with your own eyes seen the end, I should have said to you—disbelieve it all. I have not, I think, many more weeks to live, but you are young, and may forget all this."

"JOSEPH HABERDEN, M. D."

In the course of two or three months I heard that Dr. Haberden had died at sea shortly after the ship left England.

Miss Leicester ceased speaking, and looked pathetically at Dyson, who could not refrain from exhibiting some symptoms of uneasiness.

He stuttered out some broken phrases expressive of his deep interest in her extraodinary history, and then said with a better grace—

"But pardon me, Miss Leicester, I understood you were in some difficulty. You were kind enough to ask me to assist you in some way."

"Ah," she said, "I had forgotten that; my own present trouble seems of such little consequence in comparison with what I have told you. But as you are so good to me, I will go on. You will scarcely believe it, but I found that certain persons suspected, or rather pretended to suspect, that I had murdered my brother. These persons were relatives of mine, and their motives were extremely sordid ones; but I actually found myself subject to the shameful indignity of being watched. Yes, sir, my steps were dogged when I went abroad, and at home I found myself exposed to constant if artful observation. With my high spirit this was more than I could brook, and I resolved to set my wits to work and elude the persons who were shadowing me. I was so fortunate as to succeed; I assumed this disguise, and for some time have lain snug and unsuspected. But of late I have reason to believe that the pursuer is on my track; unless I am greatly deceived, I saw yesterday the detective who is charged with the odious duty of observing my movements. You, sir, are watchful and keen-sighted; tell me, did you see any one lurking about this evening?"

"I hardly think so," said Dyson, "but perhaps you would give me some description of the detective in question."

"Certainly; he is a youngish man, dark, with dark whiskers. He has adopted spectacles of large size in the hope of disguising himself effectually, but he cannot disguise his uneasy manner, and the quick, nervous glances he casts to right and left."

This piece of description was the last straw for the unhappy Dyson, who was foaming with impatience to get out of the house, and would gladly have sworn eighteenth-century oaths, if propriety had not frowned on such a course.

"Excuse me, Miss Leicester," he said with cool politeness, "I cannot assist you."

"Ah," she said sadly, "I have offended you in some way. Tell me what I have done, and I will ask you to forgive me."

"You are mistaken," said Dyson, grabbing his hat, but speaking with some difficulty; "you have done nothing. But, as I say, I cannot help you. Perhaps," he added, with some tinge of sarcasm, "my friend Russell might be of service."

"Thank you," she replied; "I will try him," and the lady went off into a shriek of laughter, which filled up Mr. Dyson's cup of scandal and confusion.

He left the house shortly afterwards, and had the peculiar delight of a five-mile walk, through streets which slowly changed from black to grey, and from grey to shining passages of glory for the sun to brighten. Here and there he met or overtook strayed revellers, but he reflected that no one could have spent the night in a more futile fashion than himself; and when he reached his home he had made resolves for reformation. He decided that he would abjure all Milesian and Arabian methods of entertainment, and subscribe to Mudie's[45] for a regular supply of mild and innocuous romance.

STRANGE OCCURRENCE IN CLERKENWELL

Mr. Dyson had inhabited for some years a couple of rooms in a moderately quiet street in Bloomsbury, where, as he somewhat pompously expressed it, he held his finger on the pulse of life without being deafened with the thousand rumours of the main arteries of London. It was to him a source of peculiar, if esoteric, gratification that from the adjacent corner of Tottenham Court Road a hundred lines of omnibuses went to the four quarters of the town; he would dilate on the facilities for visiting Dalston, and dwell on the admirable line that knew extremest Ealing and the streets beyond Whitechapel. His rooms, which had been originally "furnished apartments," he had gradually purged of their more peccant parts; and though one would not find here the glowing splendour of his old chambers in the street off the Strand, there was something of severe grace about the appointments which did credit to his taste. The rugs were old, and of the true faded beauty; the etchings, nearly all of them proofs printed by the artist, made a good show with broad white margins and black frames, and there was no spurious black oak. Indeed, there was but little furniture of any kind: a plain and honest table, square and sturdy, stood in one corner; a seventeenth-century settle fronted the hearth; and two wooden elbow-chairs and a bookshelf of the Empire made up the equipment, with an exception worthy of note. For Dyson cared for none of these things; his place was at his own bureau, a quaint old piece of lacquered-work, at which he would sit for hour after hour, with his back to the room, engaged in the desperate pursuit of literature, or, as he termed his profession, the chase of the phrase. The neat array of pigeon-holes and drawers teemed and overflowed with manuscripts and notebooks, the experiments and efforts of many years; and the inner well, a vast and cavernous receptacle, was stuffed with accumulated ideas. Dyson was a craftsman who loved all the detail and the technique of his work intensely; and if, as has been hinted, he deluded himself a little with the name of artist, yet his amusements were eminently harmless, and, so far as can be ascertained, he (or the publishers) had chosen the good part of not tiring the world with printed matter.

Here, then, Dyson would shut himself up with his fancies, experimenting with words, and striving, as his friend the recluse of Bayswater strove, with the almost invincible problem of style, but always with a fine confidence, extremely different from the chronic depression of the realist. He had been almost continuously at work on some scheme that struck him as well-nigh magical in its possibilities since the night of his adventure with the ingenious tenant of the first floor in Abingdon Grove; and as he laid down the pen with a glow of triumph, he reflected that he had not viewed the streets for five days in succession. With all the enthusiasm of his accomplished labour still working in his brain, he put away his papers and went out, pacing the pavement at first in that rare mood of exultation which finds in every stone upon the way the possibilities of a masterpiece. It was growing late, and the autumn evening was drawing to a close amidst veils of haze and mist, and in the stilled air the voices, and the roaring traffic, and incessant feet seemed to Dyson like the noise upon the stage when all the house is silent. In the square the leaves rippled down as quick as summer rain, and the street beyond was beginning to flare with the lights in the butchers' shops and the vivid illumination of the greengrocer. It was a Saturday night, and the swarming populations of the slums were turning out in force; the battered women in rusty black had begun to paw the lumps of cagmag, and others gloated over unwholesome cabbages, and there was a brisk demand for four ale. Dyson passed through these night-fires with some relief; he loved to meditate, but his thoughts were not as De Quincey's after his dose;[46] he cared not two straws whether onions were dear or cheap, and would not have exulted if meat had fallen to twopence a pound. Absorbed in the wilderness of the tale he had been writing, weighing nicely the points of plot and construction, relishing the recollection of this and that happy phrase, and dreading failure here and there, he left the rush and whistle of the gas-flares behind him, and began to touch upon pavements more deserted.

He had turned, without taking note, to the northward, and was passing through an ancient fallen street, where now notices of floors and offices to let hung out, but still about it lingered the grace and the stiffness of the Age of Wigs—a broad roadway, a broad pavement, and on each side a grave line of houses with long and narrow windows flush with the walls, all of mellowed brick-work. Dyson walked with quick steps, as he resolved that short work must be made of a certain episode; but he was in that happy humour of invention, and another chapter rose in the inner chamber of his brain, and he dwelt on the circumstances he was to write down with curious pleasure. It was charming to have the quiet streets to walk in, and in his thought he made a whole district the cabinet of his studies, and vowed he would come again. Heedless of his course, he struck off to the east again, and soon found himself involved in a squalid network of grey two-storied houses, and then in the waste void and elements of brick-work, the passages and unmade roads behind great factory walls, encumbered with the refuse of the neighbourhood, forlorn, ill-lighted, and desperate. A brief turn, and there rose before him the unexpected, a hill suddenly lifted from the level ground, its steep ascent marked by the lighted lamps, and eager as an explorer, Dyson found his way to the place, wondering where his crooked paths had brought him. Here all was again decorous, but hideous in the extreme. The builder, some one lost in the deep gloom of the early 'twenties, had conceived the idea of twin villas in grey brick, shaped in a manner to recall the outlines of the Parthenon, each with its classic form broadly marked with raised bands of stucco. The name of the street was all strange, and for a further surprise the top of the hill was crowned with an irregular plot of grass and fading trees, called a square, and here again the Parthenon-motive had persisted. Beyond, the streets were curious, wild in their irregularities, here a row of sordid, dingy dwellings, dirty and disreputable in appearance, and there, without warning, stood a house, genteel and prim, with wire blinds and brazen knocker, as clean and trim as if it had been the doctor's house in some benighted little country town. These surprises and discoveries began to exhaust Dyson, and he hailed with delight the blazing windows of a public-house, and went in with the intention of testing the beverage provided for the dwellers in this region, as remote as Libya and Pamphylia and the parts about Mesopotamia. The babble of voices from within warned him that he was about to assist at the true parliament of the London workman, and he looked about him for that more retired entrance called private. When he had settled himself on an exiguous bench, and had ordered some beer, he began to listen to the jangling talk in the public bar beyond; it was a senseless argument, alternately furious and maudlin, with appeals to Bill and Tom, and mediæval survivals of speech, words that Chaucer wrote belched out with zeal and relish, and the din of pots jerked down and coppers rapped smartly on the zinc counter made a thorough bass for it all. Dyson was calmly smoking his pipe between the sips of beer, when an indefinite-looking figure slid rather than walked into the compartment. The man started violently when he saw Dyson placidly sitting in the corner, and glanced keenly about him. He seemed to be on wires, controlled by some electric machine, for he almost bolted out of the door when the barman asked with what he could serve him, and his hand shivered as he took the glass. Dyson inspected him with a little curiosity. He was muffled up almost to the lips, and a soft felt hat was drawn down over his eyes; he looked as if he shrank from every glance, and a more raucous voice suddenly uplifted in the public bar seemed to find in him a sympathy that made him shake and quiver like a jelly. It was pitiable to see any one so thrilled with nervousness, and Dyson was about to address some trivial remark of casual inquiry to the man, when another person came into the compartment, and, laying his hand on his arm, muttered something in an undertone, and vanished as he came. But Dyson had recognized him as the smooth-tongued and smooth-shaven Burton; and yet he thought little of it, for his whole faculty of observation was absorbed in the lamentable and yet grotesque spectacle before him. At the first touch of the hand on his arm the unfortunate man had wheeled round as if spun on a pivot, and shrank back with a low, piteous cry, as if some dumb beast were caught in the toils. The blood fled away from the wretch's face, and the skin became grey as if a shadow of death had passed in the air and fallen on it, and Dyson caught a choking whisper—

"Mr. Davies! For God's sake, have pity on me, Mr. Davies! On my oath, I say—" and his voice sank to silence as he heard the message, and strove in vain to bite his lips, and summon up to his aid some tinge of manhood. He stood there a moment, wavering as the leaves of an aspen, and then he was gone out into the street, as Dyson thought silently, with his doom upon his head. He had not been gone a minute when it suddenly flashed into Dyson's mind that he knew the man; it was undoubtedly the young man with spectacles for whom so many ingenious persons were searching; the spectacles indeed were missing, but the pale face, the dark whiskers, and the timid glances were enough to identify him. Dyson saw at once that by a succession of hazards he had unawares hit upon the scent of some desperate conspiracy, wavering as the track of a loathsome snake in and out of the highways and byways of the London cosmos; the truth was instantly pictured before him, and he divined that all unconscious and unheeding he had been privileged to see the shadows of hidden forms, chasing, and hurrying, and grasping and vanishing across the bright curtain of common life, soundless and silent, or only babbling fables and pretences. For him in an instant the jargoning of voices, the garish splendour, and all the vulgar tumult of the public-house became part of magic; for here before his eyes a scene in this grim mystery play had been enacted, and he had seen human flesh grow cold with a palsy of fear; the very hell of cowardice and terror had gaped wide within an arm's-breadth. In the midst of these reflections the barman came up and stared at him as if to hint that he had exhausted his right to take his ease, and Dyson bought another lease of the seat by an order for more beer. As he pondered the brief glimpse of tragedy, he recollected that with his first start of haunted fear the young man with whiskers had drawn his hand swiftly from his greatcoat pocket, and that he had heard something fall to the ground; and pretending to have dropped his pipe, Dyson began to grope in the corner, searching with his fingers. He touched something and drew it gently to him, and with one brief glance, as he put it quietly in his pocket, he saw it was a little old-fashioned notebook, bound in faded green morocco.

He drank down his beer at a gulp, and left the place, overjoyed at his fortunate discovery, and busy with conjecture as to the possible importance of the find. By turns he dreaded to find perhaps mere blank leaves, or the laboured follies of a betting-book, but the faded morocco cover seemed to promise better things, and to hint at mysteries. He piloted himself with no little difficulty out of the sour and squalid quarter he had entered with a light heart, and emerging at Gray's Inn Road, struck off down Guilford Street and hastened home, only anxious for a lighted candle and solitude.

Dyson sat down at his bureau, and placed the little book before him; it was an effort to open the leaves and dare disappointment. But in desperation at last he laid his fingers between the pages at haphazard, and rejoiced to see a compact range of writing with a margin, and as it chanced, three words caught his glance and stood out apart from the mass. Dyson read—

"the Gold Tiberius,"

and his face flushed with fortune and the lust of the hunter.

He turned at once to the first leaf of the pocket-book, and proceeded to read with rapt interest the

The Three Impostors

HISTORY OF THE YOUNG MAN WITH SPECTACLES

From the filthy and obscure lodging, situated, I verily believe, in one of the foulest slums of Clerkenwell, I indite this history of a life which, daily threatened, cannot last very much longer. Every day—nay, every hour, I know too well my enemies are drawing their nets closer about me; even now I am condemned to be a close prisoner in my squalid room, and I know that when I go out I shall go to my destruction. This history, if it chance to fall into good hands, may, perhaps, be of service in warning young men of the dangers and pitfalls that most surely must accompany any deviation from the ways of rectitude.

My name is Joseph Walters. When I came of age I found myself in possession of a small but sufficient income, and I determined that I would devote my life to scholarship. I do not mean the scholarship of these days; I had no intention of associating myself with men whose lives are spent in the unspeakably degrading occupation of "editing" classics, befouling the fair margins of the fairest books with idle and superfluous annotation, and doing their utmost to give a lasting disgust of all that is beautiful. An abbey church turned to the base use of a stable or bakehouse is a sorry sight; but more pitiable still is a masterpiece spluttered over with the commentator's pen, and his hideous mark "cf."

For my part, I chose the glorious career of scholar in its ancient sense; I longed to possess encyclopædic learning, to grow old amongst books, to distil day by day, and year after year, the inmost sweetness of all worthy writings. I was not rich enough to collect a library, and I was therefore forced to betake myself to the reading-room of the British Museum.

O dim, far-lifted, and mighty dome, Mecca of many minds, mausoleum of many hopes, sad house where all desires fail! For there men enter in with hearts uplifted, and dreaming minds, seeing in those exalted stairs a ladder to fame, in that pompous portico the gate of knowledge, and going in, find but vain vanity, and all but in vain. There, when the long streets are ringing, is silence, there eternal twilight, and the odour of heaviness. But there the blood flows thin and cold, and the brain burns adust; there is the hunt of shadows, and the chase of embattled phantoms; a striving against ghosts, and a war that has no victory. O dome, tomb of the quick! surely in thy galleries, where no reverberant voice can call, sighs whisper ever, and mutterings of dead hopes; and there men's souls mount like moths towards the flame, and fall scorched and blackened beneath thee, O dim, far-lifted,

182

and mighty dome!

Bitterly do I now regret the day when I took my place at a desk for the first time, and began my studies. I had not been an *habitué* of the place for many months, when I became acquainted with a serene and benevolent gentleman, a man somewhat past middle age, who nearly always occupied a desk next to mine. In the reading-room it takes little to make an acquaintance—a casual offer of assistance, a hint as to the search in the catalogue, and the ordinary politeness of men who constantly sit near each other; it was thus I came to know the man calling himself Dr. Lipsius. By degrees I grew to look for his presence, and to miss him when he was away, as was sometimes the case, and so a friendship sprang up between us. His immense range of learning was placed freely at my service; he would often astonish me by the way in which he would sketch out in a few minutes the bibliography of a given subject, and before long I had confided to him my ambitions.

"Ah," he said, "you should have been a German. I was like that myself when I was a boy. It is a wonderful resolve, an infinite career. I will know all things; yes, it is a device indeed. But it means this—a life of labour without end, and a desire unsatisfied at last. The scholar has to die, and die saying, 'I know very little!'"

Gradually, by speeches such as these, Lipsius seduced me: he would praise the career, and at the same time hint that it was as hopeless as the search for the philosopher's stone, and so by artful suggestions, insinuated with infinite address, he by degrees succeeded in undermining all my principles. "After all," he used to say, "the greatest of all sciences, the key to all knowledge, is the science and art of pleasure. Rabelais was perhaps the greatest of all the encyclopædic scholars; and he, as you know, wrote the most remarkable book that has ever been written. And what does he teach men in this book? Surely the joy of living. I need not remind you of the words, suppressed in most of the editions, the key of all the Rabelaisian mythology, of all the enigmas of his grand philosophy, *Vivez joyeux*.[47] There you have all his learning; his work is the institutes of pleasure as the fine art; the finest art there is; the art of all arts. Rabelais had all science, but he had all life too. And we have gone a long way since his time. You are enlightened, I think; you do not consider all the petty rules and bylaws that a corrupt society has made for its own selfish convenience as the immutable decrees of the Eternal."

Such were the doctrines that he preached; and it was by such insidious arguments, line upon line, here a little and there a little, that he at last succeeded in making me a man at war with the whole social system. I used to long for some opportunity to break the chains and to live a free life, to be my own rule and measure. I viewed existence with the eyes of a pagan, and Lipsius understood to perfection the art of stimulating the natural inclinations of a young man hitherto a hermit. As I gazed up at the great dome I saw it flushed with the flames and colours of a world of enticement unknown to me, my imagination played me a thousand wanton tricks, and the forbidden drew me as surely as a loadstone draws on iron. At last my resolution was taken, and I boldly asked Lipsius to be my guide.

He told me to leave the Museum at my usual hour, half-past four, to walk slowly along the northern pavement of Great Russell Street, and to wait at the corner of the street till I was addressed, and then to obey in all things the instructions of the person who came up to me. I carried out these directions, and stood at the corner looking about me anxiously, my heart beating fast, and my breath coming in gasps. I waited there for some time, and had begun to fear I had been made the object of a joke, when I suddenly became conscious of a gentleman who was looking at me with evident amusement from the opposite pavement of Tottenham Court Road. He came over, and raising his hat, politely begged me to follow him, and I did so without a word, wondering where we were going, and what was to happen. I was taken to a house of quiet and respectable aspect in a street lying to the north of Oxford Street, and my guide rang the bell. A servant showed us into a large room, quietly furnished, on the ground floor. We sat there in silence for some time, and I noticed that the furniture, though unpretending, was extremely valuable. There were large oak presses, two bookcases of extreme elegance, and in one corner a carved chest which must have been mediæval. Presently Dr. Lipsius came in and welcomed me with his usual manner, and after some desultory conversation my guide left the room. Then an elderly man dropped in and began talking to Lipsius, and from their conversation I understood that my friend was a dealer in antiques; they spoke of the Hittite seal, and of the prospects of further discoveries, and later, when two or three more persons joined us, there was an argument as to the possibility of a systematic exploration of the pre-Celtic monuments in England. I was, in fact, present at an archæological reception of an informal kind; and at nine o'clock, when the antiquaries were gone, I stared at Lipsius in a manner that showed I was puzzled, and sought an explanation.

"Now," he said, "we will go upstairs."

As we passed up the stairs, Lipsius lighting the way with a hand-lamp, I heard the sound of a jarring lock and bolts and bars shot on at the front door. My guide drew back a baize door and we went down a passage, and I began to hear odd sounds, a noise of curious mirth;

then, he pushed me through a second door, and my initiation began. I cannot write down what I witnessed that night; I cannot bear to recall what went on in those secret rooms fast shuttered and curtained so that no light should escape into the quiet street; they gave me red wine to drink, and a woman told me as I sipped it that it was wine of the Red Jar that Avallaunius had made.[48] Another asked me how I liked the wine of the Fauns, and I heard a dozen fantastic names, while the stuff boiled in my veins, and stirred, I think, something that had slept within me from the moment I was born. It seemed as if my self-consciousness deserted me; I was no longer a thinking agent, but at once subject and object; I mingled in the horrible sport, and watched the mystery of the Greek groves and fountains enacted before me, saw the reeling dance and heard the music calling as I sat beside my mate, and yet I was outside it all, and viewed my own part an idle spectator. Thus with strange rites they made me drink the cup, and when I woke up in the morning I was one of them, and had sworn to be faithful. At first I was shown the enticing side of things; I was bidden enjoy myself and care for nothing but pleasure, and Lipsius himself indicated to me as the acutest enjoyment the spectacle of the terrors of the unfortunate persons who were from time to time decoyed into the evil house. But after a time it was pointed out to me that I must take my share in the work, and so I found myself compelled to be in my turn a seducer; and thus it is on my conscience that I have led many to the depths of the pit.

One day Lipsius summoned me to his private room, and told me that he had a difficult task to give me. He unlocked a drawer and gave me a sheet of type-written paper, and bade me read it.

It was, without place, or date, or signature, and ran as follows:—

Mr. James Headley, F. S. A. will receive from his agent in Armenia, on the 12th inst., a unique coin, the gold Tiberius. It bears on the reverse a faun with the legend victoria. It is believed that this coin is of immense value. Mr. Headley will come up to town to show the coin to his friend, Professor Memys, of Chenies Street, Oxford Street, on some date between the 13th and the 18th.

Dr. Lipsius chuckled at my face of blank surprise when I laid down this singular communication.

"You will have a good chance of showing your discretion," he said. "This is not a common case; it requires great management and infinite tact. I am sure I wish I had a Panurge in my service, but we will see what you can do."

"But is it not a joke?" I asked him. "How can you know—or rather, how can this correspondent of yours know—that a coin has been despatched from Armenia to Mr. Headley? And how is it possible to fix the period in which Mr. Headley will take it into his head to come up to town? It seems to me a lot of guesswork."

"My dear Mr. Walters," he replied, "we do not deal in guesswork here. It would bore you if I went into all these little details, the cogs and wheels, if I may say so, which move the machine. Don't you think it is much more amusing to sit in front of the house and be astonished than to be behind the scenes and see the mechanism? Better tremble at the thunder, believe me, than see the man rolling the cannon-ball. But, after all, you needn't bother about the how and why; you have your share to do. Of course I shall give you full instructions, but a great deal depends on the way the thing is carried out. I have often heard very young men maintain that style is everything in literature, and I can assure you that the same maxim holds good in our far more delicate profession. With us style is absolutely everything, and that is why we have friends, like yourself."

I went away in some perturbation: he had no doubt designedly left everything in mystery, and I did not know what part I should have to play. Though I had assisted at scenes of hideous revelry, I was not yet dead to all echo of human feeling, and I trembled lest I should receive the order to be Mr. Headley's executioner.

A week later, it was on the sixteenth of the month, Dr. Lipsius made me a sign to come into his room.

"It is for to-night," he began. "Please to attend carefully to what I am going to say, Mr. Walters, and on peril of your life, for it is a danger-ous matter,—on peril of your life, I say, follow these instructions to the letter. You understand? Well, to-night at about half-past seven, you will stroll quietly up the Hampstead Road till you come to Vincent Street. Turn down here and walk along, taking the third turning to your right, which is Lambert Terrace. Then follow the terrace, cross the road, and go along Hertford Street, and so into Lillington Square. The second turning you will come to in the square is called Sheen Street; but in reality it is more a passage between blank walls than a street. What-ever you do, take care to be at the corner of this street at eight o'clock precisely. You will walk along it, and just at the bend where you lose sight of the square you will find an old gentleman with white beard and whiskers. He will in all probability be abusing a cabman for having brought him to Sheen Street instead of Chenies Street. You will go up to him quietly and offer your services; he will tell you where he wants to go, and you will be so courteous as to offer to show him the way. I may say that Professor Memys moved into Chenies Street a month ago; thus Mr. Headley has never been to see him there, and, moreover, he is very short-sighted, and knows little of the topography of London. Indeed, he has quite lived the life of a learned hermit at Audley Hall.

"Well, need I say more to a man of your intelligence? You will bring him to this house, he will ring the bell, and a servant in quiet livery will let him in. Then your work will be done, and I am sure done well. You will leave Mr. Headley at the door and simply continue your walk, and I shall hope to see you the next day. I really don't think there is anything more I can tell you."

These minute instructions I took care to carry out to the letter. I confess that I walked up the Tottenham Court Road by no means blindly, but with an uneasy sense that I was coming to a decisive point in my life. The noise and rumour of the crowded pavements were to me but dumb show; I revolved again and again in ceaseless iteration the task that had been laid on me, and I questioned myself as to the possible results. As I got near the point of turning, I asked myself whether danger were not about my steps; the cold thought struck me that I was suspected and observed, and every chance foot-passenger who gave me a second glance seemed to me an officer of police. My time was running out, the sky had darkened, and I hesitated, half resolved to go no farther, but to abandon Lipsius and his friends for ever. I had almost determined to take this course, when the conviction suddenly came to me that the whole thing was a gigantic joke, a fabrication of rank improbability. Who could have procured the information about the Armenian agent? I asked myself. By what means could Lipsius have known the particular day and the very train that Mr. Headley was to take? how engage him to enter one special cab amongst the dozens waiting at Paddington? I vowed it a mere Milesian tale, and went forward merrily, turned down Vincent Street, and threaded out the route that Lipsius had so carefully impressed upon me. The various streets he had named were all places of silence and an oppressive cheap gentility; it was dark, and I felt alone in the musty squares and crescents, where people pattered by at intervals, and the shadows were growing blacker. I entered Sheen Street, and found it as Lipsius had said, more a passage than a street; it was a byway, on one side a low wall and neglected gardens, and grim backs of a line of houses, and on the other a timber-yard. I turned the corner, and lost sight of the square, and then, to my astonishment, I saw the scene of which I had been told. A hansom cab had come to a stop beside the pavement, and an old man, carrying a handbag, was fiercely abusing the cabman, who sat on his perch the image of bewilderment.

"Yes, but I'm sure you said Sheen Street, and that's where I brought you," I heard him saying as I came up, and the old gentleman boiled in a fury, and threatened police and suits at law.

The sight gave me a shock, and in an instant I resolved to go through with it. I strolled on, and without noticing the cabman, lifted my hat politely to old Mr. Headley.

"Pardon me, sir," I said, "but is there any difficulty? I see you are a traveller; perhaps the cabman has made a mistake. Can I direct you?"

The old fellow turned to me, and I noticed that he snarled and showed his teeth like an illtempered cur as he spoke.

"This drunken fool has brought me here," he said. "I told him to drive to Chenies Street, and he brings me to this infernal place. I won't pay him a farthing, and I meant to have given him a handsome sum. I am going to call for the police and give him in charge."

At this threat the cabman seemed to take alarm; he glanced round, as if to make sure that no policeman was in sight, and drove off grumbling loudly, and Mr. Headley grinned savagely with satisfaction at having saved his fare, and put back one and sixpence into his pocket, the "handsome sum" the cabman had lost.

"My dear sir," I said, "I am afraid this piece of stupidity has annoyed you a great deal. It is a long way to Chenies Street, and you will have some difficulty in finding the place unless you know London pretty well."

"I know it very little," he replied. "I never come up except on important business, and I've never been to Chenies Street in my life."

"Really? I should be happy to show you the way. I have been for a stroll, and it will not at all inconvenience me to take you to your destination."

"I want to go to Professor Memys, at Number 15. It's most annoying to me; I'm short-sighted, and I can never make out the numbers on the doors."

"This way if you please," I said, and we set out.

I did not find Mr. Headley an agreeable man; indeed, he grumbled the whole way. He informed me of his name, and I took care to say, "The well-known antiquary?" and thenceforth I was compelled to listen to the history of his complicated squabbles with publishers, who treated him, as he said, disgracefully; the man was a chapter in the Irritability of Authors. He told me that he had been on the point of making the fortune of several firms, but had been compelled to abandon the design owing to their rank ingratitude. Besides these ancient histories of wrong, and the more recent misadventure of the cabman, he had another grievous complaint to make. As he came along in the train, he had been sharpening a pencil, and the sudden jolt of the engine as it drew up at a station had driven the penknife against his face, inflicting a small triangular wound just on the cheek-bone, which he showed me. He denounced the railway company, heaped imprecations on the head of the driver, and talked of claiming damages. Thus he grumbled all the way, not noticing in the least where he was going; and so unamiable did his conduct appear to me, that I began to enjoy the trick I was playing on him.

Nevertheless, my heart beat a little faster as we turned into the street where Lipsius was waiting. A thousand accidents, I thought, might happen; some chance might bring one of Headley's friends to meet us; perhaps, though he knew not Chenies Street, he might know the street where I was taking him; in spite of his short sight, he might possibly make out the number, or, in a sudden fit of suspicion, he might make an inquiry of the policeman at the corner. Thus every step upon the pavement, as we drew nearer to the goal, was to me a pang and a terror, and every approaching passenger carried a certain threat of danger. I gulped down my excitement with an effort, and made shift to say pretty quietly—

"Number 15, I think you said? That is the third house from this. If you will allow me, I will leave you now; I have been delayed a little, and my way lies on the other side of Tottenham Court Road."

He snarled out some kind of thanks, and I turned my back and walked swiftly in the opposite direction. A minute or two later I looked round and saw Mr. Headley standing on the doorstep, and then the door opened and he went in. For my part, I gave a sigh of relief; I hastened to get away from the neighbourhood, and endeavoured to enjoy myself in merry company.

The whole of the next day I kept away from Lipsius. I felt anxious, but I did not know what had happened, or what was happening, and a reasonable regard for my own safety told me that I should do well to remain quietly at home. My curiosity, however, to learn the end of the odd drama in which I had played a part stung me to the quick, and late in the evening I made up my mind to see how events had turned out. Lipsius nodded when I came in, and asked if I could give him five minutes' talk. We went to his room, and he began to walk up and down, while I sat waiting for him to speak.

"My dear Mr. Walters," he said at length, "I congratulate you warmly; your work was done in the most thorough and artistic manner. You will go far. Look."

He went to his escritoire and pressed a secret spring; a drawer flew out, and he laid something on the table. It was a gold coin; I took it up and examined it eagerly, and read the legend about the figure of the faun.

"Victoria," I said, smiling.

"Yes; it was a great capture, which we owe to you. I had great difficulty in persuading Mr. Headley that a little mistake had been made; that was how I put it. He was very disagreeable, and indeed ungentlemanly, about it; didn't he strike you as a very cross old man?"

I held the coin, admiring the choice and rare design, clear cut as if from the mint; and I thought the fine gold glowed and burnt like a lamp.

"And what finally became of Mr. Headley?" I said at last.

Lipsius smiled, and shrugged his shoulders.

"What on earth does it matter?" he said. "He might be here, or there, or anywhere; but what possible consequence could it be? Besides, your question rather surprises me; you are an intelligent man, Mr. Walters. Just think it over, and I'm sure you won't repeat the question."

"My dear sir," I said, "I hardly think you are treating me fairly. You have paid me some handsome compliments on my share in the capture, and I naturally wish to know how the matter ended. From what I saw of Mr. Headley I should think you must have had some difficulty with him."

He gave me no answer for the moment, but began again to walk up and down the room, apparently absorbed in thought.

"Well," he said at last, "I suppose there is something in what you say. We are certainly indebted to you. I have said that I have a high opinion of your intelligence, Mr. Walters. Just look here, will you?"

He opened a door communicating with another room, and pointed.

There was a great box lying on the floor, a queer, coffin-shaped thing. I looked at it, and saw it was a mummy case, like those in the British Museum, vividly painted in the brilliant Egyptian colours, with I knew not what proclamation of dignity or hopes of life immortal. The mummy swathed about in the robes of death was lying within, and the face had been uncovered.

"You are going to send this away?" I said, forgetting the question I had put.

"Yes; I have an order from a local museum. Look a little more closely, Mr. Walters."

Puzzled by his manner, I peered into the face, while he held the lamp. The flesh was black with the passing of the centuries; but as I looked I saw upon the right cheek bone a small triangular scar, and the secret of the mummy flashed upon me: I was looking at the dead body of the man whom I had decoyed into that house.

There was no thought or design of action in my mind. I held the accursed coin in my hand, burning me with a foretaste of hell, and I fled as I would have fled from pestilence and death, and dashed into the street in blind horror, not knowing where I went. I felt the gold coin grasped in my clenched fist, and throwing it away, I knew not where, I ran on and on through by-streets and dark ways, till at last I issued out into a crowded thoroughfare and checked myself. Then as consciousness returned I realized my instant peril, and understood what would happen if I fell into the hands of Lipsius. I knew that I had put forth my finger to thwart a relentless mechanism rather than a man. My recent adventure with the unfortunate Mr. Headley had taught me that Lipsius had agents in all quarters; and I foresaw that if I fell into his hands, he would remain true to his doctrine of style, and cause me to die a death of some horrible and ingenious torture. I bent my whole mind to the task of outwitting him and his emissaries, three of whom I knew to have proved their ability for tracking down persons who for various reasons preferred to remain obscure. These servants of Lipsius were two men and a woman, and the woman was incomparably the most subtle and the most deadly. Yet I considered that I too had some portion of craft, and I took my resolve. Since then I have matched myself day by day and hour by hour against the ingenuity of Lipsius and his myrmidons. For a time I was successful; though they beat furiously after me in the covert of London, I remained *perdu*, and watched with some amusement their frantic efforts to recover the scent lost in two or three minutes. Every lure and wile was put forth to entice me from my hiding-place; I was informed by the medium of the public prints that what I had taken had been recovered, and meetings were proposed in which I might hope to gain a great deal without the slightest risk. I laughed at their endeavours, and began a little to despise the organization I had so dreaded, and ventured more abroad. Not once or twice, but several times, I recognized the two men who were charged with my capture, and I succeeded in eluding them at close quarters; and a little too hastily I decided that I had nothing to dread, and that my craft was greater than theirs. But in the meanwhile, while I congratulated myself on my cunning, the third of Lipsius's emissaries was weaving her nets; and in an evil hour I paid a visit to an old friend, a literary man named Russell, who lived in a quiet street in Bayswater. The woman, as I found out too late, a day or two ago occupied rooms in the same house, and I was followed and tracked down. Too late, as I have said I recognized that I had made a fatal mistake, and that I was beseiged. Sooner or later I shall find myself in the power of an enemy without pity; and so surely as I leave this house I shall go to receive doom. I hardly dare to guess how it will at last fall upon me; my imagination, always a vivid one, paints to me appalling pictures of the unspeakable torture which I shall probably endure; and I know that I shall die with Lipsius standing near and gloating over the refinements of my suffering and my shame.

Hours, nay minutes, have become precious to me. I sometimes pause in the midst of anticipating my tortures, to wonder whether even now I cannot hit upon some supreme stroke, some design of infinite subtlety, to free myself from the toils. But I find that the faculty of combination has left me; I am as the scholar in the old myth, deserted by the power which has helped me hitherto. I do not know when the supreme moment will come, but sooner or later it is inevitable; before long I shall receive sentence, and from the sentence to execution will not be long.

*   *   *

I cannot remain here a prisoner any longer. I shall go out to-night when the streets are full of crowds and clamours, and make a last effort to escape.

*   *   *

It was with profound astonishment that Dyson closed the little book, and thought of the strange series of incidents which had brought him into touch with the plots and counterplots connected with the Gold Tiberius. He had bestowed the coin carefully away, and he shuddered at the bare possibility of its place of deposit becoming known to the evil band who seemed to possess such extraordinary sources of information.

It had grown late while he read, and he put the pocket-book away, hoping with all his heart that the unhappy Walters might even at the eleventh hour escape the doom he dreaded.

Adventure of the Deserted Residece

"A wonderful story, as you say, an extraordinary sequence and play of coincidence. I confess that your expressions when you first showed me the Gold Tiberius were not exaggerated. But do you think that Walters has really some fearful fate to dread?"

"I cannot say. Who can presume to predict events when life itself puts on the robe of coincidence and plays at drama? Perhaps we have not yet reached the last chapter in the queer story. But, look, we are drawing near to the verge of London; there are gaps, you see, in the serried ranks of brick, and a vision of green fields beyond."

Dyson had persuaded the ingenious Mr. Phillipps to accompany him on one of those aimless walks to which he was himself so addicted. Starting from the very heart of London, they had made their way westward through the stony avenues, and were now just emerging from the red lines of an extreme surburb, and presently the half-finished road ended, a quiet lane began, and they were beneath the shade of elm trees. The yellow autumn sunlight that had lit up the bare distance of the suburban street now filtered down through the boughs of the trees and shone on the glowing carpet of fallen leaves, and the pools of rain glittered and shot back the gleam of light. Over all the broad pastures there was peace and the happy rest of autumn before the great winds begin, and afar off London lay all vague and immense amidst the veiling mist; here and there a distant window catching the sun and kindling with fire, and a spire gleaming high, and below the streets in shadow, and the turmoil of life. Dyson and Phillipps walked on in silence beneath the high hedges, till at a turn of the lane they saw a mouldering and ancient gate standing open, and the prospect of a house at the end of a moss-grown carriage drive.

"There is a survival for you," said Dyson; "it has come to its last days, I imagine. Look how the laurels have grown gaunt and weedy, and black and bare beneath; look at the house, covered with yellow wash, and patched with green damp. Why, the very notice-board, which informs all and singular that the place is to be let, has cracked and half fallen."

"Suppose we go in and see it," said Phillipps; "I don't think there is anybody about."

They turned up the drive, and walked slowly towards this remnant of old days. It was a large, straggling house, with curved wings at either end, and behind a series of irregular roofs and projections, showing that the place had been added to at divers dates; the two wings were roofed in cupola fashion, and at one side, as they came nearer, they could see a stableyard, and a clock turret with a bell, and the dark masses of gloomy cedars. Amidst all the lineaments of dissolution there was but one note of contrast: the sun was setting beyond the elm trees; and all the west and south were in flames; on the upper windows of the house the glow shone reflected, and it seemed as if blood and fire were mingled. Before the yellow front of the mansion, stained, as Dyson had remarked, with gangrenous patches, green and blackening, stretched what had once been, no doubt, a well-kept lawn, but it was now rough and ragged, and nettles and great docks, and all manner of coarse weeds, struggled in the places of the flower-beds. The urns had fallen from their pillars beside the walk, and lay broken in shards upon the ground, and everywhere from grass-plot and path a fungoid growth had sprung up and multiplied, and lay dank and slimy like a festering sore upon the earth. In the middle of the rank grass of the lawn was a desolate fountain; the rim of the basin was crumbling and pulverized with decay, and within the water stood stagnant, with green scum for the lilies that had once bloomed there; rust had eaten into the bronze flesh of the Triton that stood in the middle, and the conch-shell he held was broken.

"Here," said Dyson, "one might moralize over decay and death. Here all the stage is decked out with the symbols of dissolution; the cedarn gloom and twilight hang heavy around us, and everywhere within the pale dankness has found a harbour, and the very air is changed and brought to accord with the scene. To me, I confess, this deserted house is as moral as a graveyard, and I find something sublime in that lonely Triton, deserted in the midst of his water-pool. He is the last of the gods; they have left him, and he remembers the sound of water falling on water, and the days that were sweet."

"I like your reflections extremely," said Phillipps; "but I may mention that the door of the house is open."

"Let us go in, then."

The door was just ajar, and they passed into the mouldy hall and looked in at a room on one side. It was a large room, going far back, and the rich, old, red flock paper was peeling from the walls in long strips, and blackened with vague patches of rising damp; the ancient clay, the dank reeking earth rising up again, and subduing all the work of men's hands after the conquest of many years. The floor was thick with the dust of decay, and the painted ceiling fading from all gay colours and light fancies of cupids in a career, and disfigured with sores of dampness, seemed transmuted into other work. No longer the amorini chased one another pleasantly, with limbs that sought not to advance, and hands that merely simulated the act of grasping at the wreathed flowers; but it appeared some savage burlesque of the old careless world and of its cherished conventions, and the dance of the Loves had become a Dance of Death; black pustules and festering sores swelled and clustered on fair limbs and smiling faces showed corruption, and the fairy blood had boiled with the germs of foul disease; it was a parable of the leaven working, and worms devouring for a banquet the heart of the rose.

Strangely, under the painted ceiling, against the decaying walls, two old chairs still stood alone, the sole furniture of the empty place. High-backed, with curving arms and twisted legs, covered with faded gold leaf, and upholstered in tattered damask, they too were a part of the symbolism, and struck Dyson with surprise. "What have we here?" he said. "Who has sat in these chairs? Who, clad in peach-bloom satin, with lace ruffles and diamond buckles, all golden, a *conté fleurettes*[49] to his companion? Phillipps, we are in another age. I wish I had some snuff to offer you, but failing that I beg to offer you a seat, and we will sit and smoke tobacco. A horrid practice, but I am no pedant."

They sat down on the queer old chairs, and looked out of the dim and grimy panes to the ruined lawn, and the fallen urns, and the deserted Triton.

Presently Dyson ceased his imitation of eighteenth-century airs; he no longer pulled forward imaginary ruffles, or tapped a ghostly snuff-box.

"It's a foolish fancy," he said at last; "but I keep thinking I hear a noise like some one groaning. Listen; no, I can't hear it now. There it is again! Did you notice it, Phillipps?"

"No, I can't say I heard anything. But I believe that old places like this are like shells from the shore, ever echoing with noises. The old beams, mouldering piece-meal, yield a little and groan; and such a house as this I can fancy all resonant at night with voices, the voices of matter so slowly and so surely transformed into other shapes, the voice of the worm that gnaws at last the very heart of the oak, the voice of stone grinding on stone, and the voice of the conquest of Time."

They sat still in the old arm-chairs, and grew graver in the musty ancient air, the air of a hundred years ago.

"I don't like the place," said Phillipps, after a long pause. "To me it seems as if there were a sickly, unwholesome smell about it, a smell of something burning."

"You are right; there is an evil odour here. I wonder what it is. Hark! Did you hear that?"

A hollow sound, a noise of infinite sadness and infinite pain, broke in upon the silence, and the two men looked fearfully at one another, horror, and the sense of unknown things, glimmering in their eyes.

"Come," said Dyson, "we must see into this," and they went into the hall and listened in the silence.

"Do you know," said Phillipps, "it seems absurd, but I could almost fancy that the smell is that of burning flesh."

They went up the hollow-sounding stairs, and the odour became thick and noisome, stifling the breath, and a vapour, sickening as the smell of the chamber of death, choked them. A door was open, and they entered the large upper room, and clung hard to one another, shuddering at the sight they saw.

A naked man was lying on the floor, his arms and legs stretched wide apart, and bound to pegs that had been hammered into the boards. The body was torn and mutilated in the most hideous fashion, scarred with the marks of red-hot irons, a shameful ruin of the human shape. But upon the middle of the body a fire of coals was smouldering; the flesh had been burnt through. The man was dead, but the smoke of his torment mounted still, a black vapour.

"The young man with spectacles," said Mr. Dyson.

THE SHINNING PYRAMID

"The Shining Pyramid" was first published in the *Unknown World* (May 15 and June 15, 1895). Curiously, it was not collected until it appeared in Vincent Starrett's selection of Machen's miscellaneous stories and essays, *The Shining Pyramid* (Chicago: Covici-McGee, 1923); Machen himself gathered it into a volume of different contents (all stories) entitled *The Shining Pyramid* (London: Martin Secker, 1925). This story has also been frequently anthologized, appearing in such volumes as Arthur Neale's *The Great Weird Stories* (1929), Marjorie Bowen's *Great Tales of Horror* (1933), and Peter Haining's *The Ancient Mysteries Reader* (1976).

I

THE ARROW-HEAD CHARACTER

"Haunted, you said?"

"Yes, haunted. Don't you remember, when I saw you three years ago, you told about your place in the west with the ancient woods hanging all about it, and the wild, domed hills, and the ragged land? It has always remained a sort of enchanted picture in my mind as I sit at my desk and hear the traffic rattling in the street in the midst of whirling London. But when did you come up?"

"The fact is, Dyson, I have only just got out of the train. I drove to the station early this morning and caught the 10:45."

"Well, I am very glad you looked in on me. How have you been getting on since we last met? There is no Mrs. Vaughan, I suppose?"

"No," said Vaughan, "I am still a hermit, like yourself. I have done nothing but loaf about."

Vaughan had lit his pipe and sat in the elbow chair, fidgeting and glancing about him in a somewhat dazed and restless manner. Dyson had wheeled round his chair when his visitor entered and sat with one arm fondly reclining on the desk of his bureau, and touching the litter of manuscript.

"And you are still engaged in the old task?" said Vaughan, pointing to the pile of papers and the teeming pigeon-holes.

"Yes, the vain pursuit of literature, as idle as alchemy, and as entrancing. But you have come to town for some time I suppose; what shall we do to-night?"

"Well, I rather wanted you to try a few days with me down in the west. It would do you a lot of good, I'm sure."

"You are very kind, Vaughan, but London in September is hard to leave. Doré[1] could not have designed anything more wonderful and mystic than Oxford Street as I saw it the other evening; the sunset flaming, the blue haze transmuting the plain street into a road 'far in the spiritual city.'"[2]

"I should like you to come down though. You would enjoy roaming over our hills. Does this racket go on all day and all night? It quite bewilders me; I wonder how you can work through it. I am sure you would revel in the great peace of my old home among the woods."

Vaughan lit his pipe again, and looked anxiously at Dyson to see if his inducements had had any effect, but the man of letters shook his head, smiling, and vowed in his heart a firm allegiance to the streets.

"You cannot tempt me," he said.

"Well, you may be right. Perhaps, after all, I was wrong to speak of the peace of the country. There, when a tragedy does occur, it is like a stone thrown into a pond; the circles of disturbance keep on widening, and it seems as if the water would never be still again."

"Have you ever any tragedies where you are?"

"I can hardly say that. But I was a good deal disturbed about a month ago by something that happened; it may or may not have been a tragedy in the usual sense of the word."

"What was the occurrence?"

"Well, the fact is a girl disappeared in a way which seems highly mysterious. Her parents, people of the name of Trevor, are well-to-do farmers, and their eldest daughter Annie was a sort of village beauty; she was really remarkably handsome. One afternoon she thought she would go and see her aunt, a widow who farms her own land, and as the two houses are only about five or six miles apart, she started off, telling her parents she would take the short cut over the hills. She never got to her aunt's, and she never was seen again. That's putting it in a few words."

"What an extraordinary thing! I suppose there are no disused mines, are there, on the hills? I don't think you quite run to anything so formidable as a precipice?"

"No; the path the girl must have taken had no pitfall of any description; it is just a track over wild, bare hillside, far, even, from a byroad. One may walk for miles without meeting a soul, but it is all perfectly safe."

"And what do people say about it?"

"Oh, they talk nonsense—among themselves. You have no notion as to how superstitious English cottagers are in out-of-the-way parts like mine. They are as bad as the Irish, every whit, and even more secretive."

"But what do they say?"

"Oh, the poor girl is supposed to have 'gone with the fairies,' or to have been 'taken by the fairies.' Such stuff!" he went on, "one would laugh if it were not for the real tragedy of the case."

Dyson looked somewhat interested.

"Yes," he said, "'fairies' certainly strike a little curiously on the ear in these days. But what do the police say? I presume they do not accept the fairy-tale hypothesis?"

"No; but they seem quite at fault. What I am afraid of is that Annie Trevor must have fallen in with some scoundrels on her way. Castletown is a large seaport, you know, and some of the worst of the foreign sailors occasionally desert their ships and go on the tramp up and down the country. Not many years ago a Spanish sailor named Garcia murdered a whole family for the sake of plunder that was not worth sixpence. They are hardly human, some of these fellows, and I am dreadfully afraid the poor girl must have come to an awful end."

"But no foreign sailor was seen by anyone about the country?"

"No; there is certainly that; and of course country people are quick to notice anyone whose appearance and dress are a little out of the common. Still it seems as if my theory were the only possible explanation."

"There are no data to go upon," said Dyson, thoughtfully. "There was no question of a love affair, or anything of the kind, I suppose?"

"Oh, no, not a hint of such a thing. I am sure if Annie were alive she would have contrived to let her mother know of her safety."

"No doubt, no doubt. Still it is barely possible that she is alive and yet unable to communicate with her friends. But all this must have disturbed you a good deal."

"Yes, it did; I hate a mystery, and especially a mystery which is probably the veil of horror. But frankly, Dyson, I want to make a clean breast of it; I did not come here to tell you all this."

"Of course not," said Dyson, a little surprised at Vaughan's uneasy manner. "You came to have a chat on more cheerful topics."

"No, I did not. What I have been telling you about happened a month ago, but something which seems likely to affect me more personally has taken place within the last few days, and to be quite plain, I came up to town with the idea that you might be able to help me. You recollect that curious case you spoke to me about at our last meeting; something about a spectacle-maker."

"Oh, yes, I remember that. I know I was quite proud of my acumen at the time; even to this day the police have no idea why those peculiar yellow spectacles were wanted. But, Vaughan, you really look quite put out; I hope there is nothing serious?"

"No. I think I have been exaggerating, and I want you to reassure me. But what has happened is very odd."

"And what has happened?"

"I am sure that you will laugh at me, but this is the story. You must know there is a path, a right of way, that goes through my land, and to be precise, close to the wall of the kitchen garden. It is not used by many people; a woodman now and again finds it useful, and five or six children who go to school in the village pass twice a day. Well, a few days ago I was taking a walk about the place before breakfast, and I happened to stop to fill my pipe just by the large doors in the garden wall. The wood, I must tell you, comes to within a few feet of the wall, and the track I spoke of runs right in the shadow of the trees. I thought the shelter from a brisk wind that was blowing rather pleasant, and I stood there smoking with my eyes on the ground. Then something caught my attention. Just under the wall, on the short grass, a number of small flints were arranged in a pattern; something like this": and Mr. Vaughan caught at a pencil and piece of paper, and dotted down a few strokes.

"You see," he went on, "there were, I should think, twelve little stones neatly arranged in lines, and spaced at equal distances, as I have shewn it on the paper. They were pointed stones, and the points were very carefully directed one way."

"Yes," said Dyson, without much interest, "no doubt the children you have mentioned had been playing there on their way from school. Children, as you know, are very fond of making such devices with oyster shells or flints or flowers, or with whatever comes in their way."

"So I thought; I just noticed these flints were arranged in a sort of pattern and then went on. But the next morning I was taking the same round, which, as a matter of fact, is habitual with me, and again I saw at the same spot a device in flints. This time it was really a curious pattern; something like the spokes of a wheel, all meeting at a common centre, and this centre formed by a device which looked like a bowl; all, you understand, done in flints."

"You are right," said Dyson, "that seems odd enough. Still it is reasonable that your half-a-dozen children are responsible for these fantasies in stone."

"Well, I thought I would set the matter at rest. The children pass the gate every evening at half-past five, and I walked by at six, and found the device just as I had left it in the morning. The next day I was up and about at a quarter to seven, and I found the whole thing had been changed. There was a pyramid outlined in flints upon the grass. The chidren I saw going by an hour and a half later, and they ran past the spot without glancing to right or left. In the evening I watched them going home, and this morning when I got to the gate at six o'clock there was a thing like a half moon waiting for me."

"So then the series runs thus: firstly ordered lines, then the device of the spokes and the bowl, then the pyramid, and finally, this morning, the half moon. That is the order, isn't it?"

"Yes; that's right. But do you know it has made me feel very uneasy? I suppose it seems absurd, but I can't help thinking that some kind of signalling is going on under my nose, and that sort of thing is disquieting."

"But what have you to dread? You have no enemies?"

"No; but I have some very valuable old plate."

"You are thinking of burglars then?" said Dyson, with an accent of considerable interest, "but you must know your neighbours. Are there any suspicious characters about?"

"Not that I am aware of. But you remember what I told you of the sailors."

"Can you trust your servants?"

"Oh, perfectly. The plate is preserved in a strong room; the butler, an old family servant, alone knows where the key is kept. There is nothing wrong there. Still, everybody is aware that I have a lot of old silver, and all country folks are given to gossip. In that way information may have got abroad in very undesirable quarters."

"Yes, but I confess there seems something a little unsatisfactory in the burglar theory. Who is signalling to whom? I cannot see my way to accepting such an explanation. What put the plate into your head in connection with these flint signs, or whatever one may call them?"

"It was the figure of the Bowl," said Vaughan. "I happen to possess a very large and very valuable Charles II punch-bowl. The chasing is really exquisite, and the thing is worth a lot of money. The sign I described to you was exactly the same shape as my punch-bowl."

"A queer coincidence certainly. But the other figures or devices: you have nothing shaped like a pyramid?"

"Ah, you will think that queerer. As it happens, this punch bowl of mine, together with a set of rare old ladles, is kept in a mahogany chest of a pyramidal shape. The four sides slope upwards, the narrow towards the top."

"I confess all this interests me a good deal," said Dyson. "Let us go on then. What about the other figures; how about the Army, as we

202

may call the first sign, and the Crescent or Half-moon?"

"Ah, there is no reference that I can make out of these two. Still, you see I have some excuse for curiosity at all events. I should be very vexed to lose any of the old plate; nearly all the pieces have been in the family for generations. And I cannot get it out of my head that some scoundrels mean to rob me, and are communicating with one another every night."

"Frankly," said Dyson, "I can make nothing of it; I am as much in the dark as yourself. Your theory seems certainly the only possible explanation, and yet the difficulties are immense."

He leaned back in his chair, and the two men faced each other, frowning, and perplexed by so bizarre a problem.

"By the way," said Dyson, after a long pause, "what is your geological formation down there?"

Mr. Vaughan looked up, a good deal surprised by the question.

"Old red sandstone and limestone, I believe," he said. "We are just beyond the coal measures, you know."

"But surely there are no flints either in the sandstone or the limestone?"

"No, I never see any flints in the fields. I confess that did strike me as a little curious."

"I should think so! It is very important. By the way, what size were the flints used in making these devices?"

"I happen to have brought one with me; I took it this morning."

"From the Half-moon?"

"Exactly. Here it is."

He handed over a small flint, tapering to a point, and about three inches in length.

Dyson's face blazed up with excitement as he took the thing from Vaughan.

"Certainly," he said, after a moment's pause, "you have some curious neighbours in your country. I hardly think they can harbour any designs on your punch-bowl. Do you know this is a flint arrow-head of vast antiquity, and not only that, but an arrow-head of a unique kind? I have seen specimens from all parts of the world, but there are features about this thing that are quite peculiar."

He laid down his pipe, and took out a book from a drawer.

"We shall just have time to catch the 5:45 to Castletown," he said.

II

THE EYES ON THE WALL

Mr. Dyson drew in a long breath of the air of the hills and felt all the enchantment of the scene about him. It was very early morning, and he stood on the terrace in the front of the house. Vaughan's ancestor had built on the lower slope of a great hill, in the shelter of a deep and ancient wood that gathered on three sides about the house, and on the fourth side, the south-west, the land fell gently away and sank to the valley, where a brook wound in and out in mystic esses, and the dark and gleaming alders tracked the stream's course to the eye. On the terrace in that sheltered place no wind blew, and far beyond, the trees were still. Only one sound broke in upon the silence, and Dyson heard the noise of the brook singing far below, the song of clear and shining water rippling over the stones, whispering and murmuring as it sank to dark deep pools. Across the stream, just below the house, rose a grey stone bridge, vaulted and buttressed, a fragment of the Middle Ages, and then beyond the bridge the hills rose again, vast and rounded like bastions, covered here and there with dark woods and thickets of undergrowth, but the heights were all bare of trees, showing only grey turf and patches of bracken, touched here and there with the gold of fading fronds. Dyson looked to the north and south, and still he saw the wall of the hills, and the ancient woods, and the stream drawn in and out between them; all grey and dim with morning mist beneath a grey sky in a hushed and haunted air.

Mr. Vaughan's voice broke in upon the silence.

"I thought you would be too tired to be about so early," he said.

"I see you are admiring the view. It is very pretty, isn't it, though I suppose old Meyrick Vaughan didn't think much about the scenery when he built the house. A queer grey, old place, isn't it?"

"Yes, and how it fits into the surroundings; it seems of a piece with the grey hills and the grey bridge below."

"I am afraid I have brought you down on false pretences, Dyson," said Vaughan, as they began to walk up and down the terrace. "I have been to the place, and there is not a sign of anything this morning."

"Ah, indeed. Well, suppose we go round together."

They walked across the lawn and went by a path through the ilex shrubbery to the back of the house. There Vaughan pointed out the track leading down to the valley and up to the heights above the wood, and presently they stood beneath the garden wall, by the door.

"Here, you see, it was," said Vaughan, pointing to a spot on the turf. "I was standing just where you are now that morning I first saw the flints."

"Yes, quite so. That morning it was the Army, as I call it; then the Bowl, then the Pyramid, and, yesterday, the Half-moon. What a queer old stone that is," he went on, pointing to a block of limestone rising out of the turf just beneath the wall. "It looks like a sort of dwarf pillar, but I suppose it is natural."

"Oh, yes, I think so. I imagine it was brought here, though, as we stand on the red sandstone. No doubt it was used as a foundation stone for some older building."

"Very likely." Dyson was peering about him attentively, looking from the ground to the wall, and from the wall to the deep wood that hung almost over the garden and made the place dark even in the morning.

"Look here," said Dyson at length, "it is certainly a case of children this time. Look at that."

He was bending down and staring at the dull red surface of the mellowed bricks of the wall. Vaughan came up and looked hard where Dyson's finger was pointing, and could scarcely distinguish a faint mark in deeper red.

"What is it?" he said. "I can make nothing of it."

"Look a little more closely. Don't you see it is an attempt to draw the human eye?"

"Ah, now I see what you mean. My sight is not very sharp. Yes, so it is, it is meant for an eye, no doubt, as you say. I thought the children learnt drawing at school."

"Well, it is an odd eye enough. Do you notice the peculiar almond shape; almost like the eye of a Chinaman?"

Dyson looked meditatively at the work of the undeveloped artist, and scanned the wall again, going down on his knees in the minuteness of his inquisition.

"I should like very much," he said at length, "to know how a child in this out of the way place could have any idea of the shape of the Mongolian eye. You see the average child has a very distinct impression of the subject; he draws a circle, or something like a circle, and puts a dot in the centre. I don't think any child imagines that the eye is really made like that; it's just a convention of infantile art. But this almond-shaped thing puzzles me extremely. Perhaps it may be derived from a gilt Chinaman on a tea-canister in the grocer's shop. Still that's hardly likely."

"But why are you so sure it was done by a child?"

"Why! Look at the height. These old-fashioned bricks are little more than two inches thick; there are twenty courses from the ground to the sketch if we call it so; that gives a height of three and a half feet. Now, just imagine you are going to draw something on this wall. Exactly; your pencil, if you had one, would touch the wall somewhere on the level with your eyes, that is, more than five feet from the ground. It seems, therefore, a very simple deduction to conclude that this eye on the wall was drawn by a child about ten years old."

"Yes, I had not thought of that. Of course one of the children must have done it."

"I suppose so; and yet as I said, there is something singularly unchildlike about those two lines, and the eyeball itself, you see, is almost an oval. To my mind, the thing has an odd, ancient air; and a touch that is not altogether pleasant. I cannot help fancying that if we could see a whole face from the same hand it would not be altogether agreeable. However, that is nonsense, after all, and we are not getting farther in our investigations. It is odd that the flint series has come to such an abrupt end."

The two men walked away towards the house, and as they went in at the porch there was a break in the grey sky, and a gleam of sunshine on the grey hill before them.

All the day Dyson prowled meditatively about the fields surrounding the house. He was thoroughly and completely puzzled by the trivial circumstances he proposed to elucidate, and now he again took the flint arrow-head from his pocket, turning it over and examining it with deep attention. There was something about the thing that was altogether different from the specimens he had seen at the museums and private collections; the shape was of a distinct type, and around the edge there was a line of little punctured dots, apparently a suggestion of ornament. Who, thought Dyson, possess such things in so remote a place; who, possessing the flints, could have put them to the fantastic use of designing meaningless figures under Vaughan's garden wall? The rank absurdity of the whole affair offended him unutterably; and as one theory after another rose in his mind only to be rejected, he felt strongly tempted to take the next train back to town. He had seen the silver plate which Vaughan treasured, and had inspected the punch-bowl, the gem of the collection, with close attention; and what he saw and his interview with the butler convinced him that a plot to rob the strong box was out of the limits of enquiry. The chest in which the bowl was kept, a heavy piece of mahogany, evidently dating from the beginning of the century, was certainly strongly suggestive of a pyramid, and Dyson was at first inclined to the inept manœuvres of the detective, but a little sober thought convinced him of the impossibility of the burglary hypothesis, and he cast wildly about for something more satisfying. He asked Vaughan if there were any gypsies in the neighbourhood, and heard that the Romany[3] had not been seen for years. This dashed him a good deal, as he knew the gypsy habit of leaving queer hieroglyphics on the line of march, and had been much elated when the thought occurred to him. He was facing Vaughan by the old-fashioned hearth when he put the question, and leaned back in his chair in disgust at the destruction of his theory.

"It is odd," said Vaughan, "but the gypsies never trouble us here. Now and then the farmers find traces of fires in the wildest part of the hills, but nobody seems to know who the fire-lighters are."

"Surely that looks like gypsies?"

"No, not in such places as those. Tinkers and gypsies and wanderers of all sorts stick to the roads and don't go very far from the farmhouses."

"Well, I can make nothing of it. I saw the children going by this afternoon, and, as you say, they ran straight on. So we shall have no more eyes on the wall at all events."

"No, I must waylay them one of these days and find out who is the artist."

The next morning when Vaughan strolled in his usual course from the lawn to the back of the house he found Dyson already awaiting him by the garden door, and evidently in a state of high excitement, for he beckoned furiously with his hand, and gesticulated violently.

"What is it?" asked Vaughan. "The flints again?"

"No; but look here, look at the wall. There; don't you see it?"

"There's another of those eyes!"

"Exactly. Drawn, you see, at a little distance from the first, almost on the same level, but slightly lower."

"What on earth is one to make of it? It couldn't have been done by the children; it wasn't there last night, and they won't pass for another hour. What can it mean?"

"I think the very devil is at the bottom of all this," said Dyson. "Of course, one cannot resist the conclusion that these infernal almond eyes are to be set down to the same agency as the devices in the arrow-heads; and where that conclusion is to lead us is more than I can tell. For my part, I have to put a strong check on my imagination, or it will run wild."

"Vaughan," he said as they turned away from the wall, "has it struck you that there is one point—a very curious point—in common between the figures done in flints and the eyes drawn on the wall?"

"What is that?" asked Vaughan, on whose face there had fallen a certain shadow of indefinite dread.

"It is this. We know that the signs of the Army, the Bowl, the Pyramid, and the Half-moon must have been done at night. Presumably they were meant to be seen at night. Well, precisely the same reasoning applies to those eyes on the wall."

"I do not quite see your point."

"Oh, surely. The nights are dark just now, and have been very cloudy, I know, since I came down. Moreover, those overhanging trees would throw that wall into deep shadow even on a clear night."

"Well?"

"What struck me was this. What very peculiarly sharp eyesight, they, whoever 'they' are, must have to be able to arrange arrow-heads in intricate order in the blackest shadow of the wood, and then draw the eyes on the wall without a trace of bungling, or a false line."

"I have read of persons confined in dungeons for many years who have been able to see quite well in the dark," said Vaughan.

"Yes," said Dyson, "there was the abbé in Monte Cristo.[4] But it is a singular point."

III

THE SEARCH FOR THE BOWL

"Who was that old man that touched his hat to you just now?" said Dyson, as they came to the bend of the lane near the house.

"Oh, that was old Trevor. He looks very broken, poor old fellow."

"Who is Trevor?"

"Don't you remember? I told you the story that afternoon I came to your rooms—about a girl named Annie Trevor, who disappeared in the most inexplicable manner about five weeks ago. That was her father."

"Yes, I recollect now. To tell the truth I had forgotten all about it. And nothing has been heard of the girl?"

"Nothing whatever. The police are quite at fault."

"I am afraid I did not pay very much attention to the details you gave me. Which way did the girl go?"

"Her path would take her right across those wild hills above the house; the nearest point in the track must be about two miles from here."

"Is it near that little hamlet I saw yesterday?"

"You mean Croesyceiliog, where the children came from? No; it goes more to the north."

"Ah, I have never been that way."

They went into the house, and Dyson shut himself up in his room, sunk deep in doubtful thought, but yet with the shadow of a suspicion growing within him that for a while haunted his brain, all vague and fantastic, refusing to take definite form. He was sitting by the open window and looking out on the valley and saw, as if in a picture, the intricate winding of the brook, the grey bridge, and the vast hills rising beyond; all still and without a breath of wind to stir the mystic hanging woods and the evening sunshine glowed warm on the bracken, and down below a faint mist, pure white, began to rise from the stream. Dyson sat by the window as the day darkened and the huge bastioned hills loomed vast and vague, and the woods became dim and more shadowy; and the fancy that had seized him no longer appeared altogether impossible. He passed the rest of the evening in a reverie, hardly hearing what Vaughan said; and when he took his candle in the hall, he paused a moment before bidding his friend good-night.

"I want a good rest," he said. "I have got some work to do to-morrow."

"Some writing, you mean?"

"No. I am going to look for the Bowl."

"The Bowl! If you mean my punch-bowl, that is safe in the chest."

"I don't mean the punch-bowl. You may take my word for it that your plate has never been threatened. No; I will not bother you with any suppositions. We shall in all probability have something much stronger than suppositions before long. Good-night, Vaughan."

The next morning Dyson set off after breakfast. He took the path by the garden-wall, and noted that there were now eight of the weird almond eyes dimly outlined on the brick.

"Six days more," he said to himself, but as he thought over the theory he had formed, he shrank, in spite of strong conviction, from such a wildly incredible fancy. He struck up through the dense shadows of the wood, and at length came out on the bare hillside, and climbed higher and higher over the slippery turf, keeping well to the north, and following the indications given him by Vaughan. As he went on, he seemed to mount ever higher above the world of human life and customary things; to his right he looked at a fringe of orchard and saw a faint blue smoke rising like a pillar; there was the hamlet from which the children came to school, and there the only sign of life, for the woods embowered and concealed Vaughan's old grey house. As he reached what seemed the summit of the hill, he realised for the first time the desolate loneliness and strangeness of the land; there was nothing but grey sky and grey hill, a high, vast plain that seemed to stretch on for ever and ever, and a faint glimpse of a blue-peaked mountain far away and to the north. At length he came to the path, a slight track scarcely noticeable, and from its position and by what Vaughan had told him he knew that it was the way the lost girl, Annie Trevor, must have taken. He followed the path on the bare hill-top, noticing the great limestone rocks that cropped out of the turf, grim and hideous, and of an aspect as forbidding as an idol of the South Seas; and suddenly he halted, astonished, although he had found what he searched for. Almost without warning the ground shelved suddenly away on all sides, and Dyson looked down into a circular depression, which might well have been a Roman amphitheatre, and the ugly crags of limestone rimmed it round as if with a broken wall. Dyson walked round the hollow, and noted the position of the stones, and then turned on his way home.

"This," he thought to himself, "is more than curious. The Bowl is discovered, but where is the Pyramid?"

"My dear Vaughan," he said, when he got back, "I may tell you that I have found the Bowl, and that is all I shall tell you for the present. We have six days of absolute inaction before us; there is really nothing to be done."

IV

THE SECRET OF THE PYRAMID

"I have just been round the garden," said Vaughan one morning. "I have been counting those infernal eyes, and I find there are fourteen of them. For heaven's sake, Dyson, tell me what the meaning of it all is."

"I should be very sorry to attempt to do so. I may have guessed this or that, but I always make it a principle to keep my guesses to myself. Besides, it is really not worth while anticipating events; you will remember my telling you that we had six days of inaction before us? Well, this is the sixth day, and the last of idleness. To-night I propose we take a stroll."

"A stroll! Is that all the action you mean to take?"

"Well, it may show you some very curious things. To be plain, I want you to start with me at nine o'clock this evening for the hills. We may have to be out all night, so you had better wrap up well, and bring some of that brandy."

"Is it a joke?" asked Vaughan, who was bewildered with strange events and strange surmises.

"No, I don't think there is much joke in it. Unless I am much mistaken we shall find a very serious explanation of the puzzle. You will come with me, I am sure?"

"Very good. Which way do you want to go?"

"By the path you told me of; the path Annie Trevor is supposed to have taken."

Vaughan looked white at the mention of the girl's name.

"I did not think you were on that track," he said. "I thought it was the affair of those devices in flint and of the eyes on the wall that you were engaged on. It's no good saying any more, but I will go with you."

At a quarter to nine that evening the two men set out, taking the path through the wood, and up the hill-side. It was a dark and heavy night, and the sky was thick with clouds, and the valley full of mist, and all the way they seemed to walk in a world of shadow and gloom, hardly speaking, and afraid to break the haunted silence. They came out at last on the steep hill-side, and instead of the oppression of the wood there was the long, dim sweep of the turf, and higher, the fantastic limestone rocks hinted horror through the darkness, and the wind sighed as it passed across the mountain to the sea, and in its passage beat chill about their hearts. They seemed to walk on and on for hours, and the dim outline of the hill still stretched before them, and the haggard rocks still loomed through the darkness, when suddenly Dyson whispered, drawing his breath quickly, and coming close to his companion.

"Here," he said, "we will lie down. I do not think there is anything yet."

"I know the place," said Vaughan, after a moment. "I have often been by in the daytime. The country people are afraid to come here, I believe; it is supposed to be a fairies' castle, or something of the kind. But why on earth have we come here?"

"Speak a little lower," said Dyson. "It might not do us any good if we are overheard."

"Overheard here! There is not a soul within three miles of us."

"Possibly not; indeed, I should say certainly not. But there might be a body somewhat nearer."

"I don't understand you in the least," said Vaughan, whispering to humour Dyson, "but why have we come here?"

"Well, you see this hollow before us is the Bowl. I think we had better not talk even in whispers."

They lay full length upon the turf; the rock between their faces and the Bowl, and now and again, Dyson, slouching his dark, soft hat over his forehead, put out the glint of an eye, and in a moment drew back, not daring to take a prolonged view. Again he laid an ear to the ground and listened, and the hours went by, and the darkness seemed to blacken, and the faint sign of the wind was the only sound.

Vaughan grew impatient with this heaviness of silence, this watching for indefinite terror; for to him there was no shape or form of apprehension, and he began to think the whole vigil a dreary farce.

"How much longer is this to last?" he whispered to Dyson, and

213

Dyson who had been holding his breath in the agony of attention put his mouth to Vaughan's ear and said:

"Will you listen?" with pauses between each syllable, and in the voice with which the priest pronounces the awful words.

Vaughan caught the ground with his hands, and stretched forward, wondering what he was to hear. At first there was nothing, and then a low and gentle noise came very softly from the Bowl, a faint sound, almost indescribable, but as if one held the tongue against the roof of the mouth and expelled the breath. He listened eagerly and presently the noise grew louder, and became a strident and horrible hissing as if the pit beneath boiled with fervent heat, and Vaughan, unable to remain in suspense any longer, drew his cap half over his face in imitation of Dyson, and looked down to the hollow below.

It did, in truth, stir and seethe like an infernal caldron. The whole of the sides and bottom tossed and writhed with vague and restless forms that passed to and fro without the sound of feet, and gathered thick here and there and seemed to speak to one another in those tones of horrible sibilance, like the hissing of snakes, that he had heard. It was as if the sweet turf and the cleanly earth had suddenly become quickened with some foul writhing growth. Vaughan could not draw back his face, though he felt Dyson's finger touch him, but he peered into the quaking mass and saw faintly that there were things like faces and human limbs, and yet he felt his inmost soul chill with the sure belief that no fellow soul or human thing stirred in all that tossing and hissing host. He looked aghast, choking back sobs of horror, and at length the loathsome forms gathered thickest about some vague object in the middle of the hollow, and the hissing of their speech grew more venomous, and he saw in the uncertain light the abominable limbs, vague and yet too plainly seen, writhe and intertwine, and he thought he heard, very faint, a low human moan striking through the noise of speech that was not of man. At his heart something seemed to whisper ever "the worm of corruption, the worm that dieth not," and grotesquely the image was pictured to his imagination of a piece of putrid offal stirring through and through with bloated and horrible creeping things. The writhing of the dusky limbs continued, they seemed clustered round the dark form in the middle of the hollow, and the sweat dripped and poured off Vaughan's forehead, and fell cold on his hand beneath his face.

Then, it seemed done in an instant, the loathsome mass melted and fell away to the sides of the Bowl, and for a moment Vaughan saw in the middle of the hollow the tossing of human arms. But a spark gleamed beneath, a fire kindled, and as the voice of a woman cried out loud in a shrill scream of utter anguish and terror, a great pyramid of flame spired up like a bursting of a pent fountain, and threw a blaze of light upon the whole mountain. In that instant Vaughan saw the myriads beneath; the things made in the form of men but stunted like children hideously deformed, the faces with the almond eyes burning with evil and unspeakable lusts; the ghastly yellow of the mass of naked flesh; and then as if by magic the place was empty, while the fire roared and crackled, and the flames shone abroad.

"You have seen the Pyramid," said Dyson in his ear, "the Pyramid of fire."

V

The Little People

"Then you recognise the thing?"

"Certainly. It is a brooch that Annie Trevor used to wear on Sundays; I remember the pattern. But where did you find it? You don't mean to say that you have discovered the girl?"

"My dear Vaughan, I wonder you have not guessed where I found the brooch. You have not forgotten last night already?"

"Dyson," said the other, speaking very seriously, "I have been turning it over in my mind this morning while you have been out. I have thought about what I saw, or perhaps I should say about what I thought I saw, and the only conclusion I can come to is this, that the thing won't bear recollection. As men live, I have lived soberly and honestly, in the fear of God, all my days, and all I can do is believe that I suffered from some monstrous delusion, from some phantasmagoria of the bewildered senses. You know we went home together in silence, not a word passed between us as to what I fancied I saw; had we not better agree to keep silence on the subject? When I took my walk in the peaceful morning sunshine, I thought all the earth seemed full of praise, and passing by that wall I noticed there were no more signs recorded, and I blotted out those that remained. The mystery is over, and we can live quietly again. I think some poison has been working for the last few weeks; I have trod on the verge of madness, but I am sane now."

Mr. Vaughan had spoken earnestly, and bent forward in his chair and glanced at Dyson with something of entreaty.

"My dear Vaughan," said the other, after a pause, "what's the use of this? It is much too late to take that tone; we have gone too deep. Besides you know as well as I that there is no delusion in the case; I wish there were with all my heart. No, in justice to myself I must tell you the whole story, so far as I know it."

"Very good," said Vaughan with a sigh, "if you must, you must."

"Then," said Dyson, "we will begin with the end if you please. I found this brooch you have just identified in the place we have called the Bowl. There was a heap of grey ashes, as if a fire had been burning, indeed, the embers were still hot, and this brooch was lying on the ground, just outside the range of the flame. It must have dropped accidentally from the dress of the person who was wearing it. No, don't interrupt me; we can pass now to the beginning, as we have had the end. Let us go back to that day you came to see me in my rooms in London. So far as I can remember, soon after you came in you mentioned, in a somewhat casual manner, that an unfortunate and mysterious incident had occurred in your part of the country; a girl named Annie Trevor had gone to see a relative, and had disappeared. I confess freely that what you said did not greatly interest me; there are so many reasons which may make it extremely convenient for a man and more especially a woman to vanish from the circle of their relations and friends. I suppose, if we were to consult the police, one would find that in London somebody disappears mysteriously every other week, and the officers would, no doubt, shrug their shoulders, and tell you that by the law of averages it could not be otherwise. So I was very culpably careless to your story, and besides, there is another reason for my lack of interest; your tale was inexplicable. You could only suggest a blackguard sailor on the tramp, but I discarded the explanation immediately. For many reasons, but chiefly because the occasional criminal, the amateur in brutal crime, is always found out, especially if he selects the country as the scene of his operations. You will remember the case of that Garcia you mentioned; he strolled into a railway station the day after the murder, his trousers covered with blood, and the works of the Dutch clock, his loot, tied in a parcel. So rejecting this, your only suggestion, the whole tale became, as I say, inexplicable, and, therefore, profoundly uninteresting. Yes, *therefore*, it is a perfectly valid conclusion. Do you ever trouble your head about problems which you know to be insoluble? Did you ever bestow much thought on the old puzzle of Achilles and the Tortoise?[5] Of course not, because you knew it was a hopeless quest, and so when you told me the story of a country girl who had disappeared I simply placed the whole thing down in the category of the insoluble, and thought no more about the matter. I was mistaken, so it has turned out; but if you remember, you immediately passed on to an affair which interested you more intensely, because personally. I need not go over the very singular narrative of the flint signs; at first I thought it all trivial, probably some children's game, and if not that a hoax of some sort; but your shewing me the arrow-head awoke my acute interest. Here, I saw, there was something widely removed from the commonplace, and matter of real curiosity; and as soon as I came here I set to work to find the solution, repeating to myself again and again the signs you had described. First came the sign we have agreed to call the Army; a number of serried lines of flints, all pointing in the same way. Then the lines, like the spokes of a wheel, all converging towards the figure of a Bowl, then the triangle or Pyramid, and last of all the Half-moon. I confess that I exhausted conjecture in my efforts to unveil this mystery, and as you will understand it was a duplex or rather triplex problem. For I had not merely to ask myself: what do these figures mean? but also, who can possibly be responsible for the designing of them? And again, who can possibly possess such valuable things, and knowing their value thus throw them down by the wayside? This line of thought led me to suppose that the person or persons in question did not know the value of unique flint arrow-heads, and yet this did not lead me far, for a well-educated man might easily be ignorant on such a subject. Then came the complication of the eye on the wall, and you remember that we could not avoid the conclusion that in the two cases the same agency was at work. The peculiar position of these eyes on the wall made me enquire if there was such a thing as a dwarf anywhere in the neighbourhood, but I found that there was not, and I knew that the children who pass by every day had nothing to do with the matter. Yet I felt convinced that whoever drew the eyes must be from three-and-a-half to four feet high, since, as I pointed out at the time, anyone who draws on a perpendicular surface chooses by instinct a spot about level with his face. Then again, there was the question of the peculiar shape of the eyes; that marked Mongolian character of which the English countryman could have no conception, and for a final cause of confusion the obvious fact that the designer or designers must be able practically to see in the dark. As you remarked, a man who has been confined for many years in an extremely dark cell or dungeon might acquire that power; but since the days of Edmond Dantès, where would such a prison be found in Europe? A sailor, who had been immured for a considerable period in some horrible Chinese *oubliette*,[6] seemed the individual I was in search of, and though it looked improbable, it was not absolutely impossible that a sailor or, let us say, a man employed on shipboard, should be a dwarf. But how to account for my imaginary sailor being in possession of prehistoric arrow-heads? And the possession granted, what was the meaning and object of these mysterious signs of flint, and the almond-shaped eyes? Your theory of a contemplated burglary I saw, nearly from the first, to be quite untenable, and I confess I was utterly at a loss for a working hypothesis. It was a mere accident which put me on the track; we passed poor old Trevor, and your mention of his name and of the disappearance of his daughter, recalled the story which I had forgotten, or which remained unheeded. Here, then, I said to myself, is another problem, uninteresting, it is true, by itself; but what if it prove to be in relation with all these enigmas which torture me? I shut myself in my room, and endeavoured to dismiss all prejudice from my mind, and I went over everything *de novo*, assuming for theory's sake that the disappearance of Annie Trevor had some connection with the flint signs and the eyes on the wall. This assumption did not lead me very far, and I was on the point of giving the whole problem up in despair, when a possible significance of the Bowl struck me. As you know there is a 'Devil's Punch-bowl' in Surrey, and I saw that the symbol might refer to some feature in the country. Putting the two extremes together, I determined to look for the Bowl near the path which the lost girl had taken, and you know how I found it. I interpreted the sign by what I knew, and read the first, the Army, thus: 'there is to be a gathering or assembly at the Bowl in a fortnight (that is the Half-moon) to see the Pyramid, or to build the Pyramid.' The eyes, drawn one by one, day by day, evidently checked off the days, and I knew that there would be fourteen and no more. Thus far the way seemed pretty plain; I would not trouble myself to enquire as to the nature of the assembly, or as to who was to assemble in the loneliest and most dreaded place among these lonely hills. In Ireland or China or the west of America the question would have been easily answered; a muster of the disaffected, the meeting of a secret society, Vigilantes summoned to report: the thing would be simplicity itself; but in this quiet corner of England, inhabited by quiet folk, no such suppositions were possible for a moment. But I knew that I should have an opportunity of seeing and watching the assembly, and I did not care to perplex myself with hopeless research; and in place of reasoning a wild fancy entered into judgment: I remembered what people had said about Annie Trevor's disappearance, that she had been 'taken by the fairies.' I tell you, Vaughan, I am a sane man as you are, my brain is not, I trust, mere vacant space to let to any wild improbability, and I tried my best to thrust the fantasy away. And the hint came of the old name of fairies, 'the little people,' and the very probable belief that they represent a tradition of the prehistoric Turanian inhabitants of the country, who were cave dwellers: and then I realised with a shock that I was looking for a being under four feet in height, accustomed to live in darkness, possessing stone instruments, and familiar with the Mongolian cast of features! I say this, Vaughan, that I should be ashamed to hint at such visionary stuff to you, if it were not for that which you saw with your very eyes last night, and I say that I might doubt the evidence of my senses, if they were not confirmed by yours. But you and I cannot look each other in the face and pretend delusion; as you lay on the turf beside me I felt your flesh shrink and quiver, and I saw your eyes in the light of the flame. And so I tell you without any shame what was in my mind last night as we went through the wood and climbed the hill, and lay hidden beneath the rock.

"There was one thing that should have been most evident that puzzled me to the very last. I told you how I read the sign of the Pyramid; the assembly was to see a pyramid, and the true meaning of the symbol escaped me to the last moment. The old derivation from $\pi\upsilon\rho$, fire, though false, should have set me on the track, but it never occurred to me.

"I think I need say very little more. You know we were quite helpless, even if we had foreseen what was to come. Ah, the particular place where these signs were displayed? Yes, that is a curious question. But this house is, so far as I can judge, in a pretty central situation amongst the hills; and possibly, who can say yes or no, that queer, old limestone pillar by your garden wall was a place of meeting before the Celt set foot in Britain. But there is one thing I must add: I don't regret our inability to rescue the wretched girl. You saw the appearance of those things that gathered thick and writhed in the Bowl; you may be sure that what lay bound in the midst of them was no longer fit for earth."

"So?" said Vaughan.

"So she passed in the Pyramid of Fire," said Dyson, "and they passed again to the under-world, to the places beneath the hills."

THE WHITE PEOPLE

"The White People" was written in 1899 and first published in *Horlick's Magazine* (January 1904). It was gathered in *The House of Souls* (London: Grant Richards, 1906; New York: Alfred A. Knopf, 1922). Because of its length, it has not appeared in a great many anthologies, but it was included in Alexander Laing's *The Haunted Omnibus* (1937), Basil Davenport's *Tales to Be Told in the Dark* (1953), and Jack Sullivan's *Lost Souls* (1983), among others. H. P. Lovecraft regarded it as the second-greatest weird tale ever written, next to Algernon Blackwood's "The Willows." In the introduction to *The House of Souls* Machen claimed to have composed the work from "odds and ends of folklore."

PROLOGUE

"Sorcery and sanctity," said Ambrose, "these are the only realities. Each is an ecstasy, a withdrawal from the common life."

Cotgrave listened, interested. He had been brought by a friend to this mouldering house in a northern suburb, through an old garden to the room where Ambrose the recluse dozed and dreamed over his books.

"Yes," he went on, "magic is justified of her children. There are many, I think, who eat dry crusts and drink water, with a joy infinitely sharper than anything within the experience of the 'practical' epicure."

"You are speaking of the saints?"

"Yes, and of the sinners, too. I think you are falling into the very general error of confining the spiritual world to the supremely good; but the supremely wicked, necessarily, have their portion in it. The merely carnal, sensual man can no more be a great sinner than he can be a great saint. Most of us are just indifferent, mixed-up creatures; we muddle through the world without realizing the meaning and the inner sense of things, and, consequently, our wickedness and our goodness are alike second-rate, unimportant."

"And you think the great sinner, then, will be an ascetic, as well as the great saint?"

"Great people of all kinds forsake the imperfect copies and go to the perfect originals. I have no doubt but that many of the very highest among the saints have never done a 'good action' (using the words in their ordinary sense). And, on the other hand, there have been those who have sounded the very depths of sin, who all their lives have never done an 'ill deed.'"

He went out of the room for a moment, and Cotgrave, in high delight, turned to his friend and thanked him for the introduction.

"He's grand," he said. "I never saw that kind of lunatic before."

Ambrose returned with more whisky and helped the two men in a liberal manner. He abused the teetotal sect with ferocity, as he handed the seltzer, and pouring out a glass of water for himself, was about to resume his monologue, when Cotgrave broke in—

"I can't stand it, you know," he said, "your paradoxes are too monstrous. A man may be a great sinner and yet never do anything sinful! Come!"

"You're quite wrong," said Ambrose. "I never make paradoxes; I wish I could. I merely said that a man may have an exquisite taste in Romanée Conti,[1] and yet never have even smelt four ale. That's all, and it's more like a truism than a paradox, isn't it? Your surprise at my remark is due to the fact that you haven't realized what sin is. Oh, yes, there is a sort of connexion between Sin with the capital letter, and actions which are commonly called sinful: with murder, theft, adultery, and so forth. Much the same connexion that there is between the A, B, C and fine literature. But I believe that the misconception—it is all but universal—arises in great measure from our looking at the matter through social spectacles. We think that a man who does evil to us and to his neighbours must be very evil. So he is, from a social standpoint; but can't you realize that Evil in its essence is a lonely thing, a passion of the solitary, individual soul? Really, the average murderer, quâ murderer, is not by any means a sinner in the true sense of the word. He is simply a wild beast that we have to get rid of to save our own necks from his knife. I should class him rather with tigers than with sinners."

"It seems a little strange."

"I think not. The murderer murders not from positive qualities, but from negative ones; he lacks something which non-murderers possess. Evil, of course, is wholly positive—only it is on the wrong side. You may believe me that sin in its proper sense is very rare; it is probable that there have been far fewer sinners than saints. Yes, your standpoint is all very well for practical, social purposes; we are naturally inclined to think that a person who is very disagreeable to us must be a very great sinner! It is very disagreeable to have one's pocket picked, and we pronounce the thief to be a very great sinner. In truth, he is merely an undeveloped man. He cannot be a saint, of course; but he may be, and often is, an infinitely better creature than thousands who have never broken a single commandment. He is a great nuisance to *us*, I admit, and we very properly lock him up if we catch him; but between his troublesome and unsocial action and evil—Oh, the connexion is of the weakest."

It was getting very late. The man who had brought Cotgrave had probably heard all this before, since he assisted with a bland and judicious smile, but Cotgrave began to think that his "lunatic" was turning into a sage.

"Do you know," he said, "you interest me immensely? You think, then, that we do not understand the real nature of evil?"

"No, I don't think we do. We over-estimate it and we under-estimate it. We take the very numerous infractions of our social 'byelaws'—the very necessary and very proper regulations which keep the human company together—and we get frightened at the prevalence of 'sin' and 'evil.' But this is really nonsense. Take theft, for example. Have you any *horror* at the thought of Robin Hood, of the Highland caterans of the seventeenth century, of the moss-troopers, of the company promoters of our day?[2]

"Then, on the other hand, we underrate evil. We attach such an enormous importance to the 'sin' of meddling with our pockets (and our wives) that we have quite forgotten the awfulness of real sin."

"And what is sin?" said Cotgrave.

"I think I must reply to your question by another. What would your feelings be, seriously, if your cat or your dog began to talk to you, and to dispute with you in human accents? You would be overwhelmed with horror. I am sure of it. And if the roses in your garden sang a weird song, you would go mad. And suppose the stones in the road began to swell and grow before your eyes, and if the pebble that you noticed at night had shot out stony blossoms in the morning?

"Well, these examples may give you some notion of what sin really is."

"Look here," said the third man, hitherto placid, "you two seem pretty well wound up. But I'm going home. I've missed my tram, and I shall have to walk."

Ambrose and Cotgrave seemed to settle down more profoundly when the other had gone out into the early misty morning and the pale light of the lamps.

"You astonish me," said Cotgrave. "I had never thought of that. If that is really so, one must turn everything upside down. Then the essence of sin really is—"

"In the taking of heaven by storm, it seems to me," said Ambrose. "It appears to me that it is simply an attempt to penetrate into another and higher sphere in a forbidden manner. You can understand why it is so rare. There are few, indeed, who wish to penetrate into other spheres, higher or lower, in ways allowed or forbidden. Men, in the mass, are amply content with life as they find it. Therefore there are few saints, and sinners (in the proper sense) are fewer still, and men of genius, who partake sometimes of each character are rare also. Yes; on the whole, it is, perhaps, harder to be a great sinner than a great saint."

"There is something profoundly unnatural about sin? Is that what you mean?"

"Exactly. Holiness requires as great, or almost as great, an effort; but holiness works on lines that were natural once; it is an effort to recover the ecstasy that was before the Fall. But sin is an effort to gain the ecstasy and the knowledge that pertain alone to angels, and in making this effort man becomes a demon. I told you that the mere murderer is not *therefore* a sinner; that is true, but the sinner is sometimes a murderer. Gilles de Raiz is an instance.[3] So you see that while the good and the evil are to man as he now is—to man the social, civilized being—evil is unnatural in a much deeper sense than good. The saint endeavours to recover a gift which he has lost; the sinner tries to obtain something which was never his. In brief, he repeats the Fall."

"But are you a Catholic?" said Cotgrave.

"Yes; I am a member of the persecuted Anglican Church."

"Then, how about those texts which seem to reckon as sin that which you would set down as a mere trivial dereliction?"

"Yes; but in one place the word 'sorcerers' comes in the same sentence, doesn't it? That seems to me to give the key-note. Consider: can you imagine for a moment that a false statement which saves an innocent man's life is a sin? No; very good, then, it is not the mere liar who is excluded by those words; it is, above all, the 'sorcerers' who use the material life, who use the failings incidental to material life as instruments to obtain their infinitely wicked ends. And let me tell you this: our higher senses are so blunted, we are so drenched with materialism, that we should probably fail to recognize real wickedness if we encountered it."

"But shouldn't we experience a certain horror—a terror such as you hinted we would experience if a rose tree sang—in the mere presence of an evil man?"

"We should if we were natural: children and women feel this horror you speak of, even animals experience it. But with most of us convention and civilization and education have blinded and deafened and obscured the natural reason. No, sometimes we may recognize evil by its hatred of the good—one doesn't need much penetration to guess at the influence which dictated, quite unconsciously, the 'Blackwood' review of Keats[4]—but this is purely incidental; and, as a rule, I suspect that the Hierarchs of Tophet[5] pass quite unnoticed, or, perhaps, in certain cases, as good but mistaken men."

"But you used the word 'unconscious' just now, of Keats' reviewers. Is wickedness ever unconscious?"

"Always. It must be so. It is like holiness and genius in this as in other points; it is a certain rapture or ecstasy of the soul; a transcendent effort to surpass the ordinary bounds. So, surpassing these, it surpasses also the understanding, the faculty that takes note of that which comes before it. No, a man may be infinitely and horribly wicked and never suspect it. But I tell you, evil in this, its certain and true sense, is rare, and I think it is growing rarer."

"I am trying to get hold of it all," said Cotgrave. "From what you say, I gather that the true evil differs generically from that which we call evil?"

"Quite so. There is, no doubt, an analogy between the two; a resemblance such as enables us to use, quite legitimately, such terms as the 'foot of the mountain' and the 'leg of the table.' And, sometimes, of course, the two speak, as it were, in the same language. The rough miner, or 'puddler,' the untrained, undeveloped 'tiger-man,' heated by a quart or two above his usual measure, comes home and kicks his irritating and injudicious wife to death. He is a murderer. And Gilles de Raiz was a murderer. But you see the gulf that separates the two? The 'word,' if I may so speak, is accidentally the same in each case, but the 'meaning' is utterly different. It is flagrant 'Hobson Jobson' to confuse the two, or rather, it is as if one supposed that Juggernaut and the Argonauts had something to do etymologically with one another.[6] And no doubt the same weak likeness, or analogy, runs between all the 'social' sins and the real spiritual sins, and in some cases, perhaps, the lesser may be 'schoolmaster' to lead one on to the greater—from the shadow to the reality. If you are anything of a theologian, you will see the importance of all this."

"I am sorry to say," remarked Cotgrave, "that I have devoted very little of my time to theology. Indeed, I have often wondered on what grounds theologians have claimed the title of Science of Sciences for their favourite study; since the 'theological' books I have looked into have always seemed to me to be concerned with feeble and obvious pieties, or with the kings of Israel and Judah. I do not care to hear about those kings."

Ambrose grinned.

"We must try to avoid theological discussion," he said. "I perceive that you would be a bitter disputant. But perhaps the 'dates of the kings' have as much to do with theology as the hobnails of the murderous puddler with evil."

"Then, to return to our main subject, you think that sin is an esoteric, occult thing?"

"Yes. It is the infernal miracle as holiness is the supernal. Now and then it is raised to such a pitch that we entirely fail to suspect its existence; it is like the note of the great pedal pipes of the organ, which is so deep that we cannot hear it. In other cases it may lead to the lunatic asylum, or to still stranger issues. But you must never confuse it with mere social misdoing. Remember how the Apostle, speaking of the 'other side,' distinguishes between 'charitable' actions and charity.[7] And as one may give all one's goods to the poor, and yet lack charity; so, remember, one may avoid every crime and yet be a sinner."

"Your psychology is very strange to me," said Cotgrave, "but I confess I like it, and I suppose that one might fairly deduce from your premises the conclusion that the real sinner might very possibly strike the observer as a harmless personage enough?"

"Certainly; because the true evil has nothing to do with social life or social laws, or if it has, only incidentally and accidentally. It is a lonely passion of the soul—or a passion of the lonely soul—whichever you like. If, by chance, we understand it, and grasp its full significance, then, indeed, it will fill us with horror and with awe. But this emotion is widely distinguished from the fear and the disgust with which we regard the ordinary criminal, since this latter is largely or entirely founded on the regard which we have for our own skins or purses. We hate a murderer, because we know that we should hate to be murdered, or to have any one that we like murdered. So, on the 'other side,' we venerate the saints, but we don't 'like' them as we like our friends. Can you persuade yourself that you would have 'enjoyed' St. Paul's company? Do you think that you and I would have 'got on' with Sir Galahad?

"So with the sinners, as with the saints. If you met a very evil man, and recognized his evil; he would, no doubt, fill you with horror and awe; but there is no reason why you should 'dislike' him. On the contrary, it is quite possible that if you could succeed in putting the sin out of your mind you might find the sinner capital company, and in a little while you might have to reason yourself back into horror. Still, how awful it is. If the roses and the lilies suddenly sang on this coming morning; if the furniture began to move in procession, as in De Maupassant's tale!"[8]

"I am glad you have come back to that comparison," said Cotgrave, "because I wanted to ask you what it is that corresponds in humanity to these imaginary feats of inanimate things. In a word—what

228

is sin? You have given me, I know, an abstract definition, but I should like a concrete example."

"I told you it was very rare," said Ambrose, who appeared willing to avoid the giving of a direct answer. "The materialism of the age, which has done a good deal to suppress sanctity, has done perhaps more to suppress evil. We find the earth so very comfortable that we have no inclination either for ascents or descents. It would seem as if the scholar who decided to 'specialize' in Tophet, would be reduced to purely antiquarian researches. No palæontologist could show you a *live* pterodactyl."

"And yet you, I think, have 'specialized,' and I believe that your researches have descended to our modern times."

"You are really interested, I see. Well, I confess that I have dabbled a little, and if you like I can show you something that bears on the very curious subject we have been discussing."

Ambrose took a candle and went away to a far, dim corner of the room. Cotgrave saw him open a venerable bureau that stood there, and from some secret recess he drew out a parcel, and came back to the window where they had been sitting.

Ambrose undid a wrapping of paper, and produced a green pocket-book.

"You will take care of it?" he said. "Don't leave it lying about. It is one of the choicer pieces in my collection, and I should be very sorry if it were lost."

He fondled the faded binding.

"I knew the girl who wrote this," he said. "When you read it, you will see how it illustrates the talk we have had to-night. There is a sequel, too, but I won't talk of that."

"There was an odd article in one of the reviews some months ago," he began again, with the air of a man who changes the subject. "It was written by a doctor—Dr. Coryn, I think, was the name. He says that a lady, watching her little girl playing at the drawing-room window, suddenly saw the heavy sash give way and fall on the child's fingers. The lady fainted, I think, but at any rate the doctor was summoned, and when he had dressed the child's wounded and maimed fingers he was summoned to the mother. She was groaning with pain, and it was found that three fingers of her hand, corresponding with those that had been injured on the child's hand, were swollen and inflamed, and later, in the doctor's language, purulent sloughing set in."

Ambrose still handled delicately the green volume.

"Well, here it is," he said at last, parting with difficulty, it seemed, from his treasure.

"You will bring it back as soon as you have read it," he said, as they went out into the hall, into the old garden, faint with the odour of white lilies.

There was a broad red band in the east as Cotgrave turned to go, and from the high ground where he stood he saw that awful spectacle of London in a dream.

THE GREEN BOOK

The morocco binding of the book was faded, and the colour had grown faint, but there were no stains nor bruises nor marks of usage. The book looked as if it had been bought "on a visit to London" some seventy or eighty years ago, and had somehow been forgotten and suffered to lie away out of sight. There was an old, delicate, lingering odour about it, such an odour as sometimes haunts an ancient piece of furniture for a century or more. The end-papers, inside the binding, were oddly decorated with coloured patterns and faded gold. It looked small, but the paper was fine, and there were many leaves, closely covered with minute, painfully formed characters.

I found this book (the manuscript began) in a drawer in the old bureau that stands on the landing. It was a very rainy day and I could not go out, so in the afternoon I got a candle and rummaged in the bureau. Nearly all the drawers were full of old dresses, but one of the small ones looked empty, and I found this book hidden right at the back. I wanted a book like this, so I took it to write in. It is full of secrets. I have a great many other books of secrets I have written, hidden in a safe place, and I am going to write here many of the old secrets and some new ones; but there are some I shall not put down at all. I must not write down the real names of the days and months which I found out a year ago, nor the way to make the Aklo letters, or the Chian language, or the great beautiful Circles, nor the Mao Games, nor the chief songs. I may write something about all these things but not the way to do them, for peculiar reasons. And I must not say who the Nymphs are, or the Dôls, or Jeelo, or what voolas mean. All these are most secret secrets, and I am glad when I remember what they are, and how many wonderful languages I know, but there are some things that I call the secrets of the secrets of the secrets that I dare not think of unless I am quite alone, and then I shut my eyes, and put my hands over them and whisper the word, and the Alala[9] comes. I only do this at night in my room or in certain woods that I know, but I must not describe them, as they are secret woods. Then there are the Ceremonies, which are all of them important, but some are more delightful than others—there are the White Ceremonies, and the Green Ceremonies, and the Scarlet Ceremonies. The Scarlet Ceremonies are the best, but there is only one place where they can be performed properly, though there is a very nice imitation which I have done in other places. Besides these, I have the dances, and the Comedy, and I have done the Comedy sometimes when the others were looking, and they didn't understand anything about it. I was very little when I first knew about these things.

When I was very small, and mother was alive, I can remember remembering things before that, only it has all got confused. But I remember when I was five or six I heard them talking about me when they thought I was not noticing. They were saying how queer I was a year or two before, and how nurse had called my mother to come and listen to me talking all to myself, and I was saying words that nobody could understand. I was speaking the Xu language, but I only remember a very few of the words, as it was about the little white faces that used to look at me when I was lying in my cradle. They used to talk to me, and I learnt their language and talked to them in it about some great white place where they lived, where the trees and the grass were all white, and there were white hills as high up as the moon, and a cold wind. I have often dreamed of it afterwards, but the faces went away when I was very little. But a wonderful thing happened when I was about five. My nurse was carrying me on her shoulder; there was a field of yellow corn, and we went through it, it was very hot. Then we came to a path through a wood, and a tall man came after us, and went with us till we came to a place where there was a deep pool, and it was very dark and shady. Nurse put me down on the soft moss under a tree, and she said: "She can't get to the pond now." So they left me there, and I sat quite still and watched, and out of the water and out of the wood came two wonderful white people, and they began to play and dance and sing. They were a kind of creamy white like the old ivory figure in the drawing-room; one was a beautiful lady with kind dark eyes, and a grave face, and long black hair, and she smiled such a strange sad smile at the other, who laughed and came to her. They played together, and danced round and round the pool, and they sang a song till I fell asleep. Nurse woke me up when she came back, and she was looking something like the lady had looked, so I told her all about it, and asked her why she looked like that. At first she cried, and then she looked very frightened, and turned quite pale. She put me down on the grass and stared at me, and I could see she was shaking all over.

Then she said I had been dreaming, but I knew I hadn't. Then she made me promise not to say a word about it to anybody, and if I did I should be thrown into the black pit. I was not frightened at all, though nurse was, and I never forgot about it, because when I shut my eyes and it was quite quiet, and I was all alone, I could see them again, very faint and far away, but very splendid; and little bits of the song they sang came into my head, but I couldn't sing it.

I was thirteen, nearly fourteen, when I had a very singular adventure, so strange that the day on which it happened is always called the White Day. My mother had been dead for more than a year, and in the morning I had lessons, but they let me go out for walks in the afternoon. And this afternoon I walked a new way, and a little brook led me into a new country, but I tore my frock getting through many bushes, and beneath the low branches of trees, and up thorny thickets on the hills, and by dark woods full of creeping thorns. And it was a long, long way. It seemed as if I was going on for ever and ever, and I had to creep by a place like a tunnel where a brook must have been, but all the water had dried up, and the floor was rocky, and the bushes had grown overhead till they met, so that it was quite dark. And I went on and on through that dark place; it was a long, long way. And I came to a hill that I never saw before. I was in a dismal thicket full of black twisted boughs that tore me as I went through them, and I cried out because I was smarting all over, and then I found that I was climbing, and I went up and up a long way, till at last the thicket stopped and I came out crying just under the top of a big bare place, where there were ugly grey stones lying all about on the grass, and here and there a little twisted, stunted tree came out from under a stone, like a snake. And I went up, right to the top, a long way. I never saw such big ugly stones before; they came out of the earth some of them, and some looked as if they had been rolled to where they were, and they went on and on as far as I could see, a long, long way. I looked out from them and saw the country, but it was strange. It was winter time, and there were black terrible woods hanging from the hills all round; it was like seeing a large room hung with black curtains, and the shape of the trees seemed quite different from any I had ever seen before. I was afraid. Then beyond the woods there were other hills round in a great ring, but I had never seen any of them; it all looked black, and everything had a voor over it. It was all so still and silent, and the sky was heavy and grey and sad, like a wicked voorish dome in Deep Dendo. I went on into the dreadful rocks. There were hundreds and hundreds of them. Some were like horrid-grinning men; I could see their faces as if they would jump at me out of the stone, and catch hold of me, and drag me with them back into the rock, so that I should always be there. And there were other rocks that were like animals, creeping, horrible animals, putting out their tongues, and others were like words that I could not say, and others like dead people lying on the grass. I went on among them, though they frightened me, and my heart was full of wicked songs that they put into it; and I wanted to make faces and twist myself about in the way they did, and I went on and on a long way till at last I liked the rocks, and they didn't frighten me any more. I sang the songs I thought of; songs full of words that must not be spoken or written down. Then I made faces like the faces on the rocks, and I twisted myself about like the twisted ones, and I lay down flat on the ground like the dead ones, and I went up to one that was grinning, and put my arms round him and hugged him. And so I went on and on through the rocks till I came to a round mound in the middle of them. It was higher than a mound, it was nearly as high as our house, and it was like a great basin turned upside down, all smooth and round and green, with one stone, like a post, sticking up at the top. I climbed up the sides, but they were so steep I had to stop or I should have rolled all the way down again, and I should have knocked against the stones at the bottom, and perhaps been killed. But I wanted to get up to the very top of the big round mound, so I lay down flat on my face, and took hold of the grass with my hands and drew myself up, bit by bit, till I was at the top. Then I sat down on the stone in the middle, and looked all round about. I felt I had come such a long, long way, just as if I were a hundred miles from home, or in some other country, or in one of the strange places I had read about in the "Tales of the Genie"[10] and the "Arabian Nights," or as if I had gone across the sea, far away, for years and I had found another world that nobody had ever seen or heard of before, or as if I had somehow flown through the sky and fallen on one of the stars I had read about where everything is dead and cold and grey, and there is no air, and the wind doesn't blow. I sat on the stone and looked all round and down and round about me. It was just as if I was sitting on a tower in the middle of a great empty town, because I could see nothing all around but the grey rocks on the ground. I couldn't make out their shapes any more, but I could see them on and on for a long way, and I looked at them, and they seemed as if they had been arranged into patterns, and shapes, and figures. I knew they couldn't be, because I had seen a lot of them coming right out of the earth, joined to the deep rocks below, so I looked again, but still I saw nothing but circles, and small circles inside big ones, and pyramids, and domes, and spires, and they seemed all to go round and round the place where I was sitting, and the more I looked, the more I saw great big rings of rocks, getting bigger and bigger, and I stared so long that it felt as if they were all moving and turning, like a great wheel, and I was turning, too, in the middle. I got quite dizzy and queer in the head, and everything began to be hazy and not clear, and I saw little sparks of blue light, and the stones looked as if they were springing and dancing and twisting as they went round and round and round. I was frightened again, and I cried out loud, and jumped up from the stone I was sitting on, and fell down. When I got up I was so glad they all looked still, and I sat down on the top and slid down the mound, and went on again. I danced as I went in the peculiar way the rocks had danced when I got giddy, and I was so glad I could do it quite well, and I danced and danced along, and sang extraordinary songs that came into my head. At last I came to the edge of that great flat hill, and there were no more rocks, and the way went again through a dark thicket in a hollow. It was just as bad as the other one I went through climbing up, but I didn't mind this one, because I was so glad I had seen those singular dances and could imitate them. I went down, creeping through the bushes, and a tall nettle stung me on my leg, and made me burn, but I didn't mind it, and I tingled with the boughs and the thorns, but I only laughed and sang. Then I got out of the thicket into a close valley, a little secret place like a dark passage that nobody ever knows of, because it was so narrow and deep and the woods were so thick round it. There is a steep bank with trees hanging over it, and there the ferns keep green all through the winter, when they are dead and brown upon the hill, and the ferns there have a sweet, rich smell like what oozes out of fir trees. There was a little stream of water running down this valley, so small that I could easily step across it. I drank the water with my hand, and it tasted like bright, yellow wine, and it sparkled and bubbled as it ran down over beautiful red and yellow stones, so that it seemed alive and all colours at once. I drank it, and I drank more with my hand, but I couldn't drink enough, so I lay down and bent my head and sucked the water up with my lips. It tasted much better, drinking it that way, and a ripple would come up to my mouth and give me a kiss, and I laughed, and drank again, and pretended there was a nymph, like the one in the old picture at home, who lived in the water and was kissing me. So I bent low down to the water, and put my lips softly to it, and whispered to the nymph that I would come again. I felt sure it would not be common water, I was so glad when I got up and went on; and I danced again and went up and up the valley, under hanging hills. And when I came to the top, the ground rose up in front of me, tall and steep as a wall, and there was nothing but the green wall and the sky. I thought of "for ever and for ever, world without end, Amen";[11] and I

234

thought I must have really found the end of the world, because it was like the end of everything, as if there could be nothing at all beyond, except the kingdom of Voor, where the light goes when it is put out, and the water goes when the sun takes it away. I began to think of all the long, long way I had journeyed, how I had found a brook and followed it, and followed it on, and gone through bushes and thorny thickets, and dark woods full of creeping thorns. Then I had crept up a tunnel under trees, and climbed a thicket, and seen all the grey rocks, and sat in the middle of them when they turned round, and then I had gone on through the grey rocks and come down the hill through the stinging thicket and up the dark valley, all a long, long way. I wondered how I should get home again, if I could ever find the way, and if my home was there any more, or if it were turned and everybody in it into grey rocks, as in the "Arabian Nights." So I sat down on the grass and thought what I should do next. I was tired, and my feet were hot with walking, and as I looked about I saw there was a wonderful well just under the high, steep wall of grass. All the ground round it was covered with bright, green, dripping moss; there was every kind of moss there, moss like beautiful little ferns, and like palms and fir trees, and it was all green as jewellery, and drops of water hung on it like diamonds. And in the middle was the great well, deep and shining and beautiful, so clear it looked as if I could touch the red sand at the bottom, but it was far below. I stood by it and looked in, as if I were looking in a glass. At the bottom of the well, in the middle of it, the red grains of sand were moving and stirring all the time, and I saw how the water bubbled up, but at the top it was quite smooth, and full and brimming. It was a great well, large like a bath, and with the shining, glittering green moss about it, it looked like a great white jewel, with green jewels all round. My feet were so hot and tired that I took off my boots and stockings, and let my feet down into the water, and the water was soft and cold, and when I got up I wasn't tired any more, and I felt I must go on, farther and farther, and see what was on the other side of the wall. I climbed up it very slowly, going sideways all the time, and when I got to the top and looked over, I was in the queerest country I had seen, stranger even than the hill of the grey rocks. It looked as if earth-children had been playing there with their spades, as it was all hills and hollows, and castles and walls made of earth and covered with grass. There were two mounds like big beehives, round and great and solemn, and then hollow basins, and then a steep mounting wall like the ones I saw once by the seaside where the big guns and the soldiers were. I nearly fell into one of the round hollows, it went away from under my feet so suddenly, and I ran fast down the side and stood at the

235

bottom and looked up. It was strange and solemn to look up. There was nothing but the grey, heavy sky and the sides of the hollow; everything else had gone away, and the hollow was the whole world, and I thought that at night it must be full of ghosts and moving shadows and pale things when the moon shone down to the bottom at the dead of the night, and the wind wailed up above. It was so strange and solemn and lonely, like a hollow temple of dead heathen gods. It reminded me of a tale my nurse had told me when I was quite little; it was the same nurse that took me into the wood where I saw the beautiful white people. And I remembered how nurse had told me the story one winter night, when the wind was beating the trees against the wall, and crying and moaning in the nursery chimney. She said there was, somewhere or other, a hollow pit, just like the one I was standing in, everybody was afraid to go into it or near it, it was such a bad place. But once upon a time there was a poor girl who said she would go into the hollow pit, and everybody tried to stop her, but she would go. And she went down into the pit and came back laughing, and said there was nothing there at all, except green grass and red stones, and white stones and yellow flowers. And soon after people saw she had most beautiful emerald earrings, and they asked how she got them, as she and her mother were quite poor. But she laughed, and said her earrings were not made of emeralds at all, but only of green grass. Then, one day, she wore on her breast the reddest ruby that any one had ever seen, and it was as big as a hen's egg, and glowed and sparkled like a hot burning coal of fire. And they asked how she got it, as she and her mother were quite poor. But she laughed, and said it was not a ruby at all, but only a red stone. Then one day she wore round her neck the loveliest necklace that any one had ever seen, much finer than the queen's finest, and it was made of great bright diamonds, hundreds of them, and they shone like all the stars on a night in June. So they asked her how she got it, as she and her mother were quite poor. But she laughed, and said they were not diamonds at all, but only white stones. And one day she went to the court, and she wore on her head a crown of pure angel-gold, so nurse said, and it shone like the sun, and it was much more splendid than the crown the king was wearing himself, and in her ears she wore the emeralds, and the big ruby was the brooch on her breast, and the great diamond necklace was sparkling on her neck. And the king and queen thought she was some great princess from a long way off, and got down from their thrones and went to meet her, but somebody told the king and queen who she was, and that she was quite poor. So the king asked why she wore a gold crown, and how she got it, as she and her mother were so poor. And she laughed, and said it wasn't a gold crown at all, but only some yellow flowers she had put in her hair. And the king thought it was very strange, and said she should stay at the court, and they would see what would happen next. And she was so lovely that everybody said that her eyes were greener than the emeralds, that her lips were redder than the ruby, that her skin was whiter than the diamonds, and that her hair was brighter than the golden crown. So the king's son said he would marry her, and the king said he might. And the bishop married them, and there was a great supper, and afterwards the king's son went to his wife's room. But just when he had his hand on the door, he saw a tall, black man, with a dreadful face, standing in front of the door, and a voice said—

> Venture not upon your life,
> This is mine own wedded wife.

Then the king's son fell down on the ground in a fit. And they came and tried to get into the room, but they couldn't, and they hacked at the door with hatchets, but the wood had turned hard as iron, and at last everybody ran away, they were so frightened at the screaming and laughing and shrieking and crying that came out of the room. But next day they went in, and found there was nothing in the room but thick black smoke, because the black man had come and taken her away. And on the bed there were two knots of faded grass and a red stone, and some white stones, and some faded yellow flowers. I remembered this tale of nurse's while I was standing at the bottom of the deep hollow; it was so strange and solitary there, and I felt afraid. I could not see any stones or flowers, but I was afraid of bringing them away without knowing, and I thought I would do a charm that came into my head to keep the black man away. So I stood right in the very middle of the hollow, and I made sure that I had none of those things on me, and then I walked round the place, and touched my eyes, and my lips, and my hair in a peculiar manner, and whispered some queer words that nurse taught me to keep bad things away. Then I felt safe and climbed up out of the hollow, and went on through all those mounds and hollows and walls, till I came to the end, which was high above all the rest, and I could see that all the different shapes of the earth were arranged in patterns, something like the grey rocks, only the pattern was different. It was getting late, and the air was indistinct, but it looked from where I was standing something like two great figures of people lying on the grass. And I went on, and at last I found a certain wood, which is too secret to be described, and nobody knows of the passage into it, which I found out in a very curious manner, by seeing some little animal run into the wood through it. So I went in after the animal by a very narrow dark way, under thorns and bushes, and it was almost dark when I came to a kind of open place in the middle. And there I saw the most wonderful sight I have ever seen, but it was only for a minute, as I ran away directly, and crept out of the wood by the passage I had come by, and ran and ran as fast as ever I could, because I was afraid, what I had seen was so wonderful and so strange and beautiful. But I wanted to get home and think of it, and I did not know what might not happen if I stayed by the wood. I was hot all over and trembling, and my heart was beating, and strange cries that I could not help came from me as I ran from the wood. I was glad that a great white moon came up from over a round hill and showed me the way, so I went back through the mounds and hollows and down the close valley, and up through the thicket over the place of the grey rocks, and so at last I got home again. My father was busy in his study, and the servants had not told about my not coming home, though they were frightened, and wondered what they ought to do, so I told them I had lost my way, but I did not let them find out the real way I had been. I went to bed and lay awake all through the night, thinking of what I had seen. When I came out of the narrow way, and it looked all shining, though the air was dark, it seemed so certain, and all the way home I was quite sure that I had seen it, and I wanted to be alone in my room, and be glad over it all to myself, and shut my eyes and pretend it was there, and do all the things I would have done if I had not been so afraid. But when I shut my eyes the sight would not come, and I began to think about my adventures all over again, and I remembered how dusky and queer it was at the end, and I was afraid it must be all a mistake, because it seemed impossible it could happen. It seemed like one of nurse's tales, which I didn't really believe in, though I was frightened at the bottom of the hollow; and the stories she told me when I was little came back into my head, and I wondered whether it was really there what I thought I had seen, or whether any of her tales could have happened a long time ago. It was so queer; I lay awake there in my room at the back of the house, and the moon was shining on the other side towards the river, so the bright light did not fall upon the wall. And the house was quite still. I had heard my father come upstairs, and just after the clock struck twelve, and after the house was still and empty, as if there was nobody alive in it. And though it was all dark and indistinct in my room, a pale glimmering kind of light shone in through the white blind, and once I got up and looked out, and there was a great black shadow of the house covering the garden, looking like a prison where men are hanged; and then beyond it was all white;

and the wood shone white with black gulfs between the trees. It was still and clear, and there were no clouds in the sky. I wanted to think of what I had seen but I couldn't, and I began to think of all the tales that nurse had told me so long ago that I thought I had forgotten, but they all came back, and mixed up with the thickets and the grey rocks and the hollows in the earth and the secret wood, till I hardly knew what was new and what was old, or whether it was not all dreaming. And then I remembered that hot summer afternoon, so long ago, when nurse left me by myself in the shade, and the white people came out of the water and out of the wood, and played, and danced, and sang, and I began to fancy that nurse told me about something like it before I saw them, only I couldn't recollect exactly what she told me. Then I wondered whether she had been the white lady, as I remembered she was just as white and beautiful, and had the same dark eyes and black hair; and sometimes she smiled and looked like the lady had looked, when she was telling me some of her stories, beginning with "Once on a time," or "In the time of the fairies." But I thought she couldn't be the lady, as she seemed to have gone a different way into the wood, and I didn't think the man who came after us could be the other, or I couldn't have seen that wonderful secret in the secret wood. I thought of the moon: but it was afterwards when I was in the middle of the wild land, where the earth was made into the shape of great figures, and it was all walls, and mysterious hollows, and smooth round mounds, that I saw the great white moon come up over a round hill. I was wondering about all these things, till at last I got quite frightened, because I was afraid something had happened to me, and I remembered nurse's tale of the poor girl who went into the hollow pit, and was carried away at last by the black man. I knew I had gone into a hollow pit too, and perhaps it was the same, and I had done something dreadful. So I did the charm over again, and touched my eyes and my lips and my hair in a peculiar manner, and said the old words from the fairy language, so that I might be sure I had not been carried away. I tried again to see the secret wood, and to creep up the passage and see what I had seen there, but somehow I couldn't, and I kept on thinking of nurse's stories. There was one I remembered about a young man who once upon a time went hunting, and all the day he and his hounds hunted everywhere, and they crossed the rivers and went into all the woods, and went round the marshes, but they couldn't find anything at all, and they hunted all day till the sun sank down and began to set behind the mountain. And the young man was angry because he couldn't find anything, and he was going to turn back, when just as the sun touched the mountain, he saw come out of a brake in front of him a beautiful white stag. And he cheered to his hounds, but they whined and would not follow, and he cheered to his horse, but it shivered and stood stock still, and the young man jumped off the horse and left the hounds and began to follow the white stag all alone. And soon it was quite dark, and the sky was black, without a single star shining in it, and the stag went away into the darkness. And though the man had brought his gun with him he never shot at the stag, because he wanted to catch it, and he was afraid he would lose it in the night. But he never lost it once, though the sky was so black and the air was so dark, and the stag went on and on till the young man didn't know a bit where he was. And they went through enormous woods where the air was full of whispers and a pale, dead light came out from the rotten trunks that were lying on the ground, and just as the man thought he had lost the stag, he would see it all white and shining in front of him, and he would run fast to catch it, but the stag always ran faster, so he did not catch it. And they went through the enormous woods, and they swam across rivers, and they waded through black marshes where the ground bubbled, and the air was full of will-o'-the-wisps, and the stag fled away down into rocky narrow valleys, where the air was like the smell of a vault, and the man went after it. And they went over the great mountains, and the man heard the wind come down from the sky, and the stag went on and the man went after. At last the sun rose and the young man found he was in a country that he had never seen before; it was a beautiful valley with a bright stream running through it, and a great, big round hill in the middle. And the stag went down the valley, towards the hill, and it seemed to be getting tired and went slower and slower, and though the man was tired, too, he began to run faster, and he was sure he would catch the stag at last. But just as they got to the bottom of the hill, and the man stretched out his hand to catch the stag, it vanished into the earth, and the man began to cry; he was so sorry that he had lost it after all his long hunting. But as he was crying he saw there was a door in the hill, just in front of him, and he went in, and it was quite dark, but he went on, as he thought he would find the white stag. And all of a sudden it got light, and there was the sky, and the sun shining, and birds singing in the trees, and there was a beautiful fountain. And by the fountain a lovely lady was sitting, who was the queen of the fairies, and she told the man that she had changed herself into a stag to bring him there because she loved him so much. Then she brought out a great gold cup, covered with jewels, from her fairy palace, and she offered him wine in the cup to drink. And he drank, and the more he drank the more he longed to drink, because the wine was enchanted. So he kissed the lovely lady, and she became his wife, and he stayed all

240

that day and all that night in the hill where she lived, and when he woke he found he was lying on the ground, close to where he had seen the stag first, and his horse was there and his hounds were there waiting, and he looked up, and the sun sank behind the mountain. And he went home and lived a long time, but he would never kiss any other lady because he had kissed the queen of the fairies, and he would never drink common wine any more, because he had drunk enchanted wine. And sometimes nurse told me tales that she had heard from her great-grandmother, who was very old, and lived in a cottage on the mountain all alone, and most of these tales were about a hill where people used to meet at night long ago, and they used to play all sorts of strange games and do queer things that nurse told me of, but I couldn't understand, and now, she said, everybody but her great-grandmother had forgotten all about it, and nobody knew where the hill was, not even her great-grandmother. But she told me one very strange story about the hill, and I trembled when I remembered it. She said that people always went there in summer, when it was very hot, and they had to dance a good deal. It would be all dark at first, and there were trees there, which made it much darker, and people would come, one by one, from all directions, by a secret path which nobody else knew, and two persons would keep the gate, and every one as they came up had to give a very curious sign, which nurse showed me as well as she could, but she said she couldn't show me properly. And all kinds of people would come; there would be gentle folks and village folks, and some old people and boys and girls, and quite small children, who sat and watched. And it would all be dark as they came in, except in one corner where some one was burning something that smelt strong and sweet, and made them laugh, and there one would see a glaring of coals, and the smoke mounting up red. So they would all come in, and when the last had come there was no door any more, so that no one else could get in, even if they knew there was anything beyond. And once a gentleman who was a stranger and had ridden a long way, lost his path at night, and his horse took him into the very middle of the wild country, where everything was upside down, and there were dreadful marshes and great stones everywhere, and holes underfoot, and the trees looked like gibbet-posts, because they had great black arms that stretched out across the way. And this strange gentleman was very frightened, and his horse began to shiver all over, and at last it stopped and wouldn't go any farther, and the gentleman got down and tried to lead the horse, but it wouldn't move, and it was all covered with a sweat, like death. So the gentleman went on all alone, going farther and farther into the wild country, till at last he came to a dark place, where he heard shouting and singing and crying, like nothing he had ever heard before. It all sounded quite close to him, but he couldn't get in, and so he began to call, and while he was calling, something came behind him, and in a minute his mouth and arms and legs were all bound up, and he fell into a swoon. And when he came to himself, he was lying by the roadside, just where he had first lost his way, under a blasted oak with a black trunk, and his horse was tied beside him. So he rode on to the town and told the people there what had happened, and some of them were amazed; but others knew. So when once everybody had come, there was no door at all for anybody else to pass in by. And when they were all inside, round in a ring, touching each other, some one began to sing in the darkness, and some one else would make a noise like thunder with a thing they had on purpose, and on still nights people would hear the thundering noise far, far away beyond the wild land, and some of them, who thought they knew what it was, used to make a sign on their breasts when they woke up in their beds at dead of night and heard that terrible deep noise, like thunder on the mountains. And the noise and the singing would go on and on for a long time, and the people who were in a ring swayed a little to and fro; and the song was in an old, old language that nobody knows now, and the tune was queer. Nurse said her great-grandmother had known some one who remembered a little of it, when she was quite a little girl, and nurse tried to sing some of it to me, and it was so strange a tune that I turned all cold and my flesh crept as if I had put my hand on something dead. Sometimes it was a man that sang and sometimes it was a woman, and sometimes the one who sang it did it so well that two or three of the people who were there fell to the ground shrieking and tearing with their hands. The singing went on, and the people in the ring kept swaying to and fro for a long time, and at last the moon would rise over a place they called the Tole Deol, and came up and showed them swinging and swaying from side to side, with the sweet thick smoke curling up from the burning coals, and floating in circles all around them. Then they had their supper. A boy and a girl brought it to them; the boy carried a great cup of wine, and the girl carried a cake of bread, and they passed the bread and the wine round and round, but they tasted quite different from common bread and common wine, and changed everybody that tasted them. Then they all rose up and danced, and secret things were brought out of some hiding place, and they played extraordinary games, and danced round and round and round in the moonlight, and sometimes people would suddenly disappear and never be heard of afterwards, and nobody knew what had happened to them. And they drank more of that curious

242

wine, and they made images and worshipped them, and nurse showed me how the images were made one day when we were out for a walk, and we passed by a place where there was a lot of wet clay. So nurse asked me if I would like to know what those things were like that they made on the hill, and I said yes. Then she asked me if I would promise never to tell a living soul a word about it, and if I did I was to be thrown into the black pit with the dead people, and I said I wouldn't tell anybody, and she said the same thing again and again, and I promised. So she took my wooden spade and dug a big lump of clay and put it in my tin bucket, and told me to say if any one met us that I was going to make pies when I went home. Then we went on a little way till we came to a little brake growing right down into the road, and nurse stopped, and looked up the road and down it, and then peeped through the hedge into the field on the other side, and then she said "Quick!" and we ran into the brake, and crept in and out among the bushes till we had gone a good way from the road. Then we sat down under a bush, and I wanted so much to know what nurse was going to make with the clay, but before she would begin she made me promise again not to say a word about it, and she went again and peeped through the bushes on every side, though the lane was so small and deep that hardly anybody ever went there. So we sat down, and nurse took the clay out of the bucket, and began to knead it with her hands, and do queer things with it, and turn it about. And she hid it under a big dock-leaf for a minute or two and then she brought it out again, and then she stood up and sat down and walked round the clay in a peculiar manner, and all the time she was softly singing a sort of rhyme, and her face got very red. Then she sat down again, and took the clay in her hands and began to shape it into a doll, but not like the dolls I have at home, and she made the queerest doll I had ever seen, all out of the wet clay, and hid it under a bush to get dry and hard, and all the time she was making it she was singing these rhymes to herself, and her face got redder and redder. So we left the doll there, hidden away in the bushes where nobody would ever find it. And a few days later we went the same walk, and when we came to that narrow, dark part of the lane where the brake runs down to the bank, nurse made me promise all over again, and she looked about, just as she had done before, and we crept into the bushes till we got to the green place where the little clay man was hidden. I remember it all so well, though I was only eight, and it is eight years ago now as I am writing it down, but the sky was a deep violet blue, and in the middle of the brake where we were sitting there was a great elder tree covered with blossoms, and on the other side there was a clump of meadowsweet, and when I think of that day

243

the smell of the meadowsweet and elder blossom seems to fill the room, and if I shut my eyes I can see the glaring sky, with little clouds very white floating across it, and nurse who went away long ago sitting opposite me and looking like the beautiful white lady in the wood. So we sat down and nurse took out the clay doll from the secret place where she had bidden it, and she said we must "pay our respects," and she would show me what to do, and I must watch her all the time. So she did all sorts of queer things with the little clay man, and I noticed she was all streaming with perspiration, though we had walked so slowly, and then she told me to "pay my respects," and I did everything she did, because I liked her, and it was such an odd game. And she said that if one loved very much, the clay man was very good, if one did certain things with it, and if one hated very much, it was just as good, only one had to do different things, and we played with it a long time, and pretended all sorts of things. Nurse said her great-grandmother had told her all about these images, but what we did was no harm at all, only a game. But she told me a story about these images that frightened me very much, and that was what I remembered that night when I was lying awake in my room in the pale, empty darkness, thinking of what I had seen and the secret wood. Nurse said there was once a young lady of the high gentry, who lived in a great castle. And she was so beautiful that all the gentlemen wanted to marry her, because she was the loveliest lady that anybody had ever seen, and she was kind to everybody, and everybody thought she was very good. But though she was polite to all the gentlemen who wished to marry her, she put them off, and said she couldn't make up her mind, and she wasn't sure she wanted to marry anybody at all. And her father, who was a very great lord, was angry, though he was so fond of her, and he asked her why she wouldn't choose a bachelor out of all the handsome young men who came to the castle. But she only said she didn't love any of them very much, and she must wait, and if they pestered her, she said she would go and be a nun in a nunnery. So all the gentlemen said they would go away and wait for a year and a day, and when a year and a day were gone, they would come back again and ask her to say which one she would marry. So the day was appointed and they all went away; and the lady had promised that in a year and a day it would be her wedding day with one of them. But the truth was, that she was the queen of the people who danced on the hill on summer nights, and on the proper nights she would lock the door of her room, and she and her maid would steal out of the castle by a secret passage that only they knew of, and go away up to the hill in the wild land. And she knew more of the secret things than any one else, and more than any one

knew before or after, because she would not tell anybody the most secret secrets. She knew how to do all the awful things, how to destroy
young men, and how to put a curse on people, and other things that I
could not understand. And her real name was the Lady Avelin, but the
dancing people called her Cassap, which meant somebody very wise,
in the old language. And she was whiter than any of them and taller,
and her eyes shone in the dark like burning rubies; and she could sing
songs that none of the others could sing, and when she sang they all fell
down on their faces and worshipped her. And she could do what they
called the shib-show, which was a very wonderful enchantment. She
would tell the great lord, her father, that she wanted to go into the
woods to gather flowers, so he let her go, and she and her maid went
into the woods where nobody came, and the maid would keep watch.
Then the lady would lie down under the trees and begin to sing a particular song, and she stretched out her arms, and from every part of
the wood great serpents would come, hissing and gliding in and out
among the trees, and shooting out their forked tongues as they crawled
up to the lady. And they all came to her, and twisted round her, round
her body, and her arms, and her neck, till she was covered with writhing serpents, and there was only her head to be seen. And she whispered to them, and she sang to them, and they writhed round and
round, faster and faster, till she told them to go. And they all went away
directly, back to their holes, and on the lady's breast there would be a
most curious, beautiful stone, shaped something like an egg, and coloured dark blue and yellow, and red, and green, marked like a ser-
pent's scales. It was called a glame stone, and with it one could do all
sorts of wonderful things, and nurse said her great-grandmother had
seen a glame stone with her own eyes, and it was for all the world shiny
and scaly like a snake. And the lady could do a lot of other things as
well, but she was quite fixed that she would not be married. And there
were a great many gentlemen who wanted to marry her, but there were
five of them who were chief, and their names were Sir Simon, Sir John,
Sir Oliver, Sir Richard, and Sir Rowland. All the others believed she
spoke the truth, and that she would choose one of them to be her man
when a year and a day was done; it was only Sir Simon, who was very
crafty, who thought she was deceiving them all, and he vowed he would
watch and try if he could find out anything. And though he was very
wise he was very young, and he had a smooth, soft face like a girl's, and
he pretended, as the rest did, that he would not come to the castle for
a year and a day, and he said he was going away beyond the sea to
foreign parts. But he really only went a very little way, and came back
dressed like a servant girl, and so he got a place in the castle to wash

the dishes. And he waited and watched, and he listened and said nothing, and he hid in dark places, and woke up at night and looked out, and he heard things and he saw things that he thought were very strange. And he was so sly that he told the girl that waited on the lady that he was really a young man, and that he had dressed up as a girl because he loved her so very much and wanted to be in the same house with her, and the girl was so pleased that she told him many things, and he was more than ever certain that the Lady Avelin was deceiving him and the others. And he was so clever, and told the servant so many lies, that one night he managed to hide in the Lady Avelin's room behind the curtains. And he stayed quite still and never moved, and at last the lady came. And she bent down under the bed, and raised up a stone, and there was a hollow place underneath, and out of it she took a waxen image, just like the clay one that I and nurse had made in the brake. And all the time her eyes were burning like rubies. And she took the little wax doll up in her arms and held it to her breast, and she whispered and she murmured, and she took it up and she laid it down again, and she held it high, and she held it low, and she laid it down again. And she said, "Happy is he that begat the bishop, that ordered the clerk, that married the man, that had the wife, that fashioned the hive, that harboured the bee, that gathered the wax that my own true love was made of." And she brought out of an aumbry[12] a great golden bowl, and she brought out of a closet a great jar of wine, and she poured some of the wine into the bowl, and she laid her mannikin very gently in the wine, and washed it in the wine all over. Then she went to a cupboard and took a small round cake and laid it on the image's mouth, and then she bore it softly and covered it up. And Sir Simon, who was watching all the time, though he was terribly frightened, saw the lady bend down and stretch out her arms and whisper and sing, and then Sir Simon saw beside her a handsome young man, who kissed her on the lips. And they drank wine out of the golden bowl together, and they ate the cake together. But when the sun rose there was only the little wax doll, and the lady hid it again under the bed in the hollow place. So Sir Simon knew quite well what the lady was, and he waited and he watched, till the time she had said was nearly over, and in a week the year and a day would be done. And one night, when he was watching behind the curtains in her room, he saw her making more wax dolls. And she made five, and hid them away. And the next night she took one out, and held it up, and filled the golden bowl with water, and took the doll by the neck and held it under the water. Then she said—

Sir Dickon, Sir Dickon, your day is done,
You shall be drowned in the water wan.

And the next day news came to the castle that Sir Richard had been drowned at the ford. And at night she took another doll and tied a violet cord round its neck and hung it up on a nail. Then she said—

Sir Rowland, your life has ended its span,
High on a tree I see you hang.

And the next day news came to the castle that Sir Rowland had been hanged by robbers in the wood. And at night she took another doll, and drove her bodkin right into its heart. Then she said—

Sir Noll, Sir Noll, so cease your life,
Your heart piercèd with the knife.

And the next day news came to the castle that Sir Oliver had fought in a tavern, and a stranger had stabbed him to the heart. And at night she took another doll, and held it to a fire of charcoal till it was melted. Then she said—

Sir John, return, and turn to clay,
In fire of fever you waste away.

And the next day news came to the castle that Sir John had died in a burning fever. So then Sir Simon went out of the castle and mounted his horse and rode away to the bishop and told him everything. And the bishop sent his men, and they took the Lady Avelin, and everything she had done was found out. So on the day after the year and a day, when she was to have been married, they carried her through the town in her smock, and they tied her to a great stake in the market-place, and burned her alive before the bishop with her wax image hung round her neck. And people said the wax man screamed in the burning of the flames. And I thought of this story again and again as I was lying awake in my bed, and I seemed to see the Lady Avelin in the marketplace, with the yellow flames eating up her beautiful white body. And I thought of it so much that I seemed to get into the story myself, and I fancied I was the lady, and that they were coming to take me to be burnt with fire, with all the people in the town looking at me. And I wondered whether she cared, after all the strange things she had done, and whether it hurt very much to be burned at the stake. I tried again and again to forget nurse's stories, and to remember the secret I had seen that afternoon, and what was in the secret wood, but I could only see the dark and a glimmering in the dark, and then it went away, and I only saw myself running, and then a great moon came up white over a dark round hill. Then all the old stories came back again, and the queer rhymes that nurse used to sing to me; and there was one beginning "Halsy cumsy Helen musty," that she used to sing very softly when she wanted me to go to sleep. And I began to sing it to myself inside of my head, and I went to sleep.

The next morning I was very tired and sleepy, and could hardly do my lessons, and I was very glad when they were over and I had had my dinner, as I wanted to go out and be alone. It was a warm day, and I went to a nice turfy hill by the river, and sat down on my mother's old shawl that I had brought with me on purpose. The sky was grey, like the day before, but there was a kind of white gleam behind it, and from where I was sitting I could look down on the town, and it was all still and quiet and white, like a picture. I remembered that it was on that hill that nurse taught me to play an old game called "Troy Town,"[13] in which one had to dance, and wind in and out on a pattern in the grass, and then when one had danced and turned long enough the other person asks you questions, and you can't help answering whether you want to or not, and whatever you are told to do you feel you have to do it. Nurse said there used to be a lot of games like that that some people knew of, and there was one by which people could be turned into anything you liked, and an old man her great-grandmother had seen had known a girl who had been turned into a large snake. And there was another very ancient game of dancing and winding and turning, by which you could take a person out of himself and hide him away as long as you liked, and his body went walking about quite empty, without any sense in it. But I came to that hill because I wanted to think of what had happened the day before, and of the secret of the wood. From the place where I was sitting I could see beyond the town, into the opening I had found, where a little brook had led me into an unknown country. And I pretended I was following the brook over again, and I went all the way in my mind, and at last I found the wood, and crept into it under the bushes, and then in the dusk I saw something that made me feel as if I were filled with fire, as if I wanted to dance and sing and fly up into the air, because I was changed and wonderful. But what I saw was not changed at all, and had not grown old, and I wondered again and again how such things could happen, and whether nurse's stories were really true, because in the daytime in the open air everything seemed quite different from what it was at night, when I

was frightened, and thought I was to be burned alive. I once told my father one of her little tales, which was about a ghost, and asked him if it was true, and he told me it was not true at all, and that only common, ignorant people believed in such rubbish. He was very angry with nurse for telling me the story, and scolded her, and after that I promised her I would never whisper a word of what she told me, and if I did I should be bitten by the great black snake that lived in the pool in the wood. And all alone on the hill I wondered what was true. I had seen something very amazing and very lovely, and I knew a story, and if I had really seen it, and not made it up out of the dark, and the black bough, and the bright shining that was mounting up to the sky from over the great round hill, but had really seen it in truth, then there were all kinds of wonderful and lovely and terrible things to think of, so I longed and trembled, and I burned and got cold. And I looked down on the town, so quiet and still, like a little white picture, and I thought over and over if it could be true. I was a long time before I could make up my mind to anything; there was such a strange fluttering at my heart that seemed to whisper to me all the time that I had not made it up out of my head, and yet it seemed quite impossible, and I knew my father and everybody would say it was dreadful rubbish. I never dreamed of telling him or anybody else a word about it, because I knew it would be of no use, and I should only get laughed at or scolded, so for a long time I was very quiet, and went about thinking and wondering; and at night I used to dream of amazing things, and sometimes I woke up in the early morning and held out my arms with a cry. And I was frightened, too, because there were dangers, and some awful thing would happen to me, unless I took great care, if the story were true. These old tales were always in my head, night and morning, and I went over them and told them to myself over and over again, and went for walks in the places where nurse had told them to me; and when I sat in the nursery by the fire in the evenings I used to fancy nurse was sitting in the other chair, and telling me some wonderful story in a low voice, for fear anybody should be listening. But she used to like best to tell me about things when we were right out in the country, far from the house, because she said she was telling me such secrets, and walls have ears. And if it was something more than ever secret, we had to hide in brakes or woods; and I used to think it was such fun creeping along a hedge, and going very softly, and then we would get behind the bushes or run into the wood all of a sudden, when we were sure that none was watching us; so we knew that we had our secrets quite all to ourselves, and nobody else at all knew anything about them. Now and then, when we had hidden ourselves as I have described, she used to show me all sorts of odd things. One day, I remember, we were in a hazel brake, overlooking the brook, and we were so snug and warm, as though it was April; the sun was quite hot, and the leaves were just coming out. Nurse said she would show me something funny that would make me laugh, and then she showed me, as she said, how one could turn a whole house upside down, without anybody being able to find out, and the pots and pans would jump about, and the china would be broken, and the chairs would tumble over of themselves. I tried it one day in the kitchen, and I found I could do it quite well, and a whole row of plates on the dresser fell off it, and cook's little work-table tilted up and turned right over "before her eyes," as she said, but she was so frightened and turned so white that I didn't do it again, as I liked her. And afterwards, in the hazel copse, when she had shown me how to make things tumble about, she showed me how to make rapping noises, and I learnt how to do that, too. Then she taught me rhymes to say on certain occasions, and peculiar marks to make on other occasions, and other things that her great-grandmother had taught her when she was a little girl herself. And these were all the things I was thinking about in those days after the strange walk when I thought I had seen a great secret, and I wished nurse were there for me to ask her about it, but she had gone away more than two years before, and nobody seemed to know what had become of her, or where she had gone. But I shall always remember those days if I live to be quite old, because all the time I felt so strange, wondering and doubting, and feeling quite sure at one time, and making up my mind, and then I would feel quite sure that such things couldn't happen really, and it began all over again. But I took great care not to do certain things that might be very dangerous. So I waited and wondered for a long time, and though I was not sure at all, I never dared to try to find out. But one day I became sure that all that nurse said was quite true, and I was all alone when I found it out. I trembled all over with joy and terror, and as fast as I could I ran into one of the old brakes where we used to go—it was the one by the lane, where nurse made the little clay man—and I ran into it, and I crept into it; and when I came to the place where the elder was, I covered up my face with my hands and lay down flat on the grass, and I stayed there for two hours without moving, whispering to myself delicious, terrible things, and saying some words over and over again. It was all true and wonderful and splendid, and when I remembered the story I knew and thought of what I had really seen, I got hot and I got cold, and the air seemed full of scent, and flowers, and singing. And first I wanted to make a little clay man, like the one nurse had made so long ago, and I had to invent plans and stratagems, and to look about, and to think of things beforehand, because nobody must dream on anything that I was doing or going to do, and I was too old to carry clay about in a tin bucket. At last I thought of a plan, and I brought the wet clay to the brake, and did everything that nurse had done, only I made a much finer image than the one she had made; and when it was finished I did everything that I could imagine and much more than she did, because it was the likeness of something far better. And a few days later, when I had done my lessons early, I went for the second time by the way of the little brook that had led me into a strange country. And I followed the brook, and went through the bushes, and beneath the low branches of trees, and up thorny thickets on the hill, and by dark woods full of creeping thorns, a long, long way. Then I crept through the dark tunnel where the brook had been and the ground was stony, till at last I came to the thicket that climbed up the hill, and though the leaves were coming out upon the trees, everything looked almost as black as it was on the first day that I went there. And the thicket was just the same, and I went up slowly till I came out on the big bare hill, and began to walk among the wonderful rocks. I saw the terrible voor again on everything, for though the sky was brighter, the ring of wild hills around was still dark, and the hanging woods looked dark and dreadful, and the strange rocks were as grey as ever; and when I looked down on them from the great mound, sitting on the stone, I saw all their amazing circles and rounds within rounds, and I had to sit quite still and watch them as they began to turn about me, and each stone danced in its place, and they seemed to go round and round in a great whirl, as if one were in the middle of all the stars and heard them rushing through the air. So I went down among the rocks to dance with them and to sing extraordinary songs; and I went down through the other thicket, and drank from the bright stream in the close and secret valley, putting my lips down to the bubbling water; and then I went on till I came to the deep, brimming well among the glittering moss, and I sat down. I looked before me into the secret darkness of the valley, and behind me was the great high wall of grass, and all around me there were the hanging woods that made the valley such a secret place. I knew there was nobody here at all besides myself, and that no one could see me. So I took off my boots and stockings, and let my feet down into the water, saying the words that I knew. And it was not cold at all, as I expected, but warm and very pleasant, and when my feet were in it I felt as if they were in silk, or as if the nymph were kissing them. So when I had done, I said the other words and made the signs, and then I dried my feet with a towel I had brought on purpose, and put on my stockings and boots. Then I climbed up the steep wall, and went into the place where there are the hollows, and the two beautiful mounds, and the round ridges of land, and all the strange shapes. I did not go down into the hollow this time, but I turned at the end, and made out the figures quite plainly, as it was lighter, and I had remembered the story I had quite forgotten before, and in the story the two figures are called Adam and Eve, and only those who know the story understand what they mean. So I went on and on till I came to the secret wood which must not be described, and I crept into it by the way I had found. And when I had gone about halfway I stopped, and turned round, and got ready, and I bound the handkerchief tightly round my eyes, and made quite sure that I could not see at all, not a twig, nor the end of a leaf, nor the light of the sky, as it was an old red silk handkerchief with large yellow spots, that went round twice and covered my eyes, so that I could see nothing. Then I began to go on, step by step, very slowly. My heart beat faster and faster, and something rose in my throat that choked me and made me want to cry out, but I shut my lips, and went on. Boughs caught in my hair as I went, and great thorns tore me; but I went on to the end of the path. Then I stopped, and held out my arms and bowed, and I went round the first time, feeling with my hands, and there was nothing. I went round the second time, feeling with my hands and there was nothing. Then I went round the third time, feeling with my hands, and the story was all true, and I wished that the years were gone by, and that I had not so long a time to wait before I was happy for ever and ever.

Nurse must have been a prophet like those we read of in the Bible. Everything that she said began to come true, and since then other things that she told me of have happened. That was how I came to know that her stories were true and that I had not made up the secret myself out of my own head. But there was another thing that happened that day. I went a second time to the secret place. It was at the deep brimming well, and when I was standing on the moss I bent over and looked in, and then I knew who the white lady was that I had seen come out of the water in the wood long ago when I was quite little. And I trembled all over, because that told me other things. Then I remembered how sometime after I had seen the white people in the wood, nurse asked me more about them, and I told her all over again, and she listened, and said nothing for a long, long time, and at last she said, "You will see her again." So I understood what had happened and what was to happen. And I understood about the nymphs; how I might meet them in all kinds of places, and they would always help me, and I must always look for them, and find them in all sorts of strange shapes and appearances. And without the nymphs I could never have found the secret, and without them none of the other things could happen. Nurse had told me all about them long ago, but she called them by another name, and I did not know what she meant, or what her tales of them were about, only that they were very queer. And there were two kinds, the bright and the dark, and both were very lovely and very wonderful, and some people saw only one kind, and some only the other, but some saw them both. But usually the dark appeared first, and the bright ones came afterwards, and there were extraordinary tales about them. It was a day or two after I had come home from the secret place that I first really knew the nymphs. Nurse had shown me how to call them, and I had tried, but I did not know what she meant, and so I thought it was all nonsense. But I made up my mind I would try again, so I went to the wood where the pool was, where I saw the white people, and I tried again. The dark nymph, Alanna, came, and she turned the pool of water into a pool of fire. . . .

Epilogue

"That's a very queer story," said Cotgrave, handing back the green book to the recluse, Ambrose. "I see the drift of a good deal, but there are many things that I do not grasp at all. On the last page, for example, what does she mean by 'nymphs'?"

"Well, I think there are references throughout the manuscript to certain 'processes' which have been handed down by tradition from age to age. Some of these processes are just beginning to come within the purview of science, which has arrived at them—or rather at the steps which lead to them—by quite different paths. I have interpreted the reference to 'nymphs' as a reference to one of these processes."

"And you believe that there are such things?"

"Oh, I think so. Yes, I believe I could give you convincing evidence on that point. I am afraid you have neglected the study of alchemy. It is a pity, for the symbolism, at all events, is very beautiful, and moreover if you were acquainted with certain books on the subject, I could recall to your mind phrases which might explain a good deal in the manuscript that you have been reading."

"Yes; but I want to know whether you seriously think that there is any foundation of fact beneath these fancies. Is it not all a department of poetry; a curious dream which man has indulged himself?"

"I can only say that it is no doubt better for the great mass of people to dismiss it all as a dream. But if you ask my veritable belief—that goes quite the other way. No; I should not say belief, but rather knowledge. I may tell you that I have known cases in which men have stumbled quite by accident on certain of these 'processes,' and have been astonished by wholly unexpected results. In the cases I am thinking of there could have been no possibility of 'suggestion' or sub-conscious action of any kind. One might as well suppose a school-boy 'suggesting' the existence of Æschylus to himself, while he plods mechanically through the declensions.

"But you have noticed the obscurity," Ambrose went on, "and in this particular case it must have been dictated by instinct, since the writer never thought that her manuscripts would fall into other hands. But the practice is universal, and for most excellent reasons. Powerful and sovereign medicines, which are, of necessity, virulent poisons also, are kept in a locked cabinet. The child may find the key by chance, and drink herself dead; but in most cases the search is educational, and the phials contain precious elixirs for him who has patiently fashioned the key for himself."

"You do not care to go into details?"

"No, frankly, I do not. No, you must remain unconvinced. But you saw how the manuscript illustrates the talk we had last week?"

"Is this girl still alive?"

"No. I was one of those who found her. I knew the father well; he was a lawyer, and had always left her very much to herself. He thought of nothing but deeds and leases, and the news came to him as an awful surprise. She was missing one morning; I suppose it was about a year after she had written what you have read. The servants were called, and they told things, and put the only natural interpretation on them—a perfectly erroneous one.

"They discovered that green book somewhere in her room, and I found her in the place that she described with so much dread, lying on the ground before the image."

"It was an image?"

"Yes; it was hidden by the thorns and the thick undergrowth that had surrounded it. It was a wild, lonely country; but you know what it was like by her description, though of course you will understand that the colours have been heightened. A child's imagination always makes the heights higher and the depths deeper than they really are; and she had, unfortunately for herself, something more than imagination. One might say, perhaps, that the picture in her mind which she succeeded in a measure in putting into words, was the scene as it would have appeared to an imaginative artist. But it is a strange, desolate land."

"And she was dead?"

"Yes. She had poisoned herself—in time. No; there was not a word to be said against her in the ordinary sense. You may recollect a story I told you the other night about a lady who saw her child's fingers crushed by a window?"

"And what was this statue?"

"Well, it was of Roman workmanship, of a stone that with the centuries had not blackened, but had become white and luminous. The thicket had grown up about it and concealed it, and in the Middle Ages the followers of a very old tradition had known how to use it for their own purposes. In fact it had been incorporated into the monstrous mythology of the Sabbath. You will have noted that those to whom a sight of that shining whiteness had been vouchsafed by chance, or rather, perhaps, by apparent chance, were required to blindfold themselves on their second approach. That is very significant."

"And is it there still?"

"I sent for tools, and we hammered it into dust and fragments."

"The persistence of tradition never surprises me," Ambrose went on after a pause. "I could name many an English parish where such traditions as that girl had listened to in her childhood are still existent in occult but unabated vigour. No, for me, it is the 'story' not the 'sequel,' which is strange and awful, for I have always believed that wonder is of the soul."

A Fragment of Life

This short novel was begun in 1899; it is not clear when it was completed. An early version of it was serialized in *Horlick's Magazine* (February, March, April, and May 1904), and the final version appeared in *The House of Souls* (London: Grant Richards, 1906; New York: Alfred A. Knopf, 1922). It was separately published as *A Fragment of Life* (London: Martin Secker, 1928), but has otherwise not been reprinted aside from its appearance in reprints of *The House of Souls*. Because its supernatural or fantastic element is so attenuated, it was not included in *Tales of Horror and the Supernatural* (New York: Alfred A. Knopf, 1948), as were nearly all the other tales in this volume. In its depiction of Edward Darnell's return to Wales after many years as a clerk in London, it anticipates Machen's own migration to the small town of Amersham, Buckinghamshire, after nearly forty years in London.

I

Edward Darnell awoke from a dream of an ancient wood, and of a clear well rising into grey film and vapour beneath a misty, glimmering heat; and as his eyes opened he saw the sunlight bright in the room, sparkling on the varnish of the new furniture. He turned and found his wife's place vacant, and with some confusion and wonder of the dream still lingering in his mind, he rose also, and began hurriedly to set about his dressing, for he had overslept a little, and the 'bus passed the corner at 9:15. He was a tall, thin man, dark-haired and dark-eyed, and in spite of the routine of the City, the counting of coupons, and all the mechanical drudgery that had lasted for ten years, there still remained about him the curious hint of a wild grace, as if he had been born a creature of the antique wood, and had seen the fountain rising from the green moss and the grey rocks.

The breakfast was laid in the room on the ground floor, the back room with the French windows looking on the garden, and before he sat down to his fried bacon he kissed his wife seriously and dutifully. She had brown hair and brown eyes, and though her lovely face was grave and quiet, one would have said that she might have awaited her husband under the old trees, and bathed in the pool hollowed out of the rocks.

They had a good deal to talk over while the coffee was poured out and the bacon eaten, and Darnell's egg brought in by the stupid, staring servant-girl of the dusty face. They had been married for a year, and they had got on excellently, rarely sitting silent for more than an hour, but for the past few weeks Aunt Marian's present had afforded a subject for conversation which seemed inexhaustible. Mrs. Darnell had been Miss Mary Reynolds, the daughter of an auctioneer and estate agent in Notting Hill, and Aunt Marian was her mother's sister, who was supposed rather to have lowered herself by marrying a coal merchant, in a small way, at Turnham Green. Marian had felt the family attitude a good deal, and the Reynoldses were sorry for many things that had been said, when the coal merchant saved money and took up land on building leases in the neighbourhood of Crouch End, greatly to his advantage, as it appeared. Nobody had thought that Nixon could ever do very much; but he and his wife had been living for years in a beautiful house at Barnet, with bow-windows, shrubs, and a paddock, and the two families saw but little of each other, for Mr. Reynolds was not very prosperous. Of course, Aunt Marian and her husband had been asked to Mary's wedding, but they had sent excuses with a nice little set of silver apostle spoons, and it was feared that nothing more was to be looked for. However, on Mary's birthday her aunt had written a most affectionate letter, enclosing a cheque for a hundred pounds from "Robert" and herself, and ever since the receipt of the money the Darnells had discussed the question of its judicious disposal. Mrs. Darnell had wished to invest the whole sum in Government securities, but Mr. Darnell had pointed out that the rate of interest was absurdly low, and after a good deal of talk he had persuaded his wife to put ninety pounds of the money in a safe mine, which was paying five per cent. This was very well, but the remaining ten pounds, which Mrs. Darnell had insisted on reserving, gave rise to legends and discourses as interminable as the disputes of the schools.

At first Mr. Darnell had proposed that they should furnish the "spare" room. There were four bedrooms in the house: their own room, the small one for the servant, and two others overlooking the garden, one of which had been used for storing boxes, ends of rope, and odd numbers of "Quiet Days" and "Sunday Evenings," besides some worn suits belonging to Mr. Darnell which had been carefully wrapped up and laid by, as he scarcely knew what to do with them. The other room was frankly waste and vacant, and one Saturday afternoon, as he was coming home in the 'bus, and while he revolved that difficult question of the ten pounds, the unseemly emptiness of the spare room suddenly came into his mind, and he glowed with the idea that now, thanks to Aunt Marian, it could be furnished. He was busied with this delightful thought all the way home, but when he let himself in, he said nothing to his wife, since he felt that his idea must be matured. He told Mrs. Darnell that, having important business, he was obliged to go out again directly, but that he should be back without fail for tea at half-past six; and Mary, on her side, was not sorry to be alone, as she was a little behind-hand with the household books. The fact was, that Darnell, full of the design of furnishing the spare bedroom, wished to consult his friend Wilson, who lived at Fulham, and had often given him judicious advice as to the laying out of money to the very best advantage. Wilson was connected with the Bordeaux wine trade, and Darnell's only anxiety was lest he should not be at home.

However, it was all right; Darnell took a tram along the Goldhawk Road, and walked the rest of the way, and was delighted to see Wilson in the front garden of his house, busy amongst his flower-beds.

"Haven't seen you for an age," he said cheerily, when he heard Darnell's hand on the gate; "come in. Oh, I forgot," he added, as Darnell still fumbled with the handle, and vainly attempted to enter. "Of course you can't get in; I haven't shown it you."

It was a hot day in June, and Wilson appeared in a costume which he had put on in haste as soon as he arrived from the City. He wore a straw hat with a neat pugaree protecting the back of his neck, and his dress was a Norfolk jacket and knickers in heather mixture.

"See," he said, as he let Darnell in; "see the dodge. You don't *turn* the handle at all. First of all push hard, and then pull. It's a trick of my own, and I shall have it patented. You see, it keeps undesirable characters at a distance—such a great thing in the suburbs. I feel I can leave Mrs. Wilson alone now; and, formerly, you have no idea how she used to be pestered."

"But how about visitors?" said Darnell. "How do they get in?"

"Oh, we put them up to it. Besides," he said vaguely, "there is sure to be somebody looking out. Mrs. Wilson is nearly always at the window. She's out now; gone to call on some friends. The Bennetts' At Home day, I think it is. This is the first Saturday, isn't it? You know J. W. Bennett, don't you? Ah, he's in the House; doing very well, I believe. He put me on to a very good thing the other day."

"But, I say," said Wilson, as they turned and strolled towards the front door, "what do you wear those black things for? You look hot. Look at me. Well, I've been gardening, you know, but I feel as cool as a cucumber. I dare say you don't know where to get these things? Very few men do. Where do you suppose I got 'em?"

"In the West End, I suppose," said Darnell, wishing to be polite.

"Yes, that's what everybody says. And it is a good cut. Well, I'll tell you, but you needn't pass it on to everybody. I got the tip from Jameson—you know him, 'Jim-Jams,' in the China trade, 39 Eastbrook—and he said he didn't want everybody in the City to know about it. But just go to Jennings, in Old Wall, and mention my name, and you'll be all right. And what d'you think they cost?"

"I haven't a notion," said Darnell, who had never bought such a suit in his life.

"Well, have a guess."

Darnell regarded Wilson gravely.

The jacket hung about his body like a sack, the knickerbockers drooped lamentably over his calves, and in prominent positions the bloom of the heather seemed about to fade and disappear.

"Three pounds, I suppose, at least," he said at length.

"Well, I asked Dench, in our place, the other day, and he guessed four ten, and his father's got something to do with a big business in Conduit Street. But I only gave thirty-five and six. To measure? Of course; look at the cut, man."

Darnell was astonished at so low a price.

"And, by the way," Wilson went on, pointing to his new brown boots, "you know where to go for shoe-leather? Oh, I thought everybody was up to that! There's only one place. 'Mr. Bill,' in Gunning Street,—nine and six."

They were walking round and round the garden, and Wilson pointed out the flowers in the beds and borders. There were hardly any blossoms, but everything was neatly arranged.

"Here are the tuberous-rooted Glasgownias," he said, showing a rigid row of stunted plants; "those are Squintaceæ; this is a new introduction, Moldavia Semperflorida Andersonii; and this is Prattsia."

"When do they come out?" said Darnell.

"Most of them in the end of August or beginning of September," said Wilson briefly. He was slightly annoyed with himself for having talked so much about his plants, since he saw that Darnell cared nothing for flowers; and, indeed, the visitor could hardly dissemble vague recollections that came to him; thoughts of an old, wild garden, full of odours, beneath grey walls, of the fragrance of the meadowsweet beside the brook.

"I wanted to consult you about some furniture," Darnell said at last. "You know we've got a spare room, and I'm thinking of putting a few things into it. I haven't exactly made up my mind, but I thought you might advise me."

"Come into my den," said Wilson. "No; this way, by the back"; and he showed Darnell another ingenious arrangement at the side door whereby a violent high-toned bell was set pealing in the house if one did but touch the latch. Indeed, Wilson handled it so briskly that the bell rang a wild alarm, and the servant, who was trying on her mistress's things in the bedroom, jumped madly to the window and then danced a hysteric dance. There was plaster found on the drawing-room table on Sunday afternoon, and Wilson wrote a letter to the "Fulham Chronicle," ascribing the phenomenon "to some disturbance of a seismic nature."

For the moment he knew nothing of the great results of his contrivance, and solemnly led the way towards the back of the house. Here there was a patch of turf, beginning to look a little brown, with a background of shrubs. In the middle of the turf, a boy of nine or ten was standing all alone, with something of an air.

"The eldest," said Wilson. "Havelock. Well, Lockie, what are ye doing now? And where are your brother and sister?"

The boy was not at all shy. Indeed, he seemed eager to explain the course of events.

"I'm playing at being Gawd," he said, with an engaging frankness. "And I've sent Fergus and Janet to the bad place. That's in the shrubbery. And they're never to come out any more. And they're burning for ever and ever."

"What d'you think of that?" said Wilson admiringly. "Not bad for a youngster of nine, is it? They think a lot of him at the Sunday-school. But come into my den."

The den was an apartment projecting from the back of the house. It had been designed as a back kitchen and washhouse, but Wilson had draped the "copper" in art muslin and had boarded over the sink, so that it served as a workman's bench.

"Snug, isn't it?" he said, as he pushed forward one of the two wicker chairs. "I think out things here, you know; it's quiet. And what about this furnishing? Do you want to do the thing on a grand scale?"

"Oh, not at all. Quite the reverse. In fact, I don't know whether the sum at our disposal will be sufficient. You see the spare room is ten feet by twelve, with a western exposure, and I thought if we *could* manage it, that it would seem more cheerful furnished. Besides, it's pleasant to be able to ask a visitor; our aunt, Mrs. Nixon, for example. But she is accustomed to have everything very nice."

"And how much do you want to spend?"

"Well, I hardly think we should be justified in going much beyond ten pounds. That isn't enough, eh?"

Wilson got up and shut the door of the back kitchen impressively.

"Look here," he said, "I'm glad you came to me in the first place. Now you'll just tell me where you thought of going yourself."

"Well, I had thought of the Hampstead Road," said Darnell in a hesitating manner.

"I just thought you'd say that. But I'll ask you, what is the good of going to those expensive shops in the West End? You don't get a better article for your money. You're merely paying for fashion."

"I've seen some nice things in Samuel's, though. They get a brilliant polish on their goods in those superior shops. We went there when we were married."

"Exactly, and paid ten per cent more than you need have paid. It's throwing money away. And how much did you say you had to spend? Ten pounds. Well, I can tell you where to get a beautiful bedroom suite, in the very highest finish, for six pound ten. What d'you think of that? China included, mind you; and a square of carpet, brilliant colours, will only cost you fifteen and six. Look here, go any Saturday afternoon to Dick's, in the Seven Sisters Road, mention my name, and ask for Mr. Johnston. The suite's in ash, 'Elizabethan' they call it. Six pound ten, including the china, with one of their 'Orient' carpets, nine by nine, for fifteen and six. Dick's."

Wilson spoke with some eloquence on the subject of furnishing. He pointed out that the times were changed, and that the old heavy style was quite out of date.

"You know," he said, "it isn't like it was in the old days, when people used to buy things to last hundreds of years. Why, just before the wife and I were married, an uncle of mine died up in the North and left me his furniture. I was thinking of furnishing at the time, and I thought the things might come in handy; but I assure you there wasn't a single article that I cared to give house-room to. All dingy, old mahogany; big bookcases and bureaus, and claw-legged chairs and tables. As I said to the wife (as she was soon afterwards), 'We don't exactly want to set up a chamber of horrors, do we?' So I sold off the lot for what I could get. I must confess I like a cheerful room."

Darnell said he had heard that artists liked the old-fashioned furniture.

"Oh, I dare say. The 'unclean cult of the sunflower,' eh? You saw that piece in the 'Daily Post'? I hate all that rot myself. It isn't healthy, you know, and I don't believe the English people will stand it. But talking of curiosities, I've got something here that's worth a bit of money."

He dived into some dusty receptacle in a corner of the room, and showed Darnell a small, worm-eaten Bible, wanting the first five chapters of Genesis and the last leaf of the Apocalypse. It bore the date of 1753.

"It's my belief that's worth a lot," said Wilson. "Look at the wormholes. And you see it's 'imperfect,' as they call it. You've noticed that some of the most valuable books are 'imperfect' at the sales?"

264

The interview came to an end soon after, and Darnell went home to his tea. He thought seriously of taking Wilson's advice, and after tea he told Mary of his idea and of what Wilson had said about Dick's.

Mary was a good deal taken by the plan when she had heard all the details. The prices struck her as very moderate. They were sitting one on each side of the grate (which was concealed by a pretty cardboard screen, painted with landscapes), and she rested her cheek on her hand, and her beautiful dark eyes seemed to dream and behold strange visions. In reality she was thinking of Darnell's plan.

"It would be very nice in some ways," she said at last. "But we must talk it over. What I am afraid of is that it will come to much more than ten pounds in the long run. There are so many things to be considered. There's the bed. It would look shabby if we got a common bed without brass mounts. Then the bedding, the mattress, and blankets, and sheets, and counterpane would all cost something."

She dreamed again, calculating the cost of all the necessaries, and Darnell stared anxiously; reckoning with her, and wondering what her conclusion would be. For a moment the delicate colouring of her face, the grace of her form, and the brown hair, drooping over her ears and clustering in little curls about her neck, seemed to hint at a language which he had not yet learned; but she spoke again.

"The bedding would come to a great deal, I am afraid. Even if Dick's are considerably cheaper than Boon's or Samuel's. And, my dear, we must have some ornaments on the mantelpiece. I saw some very nice vases at eleven-three the other day at Wilkin and Dodd's. We should want six at least, and there ought to be a centre-piece. You see how it mounts up."

Darnell was silent. He saw that his wife was summing up against his scheme, and though he had set his heart on it, he could not resist her arguments.

"It would be nearer twelve pounds, than ten," she said.

"The floor would have to be stained round the carpet (nine by nine, you said?), and we should want a piece of linoleum to go under the washstand. And the walls would look very bare without any pictures."

"I thought about the pictures," said Darnell; and he spoke quite eagerly. He felt that here, at least, he was unassailable. "You know there's the 'Derby Day' and the 'Railway Station,' ready framed, standing in the corner of the box-room already. They're a bit old-fashioned, perhaps, but that doesn't matter in a bedroom. And couldn't we use some photographs? I saw a very neat frame in natural oak in the City, to hold half a dozen, for one and six. We might put in your father, and your brother James, and Aunt Marian, and your grandmother, in her widow's cap—and any of the others in the album. And then there's that old family picture in the hairtrunk[1]—that might do over the mantelpiece."

"You mean your great-grandfather in the gilt frame? But that's *very* old-fashioned, isn't it? He looks so queer in his wig. I don't think it would quite go with the room, somehow."

Darnell thought a moment. The portrait was a "kitcat"[2] of a young gentleman, bravely dressed in the fashion of 1750, and he very faintly remembered some old tales that his father had told him about this ancestor—tales of the woods and fields, of the deep sunken lanes, and the forgotten country in the west.

"No," he said, "I suppose it is rather out of date. But I saw some very nice prints in the City, framed and quite cheap."

"Yes, but everything counts. Well, we will talk it over, as you say. You know we must be careful."

The servant came in with the supper, a tin of biscuits, a glass of milk for the mistress, and a modest pint of beer for the master, with a little cheese and butter. Afterwards Edward smoked two pipes of honeydew, and they went quietly to bed; Mary going first, and her husband following a quarter of an hour later, according to the ritual established from the first days of their marriage. Front and back doors were locked, the gas was turned off at the meter, and when Darnell got upstairs he found his wife already in bed, her face turned round on the pillow.

She spoke softly to him as he came into the room.

"It would be impossible to buy a presentable bed at anything under one pound eleven, and good sheets are dear, anywhere."

He slipped off his clothes and slid gently into bed, putting out the candle on the table. The blinds were all evenly and duly drawn, but it was a June night, and beyond the walls, beyond that desolate world and wilderness of grey Shepherd's Bush, a great golden moon had floated up through magic films of cloud, above the hill, and the earth was filled with a wonderful light between red sunset lingering over the mountain and that marvellous glory that shone into the woods from the summit of the hill. Darnell seemed to see some reflection of that wizard brightness in the room; the pale walls and the white bed and his wife's face lying amidst brown hair upon the pillow were illuminated, and listening he could almost hear the corncrake in the fields, the fern-owl sounding his strange note from the quiet of the rugged place where the bracken grew, and, like the echo of a magic song, the melody of the nightingale that sang all night in the alder by the little brook. There was nothing that he could say, but he slowly stole his arm under his wife's neck, and played with the ringlets of brown hair. She never moved, she lay there gently breathing, looking up to the blank ceiling of the room with her beautiful eyes, thinking also, no doubt, thoughts that she could not utter, kissing her husband obediently when he asked her to do so, and he stammered and hesitated as he spoke.

They were nearly asleep, indeed Darnell was on the very eve of dreaming, when she said very softly—

"I am afraid, darling, that we could never afford it." And he heard her words through the murmur of the water, dripping from the grey rock, and falling into the clear pool beneath.

Sunday morning was always an occasion of idleness. Indeed, they would never have got breakfast if Mrs. Darnell, who had the instincts of the housewife, had not awoke and seen the bright sunshine, and felt that the house was too still. She lay quiet for five minutes, while her husband slept beside her, and listened intently, waiting for the sound of Alice stirring down below. A golden tube of sunlight shone through some opening in the Venetian blinds, and it shone on the brown hair that lay about her head on the pillow, and she looked steadily into the room at the "duchesse" toilet-table, the coloured ware of the washstand, and the two photogravures in oak frames, "The Meeting" and "The Parting," that hung upon the wall. She was half dreaming as she listened for the servant's footsteps, and the faint shadow of a shade of a thought came over her, and she imagined dimly, for the quick moment of a dream, another world where rapture was wine, where one wandered in a deep and happy valley, and the moon was always rising red above the trees. She was thinking of Hampstead, which represented to her the vision of the world beyond the walls, and the thought of the heath led her away to Bank Holidays, and then to Alice. There was not a sound in the house; it might have been midnight for the stillness if the drawling cry of the Sunday paper had not suddenly echoed round the corner of Edna Road, and with it came the warning clank and shriek of the milkman with his pails.

Mrs. Darnell sat up, and wide awake, listened more intently. The girl was evidently fast asleep, and must be roused, or all the work of the day would be out of joint, and she remembered how Edward hated any fuss or discussion about household matters, more especially on a Sunday, after his long week's work in the City. She gave her husband an affectionate glance as he slept on, for she was very fond of him, and so she gently rose from the bed and went in her nightgown to call the maid.

The servant's room was small and stuffy, the night had been very hot, and Mrs. Darnell paused for a moment at the door, wondering whether the girl on the bed was really the dusty-faced servant who bustled day by day about the house, or even the strangely bedizened creature, dressed in purple, with a shiny face, who would appear on the Sunday afternoon, bringing in an early tea, because it was her "evening out." Alice's hair was black and her skin was pale, almost of the olive tinge, and she lay asleep, her head resting on one arm, reminding Mrs. Darnell of a queer print of a "Tired Bacchante" that she had seen long ago in a shop window in Upper Street, Islington. And a cracked bell was ringing; that meant five minutes to eight, and nothing done.

She touched the girl gently on the shoulder, and only smiled when her eyes opened, and waking with a start, she got up in sudden confusion. Mrs. Darnell went back to her room and dressed slowly while her husband still slept, and it was only at the last moment, as she fastened her cherry-coloured bodice, that she roused him, telling him that the bacon would be overdone unless he hurried over his dressing.

Over the breakfast they discussed the question of the spare room all over again. Mrs. Darnell still admitted that the plan of furnishing it attracted her, but she could not see how it could be done for the ten pounds, and as they were prudent people they did not care to encroach on their savings. Edward was highly paid, having (with allowances for extra work in busy weeks) a hundred and forty pounds a year, and Mary had inherited from an old uncle, her godfather, three hundred pounds, which had been judiciously laid out in mortgage at $4\frac{1}{2}$ per cent. Their total income, then, counting in Aunt Marian's present, was a hundred and fifty-eight pounds a year, and they were clear of debt, since Darnell had bought the furniture for the house out of money which he had saved for five or six years before. In the first few years of his life in the City his income had, of course, been smaller, and at first he had lived very freely, without a thought of laying by. The theatres and music-halls had attracted him, and scarcely a week passed without his going (in the pit) to one or the other; and he had occasionally bought photographs of actresses who pleased him. These he had solemnly burnt when he became engaged to Mary; he remembered the evening well; his heart had been so full of joy and wonder, and the landlady had complained bitterly of the mess in the grate when he came home from the City the next night. Still, the money was lost, as far as he could recollect, ten or twelve shillings; and it annoyed him all the more to reflect that if he had put it by, it would have gone far towards the purchase of an "Orient" carpet in brilliant colours. Then there had been other expenses of his youth: he had purchased three-penny and even fourpenny cigars, the latter rarely, but the former frequently, sometimes singly, and sometimes in bundles of twelve for half-a-crown. Once a meerschaum pipe had haunted him for six weeks; the tobacconist had drawn it out of a drawer with some air of secrecy as he was buying a packet of "Lone Star." Here was another useless expense, these American-manufactured tobaccos; his "Lone Star," "Long Judge," "Old Hank," "Sultry Clime," and the rest of them cost from a shilling to one and six the two-ounce packet; whereas now he got excellent loose honeydew for threepence halfpenny an ounce.[3] But the crafty tradesman, who had marked him down as a buyer of expensive fancy goods, nodded with his air of mystery, and, snapping open the case, displayed the meerschaum before the dazzled eyes of Darnell. The bowl was carved in the likeness of a female figure, showing the head and *torso*, and the mouthpiece was of the very best amber—only twelve and six, the man said, and the amber alone, he declared, was worth more than that. He explained that he felt some delicacy about showing the pipe to any but a regular customer, and was willing to take a little under cost price and "cut the loss." Darnell resisted for the time, but the pipe troubled him, and at last he bought it. He was pleased to show it to the younger men in the office for a while, but it never smoked very well, and he gave it away just before his marriage, as from the nature of the carving it would have been impossible to use it in his wife's presence. Once, while he was taking his holidays at Hastings, he had purchased a malacca cane—a useless thing that had cost seven shillings—and he reflected with sorrow on the innumerable evenings on which he had rejected his landlady's plain fried chop, and had gone out to *flâner*[4] among the Italian restaurants in Upper Street, Islington (he lodged in Holloway), pampering himself with expensive delicacies: cutlets and green peas, braised beef with tomato sauce, fillet steak and chipped potatoes, ending the banquet very often with a small wedge of Gruyère, which cost twopence. One night, after receiving a rise in his salary, he had actually drunk a quarter-flask of Chianti and had added the enormities of Benedictine, coffee, and cigarettes to an expenditure already disgraceful, and sixpence to the waiter made the bill amount to four shillings instead of the shilling that would have provided him with a wholesome and sufficient repast at home. Oh, there were many other items in this account of extravagance, and Darnell had often regretted his way of life, thinking that if he had been more careful, five or six pounds a year might have been added to their income.

And the question of the spare room brought back these regrets in an exaggerated degree. He persuaded himself that the extra five pounds would have given a sufficient margin for the outlay that he desired to make; though this was, no doubt, a mistake on his part. But he saw quite clearly that, under the present conditions, there must be no levies made on the very small sum of money that they had saved. The rent of the house was thirty-five, and rates and taxes added another ten pounds—nearly a quarter of their income for house-room. Mary kept down the housekeeping bills to the very best of her ability, but meat was always dear, and she suspected the maid of cutting surreptitious slices from the joint and eating them in her bedroom with bread and treacle in the dead of night, for the girl had disordered and eccentric appetites. Mr. Darnell thought no more of restaurants, cheap or dear; he took his lunch with him to the City, and joined his wife in the evening at high tea—chops, a bit of steak, or cold meat from the Sunday's dinner. Mrs. Darnell ate bread and jam and drank a little milk in the middle of the day; but, with the utmost economy, the effort to live within their means and to save for future contingencies was a very hard one. They had determined to do without change of air for at least three years, as the honeymoon at Walton-on-the-Naze[5] had cost a good deal; and it was on this ground that they had, somewhat illogically, reserved the ten pounds, declaring that as they were not to have any holiday they would spend the money on something useful.

And it was this consideration of utility that was finally fatal to Darnell's scheme. They had calculated and recalculated the expense of the bed and bedding, the linoleum, and the ornaments, and by a great deal of exertion the total expenditure had been made to assume the shape of "something very little over ten pounds," when Mary said quite suddenly—

"But, after all, Edward, we don't really *want* to furnish the room at all. I mean it isn't necessary. And if we did so it might lead to no end of expense. People would hear of it and be sure to fish for invitations. You know we have relatives in the country, and they would be almost certain, the Mallings, at any rate, to give hints."

Darnell saw the force of the argument and gave way. But he was bitterly disappointed.

"It would have been very nice, wouldn't it?" he said with a sigh.

"Never mind, dear," said Mary, who saw that he was a good deal cast down. "We must think of some other plan that will be nice and useful too."

She often spoke to him in that tone of a kind mother, though she was by three years the younger.

"And now," she said, "I must get ready for church. Are you coming?"

Darnell said that he thought not. He usually accompanied his wife to morning service, but that day he felt some bitterness in his heart, and preferred to lounge under the shade of the big mulberry tree that stood in the middle of their patch of garden—relic of the spacious lawns that had once lain smooth and green and sweet, where the dismal streets now swarmed in a hopeless labyrinth.

So Mary went quietly and alone to church. St. Paul's stood in a neighbouring street, and its Gothic design would have interested a curious inquirer into the history of a strange revival. Obviously, mechanically, there was nothing amiss. The style chosen was "geometrical decorated," and the tracery of the windows seemed correct. The nave, the aisles, the spacious chancel, were reasonably proportioned; and, to be quite serious, the only feature obviously wrong was the substitution of a low "chancel wall" with iron gates for the rood screen with the loft and rood. But this, it might plausibly be contended, was merely an adaptation of the old idea to modern requirements, and it would have been quite difficult to explain why the whole building, from the mere mortar setting between the stones to the Gothic gas standards, was a mysterious and elaborate blasphemy. The canticles were sung to Joll in B flat, the chants were "Anglican," and the sermon was the gospel for the day, amplified and rendered into the more modern and graceful English of the preacher. And Mary came away.

After their dinner (an excellent piece of Australian mutton, bought in the "World Wide" Stores, in Hammersmith), they sat for some time in the garden, partly sheltered by the big mulberry tree from the observation of their neighbours. Edward smoked his honeydew, and Mary looked at him with placid affection.

"You never tell me about the men in your office," she said at length. "Some of them are nice fellows, aren't they?"

"Oh, yes, they're very decent. I must bring some of them round, one of these days."

He remembered with a pang that it would be necessary to provide whisky. One couldn't ask the guest to drink table beer at tenpence the gallon.

"Who are they, though?" said Mary. "I think they might have given you a wedding present."

"Well, I don't know. We never have gone in for that sort of thing. But they're very decent chaps. Well, there's Harvey; 'Sauce' they call him behind his back. He's mad on bicycling. He went in last year for the Two Miles Amateur Record. He'd have made it, too, if he could have got into better training.

"Then there's James, a sporting man. You wouldn't care for him. I always think he smells of the stable."

"How horrid!" said Mrs. Darnell, finding her husband a little frank, lowering her eyes as she spoke.

"Dickenson might amuse you," Darnell went on. "He's always got a joke. A terrible liar, though. When he tells a tale we never know how much to believe. He swore the other day he'd seen one of the governors buying cockles off a barrow near London Bridge, and Jones, who's just come, believed every word of it."

Darnell laughed at the humorous recollection of the jest.

"And that wasn't a bad yarn about Salter's wife," he went on. "Salter is the manager, you know. Dickenson lives close by, in Notting Hill, and he said one morning that he had seen Mrs. Salter, in the Portobello Road, in red stockings, dancing to a piano organ."

"He's a little coarse, isn't he?" said Mrs. Darnell. "I don't see much fun in that."

"Well, you know, amongst men it's different. You might like Wallis; he's a tremendous photographer. He often shows us photos he's taken of his children—one, a little girl of three, in her bath. I asked him how he thought she'd like it when she was twenty-three."

Mrs. Darnell looked down and made no answer.

There was silence for some minutes while Darnell smoked his pipe. "I say, Mary," he said at length, "what do you say to our taking a paying guest?"

"A paying guest! I never thought of it. Where should we put him?"

"Why, I was thinking of the spare room. The plan would obviate your objection, wouldn't it? Lots of men in the City take them, and make money of it too. I dare say it would add ten pounds a year to our income. Redgrave, the cashier, finds it worth his while to take a large house on purpose. They have a regular lawn for tennis and a billiard-room."

Mary considered gravely, always with the dream in her eyes. "I don't think we could manage it, Edward," she said; "it would be inconvenient in many ways." She hesitated for a moment. "And I don't think I should care to have a young man in the house. It is so very small, and our accommodation, as you know, is so limited."

She blushed slightly, and Edward, a little disappointed as he was, looked at her with a singular longing, as if he were a scholar confronted with a doubtful hieroglyph, either wholly wonderful or altogether commonplace. Next door children were playing in the garden, playing shrilly, laughing, crying, quarrelling, racing to and fro. Suddenly a clear, pleasant voice sounded from an upper window.

"Enid! Charles! Come up to my room at once!"

There was an instant sudden hush. The children's voices died away.

"Mrs. Parker is supposed to keep her children in great order," said Mary. "Alice was telling me about it the other day. She had been talking to Mrs. Parker's servant. I listened to her without any remark, as I don't think it right to encourage servants' gossip; they always exaggerate everything. And I dare say children often require to be corrected."

The children were struck silent as if some ghastly terror had seized them.

Darnell fancied that he heard a queer sort of cry from the house, but could not be quite sure. He turned to the other side, where an elderly, ordinary man with a grey moustache was strolling up and down on the further side of his garden. He caught Darnell's eye, and Mrs. Darnell looking towards him at the same moment, he very politely raised his tweed cap. Darnell was surprised to see his wife blushing fiercely.

"Sayce and I often go into the City by the same 'bus," he said, "and as it happens we've sat next to each other two or three times lately. I believe he's a traveller for a leather firm in Bermondsey. He struck me as a pleasant man. Haven't they got rather a good-looking servant?"

"Alice has spoken to me about her—and the Sayces," said Mrs. Darnell. "I understand that they are not very well thought of in the neighbourhood. But I must go in and see whether the tea is ready. Alice will be wanting to go out directly."

Darnell looked after his wife as she walked quickly away. He only dimly understood, but he could see the charm of her figure, the delight of the brown curls clustering about her neck, and he again felt that sense of the scholar confronted by the hieroglyphic. He could not have expressed his emotion, but he wondered whether he would ever find the key, and something told him that before she could speak to him his own lips must be unclosed. She had gone into the house by the back kitchen door, leaving it open, and he heard her speaking to the girl about the water being "really boiling." He was amazed, almost indignant with himself; but the sound of the words came to his ears as strange, heart-piercing music, tones from another, wonderful sphere. And yet he was her husband, and they had been married nearly a year; and yet, whenever she spoke, he had to listen to the sense of what she said, constraining himself, lest he should believe she was a magic creature, knowing the secrets of immeasurable delight.

He looked out through the leaves of the mulberry tree. Mr. Sayce had disappeared from his view, but he saw the light-blue fume of the cigar that he was smoking floating slowly across the shadowed air. He was wondering at his wife's manner when Sayce's name was mentioned, puzzling his head as to what could be amiss in the household of a most respectable personage, when his wife appeared at the dining-room window and called him in to tea. She smiled as he looked up, and he rose hastily and walked in, wondering whether he were not a little "queer," so strange were the dim emotions and the dimmer impulses that rose within him.

Alice was all shining purple and strong scent, as she brought in the teapot and the jug of hot water. It seemed that a visit to the kitchen had inspired Mrs. Darnell in her turn with a novel plan for disposing of the famous ten pounds. The range had always been a trouble to her, and when sometimes she went into the kitchen, and found, as she said, the fire "roaring halfway up the chimney," it was in vain that she reproved the maid on the ground of extravagance and waste of coal. Alice was ready to admit the absurdity of making up such an enormous fire merely to bake (they called it "roast") a bit of beef or mutton, and to boil the potatoes and the cabbage; but she was able to show Mrs. Darnell that the fault lay in the defective contrivance of the range, in an oven which "would not get hot." Even with a chop or a steak it was almost as bad; the heat seemed to escape up the chimney or into the room, and Mary had spoken several times to her husband on the shocking waste of coal, and the cheapest coal procurable was never less than eighteen shillings the ton. Mr. Darnell had written to the landlord, a builder, who had replied in an illiterate but offensive communication, maintaining the excellence of the stove and charging all the faults to the account of "your good lady," which really implied that the Darnells kept no servant, and that Mrs. Darnell did everything. The range, then, remained, a standing annoyance and expense. Every morning, Alice said, she had the greatest difficulty in getting the fire to light at all, and once lighted it "seemed as if it fled right up the chimney." Only a few nights before Mrs. Darnell had spoken seriously to her husband about it; she had got Alice to weigh the coals expended in cooking a cottage pie, the dish of the evening, and deducting what remained in the scuttle after the pie was done, it appeared that the wretched thing had consumed nearly twice the proper quantity of fuel.

"You remember what I said the other night about the range?" said Mrs. Darnell, as she poured out the tea and watered the leaves. She thought the introduction a good one, for though her husband was a most amiable man, she guessed that he had been just a little hurt by her decision against his furnishing scheme.

"The range?" said Darnell. He paused as he helped himself to the marmalade and considered for a moment. "No, I don't recollect. What night was it?"

"Tuesday. Don't you remember? You had 'overtime,' and didn't get home till quite late."

She paused for a moment, blushing slightly; and then began to recapitulate the misdeeds of the range, and the outrageous outlay of coal in the preparation of the cottage pie.

"Oh, I recollect now. That was the night I thought I heard the nightingale (people say there are nightingales in Bedford Park), and the sky was such a wonderful deep blue."

He remembered how he had walked from Uxbridge Road Station, where the green 'bus stopped, and in spite of the fuming kilns under Acton, a delicate odour of the woods and summer fields was mysteriously in the air, and he had fancied that he smelt the red wild roses, drooping from the hedge. As he came to his gate he saw his wife standing in the doorway, with a light in her hand, and he threw his arms violently about her as she welcomed him, and whispered something in her ear, kissing her scented hair. He had felt quite abashed a moment afterwards, and he was afraid that he had frightened her by his nonsense; she seemed trembling and confused. And then she had told him how they had weighed the coal.

"Yes, I remember now," he said. "It is a great nuisance, isn't it? I hate to throw away money like that."

"Well, what do you think? Suppose we bought a really good range with aunt's money? It would save us a lot, and I expect the things would taste much nicer."

Darnell passed the marmalade, and confessed that the idea was brilliant.

"It's much better than mine, Mary," he said quite frankly. "I am so glad you thought of it. But we must talk it over; it doesn't do to buy in a hurry. There are so many makes."

Each had seen ranges which looked miraculous inventions; he in the neighbourhood of the City; she in Oxford Street and Regent Street, on visits to the dentist. They discussed the matter at tea, and afterwards they discussed it walking round and round the garden, in the sweet cool of the evening.

"They say the 'Newcastle' will burn anything, coke even," said Mary.

"But the 'Glow' got the gold medal at the Paris Exhibition,"[6] said Edward.

"But what about the 'Eutopia' Kitchener? Have you seen it at work in Oxford Street?" said Mary. "They say their plan of ventilating the oven is quite unique."

"I was in Fleet Street the other day," answered Edward, "and I was looking at the 'Bliss' Patent Stoves. They burn less fuel than any in the market—so the makers declare."

He put his arm gently round her waist. She did not repel him; she whispered quite softly—

"I think Mrs. Parker is at her window," and he drew his arm back slowly.

"But we will talk it over," he said. "There is no hurry. I might call at some of the places near the City, and you might do the same thing in Oxford Street and Regent Street and Piccadilly, and we could compare notes."

Mary was quite pleased with her husband's good temper. It was so nice of him not to find fault with her plan; "He's so good to me," she thought, and that was what she often said to her brother, who did not care much for Darnell. They sat down on the seat under the mulberry, close together, and she let Darnell take her hand, and as she felt his shy, hesitating fingers touch her in the shadow, she pressed them ever so softly, and as he fondled her hand, his breath was on her neck, and she heard his passionate, hesitating voice whisper, "My dear, my dear," as his lips touched her cheek. She trembled a little, and waited. Darnell kissed her gently on the cheek and drew away his hand, and when he spoke he was almost breathless.

"We had better go in now," he said. "There is a heavy dew, and you might catch cold."

A warm, scented gale came to them from beyond the walls. He longed to ask her to stay out with him all night beneath the tree, that they might whisper to one another, that the scent of her hair might inebriate him, that he might feel her dress still brushing against his ankles. But he could not find the words, and it was absurd, and she was so gentle that she would do whatever he asked, however foolish it might be, just because he asked her. He was not worthy to kiss her lips; he bent down and kissed her silk bodice, and again he felt that she trembled, and he was ashamed, fearing that he had frightened her.

They went slowly into the house, side by side, and Darnell lit the gas in the drawing-room, where they always sat on Sunday evenings. Mrs. Darnell felt a little tired and lay down on the sofa, and Darnell took the arm-chair opposite. For a while they were silent, and then Darnell said suddenly—

"What's wrong with the Sayces? You seemed to think there was something a little strange about them. Their maid looks quite quiet."

"Oh, I don't know that one ought to pay any attention to servants' gossip. They're not always very truthful."

"It was Alice told you, wasn't it?"

"Yes. She was speaking to me the other day, when I was in the kitchen in the afternoon."

"But what was it?"

"Oh, I'd rather not tell you, Edward. It's not pleasant. I scolded Alice for repeating it to me."

Darnell got up and took a small, frail chair near the sofa.

"Tell me," he said again, with an odd perversity. He did not really care to hear about the household next door, but he remembered how his wife's cheeks flushed in the afternoon, and now he was looking at her eyes.

"Oh, I really couldn't tell you, dear. I should feel ashamed."

"But you're my wife."

"Yes, but it doesn't make any difference. A woman doesn't like to talk about such things."

Darnell bent his head down. His heart was beating; he put his ear to her mouth and said, "Whisper."

Mary drew his head down still lower with her gentle hand, and her cheeks burned as she whispered—

"Alice says that—upstairs—they have only—one room furnished. The maid told her—herself."

With an unconscious gesture she pressed his head to her breast, and he in turn was bending her red lips to his own, when a violent jangle clamoured through the silent house. They sat up, and Mrs. Darnell went hurriedly to the door.

"That's Alice," she said. "She is always in in time. It has only just struck ten."

Darnell shivered with annoyance. His lips, he knew, had almost been opened. Mary's pretty handkerchief, delicately scented from a little flagon that a school friend had given her, lay on the floor, and he picked it up, and kissed it, and hid it away.

The question of the range occupied them all through June and far into July. Mrs. Darnell took every opportunity of going to the West End and investigating the capacity of the latest makes, gravely viewing the new improvements and hearing what the shopmen had to say; while Darnell, as he said, "kept his eyes open" about the City. They accumulated quite a literature of the subject, bringing away illustrated pamphlets, and in the evenings it was an amusement to look at the pictures. They viewed with reverence and interest the drawings of great ranges for hotels and public institutions, mighty contrivances furnished with a series of ovens each for a different use, with wonderful apparatus for grilling, with batteries of accessories which seemed to invest the cook almost with the dignity of a chief engineer. But when, in one of the lists, they encountered the images of little toy "cottage" ranges, for four pounds, and even for three pounds ten, they grew scornful, on the strength of the eight or ten pound article which they meant to purchase—when the merits of the divers patents had been thoroughly thrashed out.

The "Raven" was for a long time Mary's favourite. It promised the utmost economy with the highest efficiency, and many times they were on the point of giving the order. But the "Glow" seemed equally seductive, and it was only £8. 5s. as compared with £9. 7s. 6d., and though the "Raven" was supplied to the Royal Kitchen, the "Glow" could show more fervent testimonials from continental potentates.

It seemed a debate without end, and it endured day after day till that morning, when Darnell woke from the dream of the ancient wood, of the fountains rising into grey vapour beneath the heat of the sun. As he dressed, an idea struck him, and he brought it as a shock to the hurried breakfast, disturbed by the thought of the City 'bus which passed the corner of the street at 9:15.

"I've got an improvement on your plan, Mary," he said, with triumph. "Look at that," and he flung a little book on the table.

He laughed. "It beats your notion all to fits. After all, the great expense is the coal. It's not the stove—at least that's not the real mischief. It's the coal is so dear. And here you are. Look at those oil stoves. They don't burn any coal, but the cheapest fuel in the world—oil; and for two pounds ten you can get a range that will do everything you want."

"Give me the book," said Mary, "and we will talk it over in the evening, when you come home. Must you be going?"

Darnell cast an anxious glance at the clock.

"Good-bye," and they kissed each other seriously and dutifully, and Mary's eyes made Darnell think of those lonely water-pools, hidden in the shadow of the ancient woods.

So, day after day, he lived in the grey phantasmal world, akin to death, that has, somehow, with most of us, made good its claim to be called life. To Darnell the true life would have seemed madness, and when, now and again, the shadows and vague images reflected from its splendour fell across his path, he was afraid, and took refuge in what he would have called the sane "reality" of common and usual incidents and interests. His absurdity was, perhaps, the more evident, inasmuch as "reality" for him was a matter of kitchen ranges, of saving a few shillings; but in truth the folly would have been greater if it had been concerned with racing stables, steam yachts, and the spending of many thousand pounds.

But so went forth Darnell, day by day, strangely mistaking death for life, madness for sanity, and purposeless and wandering phantoms for true beings. He was sincerely of opinion that he was a City clerk, living in Shepherd's Bush—having forgotten the mysteries and the far-shining glories of the kingdom which was his by legitimate inheritance.

II

All day long a fierce and heavy heat had brooded over the City, and as Darnell neared home he saw the mist lying on all the damp lowlands, wreathed in coils about Bedford Park to the south, and mounting to the west, so that the tower of Acton Church loomed out of a grey lake. The grass in the squares and on the lawns which he overlooked as the 'bus lumbered wearily along was burnt to the colour of dust. Shepherd's Bush Green was a wretched desert, trampled brown, bordered with monotonous poplars, whose leaves hung motionless in air that was still, hot smoke. The foot passengers struggled wearily along the pavements, and the reek of the summer's end mingled with the breath of the brickfields made Darnell gasp, as if he were inhaling the poison of some foul sick-room.

He made but a slight inroad into the cold mutton that adorned the tea-table, and confessed that he felt rather "done up" by the weather and the day's work.

"I have had a trying day, too," said Mary. "Alice has been very queer and troublesome all day, and I have had to speak to her quite seriously. You know I think her Sunday evenings out have a rather unsettling influence on the girl. But what is one to do?"

"Has she got a young man?"

"Of course: a grocer's assistant from the Goldhawk Road—Wilkin's, you know. I tried them when we settled here, but they were not very satisfactory."

"What do they do with themselves all the evening? They have

from five to ten, haven't they?"

"Yes; five, or sometimes half-past, when the water won't boil. Well, I believe they go for walks usually. Once or twice he has taken her to the City Temple,[7] and the Sunday before last they walked up and down Oxford Street, and then sat in the Park. But it seems that last Sunday they went to tea with his mother at Putney. I should like to tell the old woman what I really think of her."

"Why? What happened? Was she nasty to the girl?"

"No; that's just it. Before this, she has been very unpleasant on several occasions. When the young man first took Alice to see her— that was in March—the girl came away crying; she told me so herself. Indeed, she said she never wanted to see old Mrs. Murry again; and I told Alice that, if she had not exaggerated things, I could hardly blame her for feeling like that."

"Why? What did she cry for?"

"Well, it seems that the old lady—she lives in quite a small cottage in some Putney back street—was so stately that she would hardly speak. She had borrowed a little girl from some neighbour's family, and had managed to dress her up to imitate a servant, and Alice said nothing could be sillier than to see that mite opening the door, with her black dress and her white cap and apron, and she hardly able to turn the handle, as Alice said. George (that's the young man's name) had told Alice that it was a little bit of a house; but he said the kitchen was comfortable, though very plain and old-fashioned. But, instead of going straight to the back, and sitting by a big fire on the old settle that they had brought up from the country, that child asked for their names (did you ever hear such nonsense?) and showed them into a little poky parlour, where old Mrs. Murry was sitting 'like a duchess,' by a fire-place full of coloured paper, and the room as cold as ice. And she was so grand that she would hardly speak to Alice."

"That must have been very unpleasant."

"Oh, the poor girl had a dreadful time. She began with: 'Very pleased to make your acquaintance, Miss Dill. I know so very few persons in service.' Alice imitates her mincing way of talking, but I can't do it. And then she went on to talk about her family, how they had farmed their own land for five hundred years—such stuff! George had told Alice all about it: they had had an old cottage with a good strip of garden and two fields somewhere in Essex, and that old woman talked almost as if they had been country gentry, and boasted about the Rector, Dr. Somebody, coming to see them so often, and of Squire Somebody Else always looking them up, as if they didn't visit them out of kindness. Alice told me it was as much as she could do to keep from laughing in Mrs. Murry's face, her young man having told her all about the place, and how small it was, and how the Squire had been so kind about buying it when old Murry died and George was a little boy, and his mother not able to keep things going. However, that silly old woman 'laid it on thick,' as you say, and the young man got more and more uncomfortable, especially when she went on to speak about marrying in one's own class, and how unhappy she had known young men to be who had married beneath them, giving some very pointed looks at Alice as she talked. And then such an amusing thing happened: Alice had noticed George looking about him in a puzzled sort of way, as if he couldn't make out something or other, and at last he burst out and asked his mother if she had been buying up the neighbours' ornaments, as he remembered the two green cut-glass vases on the mantelpiece at Mrs. Ellis's, and the wax flowers at Miss Turvey's. He was going on, but his mother scowled at him, and upset some books, which he had to pick up; but Alice quite understood she had been borrowing things from her neighbours, just as she had borrowed the little girl, so as to look grander. And then they had tea—water bewitched, Alice calls it—and very thin bread and butter, and rubbishy foreign pastry from the Swiss shop in the High Street—all sour froth and rancid fat, Alice declares. And then Mrs. Murry began boasting again about her family, and snubbing Alice and talking at her, till the girl came away quite furious, and very unhappy, too. I don't wonder at it, do you?"

"It doesn't sound very enjoyable, certainly," said Darnell, looking dreamily at his wife. He had not been attending very carefully to the subject-matter of her story, but he loved to hear a voice that was incantation in his ears, tones that summoned before him the vision of a magic world.

"And has the young man's mother always been like this?" he said after a long pause, desiring that the music should continue.

"Always, till quite lately, till last Sunday in fact. Of course Alice spoke to George Murry at once, and said, like a sensible girl, that she didn't think it ever answered for a married couple to live with the man's mother, 'especially,' she went on, 'as I can see your mother hasn't taken much of a fancy to me.' He told her, in the usual style, it was only his mother's way, that she didn't really mean anything, and so on; but Alice kept away for a long time, and rather hinted, I think, that it might come to having to choose between her and his mother. And so affairs went on all through the spring and summer, and then, just before the August Bank Holiday, George spoke to Alice again about it, and told her how sorry the thought of any unpleasantness made him, and how he wanted his mother and her to get on with each other, and how she was only a bit old-fashioned and queer in her ways, and had spoken very nicely to him about her when there was nobody by. So the long and the short of it was that Alice said she might come with them on the Monday, when they had settled to go to Hampton Court—the girl was always talking about Hampton Court, and wanting to see it. You remember what a beautiful day it was, don't you?"

"Let me see," said Darnell dreamily. "Oh yes, of course—I sat out under the mulberry tree all day, and we had our meals there: it was quite a picnic. The caterpillars were a nuisance, but I enjoyed the day very much." His ears were charmed, ravished with the grave, supernal melody, as of antique song, rather of the first made world in which all speech was descant, and all words were sacraments of might, speaking not to the mind but to the soul. He lay back in his chair, and said—

"Well, what happened to them?"

"My dear, would you believe it; but that wretched old woman behaved worse than ever. They met as had been arranged, at Kew Bridge, and got places, with a good deal of difficulty, in one of those char-à-banc[8] things, and Alice thought she was going to enjoy herself tremendously. Nothing of the kind. They had hardly said 'Good morning,' when old Mrs. Murry began to talk about Kew Gardens, and how beautiful it must be there, and how much more convenient it was than Hampton, and no expense at all; just the trouble of walking over the bridge. Then she went on to say, as they were waiting for the char-à-banc, that she had always heard there was nothing to see at Hampton, except a lot of nasty, grimy old pictures, and some of them not fit for any decent woman, let alone girl, to look at, and she wondered why the Queen allowed such things to be shown, putting all kinds of notions into girls' heads that were light enough already; and as she said that she looked at Alice so nastily—horrid old thing—that, as she told me afterwards, Alice would have slapped her face if she hadn't been an elderly woman, and George's mother. Then she talked about Kew again, saying how wonderful the hot-houses were, with palms and all sorts of wonderful things, and a lily as big as a parlour table, and the view over the river. George was very good, Alice told me. He was quite taken aback at first, as the old woman had promised faithfully to be as nice as ever she could be; but then he said, gently but firmly, 'Well, mother, we must go to Kew some other day, as Alice has set her heart on Hampton for to-day, and I want to see it myself!' All Mrs. Murry did was to snort, and look at the girl like vinegar, and just then the char-à-banc came up, and they had to scramble for their seats. Mrs. Murry grumbled to herself in an indistinct sort of voice all the way to Hampton Court. Alice couldn't very well make out what she said, but now and then she seemed to hear bits of sentences, like: *Pity to grow old, if sons grow bold;* and *Honour thy father and mother;*[9] and *Lie on the shelf, said the housewife to the old shoe, and the wicked son to his mother; and I gave you milk and you give me the go-by.* Alice thought they must be proverbs (except the Commandment, of course), as George was always saying how old-fashioned his mother is; but she says there were so many of them, and all pointed at her and George, that she thinks now Mrs. Murry must have made them up as they drove along. She says it would be just like her to do it, being old-fashioned, and ill-natured too, and fuller of talk than a butcher on Saturday night. Well, they got to Hampton at last, and Alice thought the place would please her, perhaps, and they might have some enjoyment. But she did nothing but grumble, and out loud too, so that people looked at them, and a woman said, so that they could hear, 'Ah well, they'll be old themselves some day,' which made Alice very angry, for, as she said, they weren't doing anything. When they showed her the chestnut avenue in Bushey Park, she said it was so long and straight that it made her quite dull to look at it and she thought the deer (you know how pretty they are, really) looked thin and miserable, as if they would be all the better for a good feed of hog-wash, with plenty of meal in it. She said she knew they weren't happy by the look in their eyes, which seemed to tell her that their keepers beat them. It was the same with everything; she said she remembered market-gardens in Hammersmith and Gunnersbury that had a better show of flowers, and when they took her to the place where the water is, under the trees, she burst out with its being rather hard to tramp her off her legs to show her a common canal, with not so much as a barge on it to liven it up a bit. She went on like that the whole day, and Alice told me she was only too thankful to get home and get rid of her. Wasn't it wretched for the girl?"

"It must have been, indeed. But what happened last Sunday?"

"That's the most extraordinary thing of all. I noticed that Alice was rather queer in her manner this morning; she was a longer time washing up the breakfast things, and she answered me quite sharply when I called to her to ask when she would be ready to help me with the wash; and when I went into the kitchen to see about something, I noticed that she was going about her work in a sulky sort of way. So I asked her what was the matter, and then it all came out. I could scarcely believe my own ears when she mumbled out something about Mrs. Murry thinking she could do very much better for herself; but I asked her one question after another till I had it all out of her. It just shows one how foolish and empty-headed these girls are. I told her she was no better than a weather-cock. If you will believe me, that horrid old woman was quite another person when Alice went to see her the other night. Why, I can't think, but so she was. She told the girl how pretty she was; what a neat figure she had; how well she walked; and how she'd known many a girl not half so clever or well-looking earning her twenty-five or thirty pounds a year, and with good families. She seems to have gone into all sorts of details, and made elaborate calculations as to what she would be able to save, 'with decent folks, who don't screw, and pinch, and lock up everything in the house,' and then she went off into a lot of hypocritical nonsense about how fond she was of Alice, and how she could go to her grave in peace, knowing how happy her dear George would be with such a good wife, and about her savings from good wages helping to set up a little home, ending up with 'And, if you take an old woman's advice, deary, it won't be long before you hear the marriage bells.'"

"I see," said Darnell; "and the upshot of it all is, I suppose, that the girl is thoroughly dissatisfied?"

"Yes, she is so young and silly. I talked to her, and reminded her of how nasty old Mrs. Murry had been, and told her that she might change her place and change for the worse. I think I have persuaded her to think it over quietly, at all events. Do you know what it is, Edward? I have an idea. I believe that wicked old woman is trying to get Alice to leave us, that she may tell her son how changeable she is; and I suppose she would make up some of her stupid old proverbs: 'A changeable wife, a troublesome life,' or some nonsense of the kind. Horrid old thing!"

"Well, well," said Darnell, "I hope she won't go, for your sake. It would be such a bother for you, hunting for a fresh servant."

He refilled his pipe and smoked placidly, refreshed somewhat after the emptiness and the burden of the day. The French window was wide open, and now at last there came a breath of quickening air, distilled by the night from such trees as still wore green in that arid valley. The song to which Darnell had listened in rapture, and now the breeze, which even in that dry, grim suburb still bore the word of the woodland, had summoned the dream to his eyes, and he meditated over matters that his lips could not express.

"She must, indeed, be a villainous old woman," he said at length.

"Old Mrs. Murry? Of course she is; the mischievous old thing! Trying to take the girl from a comfortable place where she is happy."

"Yes; and not to like Hampton Court! That shows how bad she must be, more than anything."

"It is beautiful, isn't it?"

"I shall never forget the first time I saw it. It was soon after I went into the City; the first year. I had my holidays in July, and I was getting such a small salary that I couldn't think of going away to the seaside, or anything like that. I remember one of the other men wanted me to come with him on a walking tour in Kent. I should have liked that, but the money wouldn't run to it. And do you know what I did? I lived in Great College Street then, and the first day I was off, I stayed in bed till past dinner-time, and lounged about in an arm-chair with a pipe all the afternoon. I had got a new kind of tobacco—one and four for the two-ounce packet—much dearer than I could afford to smoke, and I was enjoying it immensely. It was awfully hot, and when I shut the window and drew down the red blind it grew hotter; at five o'clock the room was like an oven. But I was so pleased at not having to go into the City, that I didn't mind anything, and now and again I read bits from a queer old book that had belonged to my poor dad. I couldn't make out what a lot of it meant, but it fitted in somehow, and I read and smoked till tea-time. Then I went out for a walk, thinking I should be better for a little fresh air before I went to bed; and I went wandering away, not much noticing where I was going, turning here and there as the fancy took me. I must have gone miles and miles, and a good many of them round and round, as they say they do in Australia if they lose their way in the bush; and I am sure I couldn't have gone exactly the same way all over again for any money. Anyhow, I was still in the streets when the twilight came on, and the lamp-lighters were trotting round from one lamp to another. It was a wonderful night: I wish you had been there, my dear."

"I was quite a little girl then."

"Yes, I suppose you were. Well, it was a wonderful night. I remember, I was walking in a little street of little grey houses all alike, with stucco copings and stucco door-posts; there were brass plates on a lot of the doors, and one had 'Maker of Shell Boxes' on it, and I was quite pleased, as I had often wondered where those boxes and things that you buy at the seaside came from. A few children were playing about in the road with some rubbish or other, and men were singing in a small public-house at the corner, and I happened to look up, and I noticed what a wonderful colour the sky had turned. I have seen it since, but I don't think it has ever been quite what it was that night, a dark blue, glowing like a violet, just as they say the sky looks in foreign countries. I don't know why, but the sky or something made me feel quite queer; everything seemed changed in a way I couldn't understand. I remember, I told an old gentleman I knew then—a friend of my poor father's, he's been dead for five years, if not more—about how I felt, and he looked at me and said something about fairyland; I don't know what he meant, and I dare say I didn't explain myself properly. But, do you know, for a moment or two I felt as if that little back street was beautiful, and the noise of the children and the men in the public-house seemed to fit in with the sky and become part of it. You know that old saying about 'treading on air' when one is glad! Well, I really felt like that as I walked, not exactly like air, you know, but as if the pavement was velvet or some very soft carpet. And then—I suppose it was all my fancy—the air seemed to smell sweet, like the incense in Catholic churches, and my breath came queer and catchy, as it does when one gets very excited about anything. I felt altogether stranger than I've ever felt before or since."

Darnell stopped suddenly and looked up at his wife. She was watching him with parted lips, with eager, wondering eyes.

"I hope I'm not tiring you, dear, with all this story about nothing. You have had a worrying day with that stupid girl; hadn't you better go to bed?"

"Oh, no, please, Edward. I'm not a bit tired now. I love to hear you talk like that. Please go on."

"Well, after I had walked a bit further, that queer sort of feeling seemed to fade away. I said a bit further, and I really thought I had been walking about five minutes, but I had looked at my watch just before I got into that little street, and when I looked at it again it was eleven o'clock. I must have done about eight miles. I could scarcely believe my own eyes, and I thought my watch must have gone mad; but I found out afterwards it was perfectly right. I couldn't make it out, and I can't now; I assure you the time passed as if I walked up one side of Edna Road and down the other. But there I was, right in the open country, with a cool wind blowing on me from a wood, and the air full of soft rustling sounds, and notes of birds from the bushes, and the singing noise of a little brook that ran under the road. I was standing on the bridge when I took out my watch and struck a wax light to see the time; and it came upon me suddenly what a strange evening it had been. It was all so different, you see, to what I had been doing all my life, particularly for the year before, and it almost seemed as if I couldn't be the man who had been going into the City every day in the morning and coming back from it every evening after writing a lot of uninteresting letters. It was like being pitched all of a sudden from one world into another. Well, I found my way back somehow or other, and as I went along I made up my mind how I'd spend my holiday. I said to myself, 'I'll have a walking tour as well as Ferrars, only mine is to be a tour of London and its environs,' and I had got it all settled when I let myself into the house about four o'clock in the morning, and the sun was shining, and the street almost as still as the wood at midnight!"

"I think that was a capital idea of yours. Did you have your tour? Did you buy a map of London?"

"I had the tour all right. I didn't buy a map; that would have spoilt it, somehow; to see everything plotted out, and named, and measured. What I wanted was to feel that I was going where nobody had been before. That's nonsense, isn't it? as if there could be any such places in London, or England either, for the matter of that."

"I know what you mean; you wanted to feel as if you were going on a sort of voyage of discovery. Isn't that it?"

"Exactly, that's what I was trying to tell you. Besides, I didn't want to buy a map. I made a map."

"How do you mean? Did you make a map out of your head?"

"I'll tell you about it afterwards. But do you really want to hear about my grand tour?"

"Of course I do; it must have been delightful. I call it a most original idea."

"Well, I was quite full of it, and what you said just now about a voyage of discovery reminds me of how I felt then. When I was a boy I was awfully fond of reading of great travellers—I suppose all boys are—and of sailors who were driven out of their course and found themselves in latitudes where no ship had ever sailed before, and of people who discovered wonderful cities in strange countries; and all the second day of my holidays I was feeling just as I used to when I read these books. I didn't get up till pretty late. I was tired to death after all those miles I had walked; but when I had finished my breakfast and filled my pipe, I had a grand time of it. It was such nonsense, you know; as if there could be anything strange or wonderful in London."

"Why shouldn't there be?"

"Well, I don't know; but I have thought afterwards what a silly lad I must have been. Anyhow, I had a great day of it, planning what I would do, half making-believe—just like a kid—that I didn't know where I might find myself, or what might happen to me. And I was enormously pleased to think it was all my secret, that nobody else knew anything about it, and that, whatever I might see, I would keep to myself. I had always felt like that about the books. Of course, I loved reading them, but it seemed to me that, if I had been a discoverer, I would have kept my discoveries a secret. If I had been Columbus, and, if it could possibly have been managed, I would have found America all by myself, and never have said a word about it to anybody. Fancy! how beautiful it would be to be walking about in one's own town, and talking to people, and all the while to have the thought that one knew of a great world beyond the seas, that nobody else dreamed of. I should have loved that!

"And that is exactly what I felt about the tour I was going to make. I made up my mind that nobody should know; and so, from that day to this, nobody has heard a word of it."

"But you are going to tell me?"

"You are different. But I don't think even you will hear everything; not because I won't, but because I can't tell many of the things I saw."

"Things you saw? Then you really did see wonderful, strange things in London?"

"Well, I did and I didn't. Everything, or pretty nearly everything, that I saw is standing still, and hundreds of thousands of people have looked at the same sights—there were many places that the fellows in the office knew quite well, I found out afterwards. And then I read a book called 'London and its Surroundings.' But (I don't know how it is) neither the men at the office nor the writers of the book seem to have seen the things that I did. That's why I stopped reading the book; it seemed to take the life, the real heart, out of everything, making it as dry and stupid as the stuffed birds in a museum.

"I thought about what I was going to do all that day, and went to bed early, so as to be fresh. I knew wonderfully little about London, really; though, except for an odd week now and then, I had spent all my life in town. Of course I knew the main streets—the Strand, Regent Street, Oxford Street, and so on—and I knew the way to the school I used to go to when I was a boy, and the way into the City. But I had just kept to a few tracks, as they say the sheep do on the mountains; and that made it all the easier for me to imagine that I was going to discover a new world."

Darnell paused in the stream of his talk. He looked keenly at his wife to see if he were wearying her, but her eyes gazed at him with unabated interest—one would have almost said that they were the eyes of one who longed and half expected to be initiated into the mysteries, who knew not what great wonder was to be revealed. She sat with her back to the open window, framed in the sweet dusk of the night, as if a painter had made a curtain of heavy velvet behind her; and the work that she had been doing had fallen to the floor. She supported her head with her two hands placed on each side of her brow, and her eyes were as the wells in the wood of which Darnell dreamed in the night-time and in the day.

"And all the strange tales I had ever heard were in my head that morning," he went on, as if continuing the thoughts that had filled his mind while his lips were silent. "I had gone to bed early, as I told you, to get a thorough rest, and I had set my alarm clock to wake me at three, so that I might set out at an hour that was quite strange for the beginning of a journey. There was a hush in the world when I awoke, before the clock had rung to arouse me, and then a bird began to sing and twitter in the elm tree that grew in the next garden, and I looked out of the window, and everything was still, and the morning air breathed in pure and sweet, as I had never known it before. My room was at the back of the house, and most of the gardens had trees in them, and beyond these trees I could see the backs of the houses of the next street rising like the wall of an old city; and as I looked the sun rose, and the great light came in at my window, and the day began.

"And I found that when I was once out of the streets just about me that I knew, some of the queer feeling that had come to me two days before came back again. It was not nearly so strong, the streets no longer smelt of incense, but still there was enough of it to show me what a strange world I passed by. There were things that one may see again and again in many London streets: a vine or a fig tree on a wall, a lark singing in a cage, a curious shrub blossoming in a garden, an odd shape of a roof, or a balcony with an uncommon-looking trellis-work in iron. There's scarcely a street, perhaps, where you won't see one or other of such things as these; but that morning they rose to my eyes in a new light, as if I had on the magic spectacles in the fairy tale, and just like the man in the fairy tale, I went on and on in the new light. I remember going through wild land on a high place; there were pools of water shining in the sun, and great white houses in the middle of dark, rocking pines, and then on the turn of the height I came to a little lane that went aside from the main road, a lane that led to a wood, and in the lane was a little old shadowed house, with a bell turret in the roof, and a porch of trellis-work all dim and faded into the colour of the sea; and in the garden there were growing tall, white lilies, just as we saw them that day we went to look at the old pictures; they were shining like silver, and they filled the air with their sweet scent. It was from near that house I saw the valley and high places far away in the sun. So, as I say, I went 'on and on,' by woods and fields, till I came to a little town on the top of a hill, a town full of old houses bowing to the ground beneath their years, and the morning was so still that the blue smoke rose up straight into the sky from all the roof-tops, so still that I heard far down in the valley the song of a boy who was singing an old song through the streets as he went to school, and as I passed through the awakening town, beneath the old, grave houses, the church bells began to ring.

"It was soon after I had left this town behind me that I found the

Strange Road.[10] I saw it branching off from the dusty high road, and it looked so green that I turned aside into it, and soon I felt as if I had really come into a new country. I don't know whether it was one of the roads the old Romans made that my father used to tell me about; but it was covered with deep, soft turf, and the great tall hedges on each side looked as if they had not been touched for a hundred years; they had grown so broad and high and wild that they met overhead, and I could only get glimpses here and there of the country through which I was passing, as one passes in a dream. The Strange Road led me on and on, up and down hill; sometimes the rose bushes had grown so thick that I could scarcely make my way between them, and sometimes the road broadened out into a green, and in one valley a brook, spanned by an old wooden bridge, ran across it. I was tired, and I found a soft and shady place beneath an ash tree, where I must have slept for many hours, for when I woke up it was late in the afternoon. So I went on again, and at last the green road came out into the highway, and I looked up and saw another town on a high place with a great church in the middle of it, and when I went up to it there was a great organ sounding from within, and the choir was singing."

There was a rapture in Darnell's voice as he spoke, that made his story well-nigh swell into a song, and he drew a long breath as the words ended, filled with the thought of that far-off summer day, when some enchantment had informed all common things, transmuting them into a great sacrament, causing earthly works to glow with the fire and the glory of the everlasting light.

And some splendour of that light shone on the face of Mary as she sat still against the sweet gloom of the night, her dark hair making her face more radiant. She was silent for a little while, and then she spoke—

"Oh, my dear, why have you waited so long to tell me these wonderful things? I think it is beautiful. Please go on."

"I have always been afraid it was all nonsense," said Darnell. "And I don't know how to explain what I feel. I didn't think I could say so much as I have to-night."

"And did you find it the same day after day?"

"All through the tour? Yes, I think every journey was a success. Of course, I didn't go so far afield every day; I was too tired. Often I rested all day long, and went out in the evening, after the lamps were lit, and then only for a mile or two. I would roam about old, dim squares, and hear the wind from the hills whispering in the trees; and when I knew I was within call of some great glittering street, I was sunk in the silence of ways where I was almost the only passenger, and the lamps were so few and faint that they seemed to give out shadows instead of light. And I would walk slowly, to and fro, perhaps for an hour at a time, in such dark streets, and all the time I felt what I told you about its being my secret—that the shadow, and the dim lights, and the cool of the evening, and trees that were like dark low clouds were all mine, and mine alone, that I was living in a world that nobody else knew of, into which no one could enter.

"I remembered one night I had gone farther. It was somewhere in the far west, where there are orchards and gardens, and great broad lawns that slope down to trees by the river. A great red moon rose that night through mists of sunset, and thin, filmy clouds, and I wandered by a road that passed through the orchards, till I came to a little hill, with the moon showing above it glowing like a great rose. Then I saw figures pass between me and the moon, one by one, in a long line, each bent double, with great packs upon their shoulders. One of them was singing, and then in the middle of the song I heard a horrible shrill laugh, in the thin cracked voice of a very old woman, and they disappeared into the shadow of the trees. I suppose they were people going to work, or coming from work in the gardens; but how like it was to a nightmare!

"I can't tell you about Hampton; I should never finish talking. I was there one evening, not long before they closed the gates, and there were very few people about. But the grey-red, silent, echoing courts, and the flowers falling into dreamland as the night came on, and the dark yews and shadowy-looking statues, and the far, still stretches of water beneath the avenues; and all melting into a blue mist, all being hidden from one's eyes, slowly, surely, as if veils were dropped, one by one, on a great ceremony! Oh! my dear, what could it mean? Far away, across the river, I heard a soft bell ring three times, and three times, and again three times, and I turned away, and my eyes were full of tears.

"I didn't know what it was when I came to it; I only found out afterwards that it must have been Hampton Court. One of the men in the office told me he had taken an A. B. C. girl[11] there, and they had great fun. They got into the maze and couldn't get out again, and then they went on the river and were nearly drowned. He told me there were some spicy pictures in the galleries; his girl shrieked with laughter, so he said."

Mary quite disregarded this interlude.

"But you told me you had made a map. What was it like?"

"I'll show it you some day, if you want to see it. I marked down all the places I had gone to, and made signs—things like queer letters—to remind me of what I had seen. Nobody but myself could understand it. I wanted to draw pictures, but I never learnt how to draw, so when I tried nothing was like what I wanted it to be. I tried to draw a picture of that town on the hill that I came to on the evening of the first day; I wanted to make a steep hill with houses on top, and in the middle, but high above them, the great church, all spires and pinnacles, and above it, in the air, a cup with rays coming from it. But it wasn't a success. I made a very strange sign for Hampton Court, and gave it a name that I made up out of my head."

The Darnells avoided one another's eyes as they sat at breakfast the next morning. The air had lightened in the night, for rain had fallen at dawn; and there was a bright blue sky, with vast white clouds rolling across it from the south-west, and a fresh and joyous wind blew in at the open window; the mists had vanished. And with the mists there seemed to have vanished also the sense of strange things that had possessed Mary and her husband the night before; and as they looked out into the clear light they could scarcely believe that the one had spoken and the other had listened a few hours before to histories very far removed from the usual current of their thoughts and of their lives. They glanced shyly at one another, and spoke of common things, of the question whether Alice would be corrupted by the insidious Mrs. Murry, or whether Mrs. Darnell would be able to persuade the girl that the old woman must be actuated by the worst motives.

"And I think, if I were you," said Darnell, as he went out, "I should step over to the stores and complain of their meat. That last piece of beef was very far from being up to the mark—full of sinew."

III

It might have been different in the evening, and Darnell had matured a plan by which he hoped to gain much. He intended to ask his wife if she would mind having only one gas, and that a good deal lowered, on the pretext that his eyes were tired with work; he thought many things might happen if the room were dimly lit, and the window opened, so that they could sit and watch the night, and listen to the rustling murmur of the tree on the lawn. But his plans were made in vain, for when he got to the garden gate his wife, in tears, came forth to meet him.

"Oh, Edward," she began, "such a dreadful thing has happened! I never liked him much, but I didn't think he would ever do such awful things."

"What do you mean? Who are you talking about? What has happened? Is it Alice's young man?"

"No, no. But come in, dear. I can see that woman opposite watching us: she's always on the look out."

"Now, what is it?" said Darnell, as they sat down to tea. "Tell me, quick! you've quite frightened me."

"I don't know how to begin, or where to start. Aunt Marian has thought that there was something queer for weeks. And then she found—oh, well, the long and short of it is that Uncle Robert has been carrying on dreadfully with some horrid girl, and aunt has found out everything!"

"Lord! you don't say so! The old rascal! Why, he must be nearer seventy than sixty!"

"He's just sixty-five; and the money he has given her—"

The first shock of surprise over, Darnell turned resolutely to his mince.

"We'll have it all out after tea," he said; "I am not going to have my meals spoilt by that old fool of a Nixon. Fill up my cup, will you, dear?"

"Excellent mince this," he went on, calmly. "A little lemon juice and a bit of ham in it? I thought there was something extra. Alice all right to-day? That's good. I expect she's getting over all that nonsense."

He went on calmly chattering in a manner that astonished Mrs. Darnell, who felt that by the fall of Uncle Robert the natural order had been inverted, and had scarcely touched food since the intelligence had arrived by the second post. She had started out to keep the appointment her aunt had made early in the morning, and had spent most of the day in a first-class waiting-room at Victoria Station, where she had heard all the story.

"Now," said Darnell, when the table had been cleared, "tell us all about it. How long has it been going on?"

"Aunt thinks now, from little things she remembers, that it must have been going on for a year at least. She says there has been a horrid kind of mystery about uncle's behaviour for a long time, and her nerves were quite shaken, as she thought he must be involved with Anarchists, or something dreadful of the sort."

"What on earth made her think that?"

"Well, you see, once or twice when she was out walking with her husband, she has been startled by whistles, which seemed to follow them everywhere. You know there are some nice country walks at Barnet, and one in particular, in the fields near Totteridge, that uncle and aunt rather made a point of going to on fine Sunday evenings. Of course, this was not the first thing she noticed, but, at the time, it made a great impression on her mind; she could hardly get a wink of sleep for weeks and weeks."

"Whistling?" said Darnell. "I don't quite understand. Why should she be frightened by whistling?"

"I'll tell you. The first time it happened was one Sunday in last May. Aunt had a fancy they were being followed a Sunday or two before, but she didn't see or hear anything, except a sort of crackling noise in the hedge. But this particular Sunday they had hardly got through the stile into the fields, when she heard a peculiar kind of low whistle. She took no notice, thinking it was no concern of hers or her husband's, but as they went on she heard it again, and then again, and it followed them the whole walk, and it made her so uncomfortable, because she didn't know where it was coming from or who was doing it, or why. Then, just as they got out of the fields into the lane, uncle said he felt quite faint, and he thought he would try a little brandy at the 'Turpin's Head,' a small public-house there is there. And she looked at him and saw his face was quite purple—more like apoplexy, as she says, than fainting fits, which make people look a sort of greenish-white. But she said nothing, and thought perhaps uncle had a peculiar way of fainting of his own, as he always was a man to have his own way of doing everything. So she just waited in the road, and he went ahead and slipped into the public, and aunt says she thought she saw a little figure rise out of the dusk and slip in after him, but she couldn't be sure. And when uncle came out he looked red instead of purple, and said he felt much better; and so they went home quietly together, and nothing more was said. You see, uncle had said nothing about the whistling, and aunt had been so frightened that she didn't dare speak, for fear they might be both shot.

"She wasn't thinking anything more about it, when two Sundays afterwards the very same thing happened just as it had before. This time aunt plucked up a spirit, and asked uncle what it could be. And what do you think he said? 'Birds, my dear, birds.' Of course aunt said to him that no bird that ever flew with wings made a noise like that: sly, and low, with pauses in between; and then he said that many rare sorts of birds lived in North Middlesex and Hertfordshire. 'Nonsense, Robert,' said aunt, 'how can you talk so, considering it has followed us all the way, for a mile or more?' And then uncle told her that some birds were so attached to man that they would follow one about for miles sometimes; he said he had just been reading about a bird like that in a book of travels. And do you know that when they got home he actually showed her a piece in the 'Hertfordshire Naturalist'[12] which they took in to oblige a friend of theirs, all about rare birds found in the neighbourhood, all the most outlandish names, aunt says, that she had never heard or thought of, and uncle had the impudence to say that it must have been a Purple Sandpiper, which, the paper said, had 'a low shrill note, constantly repeated.' And then he took down a book of Siberian Travels from the bookcase and showed her a page which told how a man was followed by a bird all day long through a forest. And that's what Aunt Marian says vexes her more than anything almost; to think that he should be so artful and ready with those books, twisting them to his own wicked ends. But, at the time, when she was out walking, she simply couldn't make out what he meant by talking about birds in that random, silly sort of way, so unlike him, and they went on, that horrible whistling following them, she looking straight ahead and walking fast, really feeling more huffy and put out than frightened. And when they got to the next stile, she got over and turned round, and 'lo and behold,' as she says, there was no Uncle Robert to be seen! She felt herself go quite white with alarm, thinking of that whistle, and making sure he'd been spirited away or snatched in some way or another, and she had just screamed out 'Robert' like a mad woman, when he came quite slowly round the corner, as cool as a cucumber, holding something in his hand. He said there were some flowers he could never pass, and when aunt saw that he had got a dandelion torn up by the roots, she felt as if her head were going round."

Mary's story was suddenly interrupted. For ten minutes Darnell had been writhing in his chair, suffering tortures in his anxiety to avoid wounding his wife's feelings, but the episode of the dandelion was too much for him, and he burst into a long, wild shriek of laughter, aggravated by suppression into the semblance of a Red Indian's war-whoop. Alice, who was washing-up in the scullery, dropped some three shillings' worth of china, and the neighbours ran out into their gardens wondering if it were murder. Mary gazed reproachfully at her husband.

"How can you be so unfeeling, Edward?" she said, at length, when Darnell had passed into the feebleness of exhaustion. "If you had seen the tears rolling down poor Aunt Marian's cheeks as she told me, I don't think you would have laughed. I didn't think you were so hard-hearted."

"My dear Mary," said Darnell, faintly, through sobs and catching of the breath, "I am awfully sorry. I know it's very sad, really, and I'm not unfeeling; but it is such an odd tale, now, isn't it? The Sandpiper, you know, and then the dandelion!"

His face twitched and he ground his teeth together. Mary looked gravely at him for a moment, and then she put her hands to her face, and Darnell could see that she also shook with merriment.

"I am as bad as you," she said, at last. "I never thought of it in that way. I'm glad I didn't, or I should have laughed in Aunt Marian's face, and I wouldn't have done that for the world. Poor old thing; she cried as if her heart would break. I met her at Victoria, as she asked me, and we had some soup at a confectioner's. I could scarcely touch it; her tears kept dropping into the plate all the time; and then we went to the waiting-room at the station, and she cried there terribly."

"Well," said Darnell, "what happened next? I won't laugh any more."

"No, we mustn't; it's much too horrible for a joke. Well, of course aunt went home and wondered and wondered what could be the matter, and tried to think it out, but, as she says, she could make nothing of it. She began to be afraid that uncle's brain was giving way through overwork, as he had stopped in the City (as he said) up to all hours lately, and he had to go to Yorkshire (wicked old story-teller!), about some very tiresome business connected with his leases. But then she reflected that however queer he might be getting, even his queerness couldn't make whistles in the air, though, as she said, he was always a wonderful man. So she had to give that up; and then she wondered if there were anything the matter with her, as she had read about people who heard noises when there was really nothing at all. But that wouldn't do either, because though it might account for the whistling, it wouldn't account for the dandelion or the Sandpiper, or for fainting fits that turned purple, or any of uncle's queerness. So aunt said she could think of nothing but to read the Bible every day from the beginning, and by the time she got into Chronicles she felt rather better, especially as nothing had happened for three or four Sundays. She noticed uncle seemed absent-minded, and not as nice to her as he might be, but she put that down to too much work, as he never came home before the last train, and had a hansom twice all the way, getting there between three and four in the morning. Still, she felt it was no good bothering her head over what couldn't be made out or explained anyway, and she was just settling down, when one Sunday evening it began all over again, and worse things happened. The whistling followed them just as it did before, and poor aunt set her teeth and said nothing to uncle, as she knew he would only tell her stories, and they were walking on, not saying a word, when something made her look back, and there was a horrible boy with red hair, peeping through the hedge just behind, and grinning. She said it was a dreadful face, with something unnatural about it, as if it had been a dwarf, and before she had time to have a good look, it popped back like lightning, and aunt all but fainted away."

"A red-headed *boy*?" said Darnell. "I thought— What an extraordinary story this is. I've never heard of anything so queer. Who was the boy?"

"You will know in good time," said Mrs. Darnell. "It is very strange, isn't it?"

"Strange!" Darnell ruminated for a while.

"I know what I think, Mary," he said at length. "I don't believe a word of it. I believe your aunt is going mad, or has gone mad, and that she has delusions. The whole thing sounds to me like the invention of a lunatic."

"You are quite wrong. Every word is true, and if you will let me go

298

on, you will understand how it all happened."

"Very good, go ahead."

"Let me see, where was I? Oh, I know, aunt saw the boy grinning in the hedge. Yes, well, she was dreadfully frightened for a minute or two; there was something so queer about the face, but then she plucked up a spirit and said to herself, 'After all, better a boy with red hair than a big man with a gun,' and she made up her mind to watch Uncle Robert closely, as she could see by his look he knew all about it; he seemed as if he were thinking hard and puzzling over something, as if he didn't know what to do next, and his mouth kept opening and shutting, like a fish's. So she kept her face straight, and didn't say a word, and when he said something to her about the fine sunset, she took no notice. 'Don't you hear what I say, Marian?' he said, speaking quite crossly, and bellowing as if it were to somebody in the next field. So aunt said she was very sorry, but her cold made her so deaf, she couldn't hear much. She noticed uncle looked quite pleased, and relieved too, and she knew he thought she hadn't heard the whistling. Suddenly uncle pretended to see a beautiful spray of honeysuckle high up in the hedge, and he said he must get it for aunt, only she must go on ahead, as it made him nervous to be watched. She said she would, but she just stepped aside behind a bush where there was a sort of cover in the hedge, and found she could see him quite well, though she scratched her face terribly with poking it into a rose bush. And in a minute or two out came the boy from behind the hedge, and she saw uncle and him talking, and she knew it was the same boy, as it wasn't dark enough to hide his flaming red head. And uncle put out his hand as if to catch him, but he just darted into the bushes and vanished. Aunt never said a word at the time, but that night when they got home she charged uncle with what she'd seen and asked him what it all meant. He was quite taken aback at first, and stammered and stuttered and said a spy wasn't his notion of a good wife, but at last he made her swear secrecy, and told her that he was a very high Freemason, and that the boy was an emissary of the order who brought him messages of the greatest importance. But aunt didn't believe a word of it, as an uncle of hers was a mason, and he never behaved like that. It was then she began to be afraid that it was really Anarchists, or something of the kind, and every time the bell rang she thought that uncle had been found out, and the police had come for him."

"What nonsense! As if a man with house property would be an Anarchist."

"Well, she could see there must be some horrible secret, and she didn't know what else to think. And then she began to have the things through the post."

"Things through the post! What do you mean by that?"

"All sorts of things; bits of broken bottle-glass, packed carefully as if it were jewellery; parcels that unrolled and unrolled worse than Chinese boxes, and then had 'cat' in large letters when you came to the middle; old artificial teeth, a cake of red paint, and at last cockroaches."

"Cockroaches by post! Stuff and nonsense; your aunt's mad."

"Edward, she showed me the box; it was made to hold cigarettes, and there were three dead cockroaches inside. And when she found a box of exactly the same kind, half-full of cigarettes, in uncle's greatcoat pocket, then her head began to turn again."

Darnell groaned, and stirred uneasily in his chair, feeling that the tale of Aunt Marian's domestic troubles was putting on the semblance of an evil dream.

"Anything else?" he asked.

"My dear, I haven't repeated half the things poor aunt told me this afternoon. There was the night she thought she saw a ghost in the shrubbery. She was anxious about some chickens that were just due to hatch out, so she went out after dark with some egg and bread-crumbs, in case they might be out. And just before her she saw a figure gliding by the rhododendrons. It looked like a short, slim man dressed as they used to be hundreds of years ago; she saw the sword by his side, and the feather in his cap. She thought she should have died, she said, and though it was gone in a minute, and she tried to make out it was all her fancy, she fainted when she got into the house. Uncle was at home that night, and when she came to and told him he ran out, and stayed out for half-an-hour or more, and then came in and said he could find nothing; and the next minute aunt heard that low whistle just outside the window, and uncle ran out again."

"My dear Mary, do let us come to the point. What on earth does it all lead to?"

"Haven't you guessed? Why, of course it was that girl all the time."

"Girl? I thought you said it was a boy with a red head?"

"Don't you see? She's an actress, and she dressed up. She won't leave uncle alone. It wasn't enough that he was with her nearly every evening in the week, but she must be after him on Sundays too. Aunt found a letter the horrid thing had written, and so it has all come out. Enid Vivian she calls herself, though I don't suppose she has any right to one name or the other. And the question is, what is to be done?"

"Let us talk of that again. I'll have a pipe, and then we'll go to bed."

They were almost asleep when Mary said suddenly—

"Doesn't it seem queer, Edward? Last night you were telling me such beautiful things, and to-night I have been talking about that disgraceful old man and his goings on."

"I don't know," answered Darnell, dreamily. "On the walls of that great church upon the hill I saw all kinds of strange grinning monsters, carved in stone."

The misdemeanours of Mr. Robert Nixon brought in their train consequences strange beyond imagination. It was not that they continued to develop on the somewhat fantastic lines of these first adventures which Mrs. Darnell had related; indeed, when "Aunt Marian" came over to Shepherd's Bush, one Sunday afternoon, Darnell wondered how he had had the heart to laugh at the misfortunes of a broken-hearted woman.

He had never seen his wife's aunt before, and he was strangely surprised when Alice showed her into the garden where they were sitting on the warm and misty Sunday in September. To him, save during these latter days, she had always been associated with ideas of splendour and success: his wife had always mentioned the Nixons with a tinge of reverence; he had heard, many times, the epic of Mr. Nixon's struggles and of his slow but triumphant rise. Mary had told the story as she had received it from her parents, beginning with the flight to London from some small, dull, and unprosperous town in the flattest of the Midlands, long ago, when a young man from the country had great chances of fortune. Robert Nixon's father had been a grocer in the High Street, and in after days the successful coal merchant and builder loved to tell of that dull provincial life, and while he glorified his own victories, he gave his hearers to understand that he came of a race which had also known how to achieve. That had been long ago, he would explain: in the days when that rare citizen who desired to go to London or to York was forced to rise in the dead of night, and make his way, somehow or other, by ten miles of quagmirish, wandering lanes to the Great North Road, there to meet the "Lightning" coach, a vehicle which stood to all the countryside as the visible and tangible embodiment of tremendous speed—"and indeed," as Nixon would add, "it was always up to time, which is more than can be said of the Dunham Branch Line nowadays!" It was in this ancient Dunham that the Nixons had waged successful trade for perhaps a hundred years, in a shop with bulging bay windows looking on the market-place. There was no competition, and the townsfolk, and well-to-do farmers, the clergy and the country families, looked upon the house of Nixon as an institution fixed as the town hall (which stood on Roman pillars) and the parish church. But the change came: the railway crept nearer and nearer, the farmers and the country gentry became less well-to-do; the tanning, which was the local industry, suffered from a great business which had been established in a larger town, some twenty miles away, and the profits of the Nixons grew less and less. Hence the hegira of Robert, and he would dilate on the poorness of his beginnings, how he saved, by little and little, from his sorry wage of City clerk, and how he and a fellow clerk, "who had come into a hundred pounds," saw an opening in the coal trade—and filled it. It was at this stage of Robert's fortunes, still far from magnificent, that Miss Marian Reynolds had encountered him, she being on a visit to friends in Gunnersbury. Afterwards, victory followed victory; Nixon's wharf became a landmark to bargemen; his power stretched abroad, his dusky fleets went outwards to the sea, and inward by all the far reaches of canals. Lime, cement, and bricks were added to his merchandise, and at last he hit upon the great stroke—that extensive taking up of land in the north of London. Nixon himself ascribed this *coup* to native sagacity, and the possession of capital; and there were also obscure rumours to the effect that some one or other had been "done" in the course of the transaction. However that might be, the Nixons grew wealthy to excess, and Mary had often told her husband of the state in which they dwelt, of their liveried servants, of the glories of their drawing-room, of their broad lawn, shadowed by a splendid and ancient cedar. And so Darnell had somehow been led into conceiving the lady of this demesne as a personage of no small pomp. He saw her, tall, of dignified port and presence, inclining, it might be, to some measure of obesity, such a measure as was not unbefitting in an elderly lady of position, who lived well and lived at ease. He even imagined a slight ruddiness of complexion, which went very well with hair that was beginning to turn grey, and when he heard the door-bell ring, as he sat under the mulberry on the Sunday afternoon, he bent forward to catch sight of this stately figure, clad, of course, in the richest, blackest silk, girt about with heavy chains of gold.

He started with amazement when he saw the strange presence that followed the servant into the garden. Mrs. Nixon was a little, thin old woman, who bent as she feebly trotted after Alice; her eyes were on the ground, and she did not lift them when the Darnells rose to greet her. She glanced to the right, uneasily, as she shook hands with Darnell, to the left when Mary kissed her, and when she was placed on the garden seat with a cushion at her back, she looked away at the back of the houses in the next street. She was dressed in black, it was true, but even Darnell could see that her gown was old and shabby, that the fur trimming of her cape and the fur boa which was twisted about her neck were dingy and disconsolate, and had all the melancholy air which fur wears when it is seen in a second-hand clothes-shop in a back street. And her gloves—they were black kid, wrinkled with much wear, faded to a bluish hue at the finger-tips, which showed signs of painful mending. Her hair, plastered over her forehead, looked dull and colourless, though some greasy matter had evidently been used with a view of producing a becoming gloss, and on it perched an antique bonnet, adorned with black pendants that rattled paralytically one against the other.

And there was nothing in Mrs. Nixon's face to correspond with the imaginary picture that Darnell had made of her. She was sallow, wrinkled, pinched; her nose ran to a sharp point, and her red-rimmed eyes were a queer water-grey, that seemed to shrink alike from the light and from encounter with the eyes of others. As she sat beside his wife on the green garden-seat, Darnell, who occupied a wicker-chair brought out from the drawing-room, could not help feeling that this shadowy and evasive figure, muttering replies to Mary's polite questions, was almost impossibly remote from his conceptions of the rich and powerful aunt, who could give away a hundred pounds as a mere birthday gift. She would say little at first; yes, she was feeling rather tired, it had been so hot all the way, and she had been afraid to put on lighter things as one never knew at this time of year what it might be like in the evenings; there were apt to be cold mists when the sun went down, and she didn't care to risk bronchitis.

"I thought I should never get here," she went on, raising her voice to an odd querulous pipe. "I'd no notion it was such an out-of-the-way place, it's so many years since I was in this neighbourhood."

She wiped her eyes, no doubt thinking of the early days at Turnham Green, when she married Nixon; and when the pocket-handkerchief had done its office she replaced it in a shabby black bag which she clutched rather than carried. Darnell noticed, as he watched her, that the bag seemed full, almost to bursting, and he speculated idly as to the nature of its contents: correspondence, perhaps, he thought, further proofs of Uncle Robert's treacherous and wicked dealings. He grew quite uncomfortable, as he sat and saw her glancing all the while furtively away from his wife and himself, and presently he got up and strolled away to the other end of the garden, where he lit his pipe and walked to and fro on the gravel walk, still astounded at the gulf between the real and the imagined woman.

Presently he heard a hissing whisper, and he saw Mrs. Nixon's head inclining to his wife's. Mary rose and came towards him.

"Would you mind sitting in the drawing-room, Edward?" she

murmured. "Aunt says she can't bring herself to discuss such a delicate matter before you. I dare say it's quite natural."

"Very well, but I don't think I'll go into the drawing-room. I feel as if a walk would do me good. You mustn't be frightened if I am a little late," he said; "if I don't get back before your aunt goes, say good-bye to her for me."

He strolled into the main road, where the trams were humming to and fro. He was still confused and perplexed, and he tried to account for a certain relief he felt in removing himself from the presence of Mrs. Nixon. He told himself that her grief at her husband's ruffianly conduct was worthy of all pitiful respect, but at the same time, to his shame, he had felt a certain physical aversion from her as she sat in his garden in her dingy black, dabbing her red-rimmed eyes with a damp pocket-handkerchief. He had been to the Zoo when he was a lad, and he still remembered how he had shrunk with horror at the sight of certain reptiles slowly crawling over one another in their slimy pond. But he was enraged at the similarity between the two sensations, and he walked briskly on that level and monotonous road, looking about him at the unhandsome spectacle of suburban London keeping Sunday.

There was something in the tinge of antiquity which still exists in Acton that soothed his mind and drew it away from those unpleasant contemplations, and when at last he had penetrated rampart after rampart of brick, and heard no more the harsh shrieks and laughter of the people who were enjoying themselves, he found a way into a little sheltered field, and sat down in peace beneath a tree, whence he could look out on a pleasant valley. The sun sank down beneath the hills, the clouds changed into the likeness of blossoming rose-gardens; and he still sat there in the gathering darkness till a cool breeze blew upon him, and he rose with a sigh, and turned back to the brick ramparts and the glimmering streets, and the noisy idlers sauntering to and fro in the procession of their dismal festival. But he was murmuring to himself some words that seemed a magic song, and it was with uplifted heart that he let himself into his house.

Mrs. Nixon had gone an hour and a half before his return, Mary told him. Darnell sighed with relief, and he and his wife strolled out into the garden and sat down side by side.

They kept silence for a time, and at last Mary spoke, not without a nervous tremor in her voice.

"I must tell you, Edward," she began, "that aunt has made a proposal which you ought to hear. I think we should consider it."

"A proposal? But how about the whole affair? Is it still going on?"

"Oh, yes! She told me all about it. Uncle is quite unrepentant.

It seems he has taken a flat somewhere in town for that woman, and furnished it in the most costly manner. He simply laughs at aunt's reproaches, and says he means to have some fun at last. You saw how broken she was?"

"Yes; very sad. But won't he give her any money? Wasn't she very badly dressed for a woman in her position?"

"Aunt has no end of beautiful things, but I fancy she likes to hoard them; she has a horror of spoiling her dresses. It isn't for want of money, I assure you, as uncle settled a very large sum on her two years ago, when he was everything that could be desired as a husband. And that brings me to what I want to say. Aunt would like to live with us. She would pay very liberally. What do you say?"

"Would like to live with us?" exclaimed Darnell, and his pipe dropped from his hand on to the grass. He was stupefied by the thought of Aunt Marian as a boarder, and sat staring vacantly before him, wondering what new monster the night would next produce.

"I knew you wouldn't much like the idea," his wife went on. "But I do think, dearest, that we ought not to refuse without very serious consideration. I am afraid you did not take to poor aunt very much."

Darnell shook his head dumbly.

"I thought you didn't; she was so upset, poor thing, and you didn't see her at her best. She is really so good. But listen to me, dear. Do you think we have the right to refuse her offer? I told you she has money of her own, and I am sure she would be dreadfully offended if we said we wouldn't have her. And what would become of me if anything happened to you? You know we have very little saved."

Darnell groaned.

"It seems to me," he said, "that it would spoil everything. We are so happy, Mary dear, by ourselves. Of course I am extremely sorry for your aunt. I think she is very much to be pitied. But when it comes to having her always here—"

"I know, dear. Don't think I am looking forward to the prospect; you know I don't want anybody but you. Still, we ought to think of the future, and besides we shall be able to live so very much better. I shall be able to give you all sorts of nice things that I know you ought to have after all that hard work in the City. Our income would be doubled."

"Do you mean she would pay us £150 a year?"

"Certainly. And she would pay for the spare room being furnished, and any extra she might want. She told me, specially, that if a friend or two came now and again to see her, she would gladly bear the cost of a fire in the drawing-room, and give something towards the gas bill, with a few shillings for the girl for any additional trouble.

We should certainly be more than twice as well off as we are now. You see, Edward, dear, it's not the sort of offer we are likely to have again. Besides, we must think of the future, as I said. Do you know aunt took a great fancy to you?"

He shuddered and said nothing, and his wife went on with her argument.

"And, you see, it isn't as if we should see so very much of her. She will have her breakfast in bed, and she told me she would often go up to her room in the evening directly after dinner. I thought that very nice and considerate. She quite understands that we shouldn't like to have a third person always with us. Don't you think, Edward, that, considering everything, we ought to say we will have her?"

"Oh, I suppose so," he groaned. "As you say, it's a very good offer, financially, and I am afraid it would be very imprudent to refuse. But I don't like the notion, I confess."

"I am so glad you agree with me, dear. Depend upon it, it won't be half so bad as you think. And putting our own advantage on one side, we shall really be doing poor aunt a very great kindness. Poor old dear, she cried bitterly after you were gone; she said she had made up her mind not to stay any longer in Uncle Robert's house, and she didn't know where to go, or what would become of her, if we refused to take her in. She quite broke down."

"Well, well; we will try it for a year, anyhow. It may be as you say; we shan't find it quite so bad as it seems now. Shall we go in?"

He stooped for his pipe, which lay as it had fallen, on the grass. He could not find it, and lit a wax match which showed him the pipe, and close beside it, under the seat, something that looked like a page torn from a book. He wondered what it could be, and picked it up.

The gas was lit in the drawing-room, and Mrs. Darnell, who was arranging some notepaper, wished to write at once to Mrs. Nixon, cordially accepting her proposal, when she was startled by an exclamation from her husband.

"What is the matter?" she said, startled by the tone of his voice. "You haven't hurt yourself?"

"Look at this," he replied, handing her a small leaflet; "I found it under the garden seat just now."

Mary glanced with bewilderment at her husband and read as follows:—

THE NEW CHOSEN SEED OF ABRAHAM

PROPHECIES TO BE FULFILLED IN THE PRESENT YEAR

1. The Sailing of a Fleet of One Hundred and Forty and Four Vessels for Tarshish and the Isles.

2. Destruction of the Power of the Dog, including all the instruments of anti-Abrahamic legislation.

3. Return of the Fleet from Tarshish, bearing with it the gold of Arabia, destined to be the Foundation of the New City of Abraham.

4. The Search for the Bride, and the bestowing of the Seals on the Seventy and Seven.

5. The Countenance of FATHER to become luminous, but with a greater glory than the face of Moses.

6. The Pope of Rome to be stoned stones in the valley called Berek-Zittor.

7. FATHER to be acknowledged by Three Great Rulers. Two Great Rulers will deny FATHER, and will immediately perish in the Effluvia of FATHER'S Indignation.

8. Binding of the Beast with the Horn, and all judges cast down.

9. Finding of the Bride in the Land of Egypt, which has been revealed to FATHER as now existing in the western part of London.

10. Bestowal of the New Tongue on the Seventy and Seven, and on the One Hundred and Forty and Four. FATHER proceeds to the Bridal Chamber.

11. Destruction of London and rebuilding of the City called No, which is the New City of Abraham.

12. FATHER united to the Bride, and the present Earth removed to the Sun for the space of half an hour.

Mrs. Darnell's brow cleared as she read matter which seemed to her harmless if incoherent. From her husband's voice she had been led to fear something more tangibly unpleasant than a vague catena of prophecies.

"Well," she said, "what about it?"

"What about it? Don't you see that your aunt dropped it, and that she must be a raging lunatic?"

"Oh, Edward! don't say that. In the first place, how do you know that aunt dropped it at all? It might easily have blown over from any of the other gardens. And, if it were hers, I don't think you should call her a lunatic. I don't believe, myself, that there are any real prophets now; but there are many good people who think quite differently. I knew an old lady once who, I am sure, was very good, and she took in a paper every week that was full of prophecies and things very like this. Nobody called her mad, and I have heard father say that she had one of the sharpest heads for business he had ever come across."

"Very good; have it as you like. But I believe we shall both be sorry."

They sat in silence for some time. Alice came in after her "evening out," and they sat on, till Mrs. Darnell said she was tired and wanted to go to bed.

Her husband kissed her. "I don't think I will come up just yet," he said; "you go to sleep, dearest. I want to think things over. No, no; I am not going to change my mind: your aunt shall come, as I said. But there are one or two things I should like to get settled in my mind."

He meditated for a long while, pacing up and down the room. Light after light was extinguished in Edna Road, and the people of the suburb slept all around him, but still the gas was alight in Darnell's drawing-room, and he walked softly up and down the floor. He was thinking that about the life of Mary and himself, which had been so quiet, there seemed to be gathering on all sides grotesque and fantastic shapes, omens of confusion and disorder, threats of madness; a strange company from another world. It was as if into the quiet, sleeping streets of some little ancient town among the hills there had come from afar the sound of drum and pipe, snatches of wild song, and there had burst into the market-place the mad company of the players, strangely bedizened, dancing a furious measure to their hurrying music, drawing forth the citizens from their sheltered homes and peaceful lives, and alluring them to mingle in the significant figures of their dance.

Yet afar and near (for it was hidden in his heart) he beheld the glimmer of a sure and constant star. Beneath, darkness came on, and mists and shadows closed about the town. The red, flickering flame of torches was kindled in the midst of it. The song grew louder, with more insistent, magical tones, surging and falling in unearthly modulations, the very speech of incantation; and the drum beat madly, and the pipe shrilled to a scream, summoning all to issue forth, to leave their peaceful hearths; for a strange rite was preconized in their midst. The streets that were wont to be so still, so hushed with the cool and tranquil veils of darkness, asleep beneath the patronage of the evening star, now danced with glimmering lanterns, resounded with the cries of those who hurried forth, drawn as by a magistral spell; and the songs swelled and triumphed, the reverberant beating of the drum grew louder, and in the midst of the awakened town the players, fantastically arrayed, performed their interlude under the red blaze of torches. He knew not whether they were players, men that would vanish suddenly as they came, disappearing by the track that climbed the hill; or whether they were indeed magicians, workers of great and efficacious spells, who knew the secret word by which the earth may be transformed into the hall of Gehenna, so that they that gazed and listened, as at a passing spectacle, should be entrapped by the sound and the sight presented to them, should be drawn into the elaborated figures of that mystic dance, and so should be whirled away into those unending mazes on the wild hills that were abhorred, there to wander for evermore.

But Darnell was not afraid, because of the Daystar that had risen in his heart. It had dwelt there all his life, and had slowly shone forth with clearer and clearer light, and he began to see that though his earthly steps might be in the ways of the ancient town that was beset by the Enchanters, and resounded with their songs and their processions, yet he dwelt also in that serene and secure world of brightness, and from a great and unutterable height looked on the confusion of the mortal pageant, beholding mysteries in which he was no true actor, hearing magic songs that could by no means draw him down from the battlements of the high and holy city.

His heart was filled with a great joy and a great peace as he lay down beside his wife and fell asleep, and in the morning, when he woke up, he was glad.

IV

In a haze as of a dream Darnell's thoughts seemed to move through the opening days of the next week. Perhaps nature had not intended that he should be practical or much given to that which is usually called "sound common sense," but his training had made him desirous of good, plain qualities of the mind, and he uneasily strove to account to himself for his strange mood of the Sunday night, as he had often endeavoured to interpret the fancies of his boyhood and early manhood. At first he was annoyed by his want of success; the morning paper, which he always secured as the 'bus delayed at Uxbridge Road Station, fell from his hands unread, while he vainly reasoned, assuring himself that the threatened incursion of a whimsical old woman, though tiresome enough, was no rational excuse for those curious hours of meditation in which his thoughts seemed to have dressed themselves in unfamiliar, fantastic habits, and to parley with him in a strange speech, and yet a speech that he had understood.

With such arguments he perplexed his mind on the long, accustomed ride up the steep ascent of Holland Park, past the incongruous hustle of Notting Hill Gate, where in one direction a road shows the way to the snug, somewhat faded bowers and retreats of Bayswater, and in another one sees the portal of the murky region of the slums. The customary companions of his morning's journey were in the seats about him; he heard the hum of their talk, as they disputed concerning politics, and the man next to him, who came from Acton, asked him what he thought of the Government now. There was a discussion, and a loud and excited one, just in front, as to whether rhubarb was a fruit or vegetable, and in his ear he heard Redman, who was a near neighbour, praising the economy of "the wife."

"I don't know how she does it. Look here; what do you think we had yesterday? Breakfast: fish-cakes, beautifully fried—rich, you know, lots of herbs, it's a receipt of her aunt's; you should just taste 'em. Coffee, bread, butter, marmalade, and, of course, all the usual etceteras. Dinner: roast beef, Yorkshire, potatoes, greens, and horse-radish sauce, plum tart, cheese. And where will you get a better dinner than that? Well, I call it wonderful, I really do."

But in spite of these distractions he fell into a dream as the 'bus rolled and tossed on its way Citywards, and still he strove to solve the enigma of his vigil of the night before, and as the shapes of trees and green lawns and houses passed before his eyes, and as he saw the procession moving on the pavement, and while the murmur of the streets sounded in his ears, all was to him strange and unaccustomed, as if he moved through the avenues of some city in a foreign land. It was, perhaps, on these mornings, as he rode to his mechanical work, that vague and floating fancies that must have long haunted his brain began to shape themselves, and to put on the form of definite conclusions, from which he could no longer escape, even if he had wished it. Darnell had received what is called a sound commercial education, and would therefore have found very great difficulty in putting into articulate speech any thought that was worth thinking; but he grew certain on these mornings that the "common sense" which he had always heard exalted as man's supremest faculty was, in all probability, the smallest and least-considered item in the equipment of an ant of average intelligence. And with this, as an almost necessary corollary, came a firm belief that the whole fabric of life in which he moved was sunken, past all thinking, in the grossest absurdity; that he and all his friends and acquaintances and fellow-workers were interested in matters in which men were never meant to be interested, were pursuing aims which they were never meant to pursue, were, indeed, much like fair stones of an altar serving as a pigsty wall. Life, it seemed to him, was a great search for—he knew not what; and in the process of the ages one by one the true marks upon the ways had been shattered, or buried, or the meaning of the words had been slowly forgotten; one by one the signs had been turned awry, the true entrances had been thickly overgrown, the very way itself had been diverted from the heights to the depths, till at last the race of pilgrims had become hereditary stone-breakers and ditch-scourers on a track that led to destruction—if it led anywhere at all. Darnell's heart thrilled with a strange and trembling joy, with a sense that was all new, when it came to his mind that this great loss might not be a hopeless one, that perhaps the difficulties were by no means insuperable. It might be, he considered, that the stone-breaker had merely to throw down his hammer and set out, and the way would be plain before him; and a single step would free the delver in rubbish from the foul slime of the ditch.

It was, of course, with difficulty and slowly that these things became clear to him. He was an English City clerk, "flourishing" towards the end of the nineteenth century, and the rubbish heap that had been accumulating for some centuries could not be cleared away in an instant. Again and again the spirit of nonsense that had been implanted in him as in his fellows assured him that the true world was the visible and tangible world, the world in which good and faithful letter-copying was exchangeable for a certain quantum of bread, beef, and houseroom, and that the man who copied letters well, did not beat his wife, nor lose money foolishly, was a good man, fulfilling the end for which he had been made. But in spite of these arguments, in spite of their acceptance by all who were about him, he had the grace to perceive the utter falsity and absurdity of the whole position. He was fortunate in his entire ignorance of sixpenny "science," but if the whole library had been projected into his brain it would not have moved him to "deny in the darkness that which he had known in the light."[13] Darnell knew by experience that man is made a mystery for mysteries and visions, for the realization in his consciousness of ineffable bliss, for a great joy that transmutes the whole world, for a joy that surpasses all joys and overcomes all sorrows. He knew this certainly, though he knew it dimly; and he was apart from other men, preparing himself for a great experiment.

With such thoughts as these for his secret and concealed treasure, he was able to bear the threatened invasion of Mrs. Nixon with something approaching indifference. He knew, indeed, that her presence between his wife and himself would be unwelcome to him, and he was not without grave doubts as to the woman's sanity; but after all, what did it matter? Besides, already a faint glimmering light had risen within him that showed the profit of self-negation, and in this matter he had preferred his wife's will to his own. *Et non sua poma;*[14] to his astonishment he found a delight in denying himself his own wish, a process that he had always regarded as thoroughly detestable. This was a state of things which he could not in the least understand; but, again, though a member of a most hopeless class, living in the most hopeless surroundings that the world has ever seen, though he knew as much of the *askesis*[15] as of Chinese metaphysics; again, he had the grace not to deny the light that had begun to glimmer in his soul.

And he found a present reward in the eyes of Mary, when she welcomed him home after his foolish labours in the cool of the evening. They sat together, hand in hand, under the mulberry tree, at the coming of the dusk, and as the ugly walls about them became obscure and vanished into the formless world of shadows, they seemed to be freed from the bondage of Shepherd's Bush, freed to wander in that undisfigured, undefiled world that lies beyond the walls. Of this region Mary knew little or nothing by experience, since her relations had always been of one mind with the modern world, which has for the true country an instinctive and most significant horror and dread. Mr. Reynolds had also shared in another odd superstition of these later days—that it is necessary to leave London at least once a year; consequently Mary had some knowledge of various seaside resorts on the south and east coasts, where Londoners gather in hordes, turn the sands into one vast, bad music-hall, and derive, as they say, enormous benefit from the change. But experiences such as these give but little knowledge of the country in its true and occult sense; and yet Mary, as she sat n the dusk beneath the whispering tree, knew something of the secret of the wood, of the valley shut in by high hills, where the sound of pouring water always echoes from the clear brook. And to Darnell these were nights of great dreams; for it was the hour of the work, the time of transmutation, and he who could not understand the miracle, who could scarcely believe in it, yet knew, secretly and half consciously, that the water was being changed into the wine of a new life. This was ever the inner music of his dreams and to it he added on these still and sacred nights the far-off memory of that time long ago when, a child, before the world had overwhelmed him, he journeyed down to the old grey house in the west, and for a whole month heard the murmur of the forest through his bedroom window, and when the wind was hushed, the washing of the tides about the reeds; and sometimes awaking very early he had heard the strange cry of a bird as it rose from its nest among the reeds, and had looked out and had seen the valley whiten to the dawn, and the winding river whiten as it swam down to the sea. The memory of all this had faded and become shadowy as he grew older and the chains of common life were riveted firmly about his soul; all the atmosphere by which he was surrounded was well-nigh fatal to such thoughts, and only now and again in half-conscious moments or in sleep he had revisited that valley in the far-off west, where the breath of the wind was an incantation, and every leaf and stream and hill spoke of great and ineffable mysteries. But now the broken vision was in great part restored to him, and looking with love in his wife's eyes he saw the gleam of water-pools in the still forest, saw the mists rising in the evening, and heard the music of the winding river.

They were sitting thus together on the Friday evening of the week that had begun with that odd and half-forgotten visit of Mrs. Nixon, when, to Darnell's annoyance, the door-bell gave a discordant peal, and Alice with some disturbance of manner came out and announced that a gentleman wished to see the master. Darnell went into the drawing-room, where Alice had lit one gas so that it flared and burnt with a rushing sound, and in this distorting light there waited a stout, elderly gentleman, whose countenance was altogether unknown to him. He stared blankly, and hesitated, about to speak, but the visitor began.

"You don't know who I am, but I expect you'll know my name. It's Nixon."

He did not wait to be interrupted. He sat down and plunged into narrative, and after the first few words, Darnell, whose mind was not altogether unprepared, listened without much astonishment.

"And the long and the short of it is," Mr. Nixon said at last, "she's gone stark, staring mad, and we had to put her away to-day—poor thing."

His voice broke a little, and he wiped his eyes hastily, for though stout and successful he was not unfeeling, and he was fond of his wife. He had spoken quickly, and had gone lightly over many details which might have interested specialists in certain kinds of mania, and Darnell was sorry for his evident distress.

"I came here," he went on after a brief pause, "because I found out she had been to see you last Sunday, and I knew the sort of story she must have told."

Darnell showed him the prophetic leaflet which Mrs. Nixon had dropped in the garden. "Did you know about this?" he said.

"Oh, *him*," said the old man, with some approach to cheerfulness; "oh yes, I thrashed *him* black and blue the day before yesterday."

"Isn't he mad? Who is the man?"

"He's not mad, he's bad. He's a little Welsh skunk named Richards. He's been running some sort of chapel over at New Barnet for the last few years, and my poor wife—she never could find the parish church good enough for her—had been going to his damned schism shop for the last twelve-month. It was all that finished her off. Yes; I thrashed *him* the day before yesterday, and I'm not afraid of a summons either. I know him, and he knows I know him."

Old Nixon whispered something in Darnell's ear, and chuckled faintly as he repeated for the third time his formula—

"I thrashed *him* black and blue the day before yesterday."

314

Darnell could only murmur condolences and express his hope that Mrs. Nixon might recover.

The old man shook his head.

"I'm afraid there's no hope of that," he said. "I've had the best advice, but they couldn't do anything, and told me so."

Presently he asked to see his niece, and Darnell went out and prepared Mary as well as he could. She could scarcely take in the news that her aunt was a hopeless maniac, for Mrs. Nixon, having been extremely stupid all her days, had naturally succeeded in passing with her relations as typically sensible. With the Reynolds family, as with the great majority of us, want of imagination is always equated with sanity, and though many of us have never heard of Lombroso[16] we are his ready-made converts. We have always believed that poets are mad, and if statistics unfortunately show that few poets have really been inhabitants of lunatic asylums, it is soothing to learn that nearly all poets have had whooping-cough, which is doubtless, like intoxication, a minor madness.

"But is it really true?" she asked at length. "Are you certain uncle is not deceiving you? Aunt seemed so sensible always."

She was helped at last by recollecting that Aunt Marian used to get up very early of mornings, and then they went into the drawing-room and talked to the old man. His evident kindliness and honesty grew upon Mary, in spite of a lingering belief in her aunt's fables, and when he left, it was with a promise to come to see them again.

Mrs. Darnell said she felt tired, and went to bed; and Darnell returned to the garden and began to pace to and fro, collecting his thoughts. His immeasurable relief at the intelligence that, after all, Mrs. Nixon was not coming to live with them taught him that, despite his submission, his dread of the event had been very great. The weight was removed, and now he was free to consider his life without reference to the grotesque intrusion that he had feared. He sighed for joy, and as he paced to and fro he savoured the scent of the night, which, though it came faintly to him in that brick-bound suburb, summoned to his mind across many years the odour of the world at night as he had known it in that short sojourn of his boyhood; the odour that rose from the earth when the flame of the sun had gone down beyond the mountain, and the afterglow had paled in the sky and on the fields. And as he recovered as best he could these lost dreams of an enchanted land, there came to him other images of his childhood, forgotten and yet not forgotten, dwelling unheeded in dark places of the memory, but ready to be summoned forth. He remembered one fantasy that had long haunted him. As he lay half asleep in the forest on one hot afternoon of that memorable visit to the country, he had "made believe" that a little companion had come to him out of the blue mists and the green light beneath the leaves—a white girl with long black hair, who had played with him and whispered her secrets in his ear, as his father lay sleeping under a tree; and from that summer afternoon, day by day, she had been beside him; she had visited him in the wilderness of London, and even in recent years there had come to him now and again the sense of her presence, in the midst of the heat and turmoil of the City. The last visit he remembered well; it was a few weeks before he married, and from the depths of some futile task he had looked up with puzzled eyes, wondering why the close air suddenly grew scented with green leaves, why the murmur of the trees and the wash of the river on the reeds came to his ears; and then that sudden rapture to which he had given a name and an individuality possessed him utterly. He knew then how the dull flesh of man can be like fire; and now, looking back from a new standpoint on this and other experiences, he realized how all that was real in his life had been unwelcomed, uncherished by him, had come to him, perhaps, in virtue of merely negative qualities on his part. And yet, as he reflected, he saw that there had been a chain of witnesses all through his life: again and again voices had whispered in his ear words in a strange language that he now recognized as his native tongue; the common street had not been lacking in visions of the true land of his birth; and in all the passing and repassing of the world he saw that there had been emissaries ready to guide his feet on the way of the great journey.

A week or two after the visit of Mr. Nixon, Darnell took his annual holiday.

There was no question of Walton-on-the-Naze, or of anything of the kind, as he quite agreed with his wife's longing for some substantial sum put by against the evil day. But the weather was still fine, and he lounged away the time in his garden beneath the tree, or he sauntered out on long aimless walks in the western purlieus of London, not unvisited by that old sense of some great ineffable beauty, concealed by the dim and dingy veils of grey interminable streets. Once, on a day of heavy rain he went to the "box-room," and began to turn over the papers in the old hair trunk—scraps and odds and ends of family history, some of them in his father's handwriting, others in faded ink, and there were a few ancient pocket-books, filled with manuscript of a still earlier time, and in these the ink was glossier and blacker than any writing fluids supplied by stationers of later days. Darnell had hung up the portrait of the ancestor in this room, and had bought a solid kitchen table and a chair; so that Mrs. Darnell, seeing him looking over his old documents, half thought of naming the room "Mr. Darnell's study." He had not glanced at these relics of his family for many years, but from the hour when the rainy morning sent him to them, he remained constant to research till the end of the holidays. It was a new interest, and he began to fashion in his mind a faint picture of his forefathers, and of their life in that grey old house in the river valley, in the western land of wells and streams and dark and ancient woods. And there were stranger things than mere notes on family history amongst that odd litter of old disregarded papers, and when he went back to his work in the City some of the men fancied that he was in some vague manner changed in appearance; but he only laughed when they asked him where he had been and what he had been doing with himself. But Mary noticed that every evening he spent at least an hour in the box-room; she was rather sorry at the waste of time involved in reading old papers about dead people. And one afternoon, as they were out together on a somewhat dreary walk towards Acton, Darnell stopped at a hopeless second-hand bookshop, and after scanning the rows of shabby books in the window, went in and purchased two volumes. They proved to be a Latin dictionary and grammar, and she was surprised to hear her husband declare his intention of acquiring the Latin language.

But, indeed, all his conduct impressed her as indefinably altered; and she began to be a little alarmed, though she could scarcely have formed her fears in words. But she knew that in some way that was all indefined and beyond the grasp of her thought their lives had altered since the summer, and no single thing wore quite the same aspect as before. If she looked out into the dull street with its rare loiterers, it was the same and yet it had altered, and if she opened the window in the early morning the wind that entered came with a changed breath that spoke some message that she could not understand. And day by day passed by in the old course, and not even the four walls were altogether familiar, and the voices of men and women sounded with strange notes, with the echo, rather, of a music that came over unknown hills. And day by day as she went about her household work, passing from shop to shop in those dull streets that were a network, a fatal labyrinth of grey desolation on every side, there came to her sense half-seen images of some other world, as if she walked in a dream, and every moment must bring her to light and to awakening, when the grey should fade, and regions long desired should appear in glory. Again and again it seemed as if that which was hidden would be shown even to the sluggish testimony of sense; and as she went to and fro from street to street of that dim and weary suburb, and looked on those grey material walls, they seemed as if a light glowed behind them, and again and again the mystic fragrance of incense was blown to her nostrils from across the verge of that world which is not so much impenetrable as ineffable, and to her ears came the dream of a chant that spoke of hidden choirs about all her ways. She struggled against these impressions, refusing her assent to the testimony of them, since all the pressure of credited opinion for three hundred years has been directed towards stamping out real knowledge, and so effectually has this been accomplished that we can only recover the truth through much anguish. And so Mary passed the days in a strange perturbation, clinging to common things and common thoughts, as if she feared that one morning she would wake up in an unknown world to a changed life. And Edward Darnell went day by day to his labour and returned in the evening, always with that shining of light within his eyes and upon his face, with the gaze of wonder that was greater day by day, as if for him the veil grew thin and soon would disappear.

From these great matters both in herself and in her husband Mary shrank back, afraid, perhaps, that if she began the question the answer might be too wonderful. She rather taught herself to be troubled over little things; she asked herself what attraction there could be in the old records over which she supposed Edward to be poring night after night in the cold room upstairs. She had glanced over the papers at Darnell's invitation, and could see but little interest in them; there were one or two sketches, roughly done in pen and ink, of the old house in the west: it looked a shapeless and fantastic place, furnished with strange pillars and stranger ornaments on the projecting porch; and on one side a roof dipped down almost to the earth, and in the centre there was something that might almost be a tower rising above the rest of the building. Then there were documents that seemed all names and dates, with here and there a coat of arms done in the margin, and she came upon a string of uncouth Welsh names linked together by the word "ap" in a chain that looked endless. There was a paper covered with signs and figures that meant nothing to her, and then there were the pocket-books, full of old-fashioned writing, and much of it in Latin, as her husband told her—it was a collection as void of significance as a treatise on conic sections, so far as Mary was concerned. But night after night Darnell shut himself up with the musty rolls, and more than ever when he rejoined her he bore upon his face the blazonry of some great adventure. And one night she asked him what interested him so much in the papers he had shown her.

He was delighted with the question. Somehow they had not talked much together for the last few weeks, and he began to tell her of the records of the old race from which he came, of the old strange house of grey stone between the forest and the river. The family went back and back, he said, far into the dim past, beyond the Normans, beyond the Saxons, far into the Roman days, and for many hundred years they had been petty kings, with a strong fortress high up on the hill, in the heart of the forest; and even now the great mounds remained, whence one could look through the trees towards the mountain on one side and across the yellow sea on the other. The real name of the family was not Darnell; that was assumed by one Iolo ap Taliesin ap Iorwerth in the sixteenth century—why, Darnell did not seem to understand. And then he told her how the race had dwindled in prosperity, century by century, till at last there was nothing left but the grey house and a few acres of land bordering the river.

"And do you know, Mary," he said, "I suppose we shall go and live there some day or other. My great-uncle, who has the place now, made money in business when he was a young man, and I believe he will leave it all to me. I know I am the only relation he has. How strange it would be. What a change from the life here."

"You never told me that. Don't you think your great-uncle might leave his house and his money to somebody he knows really well? You haven't seen him since you were a little boy, have you?"

"No; but we write once a year. And from what I have heard my father say, I am sure the old man would never leave the house out of the family. Do you think you would like it?"

"I don't know. Isn't it very lonely?"

"I suppose it is. I forget whether there are any other houses in sight, but I don't think there are any at all near. But what a change! No City, no streets, no people passing to and fro; only the sound of the wind and the sight of the green leaves and the green hills, and the song of the voices of the earth." . . . He checked himself suddenly, as if he feared that he was about to tell some secret that must not yet be uttered; and indeed, as he spoke of the change from the little street in Shepherd's Bush to that ancient house in the woods of the far west, a change seemed already to possess himself, and his voice put on the modulation of an antique chant. Mary looked at him steadily and touched his arm, and he drew a long breath before he spoke again.

"It is the old blood calling to the old land," he said. "I was forgetting that I am a clerk in the City."

It was, doubtless, the old blood that had suddenly stirred in him; the resurrection of the old spirit that for many centuries had been faithful to secrets that are now disregarded by most of us, that now day by day was quickened more and more in his heart, and grew so strong that it was hard to conceal. He was indeed almost in the position of the man in the tale, who, by a sudden electric shock, lost the vision of the things about him in the London streets, and gazed instead upon the sea and shore of an island in the Antipodes; for Darnell only clung with an effort to the interests and the atmosphere which, till lately, had seemed all the world to him; and the grey house and the wood and the river, symbols of the other sphere, intruded as it were into the landscape of the London suburb.

But he went on, with more restraint, telling his stories of far-off ancestors, how one of them, the most remote of all, was called a saint, and was supposed to possess certain mysterious secrets often alluded to in the papers as the "Hidden Songs of Iolo Sant." And then with an abrupt transition he recalled memories of his father and of the strange, shiftless life in dingy lodgings in the backwaters of London, of the dim stucco streets that were his first recollections, of forgotten squares in North London, and of the figure of his father, a grave bearded man who seemed always in a dream, as if he too sought for the vision of a land beyond the strong walls, a land where there were deep orchards and many shining hills, and fountains and water-pools gleaming under the leaves of the wood.

"I believe my father earned his living," he went on, "such a living as he did earn, at the Record Office and the British Museum. He used to hunt up things for lawyers and country parsons who wanted old deeds inspected. He never made much, and we were always moving from one lodging to another—always to out-of-the-way places where everything seemed to have run to seed. We never knew our neighbours—we moved too often for that—but my father had about half a dozen friends, elderly men like himself, who used to come to see us pretty often; and then, if there was any money, the lodging-house servant would go out for beer, and they would sit and smoke far into the night.

"I never knew much about these friends of his, but they all had the same look, the look of longing for something hidden. They talked of mysteries that I never understood, very little of their own lives, and when they did speak of ordinary affairs one could tell that they thought such matters as money and the want of it were unimportant trifles. When I grew up and went into the City, and met other young fellows and heard their way of talking, I wondered whether my father and his friends were not a little queer in their heads; but I know better now."

So night after night Darnell talked to his wife, seeming to wander aimlessly from the dingy lodging-houses, where he had spent his boyhood in the company of his father and the other seekers, to the old house hidden in that far western valley, and the old race that had so long looked at the setting of the sun over the mountain. But in truth there was one end in all that he spoke, and Mary felt that beneath his words, however indifferent they might seem, there was hidden a purpose, that they were to embak on a great and marvellous adventure.

So day by day the world became more magical; day by day the work of separation was being performed, the gross accidents were being refined away. Darnell neglected no instruments that might be useful in the work; and now he neither lounged at home on Sunday mornings, nor did he accompany his wife to the Gothic blasphemy which pretended to be a church. They had discovered a little church of another fashion in a back street, and Darnell, who had found in one of the old notebooks the maxim *Incredibilia sola Credenda*,[17] soon perceived how high and glorious a thing was that service at which he assisted. Our stupid ancestors taught us that we could become wise by studying books on "science," by meddling with test-tubes, geological specimens, microscopic preparations, and the like; but they who have cast off these follies know that they must read not "science" books, but mass-books, and that the soul is made wise by the contemplation of mystic ceremonies and elaborate and curious rites. In such things Darnell found a wonderful mystery language, which spoke at once more secretly and more directly than the formal creeds; and he saw that, in a sense, the whole world is but a great ceremony or sacrament, which teaches under visible forms a hidden and transcendent doctrine. It was thus that he found in the ritual of the church a perfect image of the world; an image purged, exalted, and illuminate, a holy house built up of shining and translucent stones, in which the burning torches were more significant than the wheeling stars, and the fuming incense was a more certain token than the rising of the mist. His soul went forth with the albed procession in its white and solemn order, the mystic dance that signifies rapture and a joy above all joys, and when he beheld Love slain and rise again victorious he knew that he witnessed, in a figure, the consummation of all things, the Bridal of all Bridals, the mystery that is beyond all mysteries, accomplished from the foundation of the world. So day by day the house of his life became more magical.

And at the same time he began to guess that if in the New Life there are new and unheard-of joys, there are also new and unheard-of dangers. In his manuscript books which professed to deliver the outer sense of those mysterious "Hidden Songs of Iolo Sant" there was a little chapter that bore the heading: *Fons Sacer non in communem Vsum convertendus est*,[18] and by diligence, with much use of the grammar and dictionary, Darnell was able to construe the by no means complex Latin of his ancestor. The special book which contained the chapter in question was one of the most singular in the collection, since it bore the title *Terra de Iolo*,[19] and on the surface, with an ingenious concealment of its real symbolism, it affected to give an account of the orchards, fields, woods, roads, tenements, and waterways in the possession of Darnell's ancestors. Here, then, he read of the Holy Well, hidden in the Wistman's Wood—*Sylva Sapientum*[20]—"a fountain of abundant water, which no heats of summer can ever dry, which no flood can ever defile, which is as a water of life, to them that thirst for life, a stream of cleansing to them that would be pure, and a medicine of such healing virtue that by it, through the might of God and the intercession of His saints, the most grievous wounds are made whole." But the water of this well was to be kept sacred perpetually, it was not to be used for any common purpose, nor to satisfy any bodily thirst; but ever to be esteemed as holy, "even as the water which the priest hath hallowed." And in the margin a comment in a later hand taught Darnell something of the meaning of these prohibitions. He was warned not to use the Well of Life as a mere luxury of mortal life, as a new sensation, as a means of making the insipid cup of everyday existence more palatable. "For," said the commentator, "we are not called to sit as the spectators in a theatre, there to watch the play performed before us, but we are rather summoned to stand in the very scene itself, and there fervently to enact our parts in a great and wonderful mystery."

Darnell could quite understand the temptation that was thus indicated. Though he had gone but a little way on the path, and had barely tested the overrunnings of that mystic well, he was already aware of the enchantment that was transmuting all the world about him, informing his life with a strange significance and romance. London seemed a city of the Arabian Nights, and its labyrinths of streets an enchanted maze; its long avenues of lighted lamps were as starry systems, and its immensity became for him an image of the endless universe. He could well imagine how pleasant it might be to linger in such a world as this, to sit apart and dream, beholding the strange pageant played before him; but the Sacred Well was not for common use, it was for the cleansing of the soul, and the healing of the grievous wounds of the spirit. There must be yet another transformation: London had become Bagdad; it must at last be transmuted to Syon, or in the phrase of one of his old documents, the City of the Cup.

And there were yet darker perils which the Iolo MSS. (as his father had named the collection) hinted at more or less obscurely. There were suggestions of an awful region which the soul might enter, of a transmutation that was unto death, of evocations which could summon the utmost forces of evil from their dark places—in a word, of that sphere which is represented to most of us under the crude and somewhat childish symbolism of Black Magic. And here again he was not altogether without a dim comprehension of what was meant. He found himself recalling an odd incident that had happened long ago, which had remained all the years in his mind unheeded, amongst the many insignificant recollections of his childhood, and now rose before him, clear and distinct and full of meaning. It was on that memorable visit to the old house in the west, and the whole scene returned, with its smallest events, and the voices seemed to sound in his ears. It was a grey, still day of heavy heat that he remembered: he had stood on the lawn after breakfast, and wondered at the great peace and silence of the world. Not a leaf stirred in the trees on the lawn, not a whisper came ftom the myriad leaves of the wood; the flowers gave out sweet and heavy odours as if they breathed the dreams of the summer night; and far down the valley, the winding river was like dim silver under that dim and silvery sky, and the far hills and woods and fields vanished in the mist. The stillness of the air held him as with a charm; he leant all the morning against the rails that parted the lawn from the meadow, breathing the mystic breath of summer, and watching the fields brighten as with a sudden blossoming of shining flowers as the high mist grew thin for a moment before the hidden sun. As he watched thus, a man weary with heat, with some glance of horror in his eyes, passed him on his way to the house; but he stayed at his post till the old bell in the turret rang, and they dined all together, masters and servants, in the dark cool room that looked towards the still leaves of the wood. He could see that his uncle was upset about something, and when they had finished dinner he heard him tell his father that there was trouble at a farm; and it was settled that they should all drive over in the afternoon to some place with a strange name. But when the time came Mr. Darnell was too deep in old books and tobacco smoke to be stirred from his corner, and Edward and his uncle went alone in the dog-cart. They drove swiftly down the narrow lane, into the road that followed the winding river, and crossed the bridge at Caermaen by the mouldering Roman walls, and then, skirting the deserted, echoing village, they came out on a broad white turnpike road, and the limestone dust followed them like a cloud. Then, suddenly, they turned to the north by such a road as Edward had never seen before. It was so narrow that there was barely room for the cart to pass, and the footway was of rock, and the banks rose high above them as they slowly climbed the long, steep way, and the untrimmed hedges on either side shut out the light. And the ferns grew thick and green upon the banks, and hidden wells dripped down upon them; and the old man told him how the lane in winter was a torrent of swirling water, so that no one could pass by it. On they went, ascending and then again descending, always in that deep hollow under the wild woven boughs, and the boy wondered vainly what the country was like on either side. And now the air grew darker, and the hedge on one bank was but the verge of a dark and rustling wood, and the grey limestone rocks had changed to dark-red earth flecked with green patches and veins of marl, and suddenly in the stillness from the depths of the wood a bird began to sing a melody that charmed the heart into another world, that sang to the child's soul of the blessed faery realm beyond the woods of the earth, where the wounds of man are healed. And so at last, after many turnings and windings, they came to a high bare land where the lane broadened out into a kind of common, and along the edge of this place there were scattered three or four old cottages, and one of them was a little tavern. Here they stopped, and a man came out and tethered the tired horse to a post and gave him water; and old Mr. Darnell took the child's hand and led him by a path across the fields. The boy could see the country now, but it was all a strange, undiscovered land; they were in the heart of a wilderness of hills and valleys that he had never looked upon, and they were going down a wild, steep hillside, where the narrow path wound in and out amidst gorse and towering bracken, and the sun gleaming out for a moment, there was a gleam of white water far below in a narrow valley where a little brook poured and rippled from stone to stone. They went down the hill, and through a brake, and then, hidden in dark-green orchards, they came upon a long, low whitewashed house, with a stone roof strangely coloured by the growth of moss and lichens. Mr. Darnell knocked at a heavy oaken door, and they came into a dim room where but little light entered through the thick glass in the deep-set window. There were heavy beams in the ceiling, and a great fire-place sent out an odour of burning wood that Darnell never forgot, and the room seemed to him full of women who talked all together in frightened tones. Mr. Darnell beckoned to a tall, grey old man, who wore corduroy knee-breeches, and the boy, sitting on a high straightbacked chair, could see the old man and his uncle passing to and fro across the window-panes, as they walked together on the garden path. The women stopped their talk for a moment, and one of them brought him a glass of milk and an apple from some cold inner chamber; and then, suddenly, from a room above there rang out a shrill and terrible shriek, and then, in a young girl's voice, a more terrible song. It was not like anything the child had ever heard, but as the man recalled it to his memory, he knew to what song it might be compared—to a certain chant indeed that summons the angels and archangels to assist in the great Sacrifice. But as this song chants of the heavenly army, so did that seem to summon all the hierarchy of evil, the hosts of Lilith and Samael;[21] and the words that rang out with such awful modulations—*neumata inferorum*[22]—were in some unknown tongue that few men have ever heard on earth.

The women glared at one another with horror in their eyes, and he saw one or two of the oldest of them clumsily making an old sign upon their breasts. Then they began to speak again, and he remembered fragments of their talk.

"She has been up there," said one, pointing vaguely over her shoulder.

"She'd never know the way," answered another. "They be all gone that went there."

"There be nought there in these days."

"How can you tell that, Gwenllian? 'Tis not for us to say that."

"My great-grandmother did know some that had been there," said a very old woman. "She told me how they was taken afterwards."

And then his uncle appeared at the door, and they went their way as they had come. Edward Darnell never heard any more of it, nor whether the girl died or recovered from her strange attack; but the scene had haunted his mind in boyhood, and now the recollection of it came to him with a certain note of warning, as a symbol of dangers that might be in the way.

It would be impossible to carry on the history of Edward Darnell and of Mary his wife to a greater length, since from this point their legend is full of impossible events, and seems to put on the semblance of the stories of the Graal. It is certain, indeed, that in this world they changed their lives, like King Arthur, but this is a work which no chronicler has cared to describe with any amplitude of detail. Darnell, it is true, made a little book, partly consisting of queer verse which might have been written by an inspired infant, and partly made up of "notes and exclamations" in an odd dog-Latin which he had picked up from the "Iolo MSS.", but it is to be feared that this work, even if published in its entirety, would cast but little light on a perplexing story. He called this piece of literature "In Exitu Israel,"[23] and wrote on the title page the motto, doubtless of his own composition, "*Nunc certe scio quod omnia legenda; omnes historiæ, omnes fabulæ, omnis Scriptura sint de ME narrata.*"[24] It is only too evident that his Latin was not learnt at the feet of Cicero; but in this dialect he relates the great history of the "New Life" as it was manifested to him. The "poems" are even stranger. One, headed (with an odd reminiscence of old-fashioned books) "Lines written on looking down from a Height in London on a Board School suddenly lit up by the Sun" begins thus:—

> One day when I was all alone
> I found a wondrous little stone,
> It lay forgotten on the road
> Far from the ways of man's abode.
> When on this stone mine eyes I cast
> I saw my Treasure found at last.
> I pressed it hard against my face,
> I covered it with my embrace,
> I hid it in a secret place.
> And every day I went to see
> This stone that was my ecstasy;
> And worshipped it with flowers rare,
> And secret words and sayings fair.
> O stone, so rare and red and wise,
> O fragment of far Paradise,
> O Star, whose light is life! O Sea,
> Whose ocean is infinity!
> Thou art a fire that ever burns,
> And all the world to wonder turns;
> And all the dust of the dull day
> By thee is changed and purged away,
> So that, where'er I look, I see
> A world of a Great Majesty.
> The sullen river rolls all gold,
> The desert park's a faery wold,
> When on the trees the wind is borne
> I hear the sound of Arthur's horn
> I see no town of grim grey ways,
> But a great city all ablaze
> With burning torches, to light up
> The pinnacles that shrine the Cup.
> Ever the magic wine is poured,
> Ever the Feast shines on the board,
> Ever the song is borne on high
> That chants the holy Magistry—
> Etc. etc. etc.

From such documents as these it is clearly impossible to gather any very definite information. But on the last page Darnell has written—

"So I awoke from a dream of a London suburb, of daily labour, of weary, useless little things; and as my eyes were opened I saw that I was in an ancient wood, where a clear well rose into grey film and vapour beneath a misty, glimmering heat. And a form came towards me from the hidden places of the wood, and my love and I were united by the well."

THE BOWMEN

"The Bowmen" first appeared in the London Evening News (September 29, 1914), and was collected in *The Angels of Mons: The Bowmen and Other Legends of the War* (London: Simpkin, Marshall, Hamilton, Kent & Co., 1915), a slim volume of Machen's war tales and sketches that was meant to capitalize on the notoriety of "The Bowmen." The story's setting in time and place is quite vague, but it appears to deal with the very early stages of World War I. By late August 1914, the French and British forces were forced to retreat precipitously toward Paris in the wake of the advance of the German army; but in the First Battle of the Marne (September 5–12), tactical errors by the Germans allowed the Allies to hold their ground and force a German retreat, thereby robbing the Germans of a quick victory. In his long introduction to *The Angels of Mons* (see Appendix 2), Machen suggests that the tale was inspired by the Battle of Mons (August 23–24, 1914), the first battle in which the British fought the Germans, during which the British were forced to retreat; Machen also recounts the manner in which his story was accepted as a true account in spite of his repeated statements to the contrary, as various parties believed that the story dealt with "angels" (not ghostly archers, as in the story) coming to the rescue of British troops. Accordingly, the "legend" of the "angels of Mons" was born.

THE BOWMEN

It was during the Retreat of the Eighty Thousand, and the authority of the Censorship is sufficient excuse for not being more explicit. But it was on the most awful day of that awful time, on the day when ruin and disaster came so near that their shadow fell over London far away; and, without any certain news, the hearts of men failed within them and grew faint; as if the agony of the army in the battlefield had entered into their souls.

On this dreadful day, then, when three hundred thousand men in arms with all their artillery swelled like a flood against the little English company, there was one point above all other points in our battle line that was for a time in awful danger, not merely of defeat, but of utter annihilation. With the permission of the Censorship and of the military expert, this corner may, perhaps, be described as a salient, and if this angle were crushed and broken, then the English force as a whole would be shattered, the Allied left would be turned, and Sedan would inevitably follow.

All the morning the German guns had thundered and shrieked against this corner, and against the thousand or so of men who held it. The men joked at the shells, and found funny names for them, and had bets about them, and greeted them with scraps of music-hall songs. But the shells came on and burst, and tore good Englishmen limb from limb, and tore brother from brother, and as the heat of the day increased so did the fury of that terrific cannonade. There was no help, it seemed. The English artillery was good, but there was not nearly enough of it; it was being steadily battered into scrap iron.

There comes a moment in a storm at sea when people say to one another, "It is at its worst; it can blow no harder," and then there is a blast ten times more fierce than any before it. So it was in these British trenches.

The Bowmen

There were no stouter hearts in the whole world than the hearts of these men; but even they were appalled as this seven-times-heated hell of the German cannonade fell upon them and overwhelmed them and destroyed them. And at this very moment they saw from their trenches that a tremendous host was moving against their lines. Five hundred of the thousand remained, and as far as they could see the German infantry was pressing on against them, column upon column, a grey world of men, ten thousand of them, as it appeared afterwards.

There was no hope at all. They shook hands, some of them. One man improvised a new version of the battle-song, "Good-bye, good-bye to Tipperary," ending with "And we shan't get there."[1] And they all went on firing steadily. The officers pointed out that such an opportunity for high-class, fancy shooting might never occur again; the Germans dropped line after line; the Tipperary humorist asked, "What price Sidney Street?"[2] And the few machine guns did their best. But everybody knew it was of no use. The dead grey bodies lay in companies and battalions, as others came on and on and on, and they swarmed and stirred and advanced from beyond and beyond.

"World without end. Amen," said one of the British soldiers with some irrelevance as he took aim and fired. And then he remembered—he says he cannot think why or wherefore—a queer vegetarian restaurant in London where he had once or twice eaten eccentric dishes of cutlets made of lentils and nuts that pretended to be steak. On all the plates in this restaurant there was printed a figure of St. George in blue, with the motto, *Adsit Anglis Sanctus Georgius*—May St. George be a present help to the English. This soldier happened to know Latin and other useless things, and now, as he fired at his man in the grey advancing mass—300 yards away—he uttered the pious vegetarian motto. He went on firing to the end, and at last Bill on his right had to clout him cheerfully over the head to make him stop, pointing out as he did so that the King's ammunition cost money and was not lightly to be wasted in drilling funny patterns into dead Germans.

For as the Latin scholar uttered his invocation he felt something between a shudder and an electric shock pass through his body. The roar of the battle died down in his ears to a gentle murmur; instead of it, he says, he heard a great voice and a shout louder than a thunder-peal crying, "Array, array, array!"

His heart grew hot as a burning coal, it grew cold as ice within him, as it seemed to him that a tumult of voices answered to his summons. He heard, or seemed to hear, thousands shouting: "St. George! St. George!"

"Ha! messire; ha! sweet Saint, grant us good deliverance!"

"St. George for merry England!"

"Harow! Harow! Monseigneur St. George, succour us."

"Ha! St. George! Ha! St. George! a long bow and a strong bow."

"Heaven's Knight, aid us!"

And as the soldier heard these voices he saw before him, beyond the trench, a long line of shapes, with a shining about them. They were like men who drew the bow, and with another shout, their cloud of arrows flew singing and tingling through the air towards the German hosts.

* * *

The other men in the trench were firing all the while. They had no hope; but they aimed just as if they had been shooting at Bisley.

Suddenly one of them lifted up his voice in the plainest English.

"Gawd help us!" he bellowed to the man next to him, "but we're blooming marvels! Look at those grey . . . gentlemen, look at them! D'ye see them? They're not going down in dozens, nor in 'undreds; it's thousands, it is. Look! look! There's a regiment gone while I'm talking to ye."

"Shut it!" the other soldier bellowed, taking aim, "what are ye gassing about?"

But he gulped with astonishment even as he spoke, for, indeed, the grey men were falling by the thousands. The English could hear the guttural scream of the German officers, the crackle of their revolvers as they shot the reluctant; and still line after line crashed to the earth.

* * *

All the while the Latin-bred soldier heard the cry:

"Harow! Harow! Monseigneur, dear saint, quick to our aid! St. George help us!"

"High Chevalier, defend us!"

The singing arrows fled so swift and thick that they darkened the air; the heathen horde melted from before them.

* * *

"More machine guns!" Bill yelled to Tom.

"Don't hear them," Tom yelled back. "But, thank God, anyway, they've got it in the neck."

THE BOWMEN

In fact, there were ten thousand dead German soldiers left before that salient of the English army, and consequently there was no Sedan. In Germany, a country ruled by scientific principles, the Great General Staff decided that the contemptible English must have employed shells containing an unknown gas of a poisonous nature, as no wounds were discernible on the bodies of the dead German soldiers. But the man who knew what nuts tasted like when they called themselves steak knew also that St. George had brought his Agincourt Bowmen[3] to help the English.

APPENDIX
1

Introduction to *The Three Impostors* (1923)

In the course of a quarter of a century—and a little more—I have received a good many letters of serious enquiry about "The Three Impostors." My correspondents ask me in various terms and turns of phrase whether there is any foundation for the strange circumstances and tales narrated in the book. Only the other day an American clergyman wrote to me as follows: "There are few priests," he says, "that have not stumbled upon the unknown as dramatically as you depict it, not as realistically. Of course a thousand reasons prevent their publication. I know that most of these stories are very much coloured; but there are truths, stranger than even the most vivid fiction. Is it possible that these stories have, as we say, a fundamentum in re? I would be pleased indeed to know from you if I am not making too bold?"

The letter is typical of many others. I began to get them pretty soon after "The Three Impostors" was published in 1895. Then, on the whole, I was rather displeased than pleased at the question. We have our funny little ways, our amusing little points of pride and dignity, all of us, authors as well as the rest, and I was strongly inclined to resent the implication that I had embroidered rather than invented. I remember when "The Great God Pan" was issued, a friend of mine said, "I suppose it is just an old legend that was going down in your part of the country when you were a boy?" I was quite cross. I said to myself, and I daresay to others, "These barbarians can't bear to acknowledge that anybody can 'make up' anything. They know they couldn't do anything of the kind themselves and the suggestion that, for all that, the thing is done now and again annoys them." I was proud of having invented "The Great God Pan": I was not going to have the credit of that fact taken away on the strength of a legend which never existed. And so with "The Three Impostors." I wanted to impress on all enquirers that the whole thing came out of my head—I forgot to add "and Stevenson's"—and that I had taken a great deal of trouble over the tales, and that there was no foundation in fact for anything between the two covers of the book. So far, from the point of view of the touchy author; but if this had been put out of the case and I had been asked whether I thought that anything like the experience of Professor Gregg—see the "Novel of the Black Seal"—had occurred in actuality, I should have said, "Of course not!" And if a similar question had been put as to the "Novel of the White Powder," I am afraid I should have replied, "Don't talk such damned nonsense!"

And farther, if I had been asked about the general atmosphere of the book, the Arabian Nightish aspect of London, the strange encounters, the stranger disappearances, I should certainly have stated with some firmness that I had never come across anything of the sort, that no queer characters had ever crossed my track, that my walks about Soho and Islington, Barnsbury and Clerkenwell were void of all adventures. I would have said, I think, that London streets, like most things, were dull and grey and uninteresting. "And so," I might likely enough have added, "we pretend they are wonderful and enchanting, just because it's delightful to do so, just as children are always pretending and making believe."

That then, was my general attitude on these points in 1895 and for some years afterwards. I was quite sure that there was not and could not be the faintest foundation in fact for any of my tales, and I was quite sure too that London was not a bit like an Arabian Night. I hardly think that I should be quite so positive today, if I were asked these old questions all over again. So many things have happened since the mid-nineties of the last century.

As to the "Arabian" atmosphere of London, for example, I must admit modifications in my point of view. I think it was in the June of 1900 that I was sitting in the New Lyric Club in Coventry Street, taking tea with a young friend of mine. He was telling me of some singular adventures in which he was then involved. It seemed that he had made a deadly enemy and that, furthermore, this enemy was a notorious

Black Magician. This personage—who is, I may say, an actual personage—was guilty of the most hideous misdeeds.[1] In the pursuit, doubtless, of his favourite art of Black Magic he had entrapped women into his house and had suspended them naked in cupboards, hanging in the air by hooks run through the flesh of their arms. There were other tales of strange horror which I forget. But not this. My friend had offended the magician; I do not think I heard what the offence had been. But he went in dread of his life.

"He has hired a gang down Lambeth way to smash me up and kill me if possible, and he is paying each of them eight-and-six-a day."

I listened stupefied; more stupefied still when I heard of the threatening letters sealed with a "Rosicrucian Seal"[2] that had been received. I can't say whether I believed or disbelieved, or how much I believed and how much I disbelieved. I don't know to this day what relation this queer tale bore to the hard solid facts; though I must say that some years later I myself received a minatory epistle, sealed with a "Rosicrucian Seal" which I have always put down to the credit of the Adept of the Black Art. But I was not bothering about the possible truth or possible falsity of the tale that I had been told; I was thinking of its queerness, of its incongruity with the comfortable chairs of the New Lyric Club, and the view of Coventry Street as seen from the window. I do not think that I realized with whom I had been talking till I got home to my chambers in Verulam Buildings, Gray's Inn. Then I recalled my friend's face and aspect as he told his story; certain phrases came into my mind: "youngish looking man with dark whiskers and spectacles . . . of somewhat timid bearing he is pale, has small black whiskers and wears spectacles. He has rather a timid, almost a frightened expression and looks about him nervously from side to side." And so on, and so on; and it was with a shock that I realized that I had been talking with The Young Man in Spectacles, and that he came out of "The Three Impostors." I must add that I had first met him in a secret Assembly, more harmless than the gatherings of the terrible Lipsins, but quite as queer. The Young Man in Spectacles! It was astounding, but it was undeniable; and the discovery opened my eyes to the fact that Miss Lally had also come up out of the book into my life and was involving me daily in strange adventures, in meetings and encounters that would have charmed the ear of the Caliph Haroun-al-Raschid, relating as she went on her incalculable way the most wonderful and unexpected tales. Miss Lally and The Young Man in Spectacles met more than once in my rooms. Naturally, they did not recognize each other since neither had read my book. But I shall never forget the gravity with which Miss Lally related to the Young Man in Spectacles the

Appendix 1

"Novel of My Aunt, the Enchantress." The aunt, I remember, burned curious gums obtained from the East before rising into the air; and when this operation was to be performed, the room had to be hung round with curtains distant one foot from the walls, and nine inches from the ground. It was, indeed, a sumptuous fable. And, to resume the old manner for a moment: "The Young Man in Spectacles listened with the gravest attention to the history of the Enchanting Aunt, asking many questions of a highly pertinent character, and expressing himself as more particularly satisfied with the singular circumstance of the draperies before the walls of the magic chamber. He took notes on many points, and went away with a countenance which fully expressed the serious nature of the communication which he had received."

Indeed, the tale had been told with such grave earnestness, with such an attention to the smallest minutiæ of detail, that I myself could not help thinking that it was a tale about something, that it was an illumination of some sort of a text. I therefore questioned Miss Lally pretty closely after the departure of the Young Man, whereupon she informed me with happy laughter that all was quite devoid of truth. I think she had an aunt; but that was all the fact; the rest was fiction.

And the insurgence of Miss Lally and the spectacled one from the pages of the printed book was only one, amongst many, extraordinary circumstances that now gathered thick about me. One day, for example, I got a letter from my publisher asking me to call upon him. I went at once, thinking that he wished to commission a new masterpiece. He did not quite want to do that. He explained to me that he had an acquaintance; a distant cousin, if I remember, whose existence annoyed him. I forget what poor Rundle had done, so far as I know nothing in particular, beyond being there, but, anyhow, he offended the publisher and could I help? I was not asked to murder Rundle; I was simply to found a secret society. Into this the poor fellow was to be entrapped, and from the moment of his capture his life was to be a burden to him. The agents of the Society were to beset all his ways; he was to be accosted suddenly in the street and sent on impossible errands; he was to keep appointments with mysterious persons, and these appointments were to end in nothing but annoyance and deep confusion; he was to be terrified by dark threats; doom was to hover like a fiery cloud above his devoted head. Cheerfully, I undertook the business; when in an Arabian Night behave like the Arabian Nighters. But, somehow, the Secret Society was never founded; there must have been some strange intrusion of cool reason into the wild world which I inhabited, that London which I had once thought so commonplace.

It is just possible, it strikes me, that many people have found the

336

odd encounters related in "The Three Impostors," to be of a highly improbable nature. Indeed as I have confessed, I thought so myself as I was writing of them. But experience, the experiences of 1899–1900, thoroughly convinced me that I was wrong. I became subject at this time to the oddest encounters at every turning, in every quarter of London. Total strangers would accost me on one excuse or another. I have counted ten such unexpected meetings in a day. They would babble confused things, narrate odd adventures, things, I would say, without head or tail or reason, and then sink back into the great deep of the London multitude from which they had emerged. These were utter strangers and remained such; but there were others whom I knew, who were equally entertaining and extravagant; but were so only for a certain appointed season. Thus, a gentleman, who is now one of the most serious of men, used to meet me at the Café de l'Europe in Leicester Square and come home with me to my rooms in Verulam Buildings, and there discourse amazing fables, with such eloquence, weightiness, humour, vivacity, that I was convinced of the truth of every word that was uttered. What added to the charm was the fact that after ten o'clock at night my friend seldom spoke English. He addressed me in French, and I may say that, having lived a good deal in Touraine, I have heard few Frenchmen who could speak their native tongue with so pure and winning and perfect an intonation. And I heard from men familiar with German and Italian that he excelled in these tongues also; and a Spaniard could have taught him nothing of Spanish. Well, infinitely to my delight, this personage would come home with me as I say, and tell tales till far into the night. I remember a few scraps of one of these fables. It related to a well known London restaurant which we may call Pergolesi's. My friend, as he puts it, had been one of the fondatori, the earliest customers of the establishment. There were others with him, many of them well known, even famous men, in later years.

"We noticed," the story went on, "night after night, a very beautiful woman who sat in a corner, apart by herself. There was something entrancing, something almost mystic about her beauty. No one knew who she was. Somehow I succeeded—I need not trouble you with an account of the little stratagems that I may have employed—I succeeded in making her acquaintance. We became, shall I say, friends? After a few months I had reason to suppose that she was a secret agent of the Russian Government. I found myself beset with hints, with half-expressed questions. I parried them as well as I could. At last I discovered that the continuance of the lady's favour depended on my willingness to betray the secrets of my country. I refused; in spite of tears, prayers, endearments; I refused.

Appendix 1

"That night I was sitting in our drawing-room. I was in an arm-chair, facing a mirror, and in this mirror I could see reflected the curtains hanging across the entrance to an inner room. Suddenly, the lady appeared, parting the curtains. Her feet were bare. I could not hear her, but I saw her slowly advancing into the room. One hand was raised; in it there was a revolver, levelled at my head. I hardly knew what I did, but I cried out, 'Au moins, madame, tirez juste!'

"She burst into tears and the revolver fell from her hand. I never saw her from that night. She fled!"

I think it was some years before I began to hesitate to myself about this adventure. Indeed, for all I know, every word of it may be true. But I have no reason for supposing that my friend was ever acquainted with the secrets of the British Government; so . . . what could he have betrayed, if he had been willing to betray?

Still; that doesn't matter. The point is that for many months my life was more Three-Impostory than "The Three Impostors." I relished all the queer atmosphere of "Arabian" in consequence which I had enjoyed describing, though I didn't believe there ever was or would be anything like it in actuality. I was and am convinced of my error. London will turn into Bagdad in an instant: if you have the true wand of transmutation.

So much for the atmosphere of the framework of "The Three Impostors"; now as to the "foundation in fact" question, where the stories are concerned. This is a much more doubtful and difficult matter. I have attempted to deal with it in a book called "Things Near and Far." Does the impossible ever happen? Well, the utmost I would say is this; that I have had experiences which debar me from returning the absolute negative of earlier years; the years in which I was writing the book and the years afterwards. These experiences of mine were trifling enough but they suggest the possibility of far greater things and far more extraordinary things for those with the necessary qualifications. For, if you think of it, from the scratched pictures of primitive man, the images he drew on the reindeer horn, you may infer all the majesty of pictorial art, all the mighty names and the magistral achievements of the ages. There are, I believe, savage tribes who cannot count beyond ten; yet all the science of numbers is latent in that decade of theirs. The savage scratches, the savage numberings at least prove the possibility of great art and high mathematics; and so I am inclined to urge that the things which I have known may suggest the probable existence of a world very far and remote from the world of common experience.

It may turn out after all that the weavers of fantasy are the veritable realists.

APPENDIX
2

Introduction to *The Angels of Mons* (1915)

I have been asked to write an introduction to the story of "The Bowmen," on its publication in book form together with three other tales of similar fashion. And I hesitate. This affair of "The Bowmen" has been such an odd one from first to last, so many queer complications have entered into it, there have been so many and so divers currents and cross-currents of rumour and speculation concerning it, that I honestly do not know where to begin. I propose, then, to solve the difficulty by apologising for beginning at all.

For, usually and fitly, the presence of an introduction is held to imply that there is something of consequence and importance to be introduced. If, for example, a man has made an anthology of great poetry, he may well write an introduction justifying his principle of selection, pointing out here and there, as the spirit moves him, high beauties and supreme excellencies, discoursing of the magnates and lords and princes of literature, whom he is merely serving as groom of the chamber. Introductions, that is, belong to the masterpieces and classics of the world, to the great and ancient and accepted things; and I am here introducing a short, small story of my own which appeared in *The Evening News* about ten months ago.

I appreciate the absurdity, nay, the enormity of the position in all its grossness. And my excuse for these pages must be this: that though the story itself is nothing, it has yet had such odd and unforeseen consequences and adventures that the tale of them may possess some interest. And then, again, there are certain psychological morals to be drawn from the whole matter of the tale and its sequel of rumours and discussions that are not, I think, devoid of consequence; and so to begin at the beginning.

*   *   *

This was in last August; to be more precise, on the last Sunday of last August. There were terrible things to be read on that hot Sunday morning between meat and mass. It was in *The Weekly Dispatch* that I saw the awful account of the retreat from Mons. I no longer recollect the details; but I have not forgotten the impression that was then made on my mind. I seemed to see a furnace of torment and death and agony and terror seven times heated, and in the midst of the burning was the British Army. In the midst of the flame, consumed by it and yet aureoled in it, scattered like ashes and yet triumphant, martyred and for ever glorious. So I saw our men with a shining about them, so I took these thoughts with me to church, and, I am sorry to say, was making up a story in my head while the deacon was singing the Gospel.

This was not the tale of "The Bowmen." It was the first sketch, as it were, of "The Soldiers' Rest," which is reprinted in this volume. I only wish I had been able to write it as I conceived it. The tale as it stands is, I think, a far better piece of craft than "The Bowmen," but the tale that came to me as the blue incense floated above the Gospel Book on the desk between the tapers: that indeed was a noble story—like all the stories that never get written. I conceived the dead men coming up through the flames and in the flames, and being welcomed in the Eternal Tavern with songs and flowing cups and everlasting mirth. But every man is the child of his age, however much he may hate it; and our popular religion has long determined that jollity is wicked. As far as I can make out modern Protestantism believes that Heaven is something like Evensong in an English cathedral, the service by Stainer[1] and the Dean preaching.[2] For those opposed to dogma of any kind—even the mildest—I suppose it is held that a Course of Ethical Lectures will be arranged.

Well, I have long maintained that on the whole the average church, considered as a house of preaching, is a much more poisonous place than the average tavern; still, as I say, one's age masters one, and clouds and bewilders the intelligence, and the real story of "The Soldiers' Rest," with its "sonus epulantium in æterno convivio,"[3] was ruined at the moment of its birth, and it was some time later that the actual story, as here printed, got written. And in the meantime the plot of "The Bowmen" occurred to me. Now it has been murmured and hinted and suggested and whispered in all sorts of quarters that before I wrote the tale I had heard something. The most decorative of these legends is also the most precise: "I know for a fact that the whole thing was given him in typescript by a lady-in-waiting." This was not the case; and all vaguer reports to the effect that I had heard some rumours or hints of rumours are equally void of any trace of truth.

Again I apologise for entering so pompously into the minutiæ of my bit of a story, as if it were the lost poems of Sappho; but it appears that the subject interests the public, and I comply with my instructions. I take it, then, that the origins of "The Bowmen" were composite. First of all, all ages and nations have cherished the thought that spiritual hosts may come to the help of earthly arms, that gods and heroes and saints have descended from their high immortal places to fight for their worshippers and clients. Then Kipling's story of the ghostly Indian regiment[4] got in my head and got mixed with the mediævalism that is always there; and so "The Bowmen" was written. I was heartily disappointed with it, I remember, and thought it—as I still think it—an indifferent piece of work. However, I have tried to write for these thirty-five long years, and if I have not become practised in letters, I am at least a past master in the Lodge of Disappointment. Such as it was, "The Bowmen" appeared in *The Evening News* of September 29th, 1914.

Now the journalist does not, as a rule, dwell much on the prospect of fame; and if he be an evening journalist, his anticipations of immortality are bounded by twelve o'clock at night at the latest; and it may well be that those insects which begin to live in the morning and are dead by sunset deem themselves immortal. Having written my story, having groaned and growled over it and printed it, I certainly never thought to hear another word of it. My colleague "The Londoner" praised it warmly to my face, as his kindly fashion is; entering, very properly, a technical caveat as to the language of the battle-cries of the bowmen. "Why should English archers use French terms?" he said. I replied that the only reason was this—that a "Monseigneur" here and there struck me as picturesque; and I reminded him that, as a matter of cold historical fact, most of the archers of Agincourt were mercenaries from Gwent, my native country, who would appeal to Mihangel and to saints not known to the Saxons—Teilo, Iltyd, Dewi, Cadwaladyr Vendigeid. And I thought that that was the first and last discussion of "The Bowmen." But in a few days from its publication the editor of

Appendix 2

The Occult Review wrote to me.[5] He wanted to know whether the story had any foundation in fact. I told him that it had no foundation in fact of any kind or sort; I forget whether I added that it had no foundation in rumour, but I should think not, since to the best of my belief there were no rumours of heavenly interposition in existence at that time. Certainly I had heard of none. Soon afterwards the editor of *Light*[6] wrote asking a like question, and I made him a like reply. It seemed to me that I had stifled any "Bowmen" mythos in the hour of its birth.

A month or two later, I received several requests from editors of parish magazines to reprint the story. I—or, rather, my editor—readily gave permission; and then, after another month or two, the conductor of one of these magazines wrote to me, saying that the February issue containing the story had been sold out, while there was still a great demand for it. Would I allow them to reprint "The Bowmen" as a pamphlet, and would I write a short preface giving the exact authorities for the story? I replied that they might reprint in pamphlet form with all my heart, but that I could not give my authorities, since I had none, the tale being pure invention. The priest wrote again, suggesting—to my amazement—that I must be mistaken, that the main "facts" of "The Bowmen" must be true, that my share in the matter must surely have been confined to the elaboration and decoration of a veridical history. It seemed that my light fiction had been accepted by the congregation of this particular church as the solidest of facts; and it was then that it began to dawn on me that if I had failed in the art of letters, I had succeeded, unwittingly, in the art of deceit. This happened, I should think, some time in April, and the snowball of rumour that was then set rolling has been rolling ever since, growing bigger and bigger, till it is now swollen to a monstrous size.

It was at about this period that variants of my tale began to be told as authentic histories. At first, these tales betrayed their relation to their original. In several of them the vegetarian restaurant appeared, and St. George was the chief character. In one case an officer—name and address missing—said that there was a portrait of St. George in a certain London restaurant, and that a figure, just like the portrait, appeared to him on the battlefield, and was invoked by him, with the happiest results. Another variant—this, I think, never got into print—told how dead Prussians had been found on the battlefield with arrow wounds in their bodies. This notion amused me, as I had imagined a scene, when I was thinking out the story, in which a German general was to appear before the Kaiser to explain his failure to annihilate the English.

"All-Highest," the general was to say, "it is true, it is impossible to deny it. The men were killed by arrows; the shafts were found in their bodies by the burying parties."

I rejected the idea as over-precipitous even for a mere fantasy. I was therefore entertained when I found that what I had refused as too fantastical for fantasy was accepted in certain occult circles as hard fact.

Other versions of the story appeared in which a cloud interposed between the attacking Germans and the defending British. In some examples the cloud served to conceal our men from the advancing enemy; in others, it disclosed shining shapes which frightened the horses of the pursuing German cavalry. St. George, it will be noted, has disappeared—he persisted some time longer in certain Roman Catholic variants—and there are no more bowmen, no more arrows. But so far angels are not mentioned; yet they are ready to appear, and I think that I have detected the machine which brought them into the story.

In "The Bowmen" my imagined soldier saw "a long line of shapes, with a shining about them." And Mr. A. P. Sinnett, writing in the May issue of *The Occult Review*,[7] reporting what he had heard, states that "those who could see said they saw 'a row of shining beings' between the two armies." Now I conjecture that the word "shining" is the link between my tale and the derivative from it. In the popular view shining and benevolent supernatural beings are angels and nothing else, and must be angels, and so, I believe, the Bowmen of my story have become "the Angels of Mons." In this shape they have been received with respect and credence everywhere, or almost everywhere.

And here, I conjecture, we have the key to the large popularity of the delusion—as I think it. We have long ceased in England to take much interest in saints, and in the recent revival of the cultus of St. George, the saint is little more than a patriotic figurehead. And the appeal to the saints to succour us is certainly not a common English practice; it is held Popish by most of our countrymen. But angels, with certain reservations, have retained their popularity, and so, when it was settled that the English army in its dire peril was delivered by angelic aid, the way was clear for general belief, and for the enthusiasms of the religion of the man in the street. And so soon as the legend got the title "The Angels of Mons" it became impossible to avoid it. It permeated the Press: it would not be neglected; it appeared in the most unlikely quarters—in *Truth* and *Town Topics*, *The New Church Weekly* (Swedenborgian) and *John Bull*. The editor of *The Church Times* has exercised a wise reserve: he awaits that evidence which so far is lacking; but in one issue of the paper I noted that the story furnished a text for a sermon, the subject of a letter, and the matter for an article. People send me cuttings from provincial papers containing hot controversy as to the exact nature of the appearances; the "Office Window" of *The Daily Chronicle* suggests scientific explanations of the hallucination; the *Pall Mall* in a note about St. James says he is of the brotherhood of the Bowmen of Mons—this reversion to the bowmen from the angels being possibly due to the strong statements that I have made on the matter. The pulpits both of the Church and of Nonconformity have been busy: Bishop Welldon,[8] Dean Hensley Henson (a disbeliever),[9] Bishop Taylor Smith (the Chaplain-General),[10] and many other clergy have occupied themselves with the matter. Dr. Horton[11] preached about the "angels" at Manchester; Sir Joseph Compton Rickett (President of the National Federation of Free Church Councils)[12] stated that the soldiers at the front had seen visions and dreamed dreams, and had given testimony of powers and principalities fighting for them or against them. Letters come from all the ends of the earth to the Editor of *The Evening News* with theories, beliefs, explanations, suggestions. It is all somewhat wonderful; one can say that the whole affair is a psychological phenomenon of considerable interest, fairly comparable with the great Russian delusion of last August and September.

*　　*　　*

Now it is possible that some persons, judging by the tone of these remarks of mine, may gather the impression that I am a profound disbeliever in the possibility of any intervention of the superphysical order in the affairs of the physical order. They will be mistaken if they make this inference; they will be mistaken if they suppose that I think miracles in Judæa credible but miracles in France or Flanders incredible. I hold no such absurdities. But I confess, very frankly, that I credit none of the "Angels of Mons" legends, partly because I see, or think I see, their derivation from my own idle fiction, but chiefly because I have, so far, not received one jot or tittle of evidence that should dispose me to belief. It is idle, indeed, and foolish enough for a man to say: "I am sure that story is a lie, because the supernatural element enters into it"; here, indeed, we have the maggot writhing in the midst of corrupted offal denying the existence of the sun. But if this fellow be a fool—as he is—equally foolish is he who says, "If the tale has anything of the supernatural it is true, and the less evidence the better"; and I am afraid this tends to be the attitude of many who call themselves occultists. I hope that I shall never get to that frame of mind. So I say, not that super-normal interventions are impossible, not that they have not happened during this war—I know nothing as to that point, one way or the other—but that there is not one atom of evidence (so far) to support the current stories of the angels of Mons. For, be it remarked, these stories are specific stories. They rest on the second, third, fourth, fifth hand stories told by "a soldier," by "an officer," by "a Catholic correspondent," by "a nurse," by any number of anonymous people. Indeed, names have been mentioned. A lady's name has been drawn, most unwarrantably as it appears to me, into the discussion, and I have no doubt that this lady has been subject to a good deal of pestering and annoyance. She has written to the Editor of *The Evening News* denying all knowledge of the supposed miracle. The Psychical Research Society's expert confesses that no real evidence has been proffered to her Society on the matter. And then, to my amazement, she accepts as fact the proposition that some men on the battlefield have been "hallucinated," and proceeds to give the theory of sensory hallucination. She forgets that, by her own showing, there is no reason to suppose that anybody has been hallucinated at all. Someone (unknown) has met a nurse (unnamed) who has talked to a soldier (anonymous) who has seen angels. But *that* is not evidence; and not even Sam Weller at his gayest would have dared to offer it as such in the Court of Common Pleas.[13] So far, then, nothing remotely approaching proof has been offered as to any supernatural intervention during the Retreat from Mons. Proof may come; if so, it will be interesting and more than interesting.

*   *   *

But, taking the affair as it stands at present, how is it that a nation plunged in materialism of the grossest kind has accepted idle rumours and gossip of the supernatural as certain truth? The answer is contained in the question: it is precisely because our whole atmosphere is materialist that we are ready to credit anything—save the truth. Separate a man from good drink, he will swallow methylated spirit with joy. Man is created to be inebriated; to be "nobly wild, not mad." Suffer the Cocoa Prophets and their company to seduce him in body and spirit, and he will get himself stuff that will make him ignobly wild and mad indeed. It took hard, practical men of affairs, business men, advanced thinkers, Freethinkers, to believe in Madame Blavatsky and Mahatmas and the famous message from the Golden Shore: "Judge's plan is right; follow him and *stick*."

And the main responsibility for this dismal state of affairs undoubtedly lies on the shoulders of the majority of the clergy of the Church of England. Christianity, as Mr. W. L. Courtney has so admirably pointed out, is a great Mystery Religion; it is *the* Mystery Religion. Its priests are called to an awful and tremendous hierurgy; its pontiffs are to be the pathfinders, the bridge-makers between the world of sense and the world of spirit. And, in fact, they pass their time in preaching, not the eternal mysteries, but a twopenny morality, in changing the Wine of Angels and the Bread of Heaven into gingerbeer and mixed biscuits: a sorry transubstantiation, a sad alchemy, as it seems to me.

NOTES

Introduction

1. Cited in *Things Near and Far* (New York: Alfred A. Knopf, 1923), pp. 142–43.

2. H. P. Lovecraft, letter to Bernard Austin Dwyer [1932], *Selected Letters IV:1932–1934*, ed. August Derleth and James Turner (Sauk City, WI: Arkham House, 1976), p. 4.

3. *Things Near and Far*, p. 163.

4. *Hieroglyphics: A Note upon Ecstasy in Literature* (1902; rpt. New York: Alfred A. Knopf, 1923), pp. 18–19.

5. "Folklore and Legends of the North," *Literature* 3 (24 September 1898). 272.

The Great God Pan

1. Machen is quoting from the poem "Dotage," by George Herbert (1593–1633), ll. 3–4: "Chases in Arras, gilded emptinesse, / Shadows well mounted, dreams in a career."

2. Digby and Browne Faber are fictitious.

3. See *The Three Impostors*, n. 27.

4. Oswald Crollius (or Croll) (1560?–1609), German chemist and alchemist.

5. Dr. Phillips tells me that he has seen the head in question, and assures me that he has never received such a vivid presentment of intense evil. [Machen's note.]

6. "And the Devil was turned into flesh: and was made Man." A parody of the Latin Credo: *Et [deus] incarnatus est . . . et homo factus est* ("And God was turned into flesh . . . and was made Man").

7. Machen would later use the name Ambrose Meyrick for the protagonist of his novel *The Secret Glory* (1922).

8. A quotation from Solinus' *De Mirabilibus Mundi* 24: "There is universal silence throughout the day, and the place is hidden away and not without horror. It is lit up at night by fires, and a chorus of Aegipans resounds everywhere. The sounds of flutes and the ringing of cymbals are heard along the seacoast." C. Julius Solinus was a Latin grammarian of the fourth century C.E. He is describing an unspecified region in Libya.

9. I.e., the murders of Jack the Ripper in 1888.

10. If written in conventional Latin, the text would read: *Devom [archaic form of Divi] Nodenti Flavius Senilis posuit propter nuptias quas vidit sub umbra.* Nodens was a Celtic deity worshipped in ancient Britain.

The Three Impostors

1. A Triton, in Greek mythology, is the son of Poseidon (god of the sea) and the sea nymph Amphitrite. He was thought to have a human head and shoulders and a fish tail below the waist, and is customarily depicted as blowing on a conch shell.

2. Jeremy Taylor (1613–1667) was an Anglican bishop and the author of numerous significant works of theology.

3. James Russell Lowell (1819–1891), "All Saints," l. 14.

4. The publisher Richard Bentley (1794–1871) published cheap editions of British novelists under the series title "Bentley's Standard Novelists."

5. Machen is alluding to the celebrated dictum of British critic Matthew Arnold (1822–1888) that poetry is a "criticism of life," found

in several essays, including "The Study of Poetry" (*Essays in Criticism: Second Series,* 1888).

6. The term, meaning "pertaining to all the crafts," refers to a warehouse containing a variety of merchandise, chiefly furniture.

7. Tiberius (Tiberius Claudius Nero Caesar, 42 B.C.E.–37 C.E.), became emperor of Rome after the death of the Emperor Augustus in 14 C.E. and ruled until his death.

8. The reference is to a passage in Chapter 24 of Charles Dickens's *A Tale of Two Cities* (1859).

9. Champigny is a commune in the Loir-et-Cher département in north-central France. The province of Touraine was broken up in 1790 to form this and neighboring départements.

10. The reference is to Dalziel's Atlantic Telegraph Company, Ltd., a London-based telegraph company.

11. The town is fictitious.

12. A holothuria is a sea cucumber.

13. *Meditationes de Prima Philosophiae* (1641; Meditations on First Philosophy), a pioneering philosophical work by René Descartes (1596–1650).

14. The *Gesta Romanorum* (Deeds of the Romans), a collection of moral anecdotes in Latin probably assembled in the thirteenth or fourteenth century.

15. This passage suggests that Machen was drawing on his own impoverished life in London in the 1880s: "There was no fireplace in my room, and I was often very cold. . . . In the corner nearest the angle of the wall by the window I kept my provisions, that is to say, a loaf of bread and a canister of green tea. Morning and evening the landlady or 'Marry' would bring me up a tray on which were a plate, a knife, a teapot, a cup and saucer, and a jug of hot water. With the aid of a kettle and a spirit lamp. . . I made the hot water to boil and brewed a great pot of strong green tea." *Far Off Things* (London: Martin Secker, 1922), pp. 116, 118.

16. "What do I know?" This archaic French expression became the motto of the skeptical philosopher and essayist Michel de Montaigne (1533–1592).

17. Latin for "unknown land."

18. I.e., the care of horses' hooves.

19. Humphrey Prideaux (1648–1724), *The Old and New Testament Connected in the History of the Jews and Neighbouring Nations* (1716–18), commonly known as Prideaux's *Connection*.

20. Robert Estienne (1503–1559) and his sons, Henry, Robert, and François, celebrated printers in Renaissance France. "Stephanus" is a Latinization of Estienne.

21. Pomponius Mela (c. 43 c.e.), the earliest known Roman geographer. *De Situ Orbis* (On the Position of the World) is a small treatise in three books.

22. See "The Great God Pan," n. 7. Although Solinus does in fact mention the *"Sixtystone"* (*hexacontalithos: Der Mirabilibus Mundi* 31), the Latin passage is of Machen's invention.

23. The story of Sindbad the Sailor occupies the 538th–566th nights of the *Arabian Nights*.

24. Either William Pitt the Elder, Earl of Chatham (1708–1778), prime minister of England (1757–61, 1766–68), or his son, William Pitt the Younger (1759–1806), prime minister of England (1783–1801, 1804–06).

25. Literally, "no footsteps backward" (i.e., no turning back). A loose quotation from Horace, Epistles 1.1.74–75: *"Quia me vestigia terrent, / Omnia te adversum spectantia, nulla retrorsum."*

26. The Eumenides (literally, "well-meaning women").

27. *Meropes anthropes* (literally, "articulate human beings"), a phrase found frequently in Homer (e.g., *Iliad* 9.340).

28. "Turanian" refers to an ancient language formerly thought to have been used by non-Aryan and non-Semitic peoples in Asia. Cf. Machen's prose-poem "The Turanians" (in *Ornaments in Jade*, 1924). A "Shelta" is "A cryptic jargon used by tinkers, composed partly of Irish or Gaelic words, mostly disguised by inversions or arbitrary alteration of initial consonants" (*Oxford English Dictionary*). Machen uses the term here to denote a language or code understood only by a select band of initiates.

29. Sir Oliver Lodge (1851–1940), British physicist who later destroyed his reputation by credulous belief in spiritualism and telepathy.

30. The London publisher Smith, Elder & Co. paid George Eliot (1819–1880) £7000 for the book rights to her historical novel *Romola* (1862–63).

31. Robert Elsmere (1888), a best-selling novel about a clergyman's loss of faith, written by Mrs. Humphry Ward (Mary Augusta Ward, 1851–1920). There is a difficulty in ascertaining the exact number of copies because of the multitude of different editions that appeared within the first few years of the book's publication.

32. *Tit-Bits* (1881–1984) was a popular British weekly magazine founded by publisher George Newnes.

33. Machen seems to imply that the *Essays* of Sir Francis Bacon (1561–1626) were written for the courtiers of James I (r. 1603–25), but the first edition of the essays (1597) appeared six years before James I's accession. The essays are in fact largely concerned with conduct in public and political life. Expanded editions appeared in 1612 and 1625.

34. *De Re Militari* (On Military Affairs) was a treatise on military techniques and weapons written by Roberto Valturio (1405–1475) probably between 1455 and 1460 and published in 1472.

35. French for "Means of getting ahead." Machen translated a treatise by Beroalde de Verville entitled *Le Moyen de Parvenir* (1610).

36. "One hundred new tales." The play on words in French is impossible to duplicate in English.

37. Machen refers to *The Anatomy of Melancholy* (1621), a lengthy work of philosophical miscellany by Robert Burton (1577–1640).

38. The "Comédie Humaine" is a series of 91 novels written between 1827 and 1847 by Honoré de Balzac (1799–1850). The Rougon-Macquart chronicles were a series of 20 novels (1871–93) written by Emile Zola (1840–1902). Both series were relentlessly realistic, a mode of fiction of which Machen generally disapproved.

39. Latin for "sad path." The phrase is generally taken to refer to the street in Jerusalem that Jesus walked on the way to his crucifixion.

40. A *bibelot* is a finely crafted miniature book.

41. Latin for "Everything resolves into a mystery." The saying was a commonplace among the scholastic philosophers ("Schoolmen")

of the Middle Ages.

42. A paraphrase of John Keats, "On First Looking into Chapman's Homer" (1816), l. 14: "Silent, upon a peak in Darien." The reference is to the explorer Vasco Nuñez de Balboa's first glimpse of the Pacific Ocean in the province of Darién in Panama in 1513.

43. Apparently a reference to Richard Payne Knight (1750–1824), although he wrote no monograph explicitly about the witch-cult. Possibly Machen is referring to his notorious work, *The Worship of Priapus* (1786), about phallic worship in the ancient and medieval period.

44. "Taking up the chalice of the prince of darkness." The Latin phrase is in fact of Machen's own invention.

45. Machen refers to the lending library established by Charles Edward Mudie in 1842.

46. Thomas De Quincey (1785–1859), *Confessions of an English Opium-Eater* (1822).

47. "Live joyously," the title of the first book of *Gargantua et Pantagruel* (1532–64) by François Rabelais (1494?–1553?).

48. Avallaunius is a Latin name coined by Machen. His novel *The Hill of Dreams* was serialized in *Horlick's Magazine* (July–Dec. 1904) under the title "The Garden of Avallaunius."

49. French for "to say sweet nothings."

The Shining Pyramid

1. Gustave Doré (1832–1883), French artist and illustrator best known for his powerfully imaginative illustrations to Dante's *Divine Comedy* (1857–67), the Bible (1866), Milton's *Paradise Lost* (1866), and Coleridge's *Rime of the Ancient Mariner* (1870).

2. Alfred, Lord Tennyson (1809–1892), "The Holy Grail," l. 162 (also 483).

3. Gypsies are frequently referred to as "the Romany" or "the Romany people," derived from the term—*rom* or *rrom*—they use to refer to themselves.

4. In Alexandre Dumas's novel *The Count of Monte Cristo* (1844–46), the Abbé Faria is an Italian priest who is confined in a dungeon

in the island prison of the Château d'If along with the hero, Edmond Dantès.

5. The Greek philosopher Zeno of Elea (5th century B.C.E.) first propounded the paradox of Achilles and the tortoise: If, in a race, a tortoise starts out ahead of Achilles, Achilles will never be able to catch the tortoise because the latter will always have moved forward by the time Achilles has reached the tortoise's former position.

6. A dungeon.

The White People

1. Romanée-Conti was a particularly rare and expensive wine made in the Middle Ages in a small region of that name in the Burgundy district of France.

2. Caterans were fighting men in the Highlands of Scotland. Moss-troopers were disbanded soldiers from the Scottish wars of the seventeenth century.

3. Gilles de Rais (or Retz) (1404–1440) was a French nobleman and soldier who was accused of torturing, raping, and killing dozens, perhaps hundreds, of boys and girls. Some (including Aleister Crowley) believe the charges against Gilles were trumped up.

4. The critic John Gibson Lockhart (1794–1854) wrote a famously hostile review of John Keats's *Endymion* in *Blackwood's Edinburgh Magazine*. His friend Percy Bysshe Shelley later exaggerated the influence of such reviews on Keats's temperament, maintaining that Keats's subsequent decline in health stemmed from his discouragement at the reception of his work.

5. Tophet was originally a location near Jerusalem where the Canaanites were thought to have sacrificed children to Moloch. It was later used as a synonym for Hell.

6. The word *Juggernaut* is an Anglicization of the Indian word *Jagannâtha*, hence would have no etymological connection to the Greek word *Argonaut*.

7. It is not clear what biblical passage Machen is citing. The most celebrated passage relating to charity in the Bible is St. Paul's discussion in 1 Corinthians 13:2f.

8. A reference to the story "Qui sait?" (1890), usually translated as "Who Knows?"

9. In Greek mythology, "Alala!" was the war-god Ares' battle cry.

10. *Tales of the Genii* (1764) is a series of pseudo-Persian tales, written in imitation of the *Arabian Nights* by James Ridley (1736–1765).

11. The final line of the Doxology.

12. An *aumbry* was, in medieval times, a cupboard or cabinet, usually in a church and used to store chalices and other objects.

13. Troy Town was a game played by Welsh shepherds in which mazelike paths were cut into the turf in imitation of certain aspects of the Trojan War and also the Labyrinth (the Cretan maze in which the Minotaur was housed).

A Fragment of Life

1. A hair-trunk is a large trunk, usually for storing clothes or other objects, with a hair covering.

2. In this context, "kitcat" indicates the size of a portrait—not quite half-length, but showing the hands.

3. Machen's knowledge of tobaccos was exhibited in the early work of ponderous pseudo-scholarship, *The Anatomy of Tobacco* (1884).

4. French for "to stroll."

5. A seaside town on the north coast of Essex.

6. An exhibition of new technological devices was first held in Paris in 1798. Machen is probably referring to the large exhibition of 1878 or to that of 1889 (where the Eiffel Tower was unveiled) or 1900.

7. City Temple is a Nonconformist church. The church dates to 1640; the current building was built on Holborn Viaduct in London in 1874.

8. A long four-wheeled carriage, open or curtained at the sides.

9. Exodus 20:12.

10. Cf. Machen's later essay "Strange Roads" (*Out and Away*, December 1919), a poignant account of his walks in the rural countryside.

11. I.e., a female employee of the ABC (Aerated Bread Com-

pany) chain of tea shops.

12. A reference to the *Transactions of the Hertfordshire Natural History Society and Field Club* (1879f.), loosely referred to as the *Hertfordshire Naturalist*.

13. "To him that waits all things reveal themselves, provided that he has the courage not to deny, in the darkness, what he has seen in the light." The statement is by Coventry Patmore (1823–1896), British poet and theologian, and is found in his collection of aphorisms, *The Rod, the Root and the Flower* (1895).

14. "And apples not her own." Virgil, *Georgics* 2.82. In Virgil the expression relates to the grafting of one plant on to another, with the result that the original plant, to its delight, bears "alien" fruit.

15. Greek for "practice" or "training." In Christian thought, the concept refers to spiritual exercises, specifically those pertaining to self-denial.

16. Cesare Lombroso (1835–1909), Italian psychologist and criminologist who, in such works as *L'Uomo delinquente* (1876; The Criminal Man), propounded a now discredited theory that certain people were born criminals and could be detected by physiological and other features.

17. "Only incredible things must be believed." An adaptation of the axiom by the early Christian thinker Tertullian (160?–240 C.E.): *Certum est, quia impossibile est* ("It is certain because it is impossible": De Carne Christi 5), oftentimes rendered *Credo quia impossibile* [or *incredibile*] *est* ("I believe because it is impossible [or incredible]").

18. "The sacred fountain must not be turned over to common use."

19. "The Land of Iolo."

20. Literally, "the wood of the wise."

21. Lilith, originally a Mesopotamian female demon, was conceived in the biblical apocrypha as the first wife of Adam, hence a kind of witch figure. Samael, in Judaic lore, is the Angel of Death.

22. "The breaths of the infernal [creatures]."

23. A phrase from Psalms 113:1 (Vulgate) = 114.1 in the King James Version ("When Israel went out of Egypt . . .").

24. "Now I know for certain that all legends, all histories, all

fables, every Scripture is telling a story about ME."

The Bowmen

1. "It's a Long Way to Tipperary" (1912) was a music-hall song composed by Jack Judge and Harry Williams. Machen has devised an alternate final line that rhymes with the actual final line of the chorus: "But my heart's right there."

2. Evidently a reference to the so-called Siege of Sidney Street, occurring on January 2, 1911, in a street in the Stepney district of London. A criminal gang was besieged by 200 policemen for six hours; two of the gang members were killed by a fire that eventually consumed the building.

3. The battle of Agincourt, occurring on October 25, 1415, in northern France, constituted one of the greatest victories of England over France, chiefly as a result of the longbow.

Appendix 1

1. Machen is probably referring to Aleister Crowley (1875–1947), British occultist who had been involved in black magic and other activities from as early as 1896. Both he and Machen were for a time members of the Order of the Golden Dawn.

2. The Rosicrucians (Brethren of the Rose Cross) were an esoteric sect probably originating in Germany in the early seventeenth century, and chiefly involved in alchemy, astrology, and healing. British novelists William Godwin and Edward Bulwer-Lytton based several of their Gothic novels on the Rosicrucian sect.

Appendix 2

1. Sir John Stainer (1840–1901), British organist and composer whose work heavily influenced Anglican church music during the later nineteenth century.

2. Presumably the Dean of Westminster, the Anglican clergy-

man who presides at Westminster Abbey.

3. "The sound of feasters at an endless banquet."

4. Rudyard Kipling (1865–1936), "The Lost Legion," in *Many Inventions* (1893).

5. The editor of the *Occult Review* (1905–48) in 1914 was Ralph Shirley (1865–1946). Shirley wrote *The Angel Warriors of Mons* (1915), a pamphlet attempting to prove the "truth" of "The Bowmen." He had previously written *Prophecies and Omens of the Great War* (1914).

6. *Light* (1881f.), a London periodical devoted to psychic phenomena. It is still being published.

7. Alfred Percy Sinnett (1840–1921), British mystic who, with Helena P. Blavatsky, helped to found the theosophical movement. The article is entitled "Meteorites and the World Crisis" (pp. 265–71).

8. James Edward Cowell Welldon (1854–1937), Bishop of Calcutta (1898–1902), Canon of Westminster (1902–06), Dean of Manchester (1906–18), and Dean of Durham (1918–37).

9. Herbert Hensley Henson (1863–1947), Canon of Westminster (1900–15), Dean of Durham (1915–20), and Bishop of Durham (1920–39).

10. John Taylor Smith (1860–1938), Bishop of Sierra Leone (1897–1901) and Chaplain-General of the British Army (1901–25).

11. Robert Forman Horton (1855–1934), Congregational minister at the church in Lyndhurst Road, Hampstead, London (1884–1930).

12. Sir Joseph Compton-Rickett (1847–1919), Member of Parliament (1895–1919) and president of the National Federation of Free Church Councils (1915–19), an organization of Nonconformist (i.e., non-Church of England) Protestant denominations founded in 1892.

13. Sam Weller is a character in Charles Dickens's *The Pickwick Papers* (1836–37). The jovial, quick-witted Weller becomes Mr. Pickwick's valet and companion, but Pickwick's hiring of him leads to a breach of promise suit that lands both of them in prison.

Bibliography

A. Primary

Poetry

Eleusinia. Hereford, Wales: Joseph Jones, 1881. West Warwick, RI: Necronomicon Press, 1988 (*with Beneath the Barley*).

Short Stories

The Great God Pan and the Inmost Light. London: John Lane, 1894.
The House of Souls [with The Three Impostors]. London: Grant Richards, 1906.
The Bowmen and Other Legends of the War. London: Simpkin, Marshall, Hamilton, Kent & Co., 1915. New York: G. P. Putnam's Sons, 1915. Doylestown, PA: Aegypan Press, 2006.
The Great Return. London: Faith Press, 1915.
The House of Souls. New York: Alfred A. Knopf, 1922. North Stratford, NH: Ayer, 1999.
Ornaments in Jade. New York: Alfred A. Knopf, 1924. Horam, UK: Tartarus Press, 1997.

The Shining Pyramid. London: Martin Secker, 1925.

The Cosy Room and Other Stories. London: Rich & Cowan, 1936.

The Children of the Pool and Other Stories. London: Hutchinson, 1936.

Holy Terrors. Harmondsworth: Penguin Books, 1946.

Tales of Horror and the Supernatural. New York: Alfred A. Knopf, 1948. London: Richards Press, 1949. London: John Baker, 1964. St. Albans, UK: Panther, 1963 (2 vols.). New York: Pinnacle, 1971 (2 vols.), 1983. Horam, UK: Tartarus Press, 1997.

The Strange World of Arthur Machen. New York: Juniper Press, 1960.

Ritual and Other Stories. Ed. R. B. Russell. Horam, UK: Tartarus Press, 1992 (rev. ed. 1997).

The Three Impostors and Other Stories. Ed. S. T. Joshi. Oakland, CA: Chaosium, 2001.

The White People and Other Stories. Ed. S. T. Joshi. Oakland, CA: Chaosium, 2003.

The Terror and Other Stories. Ed. S. T. Joshi. Oakland, CA: Chaosium, 2005.

Novels

The Chronicle of Clemendy. London: Carbonnek, 1888. New York: Alfred A. Knopf, 1926.

The Three Impostors; or, The Transmutations. London: John Lane; Boston: Roberts Brothers, 1895. New York: Alfred A. Knopf, 1923. London: John Baker, 1964. New York: Ballantine, 1972. London: J. M. Dent, 1995 (ed. Rita Tait).

The Hill of Dreams. London: Grant Richards, 1907. New York: Alfred A. Knopf, 1923. London: Richards Press, 1954 (introduction by Lord Dunsany). London: John Baker, 1968. New York: Dover, 1986.

The Terror. London: Duckworth, 1917. New York: W. W. Norton, 1965. London: White Lion, 1973. (Also in *Tales of Horror and the Supernatural.*)

The Secret Glory. London: Martin Secker, 1922. New York: Alfred A. Knopf, 1922. [See also *Chapters Five and Six of The Secret Glory*. Horam, UK: Tartarus Press, 1991.]

The Green Round. London: Ernest Benn, 1933. Sauk City, WI: Arkham

House, 1968.

Essays and Miscellany

The Anatomy of Tobacco. London: George Redway, 1884. New York: Alfred A. Knopf, 1926.

Don Quijote de la Mancha. London: George Redway, 1887.

Thesaurus Incantatus: The Enchanted Treasure; or, The Spagyric Quest of Beroaldus Cosmopolita. London: Thomas Marvell [Arthur Machen and Harry Spurr], 1888.

Hieroglyphics: A Note upon Ecstasy in Literature. London: Grant Richards, 1902. London: Martin Secker, 1910. New York: Mitchell Kennerley, 1913. New York: Alfred A. Knopf, 1923. London: Unicorn Press, 1960.

*The House of the Hidden Ligh*t (with A. E. Waite). London: Privately printed, 1904. Leyburn, UK: Tartarus Press/Ferret Fantasy, 2003.

Dr. Stiggins: His Views and Principles. London: Francis Griffiths, 1906. New York: Alfred A. Knopf, 1925.

"Parsifal": The Story of the Holy Grail. London: General Cinematograph Agencies, [c. 1913].

War and the Christian Faith. London: Skeffington & Sons, 1915.

The Pantomime of the Year. London: Privately printed, 1921.

The Grande Trouvaille: A Legend of Pentonville. London: First Edition Bookshop, 1923.

The Shining Pyramid. Ed. Vincent Starrett. Chicago: Covici-McGee, 1923.

The Collector's Craft. London: First Edition Bookshop, 1923.

Strange Roads and With the Gods in Spring. London: Classic Press, 1924. Caerleon: Green Round Press, 1990.

Dog and Duck. London: Jonathan Cape, 1924. New York: Alfred A. Knopf, 1924.

The Glorious Mystery. Ed. Vincent Starrett. Chicago: Covici-McGee, 1924.

Precious Balms. London: Spurr & Swift, 1924. Caerleon: Friends of Arthur Machen, 1999.

A Preface to "Casanova's Escape from the Leads." London: Casanova Society, 1925.

The Canning Wonder. London: Chatto & Windus, 1925. New York: Alfred A. Knopf, 1926.

Dreads and Drolls. London: Martin Seeker, 1926. New York: Alfred A. Knopf, 1927. Salem, NH: Ayer, 1992.

Notes and Queries. London: Spurr & Swift, 1926.

A Souvenir of Cadby Hall. London: J. Lyons & Co., 1927.

Parish of Amersham. Amersham: S. G. Mason, 1930.

Tom O'Bedlam and His Song. Westport, CT: Apellicon Press, 1930.

Beneath the Barley: A Note on the Origins of "Eleusinia." London: Privately printed, 1931.

In the 'Eighties. Amersham: Privately printed, 1931.

An Introduction to John Gawsworth's "Above the River." Amersham: Privately printed, 1931.

The Glitter of the Brook. Dalton, GA: Postprandial Press, 1932.

Bridles and Spurs. Cleveland: Rowfant Club, 1951.

A Critical Essay. Lakewood, OH: Carl Swanson, 1953.

A Receipt for Fine Prose. New York: Postprandial Press, 1956.

A Note on Poetry. Wichita, KS: Four Ducks Press, 1959.

From the London Evening News. Wichita, KS: Four Ducks Press, 1959.

Guinevere and Lancelot and Others. Ed. Cuyler W. Brooks, Jr., and Michael Shoemaker. Newport News, VA: Purple Mouth Press, 1987.

Rus in Urbe and Other Pieces. Lewes, UK: Tartarus Press, 1992.

The Secret of the Sangraal. Horam, UK: Tartarus Press, 1995.

Autobiography

Far Off Things. London: Martin Secker, 1922. New York: Alfred A. Knopf, 1922.

Things Near and Far. London: Martin Secker, 1923. New York: Alfred A. Knopf, 1923.

The London Adventure. London: Martin Secker, 1924. New York: Alfred A. Knopf, 1925. London: Village Press, 1974.

Autobiography [Far Off Things and Things Near and Far]. London: Richards Press, 1951. London: Garnstone, 1974.

Published Letters

A Few Letters. Cleveland: Rowfant Club, 1932. [n.p.]: Aylesford Press, 1993.

A.L.S.: An Unimportant Exchange of Letters Between Arthur Machen and J. H. Stewart, Jr. Wichita, KS: Four Ducks Press, 1956.

Selected Letters. Ed. Mark Valentine and Roger Dobson. London: Thorsons, 1988.

Arthur Machen and Montgomery Evans: Letters of a Literary Friendship, 1923–1947. Ed. Sue Strong Hassler and Donald M. Hassler. Kent, OH: Kent State University Press, 1994.

Translations

The Heptameron of Marguerite Queen of Navarre. London: Dryden Press, 1886. London: George Routledge & Sons; New York: E. P. Dutton, 1905. New York: Alfred A. Knopf, 1924.

Fantastic Tales or the Way to Attain (by Beroalde de Verville). London: Carbonnek, 1890. New York: Boni & Liveright, 1923.

The Memoirs of Jacques Casanova. London: H. S. Nichols, 1894. 12 vols. London: Casanova Society, 1922. New York: Alfred A. Knopf, 1929 (2 vols.). New York: Albert & Charles Boni, 1932 (2 vols.). Edinburgh: Limited Editions Club, 1940 (8 vols.). New York: G. P. Putnam's Sons; London: Elek Books, 1959–61 (6 vols.). New York: Dover, 1961 (3 vols.).

Casanova's Escape from the Leads. London: Casanova Society, 1925. New York: Alfred A. Knopf, 1925.

Remarks upon Hermodactylus by Lady Hester Lucy Stanhope. London: Privately printed, 1933.

Collected Works

Works. Caerleon Edition. London: Martin Secker, 1923. 9 vols.

B. Secondary

Biographies and Bibliographies

Danielson, Henry. *Arthur Machen: A Bibliography*. London: Henry Danielson, 1923. [Annotations by Machen.]
Gawsworth, John. *The Life of Arthur Machen*. Ed. Roger Dobson. [Leyburn, UK]: Tartarus Press/Friends of Arthur Machen, 2005.
Goldstone, Adrian, and Wesley Sweetser. *A Bibliography of Arthur Machen*. Austin: University of Texas Press, 1965.
Machen, Purefoy. *Where Memory Slept: The Memoirs of Purefoy Machen*. Ed. Geoffrey Brangham. Caerleon: Green Round Press, 1991.
Reynolds, Aidan, and William Charlton. *Arthur Machen: A Short Account of His Life and Work*. London: Richards Press, 1963. Oxford: Caermaen Books, 1988.
Valentine, Mark. *Arthur Machen*. Bridgend, Wales: Seren, 1994.

General Studies

Adcock, Arthur St. John. "Arthur Machen." *In The Glory That Was Grub Street*. New York: Frederick A. Stokes, 1928, pp. 213–44.
Bjärstorp, Sara. *The Margins of Writing: A Study of Arthur Machen and the Literary Field of the 1890s*. Lund, Sweden: Department of English, Lund University, 2005.
Carr, John Dickson. "Hammock Companions" [review of *Tales of Horror and the Supernatural*]. *New York Times Book Review* (1 August 1948): 10.
Cohen, J. M. "Books and Writers." *Spectator* (20 July 1951): 100.
Eckersley, Adrian. "A Theme in the Early Work of Arthur Machen: 'Degeneration.'" *English Literature in Transition* 35 (1992): 277–87.
Gekle, William Francis. *Arthur Machen: Weaver of Fantasy*. Millbrook, NY: Round Table Press, 1949.
Goodrick-Clarke, Nicholas. "The Enchanted City: Arthur Machen and Locality." *Durham University Journal* 87, no. 2 (July 1995): 301–13.
Gorman, Herbert S. "Arthur Machen Pursues His Mystic Way." *New York Times Book Review* (16 January 1927): 5.
Gunther, John. "The Truth about Arthur Machen." *Bookman* (New York) 61 (July 1925): 571–574.

Hillyer, Robert. "Arthur Machen." *Atlantic Monthly* 179 (May 1947): 138–40.

———. "Arthur Machen." *Yale Review* 13 (October 1923): 174–76.

Jordan-Smith, Paul. "Black Magic: An Impression of Arthur Machen." In *On Strange Altars*. New York: Albert & Charles Boni, 1924, pp. 214–35.

Joshi, S. T. "Arthur Machen: The Mystery of the Universe." In *The Weird Tale*. Austin: University of Texas Press, 1990, pp. 12–41.

Krutch, Joseph Wood. "Tales of a Mystic." *Nation* (13 September 1922): 258–59.

Leslie-McCarthy, Sage. "Re-vitalising the Little People: Arthur Machen's Tales of the Remnant Races." *Australasian Victorian Studies Journal* 11 (2005): 65–78.

Lynch, Helen. "Arthur Machen." *Sewanee Review* 47 (July–September 1939): 424–27.

Matteson, Robert S. "Arthur Machen: A Vision of an Enchanted Land." *Personalist* 46 (Spring 1965): 253–68.

Miles, Hamish. "Machen in Retrospect." *Dial* 74 (June 1923): 627–30.

Owens, Jill Tedford. "Arthur Machen's Supernaturalism: The Decadent Variety." *University of Mississippi Studies in English* 8 (1990): 117–26.

Roberts, R. Ellis. "Arthur Machen." *Bookman* (London) 62 (September 1922): 240–42.

Russell, R. B., ed. *Machenalia*. Lewes, UK: Tartarus Press, 1990. 2 vols.

Sewell, Brocard, ed. *Arthur Machen*. Llandeilo, Wales: St. Albert's Press, 1960.

Shiel, M. P. "On Scholar-Artistry." In *Science, Life and Literature*. London: Williams & Norgate, 1950, pp. 95–100.

Starrett, Vincent. "Arthur Machen: A Novelist of Ecstasy and Sin." *Reedy's Mirror* (5 October 1917): 631–32. Reprinted in Starrett's *Buried Caesars*. Chicago: Covici-McGee, 1923, pp. 1–31.

Sweetser, Wesley D. *Arthur Machen*. New York: Twayne, 1964.

Symons, Julian. "Horror in the Nineties." *Books and Bookmen* 10 (March 1965): 12–13, 37.

Tierney, Myles. "The Highway to Avalon." *Bookman* (New York) 60 (October 1924): 224–26.

Tyler, Robert L. "Arthur Machen: The Minor Writer and His Function." *Approach* (Spring 1960): 21–26.

Valentine, Mark, and Roger Dobson, ed. *Arthur Machen: Apostle of Wonder.* Oxford: Caermaen Books, 1985.

———. *Arthur Machen: Artist and Mystic.* Oxford: Caermaen Books, 1986.

Van Vechten, Carl. "Arthur Machen: Dreamer and Mystic." *Literary Digest International Book Review 1* (February 1923): 36–37. In Van Vechten's *Excavations.* New York: Alfred A. Knopf, 1926, pp. 162–69.

———. *Peter Whiffle.* New York: Alfred A. Knopf, 1922. [See ch. 10.]

Wagenknecht, Edward. *Seven Masters of Supernatural Fiction.* Westport, CT: Greenwood Press, 1991.

Wandrei, Donald. "Arthur Machen and *The Hill of Dreams.*" *Minnesota Quarterly* 3, no. 3 (Spring 1926): 19–24. *Studies in Weird Fiction* no. 15 (Summer 1994): 27–30.

Wright, Cuthbert. "Far-Off Things." *Freeman* (4 April 1923): 90–92.